MW01033777

CASANOVA COWBOY

THE MONTANA MEN SERIES BOOK 2

JAMIE SCHULZ

BOOKS BY JAMIE SCHULZ

The Montana Men Series

Broken Cowboy

Casanova Cowboy

The Angel Eyes Series

Jake's Redemption

Masters' Mistress

Masters' Escape

Masters' Promise

Masters' Rebellion

Masters' Betrayal

Masters' Freedom

Casanova Cowboy

Copyright

Casanova Cowboy

This book is a work of fiction. Names, characters, businesses, organizations, places, events and incidents either are the product of the author's imagination or are used fictitiously. Any resemblance to actual persons, living or dead, events, or locales is entirely coincidental.

ISBN: 978-0-9980257-9-7

For information contact: www.thejamieschulz.com

Book Cover design by Lesia T (Germancreative) & Jamie Schulz

For Sam... I love you, sistra!

CHAPTER 1

Zackary MacEntier's cheerful gaze traveled over the small sea of people flooding his best friends' backyard meadow. Unable to hold back a smile, he admired the women in the crowd, wondering if he'd see any new faces. A little spark of hope warmed his insides as he took in their beauty and the possibility that he might find an interesting woman today—one he hadn't already dated.

Yeah, he thought with more than a little self-deprecation, *good luck with that.* He doused the tiny flame inside him—knowing the possibility to be next to impossible—but continued to appreciate the scene, nonetheless.

Zack MacEntier loved women; he'd never denied that, even to himself. He loved everything about them, from the scent of their satiny skin to the silkiness of their hair, to their big eyes, wide smiles, dainty toes, and everything in-between. He also loved getting to know their personalities. From smart and sassy, to sweet and witty, they drew him like a bee to honey, and he'd anticipated his fascination with the fairer sex would never change. He'd spent most of his adult life with more than a few different women, and he had never expected to ever *want* to limit himself to just one.

Yet, standing under the huge white tent amid the guests at his best friend's wedding, second thoughts about life-long bachelorhood once again assailed him.

Uncomfortable with his thoughts and looking for a distraction, he shifted his booted feet as he took in the familiar faces from their little town of Meriton,

Montana. Many of his ex-girlfriends were in the crowd, and oddly, it pleased him to see they'd moved on to better men than him. However, the tightness in his chest wouldn't leave him. He knew those romantic relationships had ended because things had gotten too close for his comfort—as did the ladies he'd broken it off with. Despite that, most of them were still his friends. For the longest time, he'd seen no reason to change that or to look for something more in his life. Now, at the ripe old age of thirty, something inside him seemed to have changed.

He sighed and took a sip of the drink in his hand. Had he really wanted it that way—to be single and alone forever? Not since high school had any woman made him crave more, and until recently, he hadn't thought twice about it.

Zack's gaze switched back to the bride and groom. Cade Brody danced with his new wife Addie, and Zack had never seen his friend happier. There was a brightness…a glow…a *something* that shimmered around them both. Warmth and happiness lived in their eyes and smiles, which made Zack yearn for the same kind of bliss.

"Cade's a lucky man," Aaron Monroe, one of the town's paramedic-firefighters and another of Zack's good friends, said. Just like Zack, Aaron was considered one of Meriton's most eligible bachelors. At six-foot-three, Aaron was built like a Mac truck, but he had a gentle heart…unless provoked. He was also well-liked by the ladies and, despite only moving to town almost two years ago, he had his fair share of ex-girlfriends around town, too.

"Yeah," Zack agreed, "very lucky."

Cade had found Addie by pure coincidence, and their tale sounded a bit like a stereotypical country song. At the time, Cade had been roaming far and wide to avoid any contact with his twin brother Cord. Zack wasn't entirely sure what had set the brothers on separate trails almost six years ago, but he had a suspicion it had been a woman. Whatever the case, Zack was glad to have them both together and acting like brothers again.

"Any chance she has a sister or three?" Aaron asked with a hopeful grin.

"Or maybe some cousins?" That question came from another firefighter, Hawk Hawkins—his real first name was as much of a mystery as his past.

A murmur of interest came from the six men standing with Zack, admiring the bride and groom as they twirled around the dance floor.

Zack shrugged, eyeing the crowd once again. "All I know is she's an only child."

While he spoke, his gaze fell on his sister, Emily, who stood with their mother on the opposite side of the dance floor. Janice grinned as she watched the bride and groom, but his sister's eyes were drawn in Zack's direction. The expression on her face caused the hair on the back of his neck to rise. She wasn't staring at him with that longing look on her face. It only took a second to realize her attention was focused wholly on the man at his side, and Zack's protective brother instinct went on high alert.

He glanced at Aaron as the others groaned at the lost opportunity of Addie's relations, but quickly bounced to other topics about ranching, firefighting, and the fall roundup. Aaron seemed oblivious to Emily's interest, and Zack hoped it stayed that way. He liked the man, but his reputation with women was almost as bad as Zack's. That wasn't the kind of man he wanted for his sweet, vivacious, and all too trusting sister. He'd have to keep an eye on her whenever the firefighter was around.

Emmy might be the older sibling by a couple of years, but Zack wasn't about to let her be taken advantage of by anyone.

Putting that new problem out of his mind for now, Zack went back to pondering his bachelorhood.

What did he have to offer a woman, anyway? All he knew was ranching and he enjoyed it, but the ability to work the land and the animals he loved was on the verge of ruin. He had no one to blame but himself as far as the disaster on his family's ranch was concerned. Luckily, he'd been able to keep it to himself so far, but it was only a matter of time before Emily—who worked on their ranch whenever she wasn't working in town—stopped asking what was wrong with him and started poking around. The last thing he wanted was for his mom and dad to learn about his failures. He had to figure out a way to dig himself out of the hole he'd made in their finances by reaching too far for something he knew too little about.

Aaron elbowed him to get his attention.

"What?" Zack growled as he rubbed his abused ribs.

Aaron didn't even flinch at Zack's irritated response. "I asked how the winery was doing."

Zack grunted, "It's fine."

"Going to open anytime soon?"

He gave his friend a narrow-eyed look. "At this point, I'm not sure when it will open." *If it ever will…* he thought. "We're working on it."

"It'll sure be nice to have a little more culture around here," Aaron said with a grin, hinting once again that they'd love to have a dimly lit place to take a lady for dinner, something besides Betsy's Diner or Tony's Tavern in town. "It would be really nice not to drive miles to Missoula or Helena or, God forbid, Billings, for a fun weekend."

"Yeah..." Zack sighed. He had thought the same thing at one time, too.

Having a winery on their property had seemed like such a good idea six years ago when he'd first suggested it to his father, John—who, at the time, had not yet retired from running the ranch. He hadn't been thrilled with the idea, but once Zack had explained the benefits of diversifying their income and creating local jobs, John eventually agreed—though a bit reluctantly.

The vines they'd gotten from Washington and California had taken a few years to establish and they were looking forward to producing some barrels to test and possibly sell, but the last couple of years had been lean. Almost two years ago, in preparation for the maturing plants, he'd borrowed the money to build the winery, which they had planned to eventually open to the public. Unfortunately, environmental protestors had slowed the project to almost a halt and created yet another disaster Zack had to deal with.

Last winter, someone had broken all the building's windows, which had caused the pipes to burst and the heating system to burn out. Not to mention all the damage from the water before and after it froze and the snow as it blew in through the busted windows. Repairs for the damage had taken a big chunk out of his savings he hadn't budgeted for, and though the building was mostly finished, they were nowhere near ready for customers, nor did he know how to draw in more from beyond their little town.

He had no proof the damage had been caused by the protestors, but who else would do something like that? Aside from their offensive protest signs about farming and ranching being evil, planet-killing professions, the angry shouts that were sometimes directed at him—or the snide comments they worked into conversation whenever he'd tried to speak with them—Zack wasn't exactly sure what the protestors objected to. He understood their worries about intensive farming, deforestation, and the negative effects of other practices, but Zack—and all the farmers and ranchers he knew—practiced environmental stewardship to protect their animals, the land, and wildlife.

That fact didn't seem to matter to the protestors, though. They were there every day, disrupting work, blocking roads, starting fights, or just causing mischief—among other, not-so-tame things. They were a headache that had cost him and several other ranchers a lot of money, and may even cost Zack and his family their home—or at least, be the final nail in the proverbial coffin.

With all that and the lackluster grape harvests last year, not only had Zack's self-confidence taken a hit, but so had their income. And he hadn't had the nerve to tell his family about the problem yet. He had to find a way to either increase profits with the winery or their animals before he'd be forced to sell the winery and a big chunk of land as well.

His heart clenched and a muscle ticked in his cheek. He would work it out, somehow. He had to.

Glancing at Cade and Addie again, Zack clenched his teeth and stifled an unexpected flare of jealousy. He was happy for Cade, damn it! Zack had enough on his plate without adding another doomed-to-fail romance on top of it. He could do short and sweet, but he wasn't cut out for the long haul.

Just then, Jorje Rivera walked into the huge white tent and a smile curled Zack's lips. He'd met the younger man in the town near Addie's one-time farm in Washington. He'd helped Zack defend Cade from a gang of men intent on harm during a rodeo where Addie had once lived. Zack had only been passing through, on his way back home, when he ran into Cade again for the first time in years. Jorje had been a good friend to Cade, and Zack had liked the quiet man almost instantly.

However, it wasn't Jorje who held his attention. The curly-haired brunette goddess on his arm was far more pleasing to Zack's eyes. She was lovely with smooth brown skin and big eyes that tilted gently up at the corners and looked almost green. She had plush, soft-looking lips and high cheekbones that made her appear regal—and maybe a little snooty. She wasn't dressed for the semi-casual affair, which also seemed odd. Where most of the other women wore skirts or dresses, this lovely brown-skinned goddess wore what looked like designer jeans, a floral blouse, and high heels that made her legs look impossibly long. She seemed nervous, dipping her head to hide behind her mop of wide amber-brown curls and her beautiful eyes darted around the tent as if looking for someone but dreading what she would find.

She intrigued him, and he wondered what she was doing on Jorje's arm—when last Zack heard, Jorje had been involved with Lana, a young friend of Addie's back in Washington. Zack hoped that was still the case, because this woman's pretty face and trim figure had Zack's body waking from a yearlong nap.

Had it been that long since he'd dated someone? He'd gone through most of the women in town at one time or another, and the rest hadn't interested him enough to entertain. Still, a whole year? That wasn't like him. Everyone knew he was a flirt and would often date several women in a year. He didn't want complicated; he didn't have time for it—or so he told himself. He kept things simple, and he always made sure those women enjoyed being with him for their short time together as much as he had enjoyed being with them.

But something about the woman on Jorje's arm grabbed him, made him take note of her rapid breathing and nervous eyes.

Just then, her gaze locked with his, and it was as if the world stopped on its axis. His breath seized and his heart thudded almost painfully against his ribs. An unexpected ache tightened his throat and deep inside, he felt an unmistakable pull, tugging him toward the new beauty across the room. His body leaned forward as if preparing to go to her side, but then her eyes widened and she ripped her gaze from his.

Everything crashed back in on him—the slightly too loud music, the voices of his friends, and the warm breeze that wafted through the tent. Zack swallowed hard, unsure what had just happened, and felt more off-balance than he ever had in his life.

The gorgeous woman turned to say something to Jorje, who patted her hand and replied with a smile. The beauty nodded, though she still appeared as unsure of herself as before.

A moment later, Lana came up behind Jorje and the curly-haired goddess. Tucking her arm into the other woman's free elbow, Lana grinned broadly. She glanced over at Jorje and the brunette, and got them moving toward a table on the far side of the tent.

"I don't care what you think!" a shrill voice shouted from behind where Zack and his friends stood, breaking the spell he'd fallen under when the brunette had walked in.

"I will *not* be quiet," the voice shouted again and this time, Zack recognized it. "I'll shout if I want to, and you can't stop me."

Beside Zack, Aaron mumbled a curse.

"You got that right," Zack grumbled as he turned to see Cord Brody's head down, shoulders slumped, standing stoically near one of the tent's many exits while a blonde woman waved her hands and shouted in his face.

"She's going to ruin the reception," Aaron muttered.

"No," Zack replied, "she's not." He glanced around quickly. So far, only a few of the guests had heard the shouting over the music and chatter. The bride and groom were lost in their own little world, which he was thankful for, but if the woman kept getting louder—as he knew she would—everyone would soon hear her screeching. "You and Hawk get Cord back to a table. I'll take care of Suzy."

Both men nodded as they headed toward the uncomfortable display. Zack would not let her berate Cord at his brother's wedding. Hell, he wouldn't allow it anywhere. This time she'd gone too far, and he intended to make sure she understood and learned to keep her distance.

CHAPTER 2

Izabel Silva took a deep breath to calm her rattled nerves. Peering into the huge tent at the flowers, lacy decorations, and nicely dressed, smiling people, she ducked her head and pulled back. She didn't belong here, not at a wedding she hadn't been invited to. Then again, maybe she had been invited and just hadn't been home to receive it—nor could she have been contacted on her old phone number. She'd had it disconnected months ago to stop the incessant, unwelcomed calls. You'd think a man like Chris Richards could take a hint…or blatant rejection. Then again, he was arrogant enough to always get his way, so maybe she shouldn't have been surprised by his calls.

"*Bueno, mi amiga*, are you ready to go in?" Jorje Rivera asked from her side.

Izabel jumped and pressed a hand over her rapidly beating heart. She hadn't heard Jorje's approach. She glanced over her shoulder, looking for Jorje's charming girlfriend. "Where's Lana?"

"She'll be along soon," Jorje replied with a smile and held out his crooked arm for her to slip her hand through. "She said she'd meet us inside."

Izabel bit her lip and lowered her hand from her chest to her roiling belly. She shouldn't have come here. "We can wait."

"Izzy," Jorje said, using the nickname many had used before, "you will be welcomed. I have no doubt about that."

"Well, that makes one of us," Izabel grumbled.

Jorje chuckled as he reached for her hand and tucked it into the crook of his arm. "Don't worry so much. Everything will be fine, I promise."

"I'm glad you're so sure," Izabel mumbled as they stepped into the cool shade of the huge white tent. She'd told him and Lana a little about her connection to Addie—enough for them to know she was a friend. She hadn't, however, told them how she'd basically ignored their friendship for the last three years.

The crowd inside had formed a circle to allow Addie and her new husband to open the first dance. Addie looked beautiful and happier than Izabel had ever seen her. The way she stared into her handsome husband's smiling eyes...

Izabel swallowed and looked away. She had once dreamed of a wedding of her own, but that had turned to dust the minute she found Chris with another woman. Her heart clenched as the memory filled her mind once again, and she shook her head. Why did his betrayal bother her so much? They'd been growing apart for a long time, becoming distant, almost like strangers—or maybe that had just been her. She shouldn't have been surprised that he turned to someone else, but still, she had been floored to see it in person.

She ducked her head and peeked through the curtain of her amber-brown curls. The feeling of not belonging swept over her again, and she took a step back.

Jorje gently tugged on her arm. "Where are you going, *mi amiga*? The party is this way." He angled his chin toward the inside of the tent.

She smiled, still feeling unusually awkward. "I know... It's just a bit overwhelming."

She turned back to the crowd, taking everything in, lowering her chin again to hide behind her wide curls. Her eyes swept toward the far side of the tent, over to a group of handsome men who laughed together as they talked. Seven rather tall, well-built men, but only one commanded her interest.

He was as tall as the others, broad-shouldered, and lean in the hips. He had short brown hair and a short, well-kept beard that did nothing to conceal the strong, stubborn line of his jaw and chin, but accentuated the chiseled beauty of his masculine lips. Thick, dark brows slashed over his warm brown eyes, like the color of whiskey in a clear glass by the fire. Beautiful, soulful eyes that were, right at that moment, staring directly at her.

Izabel's heart lurched in her chest and something fluttered madly in her belly. He was gorgeous...in a farm boy sort of way—well, almost any kind of way, actually. He looked like the kind of guy you'd expect to find next door, only there was something more, something heady and rich that she couldn't quite place. Her heart pressed into her ribs, compelling her to move, to cross the dancefloor, and...

And what? She didn't know this guy, didn't know anyone here but Addie—and even that connection was tenuous at best. Still, she couldn't break the connection she felt pulling her toward the handsome stranger across the room. She saw his body slant forward as if about to move in her direction.

Oh, no... her mind rebelled and she jerked her eyes away from him. She wasn't ready for that, not ready to let another man into her life.

Why not? a little voice asked. *It's been almost a year; it's time to move on.*

Ah, that was her mother's voice from a few weeks ago replaying in her mind. Mom had threatened to move to Seattle to take care of her the last time they spoke, but Izabel hadn't wanted that. She'd wanted time to herself, and she'd taken it—spent a huge chunk of her savings in doing so, but she'd finally pulled herself together and left all the pain and disappointment behind. She'd left her job, her apartment, and all her one-time, so-called friends as well.

She wanted to look back across the room, to see if the handsome cowboy still had his riveting gaze on her, but the way her skin had warmed and tingled, she knew she'd undoubtedly be locked in once more if she dared to turn his way. Instead, she turned to Jorje. "Shall we find a seat?"

Jorje smiled and patted her hand. "As soon as Lana gets here."

At that moment, Lana hooked her arm through Izabel's free elbow and smiled at them both. "Thanks for waiting," her eyes twinkled in their lively way, "but you could've found a table." She tugged them toward the seats and Izabel let her. Jorje released her other arm to follow them to a table right on the edge of the dancefloor.

"Hi, Janice," Lana said as she sat beside an older woman who smiled broadly at them. There was something about the woman, something almost familiar, as if Izabel had seen her before. Something tickled her mind, but she pushed it aside. She didn't know anyone in Montana except for Addie.

"Hello, Lana. Jorje," the woman, Janice, replied. "It's good to see you both again."

"Looks like everything came together nicely," Lana said, indicating the tent and decorations with a wave of her hand.

"Yes, it did, and thanks to you both for your help with it, too." Janice smiled and her light brown eyes shined.

"Any time," Jorje replied.

"Yes." Lana took Jorje's hand with a huge grin, then turned back to Janice. "Anything for Addie."

"And who is your friend?" Janice asked, nodding toward Izabel.

Izabel bit her lip, feeling horribly out of place and very underdressed.

"Oh, my, I'm so sorry," Lana gushed, giving Izabel an apologetic look. "I've forgotten my manners. This is Izabel. She's a friend of Addie's from Seattle."

"Ah, so good of you to come all this way," Janice said as she patted Izabel's hand. "Any friend of Addie's is more than welcome."

Izabel glanced at Jorje, who gave her an 'I told you so' look, and she found herself smiling in return.

"I'm glad to be here," Izabel said, "but I haven't seen Addie in years. She might not—"

A loud shriek came from the opposite side of the tent near the exit, drawing their attention.

Izabel's eyes widened when she saw the handsome cowboy, who had so enamored her, in a serious conversation with an overly thin blonde woman who seemed to be screaming at him. He hovered over her almost menacingly as he replied just as vehemently as the woman, but his voice was far more reserved.

"I don't care!" the woman shouted, drawing more eyes as she tried to shove past the much larger man in her way.

He glanced at the people in the tent, many of whom had turned his way, and shook his head. With his jaw clenched and his lips pressed into a firm line, he wrapped his hand around her bicep and spun her away from the tent. His arm draped across her back as he hustled her out of view, toward where the cars were parked.

"Well, that was dramatic," Janice said, pulling them back to the party. "I hope Zack gets her to leave quietly."

"Who was that?" Izabel asked as a queasy feeling filled her stomach. The display of masculine overbearance was far too familiar for her comfort.

"Just someone who shouldn't have been here," Janice said. "Zack will take care of her. I just hope Cord is okay."

Lana leaned forward, her eyes sad and intense. "Is she...?"

Janice nodded, but didn't elaborate.

Izabel was only half-listening as she squirmed in her seat. *Of course, the first man I'm attracted to in months, and he's exactly like the last.* She sighed and lowered her chin. *Maybe I have a 'type,' after all. Maybe* all *men are like that. Maybe I* am *weak...*

"I'm going to go check on Cord," Jorje said as he stood and headed over to where two other large men had escorted Cade's twin. They watched him go, and Izabel wondered what the deal was between Cord and the mysterious woman.

"Well, Izabel," Janice interrupted her thoughts, "why haven't we seen you before now?"

"Oh, I... Well, I—"

"She didn't know if she'd be welcomed," Lana explained.

Izabel's face heated when she met Janice's warm gaze.

The older woman frowned. "Whyever not?"

"Well, like I said, Addie and I haven't seen each other in a while. I didn't want to upset her or anything before her wedding."

"If I know Addie at all," Janice said slowly, "she will be thrilled to see an old friend."

"That's what *I* said." Lana smiled as she gave Izabel a one-armed hug.

Izabel was thankful for the younger woman's exuberance. Lana made her feel welcome, like she really was part of their little group.

"Will you all be staying long?" Janice asked. "I know Addie would be upset to miss seeing Izabel."

"We've been staying at the hotel by the interstate," Lana said. "More private that way. But we'll be leaving tomorrow. Jorje says he's been away too long already. He doesn't want to burden our neighbors any longer than he has to. They've been keeping an eye on the farm while we're gone."

"Good neighbors," Janice replied and turned her gaze to Izabel. "How about you, Izabel? Will you be staying for a while?"

Izabel shrugged. "I'm not sure. I guess it depends on Addie." Her heart sunk a little lower. She didn't want to move in with either of her parents, but she didn't have anywhere else to go. A part of her didn't even know why she'd come here, except that it was far away from the heartbreak and frustration she'd left back in Seattle.

"Well, I'm sure we can figure something out for you," Janice said with her motherly smile. Her warmth and acceptance surprised Izabel, but it made her feel good as well. Maybe she could find a place here or, at least, figure out where to go next—what to *do* next.

The music faded and while some dancers began to move back to their tables, others stood to take their place as the next song started.

"I appreciate that, Janice," Izabel began, "but I don't—"

"Izzy? Izabel Silva?"

Izabel froze in her seat, then slowly turned toward her old friend.

"It *is* you," Addie said with a smile. "What are you doing here?"

"I wanted to visit, but you weren't home at your old farm," Izabel explained, quickly revealing how she'd arrived, unannounced, at Addie's old place and convinced Jorje and Lana to bring her along.

Addie released her husband's hand and rushed forward to gather Izabel into a warm embrace. "I'm so glad they did. I've missed you! Cade...?" Addie stood and pulled her husband forward. "This is Izabel Silva, another of my best friends from college. Izabel, this is my husband, Cade Brody."

Lana moved over so the couple could sit at the table with them.

"I'm happy to meet you, Cade," Izabel said as Addie and Cade sat down.

"Same here," Cade said. "Addie's mentioned you a couple of times and how much she's missed you."

Izabel glanced at her old friend. "I've missed you too, Addie," she said through her suddenly restricted throat. "I'm sorry I disappeared on you."

Addie's face filled with concern. "What happened? The last I remember, you were happy with a new job and a new guy."

Izabel dropped her eyes to her hands and shrugged. "Neither of them worked out the way I'd hoped…"

"Oh, sweetie, I'm so sorry."

Izabel met her friend's gaze with a sheepish grin. "It's okay. I'm working through it. First thing I wanted to do though, was reconnect with you."

A huge smile split Addie's sweet face. "I'd love that. Are you staying in town for a while? We're only going to be gone a week, and I'd love to spend some time with you once we get back from wherever it is we're going..." She glanced at her husband, but Cade just smiled.

"I'm not telling," he said, and Addie huffed in feigned annoyance.

She leaned toward Izabel conspiratorially, but her voice was loud enough for everyone to hear. "He's been torturing me for weeks about our honeymoon. Won't tell me a thing." She glanced over her shoulder again. "He's lucky I like him so much."

Cade chuckled. "You *love* me."

"Yeah," Addie said dreamily, "I suppose I do."

"And you wanted to be surprised." He winked, and Izabel giggled. She liked Addie's husband already.

"I don't know about that," Addie grumbled and turned back to Izabel. "So how about it? Are you going to stay for a while?"

"Well…" Izabel hesitated. She didn't have a lot of money left, and if she was going to stay out of both of her parents' spare rooms, she would need something to start over with.

Addie must have guessed her dilemma because she quickly spoke up. "Of course, you'll stay with us. I mean, we won't be there for a week, but you can use our place. No need to waste money on a hotel, and I'm sure we can find someone to entertain you." She leaned in a little more. "There are tons of handsome guys here who I'm sure would love to meet you."

"I don't know about that," Izabel said quietly before she forced herself to be a little more cheery, "but I'd gladly take the offer of a room for a while. I need to figure out my next steps."

"Then it's settled. You'll stay at our place," Addie said and, sitting back in her chair, took her husband's hand. "Maybe Cord can show her around?"

Cade shook his head. "He's going to Wyoming for a few days. Remember?"

"Oh, that's right..."

"And we already have guests from out of town staying for the next few days…" He gave Izabel an apologetic smile before he met Addie's gaze. "We don't have any room."

Addie's shoulders slumped and a frown wrinkled her brow.

"She can stay with us," Janice offered. "We've got plenty of room."

Izabel turned to Janice. "I don't want to impose on you…"

"Nonsense. I'd love to have some company, and I'm sure Emily will, too."

"Emily?"

"She's Zack's second oldest sister," Addie told her with a smile. "She's a sweetheart."

Izabel nodded, though anxiety over spending time with strangers filled her chest.

"And if she'd like to check out the area, I'm sure Zack would be happy to show her around, too," Janice added. "He knows some beautiful sites around here."

"Oh, I don't want to be a bother to anyone," Izabel said, the tightness in her chest increasing. It would be easier on her own—though a lot lonelier. *But it would be nice to do something different.* She blinked, surprised by the thought. Maybe her more adventurous side hadn't died, after all.

Cade laughed at her comment and the rest of the table did, too. "Trust me," he said through his chuckles, "Zack is the last man to be bothered by spending time with a pretty woman."

Izabel lowered her gaze and felt her cheeks heat at his compliment. "Well, as long as he won't mind… I'd like to see more of the area."

"Zack would love to be your guide, honey." Janice reached over to squeeze her hand.

"Who's guide would I love to be?" a deep voice asked from behind Izabel. The sound washed over her, warming her skin—and, to her chagrin, her nipples tightened, too—as a large body leaned over to kiss Janice's cheek. "What are you volunteering me for now, Mom?" Janice's son took the empty seat beside her.

"This pretty young lady is a friend of Addie's and will be staying at our place while they're gone. I figured you wouldn't mind showing her around a bit."

His spellbinding, whiskey-colored eyes turned her way, but Izabel had already frozen in her seat. The man gazing at her now with a friendly grin on his handsome face was none other than the one she'd locked eyes with earlier. The same one who'd manhandled the blonde woman away from the reception. The overbearing one who reminded her of Chris and all her past mistakes. The man she'd already decided to avoid at all costs was now looking at her like she was a prize for him to win, with a charming smile on his handsome lips.

Spending any time with him—with this Zack—was the last thing she wanted, but how could she get out of it without insulting one or all of them?

"Well, sure. I'd be...happy to," Zack said, but Izabel thought she detected hesitation in his voice. What did he see in her that made him sound that way?

"I don't—" Izabel started to say, but Addie spoke over her, giving Izabel a side-eyed glance.

"Thank you, Zack. That would be wonderful. I was worried she'd be stuck at a hotel all alone until we got home."

He glanced between Addie and Izabel as if confused, then shrugged. "Not a problem, but it might help if I knew her name."

"Izabel," she said abruptly, a little more sharply than she'd meant. "Izabel Silva is my name, and I don't want to impose on you or your family." She gave Janice a quick smile. "I don't mind just hanging out at the hotel until Addie and Cade get back."

"Nonsense," Addie said, and Cade nodded in agreement. "There's no need for you to be bored and cooped up in town for a week. Right, Zack?"

"Yep, that's right." This time, his pleasant comment sounded more convincing. "Believe me, it's no trouble."

Izabel shifted, wanting to tell him—tell them all—to just forget it. But with everyone smiling at her, and Addie giving her that hopeful look that had always broken her resistance—and apparently, still did—she couldn't. "Well, if you're positive…"

"I sure am. It'll be fun. I'll show you around town and take you horseback riding if you'd like."

"I can't ride," Izabel said to the ground. She didn't want to spend time with this man, and she especially didn't want to do it on the back of a huge animal she'd never been around before.

"You don't ride?" He sounded shocked that she'd never forced an animal to allow her on its back.

"No," she flicked a narrow-eyed, meaningful look at Addie, "I've never had the desire to learn; that was Addie's thing."

"No problem," Zack said confidently, completely missing her meaning. "I'll teach you. It's a wonderful feeling to be out in the wild with nothing but your horse and the wide-open spaces. It's not something you should miss out on."

Izabel's head snapped up, a refusal on her lips, but once again, Addie beat her to it. "Oh, that would be great!" Addie bubbled, almost bouncing in her chair. "Then we can ride some trails when Cade and I get home. It'll be so much fun!"

Izabel stifled a groan. Addie had tried to convince her to go horseback riding when they were in college. The one time she'd agreed to go to a ranch with her friend for a long weekend, Izabel had backed out of the riding portion of the trip at the very last minute. Being a country girl had always been Addie's dream. Izabel had hated the idea of straddling a big, unpredictable animal you could only control with two thin strips of leather. She'd also hated the smell, but she had enjoyed flirting with the other cowboys while Addie went riding.

But still, this was Addie, and Izabel wanted her friend back. "That would be great." She pasted a wide grin on her lips. If she had to glue her butt in a saddle, she would do it if that's what Addie wanted. Izabel owed her that much, but how was she going to survive a whole week with a handsome, yet overbearing man? A man exactly like the one she'd left behind. A man whose smile made her skin tingle and whose eyes seemed to see deep into her soul.

He's not my type, she told herself as the conversation turned to other topics. *I don't have a type, but even if I did, it wouldn't be him.*

But deep down, she had a sinking feeling that her denials were all a lie.

CHAPTER 3

By the time the sun had dipped behind the trees, most of the guests had left the reception, wishing the new couple good luck and well wishes—and a few suggestions for their wedding night—before heading home. Zack had stayed to help clean up and was glad he did. It gave him more time to observe the gorgeous woman his mother and Addie had volunteered him to entertain for the next week. Something he was both looking forward to and dreading at the same time.

She had been beautiful from a distance, but even more attractive up close—and her eyes were the prettiest shade of green he'd ever seen. Just knowing she was looking at him had made his skin feel too tight and warm. When she'd been near, he'd detected a sweet floral scent that seemed to emanate from her. Her intoxicating scent and stunning good looks combined seemed to turn him into a tongue-tied idiot.

Grumbling to himself, Zack picked up the chairs he'd just collected and walked them over to the trailer where others were stacking them. He set them behind the accumulated stack and felt the hair on the back of his neck stir—as if someone was watching him. He turned with a dark frown that immediately melted away when he met Izabel's emerald gaze. She was standing outside the main house's sliding glass door, and just like before, their eyes locked and he could not break the connection, nor did he want to. Unlike before, however, it only lasted a second before she turned away. He grinned to himself, knowing what her interest meant. Maybe this week wouldn't be so bad, after all. And maybe she'd be a good distraction from the heavy weight on his shoulders.

That's a worry for later, he thought as he waved and said goodbye to his friends and, like several others, made his way across the main yard to where his truck was parked.

"Zack?" his mother called from behind him. "Hold on a moment, please."

He turned to see Janice jog toward him from the house. "Whoa, Mom, what's the big hurry?"

Pressing a hand to her chest, Janice exhaled several deep breaths before she spoke. "Y'all finished packing up quicker than I expected. I was worried I might miss you."

"Well, you caught me. What's up?"

"Cord's little Bethany is kicking up such a fuss, he looks like he's about to pull his hair out. I'm going to stay for a while to help him out. Would you give Izabel a ride over to our place for dinner? I promised Addie we would look after her and Cord while they're gone."

"How are you going to get home?"

Janice smiled and patted his shoulder. "Don't worry about me, baby. I'll get home just fine. Emily's already left to get dinner started, and I should be there before you sit down to eat."

Zack glanced at Izabel, who stood on the back patio, shuffling her feet and looking even more nervous than she had at the table. He'd already been volunteered to babysit the beautiful city girl—that's what she was for sure, a city girl—but he had hoped to have a few hours to get some control over his body's attraction to her before being thrust into her company again. Apparently, he wasn't that lucky. Not that he minded; he liked spending time with women—beautiful or otherwise—but the distraction she represented wasn't something he needed right now. Still, he couldn't say no to his mother. "Sure, Mom, whatever you need."

Janice grinned and patted his cheek affectionately. "You're a good son, baby. Thank you." She turned to wave Izabel over, and Zack had to stifle the groan that threatened to leave his throat as he watched her approach. His mother was saying something to her, but Zack didn't catch a single word of it over the hot blood rushing through him. *That woman has the longest legs I've ever seen,* he thought dumbly. If she had a brain to go with all that loveliness, he'd be in trouble. Her springy hair bounced around her oval face, and the small smile that curved her lips struck him like a hard jab to his belly.

"Right, son? Zack...?"

Zack blinked and shook the steamy images from his head. "Sorry, what did you say?"

Janice gave him a sly look he pretended to not understand. "I said, you'd be thrilled to take Izabel back to our place and get her settled in."

"Oh," Zack sputtered, feeling heat blossom in his cheeks, "absolutely. If you'll come with me, ma'am, I'll show you to my truck."

Janice leaned in close to Izabel and whispered something in her ear while Zack shifted in his boots, waiting for her to join him.

"Everything will be fine," Janice said, patting Izabel's hand that she still held.

Izabel smiled at her, and even though it wasn't directed his way, Zack's mouth went dry.

Oh, this is ridiculous, Zack chastised himself. *Just calm down.* He didn't go this crazy over a woman this fast. Not any woman. Ever.

She nodded. "Thank you, Janice. I appreciate your hospitality." She glanced at Zack. "Yours, too. Thank you."

He read something vulnerable in her green eyes, something almost like fear, and it made his hackles rise. *Who is she afraid of?* Something deep inside clicked and his muscles tightened, ready to battle whatever stalked her. He wanted to erase that look from her eyes, but then... Maybe she was afraid of him? He turned his head, not liking that thought at all, but also not understanding why she would feel that way about him. *She doesn't even know me.*

When his eyes returned to the two women, Izabel gave Janice a quick nod and without a glance his way, she headed toward where the vehicles were parked.

For the first time ever, he wasn't sure how to charm a woman to get her talking. Usually, it was second nature, almost like his superpower, but something about this woman had him on edge.

"I need to get my bags from Jorje's truck," she said and pointed. Zack recognized the truck Addie had sold to the younger man, along with her farm.

"No problem," he replied and followed her to the vehicle.

When they reached it, Zack lifted the two mid-sized suitcases from the truck bed as she grabbed a smaller bag from inside the cab.

When they reached his truck, he tossed the two suitcases he carried into his truck bed and held his hand out to do the same for the one she carried. She clutched it to her chest like a shield and gave him a narrow-eyed look that was almost insulting.

"I'm just trying to be helpful," he said gently.

Her expression changed and she looked down as her brown cheeks pinkened. "I'll hold on to this one for now."

He dropped his hand and shrugged. "Okay." He went to the passenger side door and opened it for her. "Hop in, and we'll get going."

She hesitated a moment before she gave him a timid, yet tight-lipped smile and slowly approached to climb inside. He sensed her reluctance to be near him and wondered why as he shut the door and went around to the driver's side. He glanced at her as he slid into the driver's seat and saw she had the soft leather bag—that could've been a large purse—on her lap, still hugging it against her body as if to protect it...or herself.

Why? he wondered as he pushed the key into the ignition.

He gave her his most charming smile, hoping to put her at ease, as he started the truck and headed out to the rural road that would take them home.

"So, Izabel..." he said, "what brings you to Montana?"

She chuckled softly and his skin prickled, appreciative of the sound.

"I guess Addie did."

"You been friends long?"

She glanced at him with narrowed eyes before focusing on the road ahead. "Yes, since college."

Zack frowned, wondering what her dark look meant, but he let it go. "Where did you go to school?" He saw her head snap to the side and her gaze almost burned the side of his face.

"Addie didn't tell you?" Her tone sounded accusatory and distrustful.

After a quick look in her direction, he shrugged it off. "It never came up."

From the corner of his eye, he saw how she stared at him for another silent moment before she shook her head, as if having an internal argument. "We met at U-Dub."

"U-Dub?"

She chuckled softly again. "Yeah, UW, the University of Washington. It's in Seattle. It's a very good school, if you're interested." She turned to stare out the side window as if brushing him off.

Does she think I'm just some dumb redneck? The tone of her voice certainly made it sound that way.

"I'm sure it is," he said, not sure how else to reply.

A mile passed with nothing but the sound of the tires humming along the pavement before he tried again. "Will you be staying in Montana long?"

He saw her shrug before she answered, "I don't know. I'm not sure there's much for me here."

Now, why did that sting?

"There's a lot more here than you might think," he told her, hoping she'd ask about it.

She only shrugged again as she stared out the side window, remaining mute.

Somewhat insulted by her lack of interest in the place he loved, he let the conversation wane and silence filled the cab for the rest of their short drive to his family's home. He sensed her reservation, as if she wanted to keep her distance, and he didn't want to seem pushy. Still, her attitude both annoyed and intrigued him, but questions only seemed to cause her to retreat more.

You just met her, he told himself. *Give her some time to get used to you...and Montana.* He had no doubt she'd fall in love with the scenery, if nothing else.

Turning into their long drive, Zack navigated the gravel road all the way to the house. He parked and pulled the key out before turning to her. "Hang on, I'll get your door."

"No need," she said as she quickly opened her door and slid to the ground.

Zack gritted his teeth, but said nothing as he hopped out of the cab, slammed the door, and grabbed her bags from the truck bed. He watched her for a moment as she stood, staring at her surroundings. He wondered how everything looked to her eyes. The look on her face said she liked it, but he wasn't sure she'd admit that...not yet, anyway.

"This way," he said and saw her startle at the sound of his voice. When she turned those big green eyes his way, his heart stuttered stupidly in his chest.

Relax, he berated himself.

"After you," she said, nodding toward the house, and Zack led the way inside. He held the door for her to enter and didn't miss how she hugged her bag closer to her chest as she entered, staying as far from him as she could. Whatever had her wound up wasn't going to be easy to get past.

It's going to be a long week, Zack sighed as he followed her inside.

CHAPTER 4

A woman with dark hair and dancing eyes turned toward her the moment Izabel entered the large ranch kitchen. She stopped in her tracks, unsure who this new person was or how to react. Zack squeezing past her got her to scurry into the room. She jumped when the stranger in front of the oven greeted them both with a big smile. "Mom *said* we were having company."

"Emmy," Zack set the luggage beside the kitchen door, "this is Izabel Silva. Izabel, this is my sister, Emily."

"So nice to meet you." Emily came forward to enfold Izabel in a warm hug. "Please, call me Emmy."

Izabel decided right then that she adored Zack's sister. She hadn't known what to expect after Zack's display with the blonde at the wedding reception, but Emmy was sweet and bubbly, and she reminded Izabel of Addie. She could see why the two women got on so well.

"Don't mind her," Zack said to Izabel with a wink. "Emmy's a hugger." He shrugged. "It's embarrassing sometimes, but we tolerate it as best we can."

"Oh, you," Emmy said as she playfully smacked her brother's brawny shoulder. "Why don't you be useful and take Izabel's bags upstairs? Then you can come down and set the table."

"Yes, ma'am," he said with a smirk and another teasing wink before he grabbed the bags and headed upstairs.

Izabel watched him go, admiring his retreat but confused by his willingness to do as his sister said.

Emmy's friendly chatter put Izabel at ease, and having Zack out of the room for a while didn't hurt, either. He bothered her, though she knew her judgment was unfair—he hadn't done anything to her to deserve being snubbed, but she couldn't get past his behavior at the reception.

"Izabel, if you wouldn't mind helping me with those," Emmy pointed to some potatoes laid out on the counter beside the large kitchen sink, "I'd really appreciate it."

Izabel grinned, liking how Emmy put her to work as if she were part of the family. "Please, call me Izzy, if you like...and I don't mind at all."

"Do you like to cook?" Emmy asked as Izabel began peeling the potatoes.

"It's not a gift I was blessed with."

"Oh..."

"Don't get me wrong. I *can* cook; I just don't love it. Do you?"

Emmy shrugged. "I don't mind it, but my older sister, Grace, *loved* coming up with new combinations." She seemed a little sad when she mentioned her sister, but Izabel didn't want to pry. "She used to spend hours looking through our mom's old cookbooks or scouring the internet for something new."

"Will Grace be joining us tonight?"

"Oh, no..." Emmy chuckled, though it sounded a little forced. "Grace is in the military. She joined after high school and hasn't been home on leave in...oh, two...no, three years now. We chat online with her sometimes, but we never know when she'll be coming home."

"I'm sorry to hear that," Izabel said, and she meant it. Having family close was important to her—maybe because she lived so far from her own now.

"It was Grace's choice," Emmy said. "She wanted to get out of this little town and find an adventure.. and it seems like she did."

Good for her, Izabel thought. Then silence fell for a long moment before she asked, "Did your mom teach you both to cook?"

A soft smile warmed Emmy's face as she nodded. "Yeah, she used to tell us we'd appreciate it one day..." she raised her eyebrows with a hint of innuendo, "and so would our husbands."

Izabel chuckled with her new friend, noticing how it sounded more natural this time.

"Who knows," Emmy said, not caring that it was a very old-fashion outlook, "she might be right."

"Maybe..." Izabel agreed with humor in her voice. "Or maybe we'll find a guy who likes to cook for *us*."

That got a laugh from Emmy. "Maybe," she said, her eyes bright and mischievous as she gently prodded, "but maybe if *you* had someone else to cook for...?"

Izabel shrugged. She had liked cooking for Chris, at least, she had at first. "Maybe you're right, too."

Emmy gave her a brilliant smile, then her eyes shifted furtively to the door where Zack had disappeared. Izabel followed her gaze, but there was no sign of the big man.

"So, what do you do for a living?" Emmy asked as she stirred the contents of a boiling pot.

Trepidation tightened Izabel's shoulders, though she didn't know why. Her career was over, but that didn't mean she had to talk about *why*. "I used to be a consultant for a high-end marketing firm in Seattle."

"Oh, that sounds interesting." Emmy paused her stirring and leaned her hip against the counter to focus her on her guest. "What kind of things did you sell?"

"I didn't exactly *sell* things...I assisted our clients in creating and implementing the best possible strategies to reach their target audience..." she tilted her head, "among other things that would help their particular brand succeed."

"Isn't that kind of like, selling?" Emmy gave her a confused look.

Izabel laughed. "Yes, I suppose in a way, it was."

"Were you good at it?"

Izabel nodded. "Yes, I guess I was."

"Sounds like you miss it."

"Sometimes." Izabel set the last of the peeled potatoes into the bowl of water by the sink. Then she took up a knife and began cutting them into cubes. "I liked the challenge of the job, but some of the politics...not so much."

"Is that why you left?"

She hesitated at Emmy's innocent question. She should've known it was coming, but somehow, she still hadn't been prepared. Anxiety knotted in her stomach, but she forced herself to relax. *There's no reason to worry about it anymore.*

"Basically," she replied. "Now, I'm looking to start over."

"Well, I guess Meriton is as good a place as any."

She cocked her head to the side. "I was thinking the same thing." They shared another chuckle, and then Izabel asked, "So what's your career of choice?"

"I'm a trauma nurse," Emmy said. "I work at a hospital in Missoula, but I also help Zack and my father on the ranch during my off time."

"A trauma nurse," Izabel said, awed. "That must be very stressful."

Emmy nodded and stirred the boiling pot. "It can be, but I like helping people."

"I'm impressed," Izabel said as she continued to cube the potatoes. "You must see a lot of terrible things in that job."

"It's not a big deal," Emmy said, "but yes, there have been some awful cases come through. But helping those people recover and live happy lives again can be very rewarding."

"You must be really good at your job, Emmy. Your family must be very proud of what you do."

Emmy grinned at her. "Thanks, I appreciate the support. and I know my family is proud of me," she glanced at the doorway behind them once more before she leaned in conspiratorially, "but there's someone else I'd really love to impress."

"Oh?" Izabel asked as a little smile tugged at her lips.

"It's a secret." She glanced toward the doorway again, and lowered her voice to a whisper. "He's a fireman in town. Only been here about two years, but I haven't gotten the nerve to approach him yet."

"Have you talked with him or know anything about the kind of man he is?" Izabel asked, hoping the other woman wasn't going to jump into something blind. In her experience, that always turned out bad.

"Oh, yes, he's a friend of Zack's. I know a little about him and have spoken to him a few times, but not seriously. He's nice, but he dates a lot like Zack does so I'm not sure how I feel about that."

Izabel wasn't sure how she felt about hearing Zack dated a lot, either. *Forget it,* she told herself. *He's just another man who thinks he's God's gift to women.*

Emmy's face darkened with doubt for a moment, but then she grinned and her soft brown eyes twinkled with mischief. "But either way, he's a fine-looking man to admire."

Izabel chuckled. "Well, I wish you luck. I hope he's a good man and soon sees what I already do."

"And what's that?" Emmy asked with a wide, curious gaze.

"A truly wonderful woman."

Emily lowered her head shyly. "Thanks. I hope he does, too."

Izabel dried her wet fingers on her pant leg and patted Emily's shoulder. "Thank you for sharing that with me."

"Sharing what?"

Both women jumped and shifted their attention to the doorway where Zack had reentered the room. He'd changed out of his dress shirt and into a black T-shirt, and it looked as if he'd stopped in the restroom to clean up before dinner.

Izabel couldn't help but notice the breadth of his shoulders or the hint of chiseled muscles beneath his cotton shirt. Izabel's lips parted as she stared, even as warmth flooded through her body. He filled the doorway and his strong presence seemed to crowd the kitchen as well.

Warning bells buzzed in Izabel's head, telling her to avoid this man at all costs. He was too much—too masculine, too powerful, too ruggedly beautiful—and not anything she wanted. Right...?

Getting herself under control, Izabel glanced at his sister and found Emily's eyes appeared nearly as wide as hers felt. Clearly, Emmy hadn't wanted Zack to know about her infatuation with his fireman friend, but how much did he actually overhear? Izabel scoured her brain for something to say as a distraction, but nothing came to mind that wouldn't draw his attention to her again. She didn't want that, even though every nerve in her body had come alive at the sound of his voice.

Thankfully, Emmy recovered far more quickly.

"Oh, nothing," Emmy said casually, as if talking about the weather. "I was just warning Izabel that you're a big flirt and not to fall for all that Zack MacEntier charm." She chuckled, waving a spatula to indicate his whole body.

Zack grinned and Izabel's heart fluttered in her chest like a flustered bird in a cage. *My goodness, the man is attractive.*

"Ah, Emmy, don't go ruining my reputation with Miss Silva." His dark eyes shifted to Izabel and something hot flickered to life in their whiskey-colored depths. "We have so much to do together, and I wouldn't want you giving her the wrong impression of me."

Emmy snorted. "I don't think anything I say could ruin your reputation any more than it is already. Besides, she's going to hear about it sooner or later, so better it comes from someone who loves you."

To Izabel's surprise, Zack chuckled at his sister's comment and stepped forward to kiss her cheek. "You are correct, dear sister." Again, his eyes fell on Izabel. "But do try to let her know of my good qualities, too."

Izabel couldn't look away. She was mesmerized by his penetrating gaze, as if he delved into her soul, looking for...what? She wasn't sure, but his bold directness unnerved her and his sweet interaction with his sister confused her. She'd expected him to be angry, to put Emmy in her place with some well-aimed, hurtful words. Instead, he'd laughed it off and showed affection rather than anger.

Emmy turned away from the stove to level a narrowed gaze on her brother. Still holding the spatula she'd been using, she placed her fists on her hip and shook her head. "Good qualities?" Emmy asked, as if questioning their existence. "Oh, you mean like how you leave your dirty clothes in the bathroom after taking a shower or how we find your smelly socks all over the house?"

Zack gave her a hurt look. "Ah, Emmy," he crooned, "that's not nice or entirely true. You know I pick up after myself, and I've only left my clothes in the bathroom a couple of times when I was late for an appointment."

"Sure..." Emmy grunted and turned back to her cooking. "Well, like I said, Izabel will figure you out soon enough. Now, please, go set the table, oh sweet brother of mine."

Zack chuckled again and dutifully did as he was told, and without a dark look or nasty comment.

Was I wrong about him? Izabel wondered as she grabbed a damp dishtowel to wipe down the counter for Emmy. *Or is he just putting on a good show for my benefit?*

She hated being so indecisive about anything, but she wasn't about to let another man in who thought he could control her. She'd already lost enough of her life already, and she vowed she wouldn't fall for another sweet-talking, good-looking jerk.

* * *

Dinner was a cheerful, delicious affair. Janice and her husband Grant had returned as Izabel and Emmy were putting the main course on the table. She entered the kitchen with a smile and praise for her children's help with dinner. She was introducing Grant to Izabel when a downcast-looking Cord Brody followed them into the kitchen. Though every bit as handsome as his twin brother Cade, the man looked exhausted. He gave them all a soft smile and thanked Emmy when she hurried to place another setting at the table for him.

"Mom said Bethany was having trouble going to sleep," Zack began after Cord had been introduced to Izabel. "Did you get her down okay?"

"Yeah," Cord said, running his fingers through his short, dark blond hair. "Thanks to your mom, Bethany's tucked in her crib for the night."

"Not alone, I hope," Izabel blurted out, and immediately wanted to bite her tongue when every set of eyes looked her way.

Cord's smile faltered, but he seemed to force it back into place as Janice replied, "No, of course not, dear. Joe Baker's watching over her. I told Cord he needed to get out of the house for a little while tonight."

Izabel pressed her lips together and glanced at Cord. Not knowing who Joe Baker was, she didn't know how to react—though, it was none of her business in the first place.

"Joe's the ranch foreman," Cord said in his quiet, unassuming voice. "He's been with us for years, and basically became a second father to Cade and me, even before our parents died."

"Yes, he fancies himself an uncle now," Grant added as he took a seat at the dinner table. "Uncle Joe is babysitting, and he couldn't be more thrilled." The others chuckled as they joined him.

Izabel dropped her gaze and wished she could sink through the floor. She shouldn't have blurted out that question; she had no right to say anything at all. She could feel the heat in her cheeks as she met Cord's gaze. "I'm sorry. I didn't mean to—"

"It's okay," Cord said. "I'm glad you care enough to ask. Some women—" He halted abruptly and cleared his throat, looking as uncomfortable as she felt, but then he continued as if he hadn't stopped, "Some people wouldn't bother. It says a lot about you. Though, being a friend of Addie's, I'm not surprised. She's told us a little about you."

Panic filled her chest. "She did?"

He nodded as he dished some food onto his plate. "Don't worry," he said, as if he'd noticed her discomfort, "she just told us about your college days, and that the two of you were very close."

"I see," Izabel murmured, staring down at her still-empty plate.

"Honestly, Miss Silva," Cord added, "as Addie's new brother and friend, I'm glad you're here. She's really missed you. I don't think she understands why the two of you had fallen out of touch."

Izabel accepted the bowl of mashed potatoes from Emmy and shook her head as she plopped a spoonful of the fluffy goodness onto her plate.

"That was entirely my fault. It wasn't a falling out; I'd just gotten a new job and became so wrapped up in my success and working my way up..." she shrugged, "and we just lost touch." She wasn't about to get into the other reason why she lost her friend, not with a room full of strangers. Besides, Addie should be the first one to hear it.

"Well, whatever the reason, I'm glad you found each other again."

Izabel met Cord's clear blue eyes—so much like his brother's—and grinned. She could tell she was going to like Addie's new brother-in-law as well. Funny that was all she felt. He was so good-looking and seemed so calm, but not even a whisper of desire stirred inside her. "That makes two of us."

"I'll second that," Zack said, raising his beer bottle in a celebratory manner. Grins spread around the table as each of them lifted their drinks to toast Izabel and Addie's renewed friendship.

Conversation ebbed and flowed as they consume their meal. They mostly discussed ranching and cattle, which Izabel knew little about. She listened anyway, hoping to garner an understanding of their way of life, just in case she was stuck here for the foreseeable future.

"Are any of you kids excited about the fair?" Janice asked as she eyed Izabel with a smile.

"What fair?" she asked.

"The county fair is coming up in a few weeks, and the state fair is at the end of the summer," Grant explained.

"Yes." Janice nodded. "There are rides and games and local vendors selling their crafts and lots of other things. It's usually a pretty good time."

Izabel smiled. "Sounds like it."

"I'm glad you think so," Emmy said, "because I'd love it if you came along. You and me and Addie and some of the other girls from town...we'll have a great time."

Swallowing her last bite, Izabel nodded. "I'd love to."

"That reminds me, Zack," Cord said as he wiped his mouth with a napkin and placed it on his empty plate. "Cade and I have something we'd like to discuss with you when he gets back."

Izabel watched Zack's brow furrow. *Damn it! How can he still be so good-looking, even when he frowns?*

"What kind of something?" Zack asked slowly.

Cord shook his head. "Cade made me promise to wait until he gets back. He's excited about it and wants to be there when we discuss it."

"Okay," Zack said, dragging out the word suspiciously as both men got up from their chairs and began clearing the table—another thing that surprised Izabel. "Can you at least tell me if it's something serious?"

"Define serious," Cord said teasingly as he began loading the dishwasher.

"Oh, you know, burning barns or angry ex-boyfriends looking to hunt me down... You know, that sort of thing." Zack didn't sound as if he was joking, but Cord laughed, anyway.

"No, nothing like that," Cord said between chuckles.

Zack brought coffee cups over to the table, along with some tea bags and then a pot of fresh coffee and a hot teakettle.

When did they do that?

"Thanks for dinner, Emmy. It was wonderful," Zack said as he set the items on the table.

"I second that," Cord added from the sink.

"Me, too," their father added with a grin as he got to his feet.

"You're all very welcome," Emmy said with a smile as her father kissed her cheek and, with goodnights all around, headed upstairs.

Zack patted her shoulder and returned to the sink with the last of the dishes.

They went back to their previous conversation, where Zack tried to pry information from Cord—and growled at Cord's mysterious replies—as they finished washing up.

Izabel watched, fascinated, having never witnessed any man doing household chores without complaint.

She must have looked as shocked as she felt because Janice leaned forward and whispered, "Close your mouth, dear. You don't want anything flying in there uninvited."

Izabel's cheeks heated as her gaze shifted to the older woman. Janice's eyes twinkled with mirth over the edge of her mug as she sipped her drink.

"Yeah," Emmy joined in, "it's only fair they clean up. We did all the cooking, and Mom—with Dad's help, of course," she smiled at her mother, "did all the work to raise us. The boys know that and do what's right."

Izabel didn't miss the way Emmy called them 'boys,' even though both men towered over her short frame.

She shook her head. "I guess I'm just not used to men helping out in the kitchen," she said before taking a sip of her herbal tea.

"Sounds like you've been hanging around the wrong kind of men," Janice said, but Izabel didn't bristle. Janice was only too correct.

Her eyes wandered to Zack as he worked with Cord. Could this man she'd thought to be overbearing and controlling be something else...something better? The kind of man she'd dreamed of finding? Could her attraction to him be a good thing? Her heart lurched at the thought, even as a voice in her head screamed at her to be wary.

Izabel raised her eyebrows and nodded at the other woman's comment. "You may be right."

But only time will tell..

Chapter 5

Zack was up before the sun the next morning, eager to get his chores done so that he had time to show Izabel around. He knew his mom, dad, and sister would be up in an hour or so too, all fancied up for church. Of course, Mom and Emmy would try to convince Zack to join them, but he wasn't much for church. His dad would understand as he used to be the same way, and he knew Zack had work to do. And today, Zack had a beautiful woman—a goddess, as he'd come to think of her—to entertain as well.

The sun was just peeking over the treetops when he'd finished mucking out the horse stalls and giving them their morning meal. He loved this time of day, when everything was just waking, looking bright and new. It was almost surreal—a dreamlike vision he witnessed daily.

He paused to gaze around their homestead and the two-story, pale-yellow house with his mother's prized flowerbeds lining the front porch. An old clematis, with years of growth, had twined its way over the deck rails and posts in a haphazard, yet polished, sort of way—thanks to his mom's attention. Its pinkish-white flowers bloomed profusely along every winding branch and provided a nice backdrop for the other multicolored flowers that made up the rest of the garden—and later, roses would fill-in when the other flowers faded. The small green patch of lawn was framed by the gravel driveway that wound its way to the country road, and overhead, the sky was a clear, warm blue, hinting at the beautiful summer day to come.

Happiness and pride filled his chest, and he smiled as he slid the door closed on the matching pale-yellow barn. The fields beyond where the horses ran, played, and fed on the early summer grasses looked inviting, and he considered riding over to the winery to check on things. Then he remembered that Izabel had said she didn't ride, and he reconsidered.

He shook his head. He'd give her some lessons while she was here. *Everyone should ride, at least once.*

Dusting himself off, he crossed the dooryard, in a hurry to get washed up. He told himself that the grinding knots of anxious excitement were only because he had a lot to do today, and not because a beautiful woman would be sitting at the table with him, her sparkling green eyes watching him, sometimes smiling with reservation. He wasn't sure if that was just because she didn't know him yet, or if she feared him for some reason he couldn't fathom. Either way, he planned to find out.

He would also make sure she smiled more. She had a lovely smile that made her look happier, of course, but she also appeared younger when her plush lips pulled back and her white teeth flashed in a wide, honest grin.

The image made his body tighten, and he felt an unexpected twitch in his jeans that he immediately shut down. She *was* attractive, but she was also a good friend of Addie's, and he didn't want to upset Izabel by coming on too strong.

Wait... What? He halted as he pulled open the door to the mudroom. *When did I decide I wanted more with her?* Was he thinking about asking her out? Going on a date? He hadn't been on a date in almost a year. Hell, the last woman he'd gone dancing with was the woman he'd met at the fair when he ran into Cade in Washington. He'd been too busy over the last year trying to dig his way out of debt to spend much time courting women.

That thought brought his womanizing youth to mind and the old nickname that had been bestowed upon him, much to his chagrin.

Many years ago, when Zack was just out of high school, his friends had started calling him Casanova as a joke that held a little too much truth. He'd been foolishly proud of that moniker, but over the long years since, something in him had changed. Now he cringed anytime someone used that old nickname, and knowing all the mistakes he'd made to earn it brought more than a little shame. Yes, he liked women and had dated several in the past—stupidly, sometimes more than one at a time, though he'd learned that lesson the hard way—but for the last few years, he'd avoided the women in or around town. It made things awkward when the relationship eventually ended and, though most of them were still friends, he had enough local exes as it was—even one or two who would happily slap his face or verbally run him down if anyone would listen.

Izabel was beautiful, but he had more important things to do than chase her. He could be a friend though, and as long as things stayed that way, he wouldn't be distracted.

* * *

Who the hell am I kidding? Zack thought as his truck trundled down their dirt drive an hour later. From the corner of his eye, he could see Izabel's wide, caramel-brown curls bounce with every pothole or dip, making him more aware of her than he wanted to be. What he *did* want was to reach over and test the springiness of the soft mound of fluffy hair, to feel its silky texture, to bury his face in it and fill his lungs with her scent. The images that swirled in his mind and the heat pumping in his blood at just the thought had him grasping the truck's steering wheel in a white-knuckled grip and doing his best not to growl with need.

This woman was the biggest distraction he'd ever met!

She had yet to say a word since they'd crawled into the cab. He'd seen the hesitation in her step as she'd approached him outside the house and the odd look she'd turned his way when he'd opened the passenger side door. Her quiet 'thank you' had been the only words to pass her plush lips in the last five minutes, and Zack wracked his brain for some topic that wouldn't make her pull away further. He wanted to get to know her, wanted to hear about her life, and what made her so distant. She'd seemed more open and natural with Addie at the wedding reception, and even with his family last night, though there had been some reticence then too, and he wanted to know why. But he couldn't just—

"How big is your ranch?"

Zack jumped at her quiet question and glanced over in surprise before his eyes darted back to the road. He rubbed the back of his neck and told himself to calm down. "We have about five thousand acres."

Finally, she turned her wide green eyes on him. "Wow! That's a lot of land."

He shrugged. "Not really…not by Montana standards, anyway. It's only a little over average for the ranchers around here, but we do graze on some leased land as well, so we have a few more cattle than normal."

"How many is a few more?" Izabel asked, sounding more curious than before.

"Well," he said as he made a turn onto the paved state route toward town, "right now we have close to a thousand animals."

"That many?" she asked and he smiled, glad to have a conversation going.

"How do you manage it all alone?"

"I don't do it alone," he said. "We have a couple of hired hands who do some of the work, Emmy does things when she can, and our neighbors help out when there's too much for us to do by ourselves. Like in the fall, when we have to round up the cattle for market or to get them out of the hills for the winter, and we do the same for them when they need us."

"Your neighbors? Like Addie and Cade?"

"Yes, and Cord, Joe their foreman, and several others around here."

She nodded, but didn't comment further.

"Have you spent any time around a ranch before?" he asked, wanting to hear more of her sweet voice and to learn as much about her as he could.

Izabel laughed—the sound like warm water washing over his skin—and it left goosebumps in its wake. "Only once," she said, still chuckling. "Addie dragged me to a dude ranch in Canada once when we were in college, but she couldn't get me on a horse."

"I think they call them guest ranches now."

"Whatever," she said with a dismissive wave that made Zack chuckle. "It was a nice enough place, and it was filled with *dudes*."

Zack thought he caught a touch of humor in her comment and grinned.

"Why didn't you go riding?" he teased. "Too scared?"

"Damn straight," she replied. "Those creatures are beautiful but *huge,* and all those cowboys would give me to control it were two little strips of leather! No, thanks."

Zack chuckled. "Well, there's a little more to it than 'two little strips of leather.'"

She turned her narrowed green eyes his way. "Like what?"

He paused to turn onto another dirt road. "Well, you use your feet, your knees and thighs, your hands, your butt...basically, your whole body can be used to control the horse. You use your voice and emotions, too."

"Emotions?" she asked, disbelievingly. "What do emotions have to do with anything?"

"Animals can sense your moods and will react to them," Zack informed her. "To control a horse or any animal, you must first control yourself."

"Hmm." She pressed her lips together and turned to look out her window again.

"What?" Zack asked, because he wanted to know and he wanted to keep her talking.

"I'm not sure I believe you."

Zack grinned. "Well, I'll just have to show you this afternoon."

She glanced at him, her brows raised. "Show me?"

"Yeah, I'm going to give you your first lesson today." He didn't know when he'd decided that, but he intended to see it through.

"I don't need riding lessons," she snipped, crossing her arms over her chest.

"I thought you were going riding with Addie when they get back?" he asked, noting how her plush, dusky-pink lips compressed into a tight line. "How are you going to do that without lessons?"

She huffed and looked out the window, clearly unwilling to discuss it further, but Zack had another question.

"Why don't you like me?"

She turned toward him and he glanced at her.

"What are you talking about?"

"You don't even know me, but you seemed determined not to like me," he said. "I just wondered why?"

He chanced another peek in her direction and saw surprise and something else on her face.

"It's not that I don't like you..." she said, dropping her hands in her lap. "You just remind me of someone I don't want to think about."

His shoulders shifted. He didn't like that idea. "How so?"

She sighed and looked out the window. "You remind me of my ex-fiancé."

"Ah, so he was a ruggedly handsome fellow, too." He'd hoped a little teasing might lighten her mood.

She opened her mouth as she turned his way, but appeared to think twice about her reply when she met his grin. Instead of ripping his head off—as it seemed she'd intended—she sat back in the seat and lifted her chin. "I suppose you could say that." Her lips curled at the corners and they shared a mutual smile. Warmth settled in Zack's chest, knowing she was joking right along with him.

A comfortable silence settled over them and an internal tug pulled at Zack. He wanted to know more, but he'd gotten a little from her and she seemed to need the quiet. Still, he had one more thing to say.

"Whatever he did," Zack said, referring to her ex, "he's a fool to have hurt you, and I'm sorry it happened."

He heard the hitch in her breathing, but didn't turn her way, suddenly feeling uncomfortably shy. *Now, why is that?* He was never shy. What was it about this woman that had his emotions bouncing all over the place?

"Thank you," she said and something in her voice drew his gaze to hers and his belly tightened with dread.

"What's wrong?"

She shook her head and tried to blink away the tears, a half-hearted smile pulling at her lovely mouth. "Nothing's wrong," she explained. "I'm grateful, that's all."

His frown grew darker and more confused. "Grateful?"

"Yes, most men would've wanted to know more, expected me to tell them everything."

Zack shrugged. "You'll tell me when you're ready." And he had no doubt about that. Women loved to talk to him, had told him several times that he was a good listener. He wanted to know more about Izabel, but he knew he must wait for her to make that choice.

"You're a bit arrogant, aren't you?" She sounded annoyed.

"It's not arrogance," he turned his dark eyes toward her, wanting her to see the truth of his next statement, "it's respect. I won't push you more than you're willing to go. Not in riding, or talking, or anything else, but I will ask questions and I *will* challenge you. It's up to you whether you answer them or not."

She blinked at him, her lips slightly parted as if she couldn't believe what he'd just said.

What kind of men had she been hanging around? What kind of man had her ex-fiancé been that she had such a hard time trusting him now? What kind of hurt was she carrying to put that look of doubt in her pretty green eyes?

Zack didn't have an answer for any of the dozens of questions that crowded his mind, but he knew now wasn't the time to pursue them. Izabel needed coaxing, gentleness, and patience before she would trust him, and Zack intended to give her everything she needed...and maybe a little more, too.

CHAPTER 6

Izabel squirmed in her seat, unsettled by the big cowboy beside her as he navigated his truck down the dirt road toward his family's winery.

Had he really just given her control of their interactions? Had he really implied that he respected her and her feelings? Why wasn't he demanding to know what had happened? He'd picked up on her unease more readily than she'd expected, but she hadn't thought he'd confront her with it and then tell her she was right.

Well, not exactly that. But in not so many words, he had let her know her feelings mattered. Her distrust of men—of him—mattered. Maybe she didn't have to be so cautious. Maybe she could relax her guard a little and see how things went.

She chanced a quick peek at him. The man was gorgeous and she'd always been attracted to tall men, but not usually ones as rugged-looking as Zack. If she had a 'type' at all, it was the tall, lean, businessman type, with a nice suit, shiny gold accessories, and highly polished leather shoes. Zack was as far from that as a man could get, yet, she couldn't deny the pull she felt, drawing her toward him like a magnet to metal. The man looked hard as granite and strong as a bull, and his whiskey-colored gaze seemed to see deep into her soul...

He sees too damn much! It was unnerving how astute he could be.

"I see," she murmured, unable to think of anything else to say in response to his comments about challenging her without pushing.

He glanced at her and she met his gaze. "I won't hurt you, Izabel, and I won't let anyone else hurt you, either." He refocused his attention on the road, his hands shifting on the steering wheel. Izabel couldn't help but notice how the muscles in his forearms—exposed by his rolled-up sleeves—flexed beneath his bronzed skin and the size of his powerful hands. A flash of what those warm, calloused hands would feel like as they rasped over her skin, caressing her in all the right ways, stole her attention. A pleasant heat flushed through her body, leaving her skin tingling, desperate to touch and be touched.

She banished the wayward thoughts with a shake of her head and opened her mouth to tell him she could take care of herself—she'd been doing it for years—but the words wouldn't come. Something in the tone of his low voice and the honesty in his whiskey eyes wrapped around her like a velvet caress and warmed her in ways nothing else ever had.

She turned away, disturbed by the feelings he engendered inside her and by the intensity of her attraction to this man she barely knew. Staring out the side window, she couldn't help but wonder once more if she'd judged him too quickly.

A curse exploded from Zack's lips, and Izabel jumped in surprise. She huddled against the truck's door as she turned to find a dark frown marring his handsome features.

"What?" she asked, unsure what had caused his outburst.

He raked his fingers through his hair and mumbled something to himself, then flicked an apologetic look her way. "Sorry, I didn't mean to startle you." He nodded toward the front of the truck as it slowed. "The damn protestors are back, and they're not supposed to be up here. This is private property. *My family's* property."

He sounded angry, yet she couldn't help but ask, "Why? What are they protesting?"

Zack shook his head. "They claim they're here to protect the land, but that doesn't make sense." He waved a hand toward them. "Just look at the mess they've made."

A group of fifty or so people marched and milled around the side of the road with posters that read 'Cows are Killing Our Planet' and 'Save the Earth.' But that wasn't what Zack had indicated and Izabel nodded, understanding his meaning. Not only had the protesters' vehicles carved deep grooves into the grass near the sign indicating the MacEntier Winery was not far away, but wrappers, cups, and paper littered the area.

Zack grumbled another curse as he shifted into park and turned the ignition off. He sighed and looked at Izabel. "This might get a little ugly," he told her as he pulled the latch to open the door.

"Wait." She grabbed hold of his arm to stop him. "What do you mean, ugly?"

He glanced at her hand on his arm and grinned. His whiskey-colored eyes met hers, and she felt the connection sink beneath her skin as something hot stirred low in her belly. Her breath caught when he took her hand in his and brought her fingers to his mouth. He kissed her knuckles slowly, his eyes daring her for more. Her body leaned toward him, all thought and fear burned away by the fire he lit inside her with just a look and the soft, sweet press of his warm, chiseled lips.

"Don't worry, darlin'," he murmured as he released her and slid out of the truck. "I'll be right back."

He closed the door and turned toward the protestors. "Y'all need to leave," he shouted, and Izabel blinked, feeling dazed and somewhat disorientated.

Had she just allowed him to kiss her hand? Did he actually do that? Who does that anymore? And why had she longed for him to do so much more? What was wrong with her? Hadn't she learned to stay away from men like him? Men who took and demanded more than their share...

But that was unfair, not only to Zack but to herself. Sure, she was attracted to him—who wouldn't be, the man oozed sexual appeal—but she had it under control, and Zack hadn't done anything to make her think he intended to demand anything more than friendship. Though he had startled her with his loud curse and made her feel small and vulnerable with his sheer size, he couldn't help the breadth of his shoulders or the length of his long legs—from what she'd seen, he took after his father in that way.

Now she watched as he waved his arm and argued with several protestors blocking the road to the winery. She'd been somewhat excited to see their setup—having been to several wineries in the past for her previous job—and she was very curious to learn what they had planned. But as the argument outside grew more heated, her previous assumptions reasserted themselves and she wondered what darkness hid beneath Zack MacEntier's handsome exterior.

"Go ahead, call the damn cops!" one of the protestors shouted at Zack's back a few minutes later as he shook his head and marched back to the truck. His back stiffened at the comment and he paused briefly, but then he kept walking. Jaw firmly clenched, his face looked as if it had been carved from granite when he yanked open the door and slid into the seat beside her. His overwhelming size struck her again, and her newly dredged-up doubts had her sliding away from him.

He glanced at her, taking in her hunched shoulders and wide gaze, and his face softened. "I'm sorry you had to see that," he said as he swiped his phone off the dashboard. "They're not exactly the friendly type."

"Have you..." She hated the hesitation in her voice. Straightening her shoulders, she cleared her throat. "Have you argued with them before?"

He chuckled mirthlessly and nodded as he turned on his phone and dialed a number. "Yeah," he said, "several times. Some of them aren't bad, but that big guy with the bushy beard seems to be spoiling for a fight."

She'd seen the man he described step into Zack's space as they argued. They'd stood practically nose-to-nose, and the other man *had* looked as if he wanted Zack to hit him.

"Is it always like this?"

He shook his head as he lifted the phone to his ear. "No, like I said, some of them are okay—" He halted as another voice spoke over his phone. "Hey, Josh," Zack smiled as he spoke, "you anywhere near my place?"

He paused as the Josh-person spoke on the other end of the call.

"Yeah, the protestors again. They're on our property; the same place as last time." Another short pause followed. "I don't know. Could you just come and get them out of here? Maybe give them a fine or something?"

Josh must've said something he didn't like because Zack muttered another curse. "All right, just make 'em leave then. They won't listen to me and keep trying to start a fight." He listened briefly and nodded. "Yeah, I'll be here. Just hurry."

He ended the call and tossed his phone back onto the dash. They sat in uncomfortable silence, Zack glowering at the protestors while the bearded man made vulgar hand gestures and cursed at Zack. After a couple of minutes, the man seemed to notice that someone else was in the truck. He leaned to the side to get a look at Izabel, and the cruel smile that lit his face made her sit back in her seat. Chills raced up her spine as she froze in place and suddenly, she was back in Seattle, hiding in the bathroom from Chris and his endless admonishments. The hard, sharp edges to his words never failed to cut her down, and they only got worse the longer she'd been with him.

She'd been in that situation so many times, and she kept telling herself that he just wanted everything to be perfect for this thing or that event because he worked so hard at making everyone happy. It took her far too long to realize that he made everyone happy...but her.

From the corner of her eye, Izabel saw Zack lean forward. Eyeing the man ogling her, Zack shook his head, surprising Izabel once again. Apparently giving up on trying to upset her, the protestor went back to shouting insults at Zack.

The man beside her sighed and turned toward her, warming her a little when she met his amber gaze. She read anger, embarrassment, and remorse in the warm brown depths. "You're safe," he said with a nod and soft smile that she couldn't help but return.

The tension in her shoulders loosened and she released the breath she hadn't known she'd been holding. How did he know she'd needed to hear those words? And why did he act as if he were her protector? Would he want something from her now in return for his kindness?

"Are you okay?"

She blinked and realized she'd been staring at him. Her hand trembled slightly as she pushed a stray curl out of her face. Silently cursing her trepidation, she nodded and looked away. "I'm fine."

"I told you I wouldn't let anyone else hurt you, either," he said, and she met his gaze once more. "And I mean what I say."

She frowned. Had he guessed her thoughts or did she accidentally say them out loud.

"Do you believe me?" he asked, looking almost desperate for her affirmative answer.

Yes, yes, yes, echoed inside her head, but all she could do was stare at him. Part of her wanted to scoot closer, to feel his heat and the hard strength of his body, while another part wanted to run but couldn't move. Struggling to pull herself together, she opened her mouth but wasn't sure what she would say. Luckily, she was saved from having to say anything when the red and blue lights of the sheriff's vehicle flashed behind them.

Zack glanced over his shoulder out the back window. "Good, he's here." He leaned over and brushed his fingertips over her cheek, leaving a trail of fire on her skin. All she wanted was to lean into his touch, but she fought the temptation. "I'll be right back." After an intense pause—during which she couldn't look away or move, her heart thudding heavily in her throat—he dropped his hand. "Will you be okay in here for a while?"

She nodded, still too scattered by her reaction to his touch to put words together.

"Good," he said and hopped out of the truck. "Please stay in the truck."

She nodded, having no intention of leaving the meager safety of the cab.

He gave her a quick, reassuring smile, then closed the door and turned to the deputy—who must be the Josh-person Zack had spoken to on the phone.

What the hell is wrong with me? Why were her emotions so chaotic? One minute she felt wary of Zack and the next, she wanted to curl up in his lap and let him hold her...and possibly do more. She'd never been this befuddled by a man before, nor had she ever been so willing to trust one she barely knew.

She watched as he greeted the deputy and cringed as more loud shouts came from the crowd. Izabel didn't see who the voice belonged to, but she guessed the shouts had come from the bearded man again. Zack exchanged a few words with the deputy, then stepped back as Josh turned to the crowd.

"All right," he said loudly to the group in general, "you all know you can't be here."

"We have a right to assemble and protest," the bearded man replied.

Josh nodded. "Yes, you do, but not on private property. You're just lucky the owner doesn't want to press charges. Now, y'all pack up your stuff and head down to the main road."

"That won't do anything!" another protester yelled while several others joined in with similar complaints.

"If you stay," Josh warned, "then I'll have to arrest you for trespassing. Is that what you want?"

The crowd thought this over for a moment, but when another sheriff's vehicle appeared coming up the hill, they seemed to think better of the situation.

"Come on, folks," Josh cajoled as the other deputy approached. "Mr. MacEntier has a right to his privacy and to build whatever he wants on his land as long as he has the permits to do so, which," his volume increased when some of the protestors began to speak over him, "he does. So, get your things and move on. Now."

The crowd grumbled and looked less than enthused, but they did as Josh ordered.

The second deputy kept an eye on things as Zack exchanged a few more words with Josh. As she watched, the two men turned to approach the truck, and Zack opened the door when they reached it.

"Izabel," he said quietly, "I'd like you to meet a friend of mine. This is Joshua Barrett. Josh, this is Addie's friend, Izabel Silva."

Josh's smile transformed his face and she blinked in surprise. When she'd first seen him, he'd looked handsome, though brooding and serious, carrying himself like a cop or...a soldier. But now, with that gentle grin and the dimples in his cheeks, he looked like the farm boy next door—the one every girl had wanted in high school and for long after, too. His strong jaw was clean-shaven, and his blue eyes sparkled in the early morning sunshine.

"Morning, ma'am," he said in a deep, gravelly voice she imagined had melted the hearts of dozens of women. "Nice to meet you."

Strangely, neither Josh's good looks nor his sexy voice did anything for her, but she smiled a greeting just the same. "You too, deputy. Thank you for coming to our rescue."

Zack straightened a bit and glanced at his friend before shaking his head.

Had she offended him?

Josh chuckled and slapped Zack on the shoulder. "No problem, ma'am. I'm always glad to help a friend in need."

Zack rolled his eyes. "Give it a rest, *buddy*."

Josh laughed again.

The other deputy—a shorter and stockier man than either Zack or Josh, and not anywhere near as attractive—approached, since the protestors had piled into their cars and slowly drove away.

"So we'll see you Friday night?" the new man asked Zack.

"I suppose," Zack grumbled as he climbed into the cab and slouched behind the wheel.

"Tell Emmy to join us, too. Who's your friend," the second deputy asked as he grinned at Izabel, his dark eyes smiling as much as his mouth.

"Izabel, this is David," Zack said by way of introduction.

"Nice to meet you, ma'am," David said with a tip of his hat.

She gave him a bright smile, which seemed to irritate Zack, though she didn't understand why.

"You're welcome to join us on Friday, too," David offered.

She started to say she couldn't possibly, but Zack interrupted, practically growling. "Back off, Dave."

Izabel glared at him, but Zack wouldn't meet her eyes. Why did he seem so annoyed? Did he think to run off every man she smiled at, because she'd had enough of that for a lifetime. Suddenly, she wanted to assert her independence in whatever way she could.

"That would be nice," she said sweetly and smiled at Zack's surprised look. "I'm sure Emmy and I will have a great time. Thank you...Dave."

"Great," Dave said a little more exuberantly than Izabel liked. "Now, if we could just convince this big guy to join us..." He slapped Josh on the back good-naturedly.

Josh's expression turned pensive and he shrugged. "We'll see."

"Yeah, so you keep saying," Dave muttered as he stepped back and looked around. "Appears they're all gone, so we should get going, too." He glanced at Josh, who nodded, then Dave said goodbye to Zack and tipped his hat to Izabel before returning to his car.

Josh shook his head.

"You don't want to join us Friday?" Zack asked as if something were amiss.

Josh's eyes flicked toward Izabel before he answered, "It's not that. I've been gone a long time. Things...aren't what they once were."

Zack nodded. "Maybe they'll get better if you stop hiding."

Josh frowned and glanced at Izabel again. "We'll talk more later," he said to Zack, then nodded to Izabel. "A pleasure, ma'am."

"Call me Izzy, please, and the pleasure was all mine."

He grinned again, then stepped away to return to his vehicle.

Zack straightened in the seat and leaned forward to start the truck. "So, you ready for the grand tour?" he asked, seeming oddly eager.

Izabel wasn't sure what to think of his suddenly happy grin. "Sure."

"All righty, the winery is just down the hill. You can see it from here," he said, pointing. She could see a wooden building snuggled between two hills. It looked out over a short, wide valley that appeared to be filled with grape vines that snuggled up to another set of foothills, with the Rocky Mountains in the distance.

"It's beautiful," she said and meant it. The view alone would bring people from all over just to see it.

"I'm glad you like it." He shifted into drive and started down the hill. "It's taken a lot of work to get this far, and I'm hoping to have it finished this summer."

Something in his voice made her look at him sharply. Did he have doubts? From what she could see so far, this place had loads of potential, and her marketing mind went into overdrive with the possibilities. She could sell this as a winery, or a bed and breakfast, or...all kinds of other things.

Should she tell him?

Zack seemed proud of the work he'd put into it, but there was something else—something dark underlying his pride—that made her hold her tongue.

His odd mood swings were giving her whiplash. First, he ran hot, then cold, then hot again, and it unnerved her. Maybe he was just the type of man she'd thought him to be.

Her heart cringed at the thought, but she ignored it. Listening to her heart was what had caused her so many problems before, and she wasn't going to repeat them now. She came to Montana for a fresh start, and that certainly did not include a big, moody cowboy or stepping back to save a man's feelings or his pride.

This time, it was all about her.

CHAPTER 7

The sun was warm on Izabel's shoulders as she stood outside the MacEntier's pale yellow barn. She leaned against a corral post not far from the wide doors where Zack had faded into the shaded interior. Shoving her hands into her pockets, she kicked a pebble with the black toe of her fashionable half-boots. She'd thought about following him, but considering how her body had responded to his nearness during their tour of the winery that morning, she figured keeping her distance would be the wiser choice.

They'd returned from the winery hours ago, and Zack had disappeared for a while to take care of some other duties. Izabel had silently thanked him for the respite. Her body had practically buzzed with awareness on their way back to the house, and it had taken the rest of the morning to calm herself down.

She shook her head and kicked at another stone. There *was* something wrong with her. He'd had her hot and bothered from the moment he'd touched her in the truck until long after they'd returned. *Why had I allowed him to do that?* She wasn't normally so easy to tantalize, but Zack had made her heart race with nothing more than a dimpled smile and the flame in his whiskey eyes. Then he'd touched her cheek and her whole body lit up like a billboard at midnight, causing her to shift in her seat all the way back to the house.

After a few hours alone, she'd gotten her wits about her and had her aching body back under control, but the moment he'd knocked on her door, her heart had taken off like a shot and her skin was instantly too warm and too sensitive.

Something was definitely wrong with her.

On top of that, he was going to make her ride a horse! She knew nothing about horses or any other farm animal, but Zack had insisted. He'd reminded her once again about her promise to learn enough to go riding with Addie when she returned in a few days.

A few more long country days with Zack.

She bit her lip and stifled a groan. What was it about him that got under her skin so easily? He hadn't done anything too forward or even flirted with her much, but she couldn't help the nervous flutter in her stomach whenever he was near.

"Okay," Zack called as he led a pale-colored horse from the barn into the corral. "Are you ready to meet your mount?" He met her gaze and her knees began to shake.

*I can*not *do this,* Izabel thought as she stared at the big, pale-yellow-colored animal standing placidly beside Zack.

He grinned and waved her inside. "Come on in. She won't bite."

Izabel felt her eyes widen and she shook her head frantically.

Zack frowned. "Are you afraid?" His voice sounded surprised and his expression turned to concern.

"Maybe a little," Izabel confessed.

Zack tied the reins to a nearby fence post, then sauntered toward her.

Izabel eyed the big animal, not interested in getting any closer. The creature could run her over and stomp her to death with those sharp hooves if it wanted to. From the corner of her eye, she saw Zack approach and then step through the fence rails—all masculine power and cowboy grace. Part of her perked up at the idea of his closeness, while another part felt as leery of him as the horse. At that moment, however, Zack seemed the lesser of the two dangers and she allowed herself to lean toward him. She thought better of that action when his leather, horse, and rugged man scent tickled her nose. She refused to look at him, afraid of what he would see, but he didn't give her a choice when his rough fingertips gently turned her chin toward him.

When her eyes met his, he smiled, his dimples flickering beneath his neatly trimmed beard. "I won't let anything happen to you," he said softly, his deep voice sending a shudder shimmying up her back. "Come on." He took her hand—sending fiery tingles up her arm—and led her into the corral. "Let me introduce you to Summer."

Izabel couldn't take her eyes off him. The tiny flame in his eyes and the warmth of his smile drew her in, and she followed without another thought. The next thing she knew, she stood directly beside the big beast with Zack behind her. One of his large hands slowly swept over the horse's neck, while his bicep pressed into Izabel's shoulder and his musky scent surrounded her. The animal turned its head toward them, made a soft, pleasant sound, and turned back to the yard. Izabel stepped back with the animal's initial movement but came up short against the solid wall of Zack's chest.

"It's okay," he said quietly, his free hand brushing along her arm as if to soothe her fears. "She's a sweet girl. Aren't you, Summer?"

The horse made a sound like a chuckle and Zack laughed with her.

Izabel's lips curved upward, surprised by her reaction to Zack's gentle voice and warm touch. Apparently, he had as much of a calming effect on Izabel as he did on the horse. She only hoped the mare wouldn't get as wild as Zack sometimes made Izabel feel.

"This is Summer," he said in a gentle voice as he patted the horse's neck, clearly oblivious to the riot of sensations his nearness awoke inside Izabel. "She's been with us for twelve years, and you'll never meet a gentler mare. And she likes having her ears scratched."

To Izabel's alarm, Zack took her hand in his much bigger one and pressed her palm flat against the horse's neck. Izabel's first inclination was to pull her hand back, but Zack's work-roughened palm held hers in place. The next thing she noticed was the warmth of the muscled neck and the smoothness of the short hair as he slowly dragged Izabel's palm down to the horse's shoulder. He brought her hand back up and repeated the motion for several strokes. The movement soothed Izabel in a way she couldn't understand. She no longer wanted to put distance between herself and the large horse, and the fear that had gripped her at first had melted away—including her unease at being so close to the man behind her.

He released her hand and placed his on her shoulder. The action felt more right than anything she could recall for some time. Yes, her body warmed and tingled, and the desire to turn toward him—to run her hands up his chest and around his neck—almost overwhelmed her, but she banished it.

You barely know him, she told her body, though it didn't seem to matter. Folding her arms over her chest, she stared at the horse, wondering how safe it was to stand this close to such a large animal.

"What do you think?" Zack whispered. His warm breath tickled her ear and swept forward to caress her cheek. She glanced at him over her shoulder and met his knowing grin. He'd caught her off guard, and he'd done it on purpose.

Well, at least she was no longer wondering how it would feel if the horse decided to step on her toes.

She turned away. "I think I'm not a horse person."

He chuckled, low and deep, and her stomach stupidly fluttered at the sound. "That's just because you don't know any. So, just like getting to know me, once you learn a little more about them, I promise, you won't be able to stay away."

She frowned. Was he talking about the horses or himself? The tone of his voice made it hard to tell. *Is he flirting with me?*

"Okay," he said, stepping back and placing one hand on the horse's rump and the other on his hip. "I'll give you some do's and don'ts about horses, and then we'll get you in the saddle so you can get a feel for what it's like."

"Really? That fast? I mean, I petted it... Isn't that enough for one day?"

He grinned and something warm and liquidy pooled low in her belly. Why did she want to rasp her nails along his strong, bearded jaw?

"That's only a tiny step. I want to give you a little confidence in the saddle before we're through for today."

She groaned, but she also felt a little thrill. Not only would she be spending more time with Zack, but she'd also be working to overcome another of her fears as well. "All right."

For the next few minutes, Zack went over the steps for riding a horse—everything from how and on which side to mount, to how to hold and use the reins. His knowledge about horses amazed her, and she listened with rapt attention—not just because she wanted to be informed about what to expect or what to do in a given situation, but because his obvious enjoyment of the topic was contagious.

"You really like horses, don't you?" she asked, interrupting his explanation of how to use her knees to control the animal's speed and direction.

His grin lit up his eyes. "Yeah, I always have. My mom says when I turned five, I nagged everyone to teach me to ride. I couldn't wait to get into a saddle and take off like all my old cowboy heroes."

She tilted her head. "Cowboy heroes?"

His brows drew down and a look of concern filled his gaze. "Yeah...you know, Gene Autry, Gary Cooper, *the Duke*."

She shook her head. Westerns weren't high on her list of favorites, something she blamed her father for.

Zack stared at her in disbelief. "You've never heard of the Duke?"

She shook her head.

"How about John Wayne?"

Another shake of her head.

"James Garner? Steve McQueen?"

She lowered her eyes and shook her head once more. "I've never been much of a Western fan."

He slapped his chest and stumbled back a few steps, looking shocked. "Oh, you wound me," he said dramatically.

She chuckled at his theatrics.

"How can anyone not know John Wayne?" he muttered.

She drew her eyebrows together. "Me, all right? I don't know who he is."

"Was," Zack said with a half-grin.

"Was?"

Zack slipped his arm around her shoulders and gave her a little squeeze. "Yeah. He died back in 1979."

"Oh," she said, strangely unfazed by his nearness. "I'm...sorry? That's way before my time."

He chuckled at her confused tone. "Mine too, but it's okay. My dad's a big fan of old Westerns, and I guess it rubbed off on me. We used to watch them every Saturday afternoon when I was growing up. Something about that time with my dad was...special. You know?"

Izabel's heart squeezed, envious of his relationship with his father—something she never had.

He shrugged. "Not many people our age remember those names." His arm dropped from her shoulders and he stepped back. "It just means we'll have something to do tomorrow night."

Placing her hands on her hips, she glared up at him. "Were you teasing me or just testing me?"

He turned the heat of his warm whiskey eyes on her and winked. "Maybe a little of both."

A shiver started in Izabel's belly as Zack turned away to fiddle with part of the saddle. What was it with this man? Why did he make her feel safe and terrified at the same time?

"Okay," Zack said, turning back to her, "let's get you in the saddle." He stepped back and motioned for her to approach the horse's side.

Izabel's eyes widened. "Already?"

"Sooner's better than later."

"But..." She glanced between him and the horse a few times before she settled on him. "Would you show me first?"

His grin returned. "Of course. I'm sorry, I should've started with that, but I seemed to be a bit distracted this afternoon."

He gave her a quick wink—his eyes dropping to her lips—and Izabel's cheeks heated. He meant her, that she distracted him—and not because she asked too many questions. How did she feel about that?

Still debating that question, she watched as he stuck his booted foot into the metal loop at the end of a long leather strap attached to the saddle's seat that he'd called a stirrup, carefully describing the steps required to mount. He reached up to grip the horn at the front of the saddle and, with an easy display of strength and grace, he slowly hauled himself into the saddle. Sitting with his back straight and the heels of his boots angled downward, Zack gazed at her with another happy grin. "See," he said, "nothing to it." He swung his large frame back to the ground and faced her. "Your turn. Do you remember what else I told you about mounting?"

She nodded and repeated his earlier direction, "Always mount from the left."

"Yes," he said, sounding pleased, which warmed the flutter that still danced in her stomach. "Now, put your left foot in the stirrup." He held the item still for her to tuck her boot into. "Good. Next, grab the pommel." She had to grab his shoulder and hop on one foot to keep from tumbling backward.

His big hand on her back balanced her and she smiled her thanks. Feeling out of place and discombobulated by his touch and the hard muscles shifting beneath her hand, she couldn't help but wonder again, *Why the heck am I doing this?*

The reassuring grin he rewarded her with was one answer to that question.

"Okay, Izzy, just like I showed you. Pull yourself up while swinging your leg over the horse's rump to get your butt in the seat. You can do it."

She glanced at him over her shoulder, suddenly afraid. "What if I fall?"

"I'll be right here," he said, his expression serious. "If you slip, I'll catch you. I won't let you fall."

Her lips trembled slightly, but they stretched into what she hoped looked like a smile.

"You *can* do this."

She nodded. How did he always seem to know what she needed to hear? She could do this. She might be a city girl, but she used to be able to do anything. When did she become this silly, timid woman?

Dumb question, she told herself. She knew exactly when.

Pushing aside the bad memories, she focused on the instructions Zack had given her. Bouncing on one foot, she timed her leap and pulled. She blinked in surprise when she realized she'd done it.

I'm in the saddle!

What had she been so afraid of? Why had she doubted herself so much?

"Good job!" Zack cheered. "See, I told you, you could do it."

She bit her lip before her mouth curled into a huge smile. "You were right." As she met his gaze, an undefinable emotion passed over his face, as if he'd been stunned, but then he blinked and it was gone.

Good, she thought. *It's about time I caused a reaction in him.* She was tired of this one-sided attack of his overabundant charm.

A muscle in his jaw twitched as he stared up at her, clear appreciation in his eyes, and a feeling of feminine power swirled inside her. She shouldn't like the way he looked at her, but she did. It should have set off alarm bells inside her, but it didn't. She just felt warm and appreciated—and not just for her looks, but for her abilities as well.

He broke their connection, dropping his eyes and clearing his throat. "Okay, now that you're up there," his voice was slightly raspy, "how about taking a few laps around the corral?"

Her first inclination was to decline, but then she remembered that an hour ago she'd been terrified of climbing onto the horse's back. She thought of how Zack had explained everything, encouraged her when she tried, and praised her success. Then he promised not to let her fall. She straightened her spine. "Sure. I'll give it a go."

He grinned as he stepped over to the horse's head. "How about you, Summer? You ready to take this greenhorn around the corral? Just a little stroll to show her what a nice gal you can be."

Izabel watched him as he spoke to the horse, stroking the mare's jaw and neck before lightly scratching behind her ears. He'd been so patient with her and her fear of the animal on which she now sat. It seemed ridiculous now as he treated the mare with the same patience and gentle care as he'd shown her.

"You're good with horses," she said slowly, then blinked, surprised to have said the words out loud.

His lips curled upward and the dimples in his cheeks appeared. *Is that a blush on his cheeks?* He wouldn't meet her eyes. "I love them and they love me." It was a simple reply, but his words and tone said a lot about him.

"It certainly looks that way. You ever consider working with them?" Izabel asked and he looked up. It was her turn to smile when she noted the tips of his ears turned red as he dropped his gaze and stepped back.

He nodded. "Yeah, someday I'd like to do just that."

"Sooner's better than later," she teased him with his earlier words.

"Yeah, well..." he looked away, "sometimes it's not."

Izabel sensed his mood change, but didn't know why. She opened her mouth to apologize, hoping to see his smile return, but he beat her to it.

"All right," he said with a forced grin while rubbing his hands together. "To get Summer to move forward, just tighten your lower leg, brush your heel against her side, and be prepared for her to move."

Saddened by whatever pain had stolen his good cheer, Izabel nodded and tried to do as he'd instructed, but the horse only shuffled a few steps and tossed her head as if unsure what to do.

"No, no. Hold up." Zack came forward and gripped the halter to settle Summer down and then looked at Izabel. "When you close your lower leg, don't move any other part of your body."

Izabel frowned. "I didn't."

"You leaned forward and your hands pulled backward," he said, sliding his hand soothingly along Summer's sleek neck. "You're confusing her with too much movement. It's important that nothing else moves but your lower leg." He stepped back once more. "Okay, try again."

Izabel clenched her jaw in concentration, focusing on her ankles and feet, pulling them inward while holding the rest of her body still. The next instant, Summer stepped forward, slowly moving around the edge of the corral.

"Okay, now let your legs relax and just sway with the horse."

She did as he instructed and the horse walked on.

Grinning broadly, Izabel looked over at her handsome instructor. "I did it!"

He crossed his arms over his chest, looking ridiculously proud. "You certainly did. You want to try one more step?"

Eager for more—and feeling more like her old self—she nodded and Zack gave her instructions on how to get the horse to trot and then back to a walk again. They completed several rounds of these transitions before Zack called a halt.

Izabel laughed—had been laughing on and off the whole time. She felt exhilarated, happy, *alive*. Why had she never done this before?

"You're a natural," Zack said as he pulled the reins from her hands and tossed them round the top rung of the corral fence.

"It was so much easier than I thought it would be."

"You still have a lot to learn," he warned.

She nodded. "I know."

"Are you still afraid of her?"

Izabel stared back at him in confusion, unsure of what he referred to, but then she realized and leaned forward to pat Summer's neck affectionately while shaking her head. "No, not like I was."

"Don't lose all your caution about them," he said, sweeping his big hand over the mare's neck. "Horses can be dangerous, but as long as you are careful and don't get too cocky," he grinned, "then you'll be just fine."

"No problems there," she replied.

"Good. You've been up there for almost an hour. I know you've never spent time in a saddle, so your legs might be a little wobbly. Do you think you can dismount on your own?"

She frowned. "I...think so."

"Okay, then go ahead," he said as he positioned himself beside the horse. "I'll be right here if you need any help."

Grateful for his calming presence—not to mention his big, strong, capable body—Izabel lifted her butt from the saddle by settling her boots in the stirrups and straightening her legs. Surprisingly, her knees and thighs shook and suddenly, she wasn't so sure she could do what Zack had shown her earlier.

Don't be ridiculous, she scolded herself. *You got up here; you sure as heck can get back down.*

Doing her best to control her shaky legs, she swung her right leg back and over the horse's rump and began easing herself down with her left. Unfortunately, her left leg didn't hold and the heel of her right boot slapped against Summer's hindquarters, startling the horse and causing her to sidestep abruptly. Izabel lost her handhold on the saddle and felt herself falling backward—with her foot stuck in the stirrup.

She squeezed her eyes tight, waiting for the unpleasant shock of hitting the ground. When she landed, however, it *was* against something hard, but it wasn't the ground, nor did it hurt.

She opened her eyes to find Zack staring down at her as he cradled her against his broad chest.

"I told you I wouldn't let you fall," he said, his low voice huskier than normal.

Her heart squeezed at his words, but it was the warmth in his eyes that started the fire in her blood.

"Thank y-you," she stammered, feeling self-conscious and wondering where her caution where men were concerned had gone. None of her normal hesitation or fear of a man's nearness, no creeping feeling at his touch, no panicked need to scuttle away from him. Apparently, Zack didn't worry her any longer. Maybe he was a bit high-handed at times, but this man, who treated her and the animals in his care with such kindness and patience, was nothing like what she'd expected. "You can put me down now."

"Your foot's still stuck in the stirrup," he said, his eyes still locked on her face.

She glanced down and wiggled her leg until she freed herself from the metal ring. Then she turned back to him, locking her gaze with his eyes that still burned with a heat that made her skin tingle. "I'm free now," she murmured. It was the only thing she could think of to say.

He stared for another long moment, then nodded and slowly released her legs. Her knees buckled under her weight—or maybe she just wanted his arms around her again—and he pulled her close to keep her from tumbling to the ground.

"Easy, now," he all but whispered as he gathered her close, pulling her against him and holding her a little tighter than necessary.

She met his gaze and couldn't look away. Her hands rested against the hard wall of his chest and her whole body warmed with the heat radiating from his. A tremor swept through her that had nothing to do with her unstable legs. His gaze searched her face and then landed on her lips. She could feel the rapid pounding of his heart beneath her palm, but it was the flare of desire in his eyes that made her breath catch in her throat.

Is he going to kiss me? Everything inside her quivered with an odd mixture of anxiety and anticipation. *Do I want him to kiss me? Am I even ready for another man's kiss?*

She licked her lips. It would be so easy to slip her hands up around his neck, to lean into all those hard muscles and offer her mouth as encouragement to him, but she hesitated. Unsure of herself. Unsure of him. Being close was one thing, but kissing was a whole other world.

A moment later, he loosened his hold and released her, though he still gripped her elbows. "Are you okay to stand on your own?"

She nodded and he let her go. Her arms fell heavily to her sides and something like disappointment tightened her chest.

Zack murmured some soothing words to Summer as he pulled the reins from the fence. Then he turned to Izabel with what looked like a forced smile and her heart sunk a little lower. "Well, that's it for your first lesson. You should be proud. You did very well."

She smiled despite the awkwardness that fluttered between them. "When's my next one?"

"Day after tomorrow, I think," he said as he began to lead the horse back to the barn.

Her shoulders drooped a little as uncertainty weighed them down. Did he want to avoid her and the odd awkwardness between them now? "So long? Why not tomorrow?"

"I've got some work to do tomorrow, and believe me, you're going to want to take it slow until your body gets used to riding. I'm sure Emmy will be happy to have you tag along with her while I'm gone."

"What about the movie?" She nearly slapped her hand over her mouth. She hadn't meant to remind him of his earlier comment. *What am I doing?*

He frowned and cocked his head slightly.

Right. He didn't remember that he'd threatened to make her watch a Western with him tomorrow night.

"Ah, yes," he suddenly said, his lips curving upward in a big smile. "The Western. I've got just the one in mind. You'll love it." He glanced at the horse, then up at the darkening sky, and back to Izabel. "I'm going to take care of Summer and some other chores, but you should head on in. I'm sure Emmy would love the company."

"I will," she said, feeling stupidly breathless that he'd remembered—he even seemed happy to spend more time with her. "Thanks for the riding lesson. I'm looking forward to more."

His smile slipped slightly, but then his eyes brightened and one side of his mouth quirked up. "Happy to oblige you anytime." He winked. "See you at dinner." Then he turned and went into the barn with the mare right behind him.

The suggestive tone in his voice and that crooked grin of his did something to her insides, made her even more warm and fluttery than before—as if she would either melt with heat or take flight.

He's a good one, she thought. A gentleman in cowboy boots and work-worn Wranglers, but did that—and her body's unexpected attraction to him—mean she should follow where it led? Did she want to?

The undeniable pang of longing in her chest gave the answer, but how did a man-shy woman go about asking a cowboy for a kiss?

Chapter 8

Meriton was not exactly what Izabel had expected, with people bustling around and all sorts of shops lining the streets in the main part of town—including a tractor dealership, a real estate office, a funeral home, a movie theater, schools, and so much more, all rimmed by trees, open land, and mountains. Up the road to the north, a huge water tower sat atop a low hill on four steel legs and could be seen standing tall against the brilliant blue June sky. Emblazoned on its white, rounded wall was the town's name, written in navy blue letters that appeared to be at least six feet high.

Before today, she'd only seen the small portion of Meriton near the motel where she'd stayed with Jorje and Lana, and that had been out by the interstate. She'd thought the town center would be quiet and dead with not much to do, but she'd been mistaken. It *was* a small town, but from what she'd seen so far, Meriton had a lot going for it in addition to its active population with so many friendly faces. Everywhere they went, they ran into another friend of Emmy's, who seemed to know everyone.

"Well, I *have* lived here my whole life," Emmy had said when Izabel commented on this fact. "It's kind of hard *not* to know people around here."

"I suppose so," Izabel said, grinning at the elder lady—Mrs. Edwards—with whom Emmy had just passed the last fifteen minutes explaining Izabel's presence in their little town and her connection to Addie. It appeared many people were happy about Addie's marriage to Cade Brody.

"Now, if they could just get his brother to straighten himself out and find a nice girl..." Mrs. Edwards had said about Cord Brody, then sighed and shook her head. "Such a shame he got mixed up with that Suzy woman. She's always been trouble."

Izabel wondered what that meant, but she didn't ask. Emmy glanced at her nervously, looking uncomfortable, and swiftly changed the subject.

Once they said their goodbyes to Mrs. Edwards, they continued on their way, and Izabel once again had to hold back a moan of discomfort from her aching legs and backside.

"Whew." Emmy shifted a glance in Izabel's direction and grinned. "Mrs. Edwards must've had something else she needed to take care of."

Izabel frowned. "Why do you say that?"

"She's a very nice lady, but..." Emmy shrugged and her grin broadened. "She's such a gossip. I didn't think we were going to get away from her so quickly. And I didn't want her to regale you with all the bad parts about living in a small town. I'm surprised she didn't grill you about your status as a single woman." Emmy chuckled. "You probably would've had half a dozen guys knocking on the door tomorrow, looking for a date—and all from Mrs. Edwards' not-so-subtle invitation."

"But it's not her house, and I'm not her friend."

Emmy's lips thinned. "Doesn't matter. Everyone knows everyone and their business around here. It's hard to keep a secret, and the old ladies love," she drew out the word dramatically, "a great love story."

"Oh." Izabel stared at the ground and tried not to grimace. "Well, they'd be disappointed. I'm not in the market for a man."

"No?" Emmy asked, a little too innocently.

"No. I'm not like you, Emmy. I don't have a shiny knight willing to take me away from my dull life or to save me from my well-meaning, yet pushy, mother."

"I thought you got on with your mom...?"

Izabel nodded, remembering she'd told Emmy a bit about her mom on the way into town. "We are, but she's never been good at keeping her opinions to herself. She wants me to be happy, but she doesn't understand why I left my ex."

"Why did you?"

She glanced at her new friend and sighed. "It's a long story, but suffice it to say, he wasn't who I thought he was and he couldn't make me happy."

All he did was make me miserable, she thought but kept it to herself.

Emmy's eyes softened and shimmered a bit. "Oh, I'm so sorry to hear that."

Izabel pressed her lips together, acknowledging Emmy's comment with a dip of her head, but she wouldn't say more. She wasn't ready to talk about that yet, at least, not with Emmy.

"I'd thought..."

"You'd thought, what?"

Emmy shrugged. "You and Zack seemed to get along so well. I thought maybe you and he might...?"

Izabel shook her head. "It's a little early for that, don't you think? It's only been a few days, and I barely know your brother."

Emmy nodded and something in her countenance told Izabel there was more.

"What?"

Emmy looked up as if startled, but shrugged. "I'm just worried about him... I have been for a long time."

Izabel frowned. "He seems fine to me."

A soft chuckle escaped Emmy's lips. "He always *seems* fine, and if you asked him, he'd say he was fine, but I know he's not. Something's bothering him and I think...I think he's finally grown unhappy with his personal life."

"What do you mean?"

Emmy sighed. "I'm not sure exactly, but Zack used to be the biggest Casanova in town. His friends even gave him that nickname years ago, but he doesn't seem to enjoy the notoriety like he used to."

"I see." Another womanizer she'd be smart to avoid.

Emmy must have heard the censure in Izabel's voice, because her wide brown eyes glanced at Izabel and she reached out to stop her. "Don't get me wrong. Zack's always been a good guy and a great brother, he just..." Emmy sighed. "His is a long story too, but let's just say his heart suffered early in life, and he barricaded himself off from anyone who got too close."

"That's happened to a lot of people," Izabel sympathized. "They usually work it out."

"Yes, but I'm afraid he's waited too long, become too entrenched. People expect him to be and act a certain way, but that isn't who he is anymore. At least, he seems different to me now, but then again, I'm his sister. Maybe I'm just seeing what I want to see."

"Maybe," Izabel said, wrapping her arm around Emmy's and starting them walking again. "Then again, who would know him better than a caring, older sister?"

Emmy gave her a grateful smile. "Yeah, maybe... And maybe it'll make *you* feel better to know that I don't have a white knight, either," Emmy said in a small voice—returning them to Izabel's previous comment.

"What about that sexy fireman waiting in the wings to sweep you into his arms and take you away from all this." She waved her hand in a wide circle over her head, indicating the whole town.

Emmy's brows lowered and she blinked. "I never said that. I barely know him, and he doesn't seem to know that I exist as anything other than Zack's sister." Then a smile split her face and a mischievous twinkle entered her eyes. "But I plan to change that someday."

Emmy's cocky grin had instantly reminded Izabel of Zack. Just the thought of him had her pulse fluttering and warmth flooding her body. A little thrill of excitement knowing she'd see him tonight made her rethink her words about barely knowing him. Apparently, the rest of her wanted to get to know him very much.

He'd been gone before breakfast, off to take care of the errands he'd told her about the day before. The morning meal hadn't been the same without Zack's handsome face and quick smile, but Emmy had filled in a few gaps with her happy chatter before she and Izabel headed into town.

Their trip had been a bit of an adventure so far—and even more of a culture shock for Izabel. She'd never been to a small town—the closest she'd ever come were the suburbs of Seattle, which would never be classified as 'small.' She hadn't thought there'd be much for her here, and she'd not looked forward to the boredom she'd expected, but she'd been pleasantly surprised. Even more so today, after the fun she and Emmy had in the clothing shops they'd visited. The post office had been interesting, with all the friendly chitchat and gossip, as had their quick stop at the feed store. She'd met so many of Emmy's friends and neighbors that the faces had begun to blur together, and there was no way she would remember all their names. In no small part because, the whole time, Zack had been in the back of her mind, floating forward whenever she saw something that reminded her of him or Emmy mentioned him in passing.

Now, as the sun sank closer to the mountaintops, Izabel found herself thinking about him more and more, vibrations of eager anticipation humming in her belly. A smile curled her lips as she sauntered along the sidewalk as Emmy returned their conversation to her rendition of the town's history. But all Izabel could think about was how it felt to be held in Zack's arms, surrounded by his addictive scent, and warmed by his large, hard body all around her. She couldn't wait to spend some more time alone with the man she was learning to trust...maybe even a little more. She certainly found him attractive.

"Come on, Izzy," Emmy said as she hurried down the sidewalk. "The coffee shop is just around the corner."

* * *

An hour later, Izabel had discovered another reason to fall in love with this little town. The coffee shop they'd stopped in was more like a bistro or small café, with bare brick walls covered in tasteful art and old-fashioned signs. The tabletops were wooden, the chairs artistic with thin wrought-iron backs and legs, and soft, cream-colored cushioned seats. The whole scene reminded her of a painting of a French bistro she'd once seen.

And the food... The sandwiches they'd purchased were simple but flavorful, and the dessert—lemon custard that was so sweet and creamy, it was like pudding, and chocolate cream puffs, so light and delicate, each bite melted on her tongue—rivaled those she'd had at the best restaurants in Seattle.

Emmy groaned as she downed the last of her custard. "Oh, how I love this place! Didn't I tell you their lemon custard was to die for?"

Removing the remnants of her custard from her spoon with her tongue, Izabel nodded in agreement. "You weren't exaggerating," she said between licks. "This is amazing! And the coffee...?" She moaned in pleasure as she took a sip of her iced mocha brava, then licked her lips. "So good."

"I know," Emmy said as she pushed her empty dishes away. "I wish I could make a dessert this good."

Izabel nodded, wholeheartedly agreeing. If she could cook like this, she'd eat at home every night. She'd also be considerably rounder than she was now.

Maybe then, Chris would've been better to me...would've appreciated me more, she thought and then blinked. *Where the hell did that come from?* She didn't need to make frilly food for a man to treat her right. The next man she got involved with would have to take her as she was or take a hike. She would never hide parts of herself to keep the peace ever again. She nodded to herself as Emmy stood and grabbed her blended frappuccino.

"We should probably get back," Emmy said. "Mama's visiting a sick friend and asked me to make dinner tonight."

"Of course." Izabel got to her feet and grabbed her caffeinated beverage. "I'd be happy to help, if you like...?"

Just inside the front door, Emmy spun on her heel and her puckered brows made her concern evident. "You don't have to, you know. You're a guest, and Zack won't—"

Izabel smiled and waved her free hand in the air, dismissing Emmy's worries. "I don't mind," she said. "After you kept me company all day, it's the least I could do."

Emmy sipped her coffee. "Well, in that case," she grinned, "I'd love some extra hands in the kitchen."

The tiny bell above the door jingled just as Emmy turned to head outside. The ensuing collision sent her nearly full drink splashing everywhere, but mostly all over the tall, dark, and very handsome stranger who'd just entered the bistro.

Cursing, the man shook his arms in an attempt to rid them of the iced coffee that now dripped from his chin and had plastered his pale blue T-shirt to his very broad chest. Izabel couldn't help but notice the hint of chiseled muscle beneath the wet, clingy garment. She also couldn't miss the look of horror on Emmy's face, especially when the man's dark frown turned on her.

"Oh, I-I'm so-so sorry," Emmy stuttered as she grabbed her crumpled, empty cup from the ground and hurried over to throw it away. She then grabbed two handfuls of napkins from the counter and rushed back to begin dabbing at the man's soaked shirt. "I'm s-so clumsy..."

The whole scene would've been quite humorous if Emmy hadn't looked as if she were about to cry. Emmy's reaction and the earlier description she'd given of the man she adored from afar led Izabel to believe that this was Zack's friend, the fireman Aaron.

After his surprised curse, Aaron hadn't said a word. He just stood there, dripping, watching as Emmy scurried around and attempted to dry him off with two handfuls of napkins. His frown had slipped away and Izabel was certain the corners of his mouth curved upward ever-so slightly.

At least, he's a good sport.

Emmy didn't seem to notice as she continued to mumble apologies and swipe at Aaron's soaked clothes. She'd finished his chest and had moved to his flat belly in a few seconds, clearly too flustered to notice that her ministrations were dipping well beneath his belt.

Something like interest flashed in his eyes, and then his brows dipped down again as Emmy peeled away some of the wet napkins and then continued her attempt to dry his jeans.

In a flash, his large, strong hands gripped Emmy's wrists and held them from his body.

Emmy's eyes snapped upward, and Izabel couldn't help her own slight grin as her friend's rosy cheeks turned scarlet.

"It's okay, Emmy," Aaron said, his voice a deep, smooth baritone. "It's just coffee. It was a bit cold, but I've been doused with worse. Don't worry about it."

"But..." Emmy's eyes flicked down to his damp clothes. "You're clothes are ruined. At least, let me wash them for you?"

He grinned again, and Izabel saw something dark and a bit lusty fill his gray eyes. "I don't think the middle of town would be the best place for me to disrobe, do you?" he said so softly that Izabel almost didn't hear the words.

She hadn't thought that Emmy's face could get any redder, but she'd been wrong.

"Well, I-I meant—"

He released Emmy's wrists and rested his hands on her shoulders as he bent in closer. "I know what you meant," he said softly, clearly trying to put Emmy at ease. "I was just teasing, and it's okay. I can wash my own clothes."

"Let m-me make it up t-to you...some-somehow," Emmy said as she gazed up at him as if mesmerized. "Washing them w-would be the least I c-could do for ruining them and your d-day."

He smiled what had to be his most charming smile and leaned in to whisper something in Emmy's ear that Izabel couldn't hear.

Emmy's eyes widened and a little gasp spilled through her parted lips, and Izabel swore the roots of her friends hair turned red, along with the rest of her face.

He let her go and stood tall. "Your choice," he said as he wiped his hands on his jeans. "Let me know what you decide. I'm sure whatever you come up with will be just fine, though, but like I said, it's not a big deal."

With that, he grinned, nodded at Izabel, and left the bistro.

Izabel reached out to touch Emmy's shoulder and she jumped as if scalded. She turned her amber eyes—so much like her brother's—to Izabel with a look of stunned surprise on her face.

"What did he say?" Izabel asked.

Emmy wet her lips and swallowed. "He... He said I could make him dinner."

"Like a date? Well, that's great!" Izabel said, happy for her friend's good luck, but something in Emmy's eyes made her pause. "It *is* a good thing, right?"

Emmy nodded, still seeming shocked by the whole incident. "Apparently, the guys at the fire station aren't very good cooks. He said he hasn't had a really good homemade meal in years."

"Well, he's in for a real treat, then."

"I guess."

Izabel shook her head. "No guessing about it. You ever heard of winning a man's affection through his stomach? And Em...the way he looked at you?" Izabel waved her hand in front of her face as if it were a fan. "Whew...so hot!"

"What do you mean?"

"You didn't notice?"

"Notice what?"

"There was definite interest in his eyes, Emmy. I have no doubt."

Emmy shook her head. "I don't know. He'd never paid any attention to me before—not like *that,* anyway—and he's almost as much of a flirt as my brother once was...is...sometimes. I don't know."

Izabel wasn't sure what to say about that, but she was certain how attracted Aaron had been to her friend.

"Come on," she said as she spun her friend toward the door. "Let's get you home. You need to change into something dry yourself."

The way Emmy's brow puckered when she glanced down at her wet shirt almost made Izabel chuckle. Emmy crossed her arms over her chest, suddenly realizing what the soaked garment displayed, and groaned as they headed outside. "I hadn't even noticed..."

"It's okay," Izabel said, rubbing her friend's arm comfortingly. "If you give me the keys and direct me, I'll drive us back to the ranch."

Emmy nodded and handed over the keys, but she still looked as if she was stuck between joyful and humiliated by everything that had happened.

Izabel could understand that. She'd had a few embarrassing moments with her ex-fiancé, but nothing as cute as what she'd just witnessed between Emmy and Aaron. But Izabel had put all that behind her, and she would be strong again. She would be herself, *find* herself again. And she didn't need a man's help to do that, either.

Then she thought of the way Zack had looked at her yesterday as he held her in his arms. Nothing had existed for her at that moment. The horse, the barn, the dust had all disappeared when she'd met his gaze; the man, his warm body, and the tightening inside her were all she knew. She'd been so aware of him and of every inch where their bodies touched that her nerve endings had been snapping with the need for him to touch her everywhere.

Izabel held in her groan of embarrassment. Had she looked as besotted as Emmy had, staring up at the man she adored? Had she appeared so taken with the man as to invite the kiss she'd been so sure Zack had wanted to place on her waiting lips? *Oh, God, I hope not,* she thought, but she was lying to herself.

Izabel could only hope that she had been better at hiding her emotions when she looked into Zack's warm, whiskey-colored eyes. Because she knew if he'd pressed his mouth to hers as he held her under the warm setting sun, Izabel would've kissed him back with everything she had.

And *that* scared her to death.

CHAPTER 9

The sun had fallen behind the jagged peaks of the Rockies by the time Zack turned his old truck down the bumpy drive to the family ranch house. He'd stayed away as long as he could, checking on the progress at the winery and then looking in on the Brodys' ranch during the brothers' absence. They hadn't actually needed his help—in fact, their foreman Joe Baker had given him an odd look when Zack had offered his assistance—but he'd needed a reason to be away from his ranch and the heady temptation of a goddess with green eyes, warm brown skin, and wide amber-tinted curls.

He'd never been so unsettled by a beautiful woman, nor had one tugged at his heart the way Izabel did. He raked his fingers through his damp hair as the truck bounced over the gravel. His nervous stomach tightened as what he would face after dinner filled his head once more.

Tonight, he'd promised to watch a movie with Izabel. To sit in a dark room, alone with a woman he found...appealing. No, she was more than that; she was amazing. Strong yet vulnerable, she'd impressed him with her iron backbone during her first riding lesson. He'd seen the stark fear in her eyes, the total lack of confidence in herself and her abilities. But as he'd slowly encouraged and challenged her, she'd blossomed, and he'd been fascinated by the change. As he watched her inner courage manifest, he'd stood taller, proud of her, and honored that she'd shared those moments with him.

All of that had been fine, except when she'd fallen during her dismount and landed right in his arms. God, she'd felt good, soft and light against his chest, and she'd smelled sweet—a faint hint of roses and sugar cookies. How he longed to hold her close again, to bury his nose in her sweet-smelling hair and trace the gentle curves of her lovely body with his calloused hands. He wanted to pull her in for a lasting kiss that would lead to more kisses, then peel away her clothing to expose more of her luscious caramel skin, to taste it and savor her...

"Ah, hell!" He slammed his hand on the steering wheel and adjusted the sudden discomfort in his jeans. He shook his head. *What am I thinking?*

He had nothing to offer except a horrid reputation that would send a cautious woman like Izabel running for the hills the moment she heard the whole of it. She'd been right to be wary of him. He was the Meriton Casanova, and no matter how hard he'd tried to live it down, his prior behavior always came back to haunt him. But no matter how much he castigated himself for all his past mistakes, he couldn't extinguish the need that hummed through his body whenever Izabel was near.

A small cloud of dust kicked up around his tires when he parked the truck in his normal spot near the house. Grabbing his hat from the passenger seat, he stepped out of the cab and slammed the door behind him. The cowboy hat hung from his fingers as he surveyed the dooryard and fields beyond the barn. None of the horses were out, which meant one of his family members had already taken care of the evening chores. He had no other option than to go inside and face whatever awaited.

He swiped at his dirty jeans before he reached for the mudroom door and pulled it open, not trying to hide his arrival. Anyone in the kitchen or dining room could see him enter if the inside door was open, which, unfortunately, it was.

"Where the heck have you been?" Emmy asked in an accusatory voice. "I held supper as long as I could, but now you'll have to eat it cold."

"Sorry, Emmy," he said over his shoulder as he stopped at the mudroom sink to wash his hands. "I already ate. Didn't you get my message?"

Emmy's head tilted and her fists rested on her hips when Zack turned around, drying his hands on a nearby towel.

"Clearly, I didn't," she said. "What kept you so long? I thought you had a date with Izabel tonight?"

Zack's eyes widened on his sister's grinning face. *What the hell...?*

"I never said it was a date," Izabel said from the counter that separated the kitchen from the living room to his right.

Zack's gaze snapped to her face. Her cheeks turned rosy under his watchful gaze and she squirmed a little on the stool where she sat.

"I only said that he'd mentioned watching a movie tonight, Emmy, and you know it."

Emmy's grin never left her lips. "Oh, well, it's kind of the same thing. Besides," she tapped Zack's arm with the spatula she'd just dried with the towel on her shoulder, "it's rude to be late for an event *you* suggested."

Zack felt heat crawl up his neck and onto his face. Leave it to his sweet sister to make more out of his suggestion that it was and then scold him for being late.

He pasted on his best awe-shucks grin and kissed Emmy's cheek.

"Sorry, sis," he murmured, then turned to Izabel, whose eyes widened slightly before she licked her lips. He stared at that tiny movement—she was unable not to—and felt that same, all-encompassing need to taste those full, succulent lips.

"You should be," Emmy said, breaking the spell he'd fallen under.

He chuckled. "Of course, my apologies for keeping you ladies waiting, but if you'll give me twenty minutes, I'll get cleaned up and then we can get started."

Emmy's lips thinned and she gave him a look that clearly stated he should've gotten home sooner so they wouldn't have to wait again.

"No problem," Izabel said, coming around the counter and into the kitchen. "I'll help Emmy finish cleaning and wait for you in the living room."

The tip of her pink tongue slid over her lips once more, and Zack's body tightened. His hand twitched with the need to touch her cheek, to sweep his thumb over the fullness of her lower lip. If his sister hadn't been standing there, watching them, something more might have happened, but he felt her eyes on him and the sensation kept his hands at his sides.

"Shouldn't you be heading upstairs?" Emmy asked with an all too knowing smile.

He gave her a dark look that promised retribution for her teasing later.

"Yeah," he muttered as he headed for the stairs, "but don't wait for me. I've seen that movie a hundred times. I know it by heart. Go ahead and start it, I'll be down soon."

* * *

After the quickest shower he'd ever taken, Zack pulled on a pair of clean, well-worn jeans and a blue T-shirt he didn't bother to tuck in before he headed back downstairs. He could hear the familiar dialog from the movie as he made his way down the stairs, and he couldn't help the grin of expectation on his lips. He loved this film. He only hoped Izabel would like it as well.

His steps halted abruptly.

Why?

Other than being a good host, why would he care if she liked it or not? Why did it seem to mean so much to him? This wasn't a date, and he had no one to impress. He told himself that, but the little voice in the back of his head said differently. Pushing it away, along with the odd sensation of excitement churning in his gut, he ignored the voice and hurried into the living room, where he paused and took in the scene.

Emmy had apparently decided to join them and sat in their father's chair with her feet tucked beneath her. Her eyes sparkled when she met his gaze, and he stifled a growl of annoyance when she winked at him. He knew what she was up to, but her assumptions were wrong. Izabel needed more than a one-time, love 'em and leave 'em cowboy with nothing to his name but his stake in this ranch and an old truck. It didn't matter how much Emmy teased, he would not give in to her goading.

Instead, he rolled his eyes and turned to the couch where Izabel sat, curled up much like his sister, with her long legs bent and a square throw pillow held in her lap. Her eyes were glued to the screen as the Duke's character introduced a cat named General Sterling Price as his nephew to the young girl on the screen. Zack grinned at the TV, then turned back to Izabel. She glanced at him, a gentle smile curling her sweet lips before she turned back to the film. She seemed interested in the storyline and that insight puffed up his chest a bit. Then, realizing he was staring, Zack looked away and quickly took the only seat available to him—on the couch, beside Izabel.

Her faint rose scent instantly filled his senses, and he slanted a glare at his sister. Emmy hid a giggle behind her hand and took a sip of water from a glass she'd been holding.

Zack sat back and soon, his long, hard day, coupled with the warmth from the shower, had him sinking into the couch cushions and yawning. He stifled it the best he could and focused on the TV...or at least he tried to. He loved this movie, but inhaling Izabel with every breath was torture. Still, she seemed to be enjoying it so far, so he settled in and tried to keep his eyes open and his baser needs under control.

* * *

An insistent bell kept ringing somewhere in the background, but Zack couldn't pull his gaze away from the beautiful goddess before him. Izabel's brilliant smile and the twinkle of promise in her clear green eyes had him trapped.

She ran her fingers up his chest and along his jaw, leaving a line of fire in their wake. He wanted to crush her to him, to take her mouth, and to show her how much he desired her. But before he raised a hand, her fingers dived into his hair and she pulled herself closer. Her body arched into his, pressing her lovely breasts into him and setting his blood on fire.

Almost afraid he would frighten her, he wrapped his arms around her, pulling her small form fully against him. Instead of shying away, Izabel tugged his head down to meet her waiting mouth.

He groaned as her tongue traced his lips and he shifted to get closer to the gorgeous woman in his arms...

"Zack," a discordant voice called. He tried to ignore it, but the persistent tone wouldn't leave. "Zack, get up."

"Go away," he muttered, trying to recapture the feel of Izabel in his arms.

"Zack!" Emmy shouted and shoved his legs off the coffee table where he'd put them earlier.

"What?" he growled as he lurched to the side. Blinking in confusion, he sat up and glared at his sister. "What's wrong with you?"

"Nothing," Emmy said with a mischievous grin. "I just didn't want you to embarrass yourself in front of Izzy."

Izzy? He blinked again, sleep slowing his addled brain, then it all came to him in a rush. *Izabel.* She was sitting right beside him on the couch. They'd been watching a movie. He'd fallen asleep and he'd dreamed about her...

Oh, God, did I say something in my sleep?

Heat flooded his face.

Emmy laughed as she turned and hurried toward the kitchen.

He held back a groan. *Emmy knew something, but what, exactly?*

After the dream he'd been having, not to mention the telltale signs of how it affected him still visible in his jeans, the last thing he wanted was to meet Izabel's gaze, but he wasn't a total coward. He dared a peek in her direction and she smiled and wiggled her fingers at him in greeting. She looked even more beautiful than he'd dreamed. His pulse picked up and breathing suddenly became difficult.

"Hello," she said, the hint of a smile on her sweet lips.

"Hey there," he grumbled, grabbing a throw pillow from the floor to drop on his lap before he straightened himself on the couch. *I am such an idiot!*

"How was your nap?"

He cleared his throat and glanced at her again, but there was no sign of humor or disgust on her face. "It was...fine."

"Bye," Emmy shouted from the kitchen. "I'll see you both tomorrow."

Wait...what? He jerked around to look back at his sister. "Where are you going?"

"The hospital called; they need me to cover a shift."

"Oh, okay," he muttered, now feeling even sillier. He knew she sometimes got called in at night.

"Don't worry," she said with a wave, "I'll be back in the morning."

"Be careful," he said a little too gruffly.

Emmy giggled. "Have a good night, you two."

Zack slouched into the couch and, dropping his head back, closed his eyes and exhaled.

"You seem tired," Izabel said quietly.

His lids snapped open and he turned his head toward her. With a slow grin, he nodded. "A little, but I don't mind staying up a bit longer if you're not tired."

"Maybe just a little longer. If you really don't mind...?"

Zack straightened and turned toward her, placing his arm across the back of the couch—his hand close enough that her soft curls brushed his fingers. "I don't mind at all."

She smiled and lowered her eyes shyly before meeting his gaze again. "I loved the movie," she said with a big grin. "Do you have any more like it?"

"Tons," he replied. "And you're welcome to watch them anytime you like...with me or not."

"Thanks."

Zack searched his mind for something else to say, but came up empty. He heard her shift on the couch, but didn't look up.

"So," she murmured, "will we have another riding lesson tomorrow?"

He met her gaze and caught the hopeful expression on her face. "You actually *want* another one?"

She nodded enthusiastically.

"I wasn't sure after your fall."

"It wasn't the horse's fault. Besides," she said quickly, then lowered her gaze briefly, "I kind of liked it." Her eyes widened, obviously remembering how he'd held her after she fell. "The ride, I mean."

She wasn't the only one who'd thought about their embrace. The memory of her cradled in his arms sent a jolt through his body. He wanted to touch her, feel the smooth warmth of her skin. His hand practically itched to close the short distance to caress her cheek, but he pressed it flat against the couch's back cushion and kept himself in check.

"Really? But you were so against it..."

"I know." She shrugged. "It surprised me, too."

"Well," he straightened up, "in that case, the next nice day we have, I think we'll take a short ride into the hills, maybe have a picnic while we're there."

A picnic? He winced inwardly. *Where did* that *come from?*

Her eyes widened. "Do you really think that's a good idea? I mean, I've only been on a horse once."

He tilted his head, assessing her nervousness. "I think you can handle it." He risked a little tug on a stray curl. "Sometimes it's best to just jump right in. Besides, I've been riding my whole life; I won't let anything happen to you."

A rosy blush colored her cheeks and Zack thought she looked even prettier than before.

"I know you won't," she said, meeting his gaze boldly and reaching out to place her hand on his bent leg. "Thank you, for all the time you're spending with me and the lessons, too. I know it wasn't what you'd planned to do this week, nor was it your responsibility, but I really appreciate it...and I think a picnic tomorrow would be really...nice."

The heat of her small hand soaked through his jeans and slammed into his groin with the force of a runaway truck. For a moment, he couldn't breathe, couldn't think, he could only stare at her delicate fingers resting against his leg. Then he cleared his throat awkwardly. "No problem." His voice came out like a croak, so he coughed and tried again. "Really, I don't mind, but another lesson might have to wait a day or two. We got rain coming in tonight."

Her answering smile nearly knocked him over, and the urge to touch her had him leaning in her direction.

"You're very generous," she said as her eyes dropped to his mouth. She licked her lips and looked up again. Her gaze was direct, but the stiffness in her shoulders made her still seem nervous. "How about I...help you with some chores while we wait for the sun to return?"

Is she feeling the pull, too? Was she lingering beside him because she wanted to kiss him as much as he wanted to kiss her? Was she trying to come up with more reasons to spend time with him?

He took a chance and brushed his knuckles against her cheek. She tilted her head into his hand, closed her eyes, and sighed. Zack's heart skipped a beat. He pushed his hand into her silky hair and moved a little closer.

"Izabel," he whispered, his whole body humming with total awareness of her.

She met his gaze with soft, languid eyes, darkened with desire, and her lips parted. A look he'd seen many times before, but from her, it meant so much more. He didn't know what, but he wasn't in the mood to evaluate it.

With his hand behind her head, he asserted some slight pressure to draw her closer. She didn't resist, but lifted a hand to his chest as she leaned toward him. His heart thundered beneath her fingers and he felt the distance between them like an ache banding his chest, his nerve endings zapping with anticipation. Only a little farther and she'd be in his arms, her soft breasts pressed into his chest, and her lush lips on his as he tasted his gorgeous goddess for the first time.

She'd nearly fallen against his chest, their lips mere inches from each other, when the light above the stairs came on.

They sprung apart, and Izabel began brushing her hair as if he'd been tangling his fingers in its springy softness for hours. Zack grumbled a curse about living with family as he got up and reached for the TV remote Emmy had left on the chair.

"Hello you two," his mother said from the entry to the living room. "What are you doing up so late?"

Zack glanced at his watch to see it was almost midnight. He hadn't been up till the wee hours in a long time. He could see Izabel from the corner of his eye. She looked worried, as if they'd done something wrong. *Now why would she think that?*

"We just finished a movie," he said as he turned off the TV and dropped the remote onto the coffee table. "We were just heading to bed."

Izabel gasped softly. A glance at her widened eyes told him how his words might be misconstrued, and he stumbled to clarify. "I mean, w-we were heading up to go to...to..."

"Sleep," Izabel finished for him as she got to her feet.

Why am I acting like a schoolboy caught with his first girl?

"Oh," his mother said, "well, goodnight then." She headed into the kitchen.

Zack frowned, thinking his mother looked tired, which, considering the time, wasn't surprising, but she also appeared paler than normal, too. Late-night trips to the kitchen weren't typical for his mom and the combination had Zack's heart clenched with worry. He wasn't ready to lose another person he cared about.

"Is everything okay, Mom?" Zack asked as he came around the couch.

"Yes, honey, I'm fine," she said as she pulled a glass from the cupboard. "I just needed some water. You two go on to bed."

"Are you sure?"

Janice glanced at her son, a small wrinkle between her brows. "I'm fine, honey. My throat's just a little dry." She smiled at him reassuringly. "No cause for worry. Go on to bed. You've got early chores tomorrow, and I'm right as rain."

"Okay," he said, the tightness in his chest loosening as he crossed the room to kiss her cheek. "Love you, Mom."

"Love you too, sweet boy. Goodnight."

Swallowing the awkwardness that had him wanting to run from the room, Zack turned to Izabel with a gesture to proceed him.

"Goodnight, Janice," she said to his mother before turning to climb the stairs.

Janice replied, but Zack was too focused on watching Izabel climb the stairs to hear it. The slow sway of her sweet bottom hypnotized him and made his mouth water.

What are you doing? he asked himself as they reached the landing and headed to their respective rooms. *I'm supposed to entertain her, not lust after her like a lovesick pup.*

"Goodnight, Zack," Izabel said quietly and he met her reticent gaze. Apparently, their almost-kiss on the couch wasn't going to continue here.

He'd almost held her in his arms again, almost tasted those luscious lips. He mentally shook himself. They might've both been tired and caught up in the moment, but it was over now.

"Goodnight, Izabel," he said. "Sleep well. If you really want to help with chores, dress warm... Tomorrow's supposed to be a soaker."

Something hot and needy flickered in her eyes, but it was gone so fast he thought he'd imagined it.

"I'm looking forward to it," she said as she pushed open her door. "You sleep well, too." She smiled. "I can still count on you to keep me safe, right?"

He nodded.

"And the next nice day we'll go for a picnic?"

He nodded again, but inside he groaned. *Why the hell did I suggest that ride?*

Because you want to be alone with her, his inner voice replied.

"Good," she said with a tired smile. "I am really looking forward to seeing more of Montana's natural, rugged beauty."

Again, something flickered in her eyes as he grinned, but she lowered her gaze as she slowly closed the door before he could read the expression.

Yes, he wanted to be alone with her where no one would interrupt.

But does she want the same thing?

You'd think the Meriton Casanova would be more certain of a woman's interest, but Izabel was a puzzle. Sometimes it seemed she wanted his touch and other times... He shook his head. Either way, he now had a picnic to plan and a whole afternoon to try to determine if he was right about her wanting him or getting his face slapped for being too forward. Luckily, or maybe not, the rain gave him a couple of days to think about it.

He pushed open his bedroom door and then closed it behind him, thoughts of Izabel still spinning through his mind. He tried to push them aside as he stripped off his clothes and crawled into bed, but one thought kept coming back to start them all rolling again.

Izabel is in bed just down the hall...

He groaned and threw his arm over his eyes. Tonight, sleep would be a long time coming.

CHAPTER 10

Izabel woke to a thin shaft of sunlight streaming through the frilly, dark blue drapes in her borrowed room and rolled onto her back to avoid the glare. According to Emmy, the room belonged to their oldest sister Grace, who had left for the Marines shortly after high school several years before. Though as neat as a pin, small reminders of a younger Grace's one-time occupancy could be found everywhere. Clothes that were nearly a decade old in fashion hung in the closet and a small bouquet of flowers, dead and dried, dangled from a hook beside her cream-colored dresser's mirror. The sky-blue walls were dotted with images and posters of famous people who were about as old as the clothes in the closet. The only image that seemed timeless was the Marines recruiting poster that adorned the back of her bedroom door.

Several photographs of a girl, who looked a great deal like Emmy and Zack—Grace, Izabel guessed—with a large, reddish-colored horse were mixed in as well. Her smile was wide and infectious, but there was one photo where she'd seemed sad, as if she were leaving, never to return home. The photo had been taken in front of the barn with the same big red horse, a small suitcase sat beside an older version of Grace, and she had lifted a hand in farewell. That image intrigued Izabel and caught her glance again this morning as she lay in bed.

Had Grace been about to leave on her first adventure in life, one she'd clearly planned—based on the Marine in his dress uniform that decorated her bedroom door. And if so, why did she look so despondent in that photo? Was she that upset to leave home and her family? Worried about her future? Already missing a boyfriend she'd be leaving behind? Izabel couldn't guess, but something about the girl's expression called to her. It made Izabel want to throw her arms around the young woman to comfort her somehow and tell her everything would work out right.

Maybe I'm just projecting, she thought, pushing off the blue blankets—keeping with the room theme of various blues with cream accents. Sitting up, she stretched languorously and thought back on the times she had wished for someone to comfort her. Addie had been there for many of those occasions, but then Izabel had met Chris Richards shortly after they'd graduated college and everything changed.

Dropping her hands to her lap, Izabel stared at the pale blue throw rug beside the bed, her mind spinning into the past.

Charming, suave, and handsome, Chris had been a few years older than Izabel, and he had completely swept her off her feet. In a very short time, not only had she stopped hanging out with her friends—Addie included—but she'd moved in with Chris, and they'd begun to build a life together. Izabel had thought she'd found the one and had jumped in with both feet, not paying any attention to the warning signs. Oh, she'd noticed them—of course, she had—but he'd always had a reason for the uncomfortable things he did and said, and she—the stupid young woman she'd been—had believed in him and in their relationship so much that she'd waved it all aside. To her eternal regret.

Shaking her head at her previous self, Izabel stood and made the bed.

She would never be that foolish again. Coming here had been the first...well, second, step in getting her life back. Thankfully, Addie didn't hold a grudge, or at least, she didn't appear to at the reception.

"Maybe she'd just been too deliriously happy to remember how I'd ignored her for so long," Izabel grumbled as she took her clothes out of her suitcase and got dressed.

When she reached for the pair of western boots Emmy had loaned her, she paused. Thoughts of Zack tumbled through her mind. His kindness and patience during her first riding lesson two days ago, his charmingly crooked smile when he teased her, and the soul-deep sincerity in his eyes when he reassured her. Then there was how she'd felt in his arms—small, safe, and protected. The other night, after the movie, she'd wanted to feel his arms around her again, had wanted to taste his lips and see what it would be like. The look in his eyes had told her he'd wanted the same thing. That knowledge had urged her on, had taken hold of her limbs and made her touch him, to flirt and act a little coy.

She blew out a breath and grabbed the boots off the floor.

Thank goodness for Janice and the sudden burst of light. Her timely appearance had saved Izabel from yet another terrible mistake. Despite his kindness and his, so far, gentlemanly behavior toward her, Zack was an unrepentant flirt. Izabel didn't have any business messing around with him. She'd barely gotten her life back, having pried it from the grasping fingers of a controlling man, and she didn't need to jump back in with yet another mistake.

An image of Zack's warm amber gaze floated through her head. She sighed, remembering how his gentle voice had soothed her fears about the horse, and the pride that had clearly shone in the depths of his eyes had given her the first taste of self-confidence she'd felt in a very long time. And his body...

"Don't even get started," she told herself, but it didn't work.

His body was hard, strong, and so damn warm, she'd wanted to cuddle up alongside him. In fact, she'd fallen asleep the last two nights envisioning his chest against her back and those brawny arms wrapped around her. Letting him hold her, even for a few moments, had felt like heaven, and she couldn't help but relive that feeling at night.

Pushing aside the rush of warmth that filled her chest, she pulled the first boot onto her foot and picked up the second.

Something drew her to Zack. She felt it whenever he was around, and despite her best efforts to remember why she didn't want to get involved with the Casanova he'd been dubbed, she kept thinking about what he'd said.

'I won't hurt you, Izabel, and I won't let anyone else hurt you, either.'

His expression had been all seriousness and his eyes... His eyes had simultaneously begged and demanded, as if he desperately wanted her to believe him. And she wanted to, but she needed to take it one baby step at a time, not dive into the warm, sexy pool that was Zack MacEntier. Even Emmy had warned her about his philandering, but then, she'd also talked about his many good sides and an old heartbreak, too. What had happened when he was a younger man that he still lived his life based on that mysterious event so long ago?

Part of her wanted to ask, but the wary side wouldn't let her. "It's none of my business," she muttered. Jerking on the last of her borrowed boots, Izabel got to her feet and headed downstairs, determined not to dwell on it or Zack.

After the last couple of days of nothing but lightning, thunder, and lots of rain, Izabel was glad the sun had already risen this morning. *Maybe it'll dry up all the dang mud!*

She'd never imagined how much work it took to run a ranch, but yesterday had given her a much clearer understanding. She'd followed Zack around for half a day while it rained harder than she'd ever seen. Even with her borrowed slicker, she'd been soaked and exhausted by the time they went in for lunch. Of course, he'd noticed her lack of energy and had taken pity on her, though not without some teasing.

"Need some new batteries?" he'd asked as they'd finished clearing the table.

She'd frowned as she followed him to the mudroom. "Batteries?"

"Yeah." He chuckled as he took his long coat off a hook. "You seem to be dragging a bit. I thought I'd worn you out with all the stall mucking and that maybe you needed a little power up." He'd wiggled his eyebrows suggestively and her stomach flipped over at the dirty thoughts that ran through her head—not to mention the brilliant, dimpled smile that had adorned Zack's face.

She snorted. "I'm fine. Besides, I should do something around here for all your hospitality."

"You sure *are* fine," he said as she stopped beside him to grab her borrowed jacket.

She didn't miss the not-so-subtle emphasis on the word and wondered about it.

He'd stopped her from taking the jacket with a hand on the hook where it was hung. Then he lifted his other hand to gently tug at one of her curls.

"You've already been a big help this morning; there's no need for you to go out in this mess again." He glanced out the window at the sheets of rain still pelting the earth.

She'd hesitated. Was he trying to get rid of her?

"Emmy's still asleep, but I'm sure she or my mom wouldn't mind some company." He raised his voice to reach into the kitchen, where Janice stood beside the sink. "Right, Mom?"

"Sure, honey," Janice replied distractedly, but then looked up. "Wait... What am I agreeing to?"

"You're going to help at the retirement center in town today, aren't you?" he'd asked and she nodded. "Could Izabel tag along?"

Janice had smiled brightly. "Of course. They'll love a new face, and a pretty one at that."

Heat had flooded her face at that comment. Zack merely grinned and winked. "See, I told you." Then he'd headed out into the rain, leaving Izabel with his mom.

She had felt a little bereft when he walked away without her, but his maneuvering had annoyed her, too.

Janice's cheerful chatter on the way to town, however, helped alleviate Izabel's annoyance with Zack.

"I'm so glad you agreed to come along today," Janice had said. "They enjoy it when I come to visit, but they're going to love having a new person to talk to."

"I've never done anything like this before," Izabel had confessed. "What do I do?"

Janice chuckled. "Just be yourself, honey. They love hearing about life outside their little world."

"But what do I say?"

"Whatever you feel comfortable with," Janice replied with a shrug. "If you have a problem just let me know. Some of the gentlemen can be a bit...flirtatious. Don't take it seriously, but don't let them have free rein, either. They love to tease, but they like it even more when the tables get turned. It's a challenge for them, if you know what I mean."

"So I should just stand my ground. Is that what you mean?"

Janice glanced at her as they turned into the center's parking lot, but didn't speak immediately. The windshield whippers slapped out a tempo, whisking away the heavy rain as Janice parked her small SUV. Then she turned to Izabel and reached out the pat her shoulder. "Give as good as you get," she said, gathering up her purse, "and just be your sweet-self otherwise. You'll be fine, honey."

Her encouragement hadn't eased Izabel's concerns much, but she'd appreciated the effort. Still, once she and Janice had entered the retirement center, and Izabel was introduced to all the nice people there, she had to admit, those folks were a lot more fun than slogging through mud in the pouring rain.

A couple of hours after they'd arrived, she'd sat with Janice and some of the other residents in the common room, playing bingo while a few of the older gentlemen complimented her and flirted audaciously.

"Sweetie, I'm telling you, they're useless. A nice girl like you...you don't want one of those young bucks running around town now. I got a feeling you need a man's man," a spry octogenarian said with a crooked smile that reminded Izabel of Zack's charming grin. "You're too beautiful for those youngsters. I'll bet too smart and sophisticated as well." He nodded as if confirming the fact.

"Well, I don't know about that, Jacob..." she'd said with a laugh. "I don't know if I'm looking for anyone right now."

Everyone at the table pooh-poohed that comment. Then Jacob leaned a little closer and lowered his voice. "If any of those rascals mistreat you, you know where to go. I'll be right here, waiting."

She hunched her shoulders and leaned in, mimicking his whisper. "Aren't I a little young for you?"

He harrumphed at that. "No way. I might look like a crotchety old fart, but I can still out-work and out-drink those young fools any day. And I have the experience to know how to treat a lady right." He winked and then nodded again as if she'd agreed.

She'd chuckled awkwardly and blushed profusely at his suggestive comment. One of the other ladies at the table noted the change.

"Jacob," the lady stated sternly, "you leave that poor young woman alone. She doesn't need you whispering sweet-nothings—and I do mean *nothings*—in her ear."

Jacob had grumbled under his breath and his cheeks reddened, but he kept chatting with Izabel—although, a trifle less flirtatiously.

That had been only one of the incidents of shameless flirting at the center, but she'd enjoyed her time there quite a lot. Even if it had felt as if Zack had made the choice for her, she'd still been thankful for the experience.

"So did you have a good time?" Janice had asked on the drive back home.

"Yes, it was a lot of fun." She laughed surprised that it was the truth. "Those guys are crazy flirts."

Janice smiled. "Yes, they are, but you seemed to hold your own with them. I'm sure they'd love another visit sometime, if you feel up to it."

Izabel grinned. "I think that can be arranged."

A comfortable quiet had settled in the cab until Janice spoke again. "So how are you and Zack getting on?"

Izabel glanced at the older woman, wondering if there was something more behind the question. "We're doing fine. He's giving me riding lessons and letting me help take care of chores while I'm here."

"Oh, honey," Janice said as if shocked, "you're a guest. You don't have to do any chores."

Izabel had turned toward the driver's seat and reached out to touch Janice's arm reassuringly. "But I want to. It makes me feel like a little less of a burden."

"Sweetie," Janice had said with a slight shake of her head, "you are no burden. Heck, his father and I would love it if the two of you spent more time together."

Izabel's eyebrows climbed to her hairline, and her voice squeaked a little when she asked, "Who? Me and Zack?"

"Sure," Janice replied. "He seems to smile more whenever you're around, and I've noticed you blushing in his presences a time or two." She glanced at Izabel. "Zack's a good boy, no matter what his past or that silly nickname says about him."

"You know about that?"

"Of course," Janice had replied as they bumped over their rough gravel driveway. "I'm not deaf or blind. I know he's been lost. But lately, he seems to be finding his way back to his old self, and to us."

Izabel had nodded, but she felt a bit uncomfortable talking about Zack with his mother. So she said no more as they parked in front of the MacEntier's adorable house, then dashed through the rain to the front door beneath the wide, covered deck.

That had been yesterday. Now, she paused on the stairs to examine the collage of family photos on the wall, unsurprised to find that Zack had been a handsome young man. His sisters were just as pretty and they all looked happy. His parents clearly loved each other from the expressions on their faces, too.

As a young girl, Izabel's family life had been strained. Looking at the multitude of cheery family pictures on the MacEntier's wall caused a pang in the area around her heart. What she'd have given to have a more loving and involved father.

Despite the discomfort of her memories, all the wonderful photos made the corners of her lips curl upward as she slowly continued down each step.

When Izabel reached the bottom of the stairs, with a smile still on her face, she turned into the kitchen, looking forward to seeing Zack again.

Her heart sank when only Emmy sat at the table.

"Good morning," Emmy said with a smile. "There's still plenty of breakfast if you're hungry."

She returned her friend's greeting as she quickly looked around.

"Everyone headed out early," Emmy said and took a sip of coffee from her mug, "and I'm going back to the hospital as soon as I finish my coffee."

"Oh," Izabel murmured before she went to grab a plate from the cupboard.

"Is something wrong?" Emmy asked. "If Zack did something stupid—"

"No, no," Izabel corrected. "It's nothing like that. I wanted to talk with him about another lesson today."

"Oh." Emmy sat up a little straighter. "Well, he said he should be back around eleven."

Izabel glanced at the clock on the stove. *Just after nine,* she thought. *I can fill two hours without his help.*

"Do you two have anything else planned?"

Izabel shot her a suspicious look. *Did Zack say something to her about the other night?*

"Why do you ask?

Emmy shrugged and stood, then picked up her plate and took it to the washer. "No reason. Zack seemed a little flustered and your face fell the minute you came around the corner. Are you sure he didn't upset you somehow?"

Izabel took a bite of the pancakes she'd taken from the oven, where they'd been warming. She did it to give herself a little time to think, but the wonderful flavors of buttermilk and homemade huckleberry syrup made her hum with approval.

"Oh, my... These are really good."

"Mom's secret recipe. Ask her about it tonight," Emmy said with a smile, then she gulped down the rest of her coffee, wiped her mouth with a napkin, and put the mug into the dishwasher. Then she turned around, and with a hand on her hip, she pinned Izabel with a narrowed gaze. "*You* didn't answer my question."

"Well..." Izabel choked on the pancake she'd just swallowed. "Well," she began again, "we were talking about taking a ride through the hills."

Emmy's sudden smile lit up the room. "That's great! He must believe you're capable or he wouldn't risk that so soon. You're going to love it."

Izabel smiled. She *was* looking forward to seeing a little more of the area.

"Now, in twenty words or less—since I really do need to run—why did you look so down when you saw Zack wasn't here?" Emmy tilted her head. "Are you interested in my brother?"

"What?" Izabel coughed on another bite of pancake and took a sip of her coffee. "Where did that come from? I just thought he might've forgotten, is all. I was looking forward to riding again."

"I think that might've been just over twenty words," Emmy teased as she grabbed her keys off the counter. "Too bad, though. I'm still hoping you might be the one he straightens his life out for."

Izabel shook her head. "Emmy..." her voice, though steady, came out low and a bit admonishing, "I've told you, I—"

Emmy waved her hands in a placating gesture. "I know. I know. But a sister can still hope."

Izabel sighed.

"I'll see you tonight," Emmy said with a big smile, then disappeared out the door.

Why does she think it'd want to get involved with her brother? After all the things she told me about his womanizing ways, you'd think she meant to frighten me away.

Once upon a time, Izabel hadn't been afraid of anything, and a guy like Zack might've been a challenge or an interesting diversion, but not anymore. Everything seemed to frighten her—especially men—and she hated it. Where was that girl who had wanted to take on the world, who did and had won? Izabel had thought she was gone, lost to the disaster that had been Chris Richards.

But being here with these people—not to mention Zack's attention and positive encouragement—she was starting to feel like herself again. Maybe she should take another step on the road to healing. Maybe a short, sizzling tryst was just what she needed.

The smile Zack had given her every time she'd correctly performed one of his instructions during her riding lesson popped into her head. She could hear the praise he'd given so freely. That, and the flame in his eyes that had ignited into an inferno when she'd touched his leg after the movie had combined to unearth a portion of the strong woman she'd once been. But more than that, he touched her in a way she couldn't define, and part of her wanted to touch him, kiss that sexy mouth of his, and see what happened next.

Something fluttered in her chest and the heat it created coiled downward to fuse into a pulsing pool of need low in her belly.

"This is such a bad idea..." she muttered to the empty room.

What if something went wrong? What if she fell hard and didn't want it to end? What if he broke her heart all over again?

The heat in his whiskey eyes when he'd stared at her mouth had her wiggling in her chair, and she slammed down her fork. "What am I thinking?"

But she knew. She was already more than just a little attracted to the Meriton Casanova. With him, she wanted more than heated looks and casual touches. But what would happen after she gave in to her desires?

She pressed her lips together and silently shook her head. She had absolutely no idea.

CHAPTER 11

Huge fluffy clouds floated across the bright blue sky as Zack encouraged his horse up the hillside behind Izabel. Thanks to the return of the hot weather, everything—including the dirt path they currently followed—had dried out, and as they rode, the horses' hooves raised a small cloud of dust around them that Zack vainly attempted to wave away with his hand. The path they followed had been well-worn over the years, so she had no problem following it without much direction. Zack, however, was having a hard time keeping his eyes from her slim form as her denim-clad rear gently rocked in the saddle. He'd never been so jealous of a hunk of leather in his life.

Izabel had taken to riding like she'd been born for it, as if she'd already spent hours becoming used to the gentle sway of a horse's gait. Her comfort with the animals had also improved. When they'd gone to the barn to saddle the horses, she'd gone right into Summer's stall to slide her hand down the mare's sleek neck, talking to the horse like a friend, rather than a monster she feared.

Izabel had changed a good deal over the short week she'd spent with him and his family. He could see her increased confidence in other areas as well and loved seeing her smile more often. Her boosted self-assurance made his chest fill with pride for her. Whatever had caused her wariness when she first arrived seemed to be fading, and the vibrant, strong woman he had sensed beneath her unease had begun to emerge. She was still cautious, but she no longer seemed to fear him, which pleased him on so many levels that he refused to examine any of them too closely.

Though, now it was his turn to worry. The incident with her after the movie kept playing in his head, especially at night—which was frustrating in more ways than one. He even dreamed about her and that evening on the couch—that his mother hadn't come downstairs to interrupt what had promised to be something unbelievably hot. In his dream, their lips had met and the explosion of sensation from that fantasy had lingered upon his waking.

Unfortunately, his dream of kissing her had yet to be fulfilled, and he couldn't stop reminiscing about that night when their lips had been only a couple of inches apart and everything in him had ached to close the distance. He'd felt her warm breath on his cheek and the curves of her slim body pillowed against his chest. One or two more seconds, and he would've finally tasted her sumptuous lips, discovered if she tasted like the sweet cookies her scent brought to his mind.

"Stay to the right," he instructed as Izabel's horse came to a fork in the path.

She glanced at him over her shoulder, an enormous grin adorning her sensual mouth. He swallowed the groan that suddenly clogged his throat and tried to keep the rest of his body in check, too.

"So, where are we going?" she asked, facing forward once more.

"You'll see when we get there," he teased.

"I think you like frustrating me," she replied.

Is she flirting with me?

"No, darlin', I would *never* frustrate *you*," he said, letting the innuendo ring clearly in his voice.

She giggled and the sound prickled his skin, sending another shot of heat straight to his cock.

Suppressing a groan of frustration, he stood in the stirrups briefly to relieve the sudden tightness in his jeans.

He liked this playful side of her, but his body's reaction to her nearness, her voice, her rose and vanilla scent—to *all* of her—was out of control. Hell, he wanted to be a gentleman with her, to give her time to get used to him, to get to know him better, but the urgent need to touch her made that almost impossible. It also terrified him a little.

He'd always been able to keep his senses under control, had always been the one to initiate and end every relationship. But with Izabel, he had no idea what he was doing, let alone whether she wanted him. Well, maybe he knew a little... The way she sometimes looked at him told him all he needed to know about her attraction to him, but being around her made him feel like he had electricity sizzling all over his skin. His hands itched to test the softness of her cheek, to see if it was as warm and smooth as he remembered. He wanted to plunge his hands into her hair to see if it was just as silky as it had been that night after the movie. He wanted to take the next step, to hold her close and kiss her silly…or to have her kiss him.

Either way, it would be wonderful.

Up ahead, Izabel's horse entered the clearing he'd been steering them toward for the last forty minutes, and he heard her astonished gasp. This ride was a short, relatively easy one, but the view, he knew, was stunning.

Coming to a stop beside her, Zack saw her mouth open in surprise and her eyes widen with wonder.

"It's beautiful," she said, her gaze riveted on the valley that stretched below their vantage point.

Zack stared out at the rolling green foothills and tried to see it through her eyes. The deep green of the conifer trees, the lighter greens of the grass, dots of color where patches of wildflowers grew, and the darker, grayish-blue of the tall, white-tipped mountains far in the distance. Between the evergreen hills was a narrow valley, filled with long grasses that swayed gently with the wind and where the sun left dark splotches of shade that faded and reappeared with the movement of the cotton-candy-like clouds overhead.

She was right, it was a beautiful sight—and one he'd never get tired of seeing.

"What am I looking at," Izabel asked, glancing at him for the first time. "Is this *all* your land?"

He sat a little taller as pride swelled within him. He loved their ranch and he was glad she was so struck by the view.

"Most of it, but we do border a national park to the northwest," he replied as he pointed in that direction, and then swung around, pointing again. "Meriton is off that-a-way, and just past those foothills to the west is the winery we visited. The Brodys' ranch is a little farther beyond that. Their property line is the longest we share with a neighbor. We also share water rights with them."

Izabel's gaze followed where he indicated, nodding her understanding, but then she sat forward in her saddle and pointed downhill at a winding stand of white-trunked aspen, wildflowers, and tall grass. "Is that a river?" Her eyes were round with interest when she looked his way.

"Good eye," he said, impressed. "Yeah, it's Colson Creek, named after some prospector or mountain man from a couple of hundred years ago. No one's sure, but it's a nice story. It must have grown considerably since then."

Her brow wrinkled as she gazed at the area. "Why do you say that?"

"Well, it's more like a river than a creek, wide and deep in some areas, and a little farther up the valley, there's a place where you can see where it changed paths when another larger waterway joined it. It has a pretty strong current, and it supplies enough water for our animals and some irrigation, too."

"Can we go there? I'd love to see it up close. Maybe ride up to the place you just described?"

Zack hesitated. The ride would be a long one, and from this overlook, harder than she was ready for right now. "Sure, but not today." Her lips tugged down in disappointment and a weight settled in his chest. Upsetting her was the last thing he wanted. "Maybe we could drive out there another time. It's a bit of a ride from here," he explained, "and we've a ways to go to get home. I don't want to overtax you in the saddle again so soon."

She nodded. "You're always thinking of me."

"You have no idea," he mumbled to himself, but the way she glanced at him made him believe she'd heard and his neck grew hot.

"So, shall we picnic here?" she asked, indicating a clear area beneath a nearby stand of pine trees off to their left, and thankfully, leaving his comment alone.

"I think that's a great idea."

She smiled at him and his heart thudded against his ribs so hard he'd swear it left a bruise. Following Izabel's mare toward the shaded area, Zack absently rubbed at his chest, trying to will away the throbbing ache.

The horses stepped easily over the grayish-white limbs and trunks of the scattered deadfall beneath the trees' high boughs until they reached the area Izabel had chosen within the grove.

"Would you like help dismounting?" he asked after he quickly swung down from his horse's back.

"No, I want to try it myself," she said with a gentle upturn of her lips, "but thank you for the offer."

"Just wanted to make sure," he said as he tied the reins of the buckskin gelding he rode to a low branch near some brush. Izabel followed his example, but he made sure to be close by should she need him.

Once on the ground, she walked around the small area while Zack pulled out a blanket and the bag of food he'd asked his mother to put together for this occasion.

The thought of his mom almost made him groan. The twinkly-eyed smile she'd given him when he explained why he wanted the meal had been a sure sign she thought something was in the works.

"It's not what you think," he had grumbled as she handed him the bag filled with food.

"Of course it's not, honey," she murmured as she reached up to pat his cheek affectionately.

Shaking his head at the memory, he spread out the multicolored Navajo blanket he'd brought and placed the bag of food on top, then went back to his horse to snag the extra water bottles he'd stored in his saddlebags.

When he returned, Izabel was already on the blanket, pulling out the wax-paper-wrapped sandwiches and other items for their meal.

"Wow, you did all this?" She looked up at him, her clear green eyes full of wonder.

He chuckled. "I wish I could take the credit, but my mom was nice enough to set it up for us last night."

"Oh, well, that was nice of her," she said and hurried on, "and you, too, since I assume you asked her to do so."

"Yes, I did," he said as he handed her a water bottle and then sat beside her. "But only because I had some things to finish this morning before we left. I can whip up a mean picnic if I had the time to do it."

She grinned. "I have no doubt about that."

Zack's heart was doing strange things, fluttering around his chest like a caged bird every time she looked his way. *Get ahold of yourself,* he thought. *This is just a friendly lunch, and you're just a tour guide, not her date.*

They ate in companionable silence, gazing out at the sun-dappled valley.

"Are you planning to stay in Meriton?" he asked suddenly. The question had occurred to him before, but he'd kept it to himself. It really was none of his business, and he had no idea why it tumbled out of his mouth now.

"I'm not sure. I'm more of a city girl," she glanced at him and his breath caught in his throat, "but I think I'd like to stay here. Though," she shrugged, "I suppose it depends."

"On what?" He popped the last bite of his sandwich into his mouth and quickly chewed as he laid down on his side, head resting on his hand to look up at her.

"On whether I can find work, either local or online. And..." She shot a quick glance at him. "Well, I'm not sure how things will go with Addie."

Zack frowned. "What do you mean? She looked thrilled to see you at the reception."

"Yes, well, maybe. It's been a long time since we've spoken, and I've done some things..."

"Things?" he asked gently when her words petered out.

She nodded. "I basically ignored our friendship for several years. She wasn't the only one, of course, and some of the others weren't so forgiving... But

Addie has always been the most important. Still is, I guess. Otherwise, I wouldn't be doing this with you."

He tilted his head. "And what are you doing with me?"

She glanced at him and he wanted to sink into the ground. *Why did I ask that?*

Izabel just chuckled. "Riding," she said. "It's something Addie loves, but I never understood why...until now." She smiled at him and his heart, once again, fluttered erratically.

He wasn't sure if she was flirting with him or not, but he'd take the coy smiles either way.

"Is there anything else you're doing with me?"

Her eyes fell to her lap as she rolled up the crumbs in her empty wax paper and her dusky cheeks turned a pretty rose color. "I'd...like to," she said so softly, he'd almost missed it.

Those words had him sitting up and leaning closer. He brushed his knuckles over her cheek and her head tilted into his touch. She sighed and all the blood that had been pulsing in his body raced south of his belt.

Is she implying what I think she is...? She seemed to be, but she'd been so wary and nervous around him at first. He didn't want to rush in now—not after all the time it took to get here—and be wrong. A rejection from Izabel might break a part of him.

"I'd like to kiss you right now, goddess," he said, his voice a low rasp of desire.

Her eyes narrowed. "Goddess?"

"Yeah, my beautiful, golden goddess. It was the only thing I thought of the first time I saw you."

"Really?"

"Yes, really. Now," he leaned in a little closer, "about that kiss..."

Her gaze brightened and her full lips curled upward ever so slightly. "I'd...like that, too."

Heat flooded his body and the need to clutch her to him burned like never before, but something warned him to go slow. "Are you sure that's what you want?"

She nodded, licking her lips. Her gaze dropped to his mouth and then lifted to his eyes. "Yes..."

That was enough for him. He leaned in—her rose and vanilla scent overwhelming his senses, making his body go wild—and pressed his lips to hers.

Chapter 12

Izabel closed her eyes as Zack's perfect, masculine mouth lowered toward hers. Her lips parted in eager, yet cautious anticipation, her whole body alive with the tingles of expectation. She wanted this. Oh, how she wanted this! She'd been dreaming about his lips and how they would feel, how he would taste as their tongues met in the dance of desire. How all that hard, unyielding muscle would press against her. Her hands itched, desperate to touch him, to drive her fingers through his short brown hair and drag him closer, but she waited for the gentle pressure of his lips.

Her heart raced as she leaned toward him, hoping to close the distance a little more quickly. His warm breath feathered against her face and she knew he couldn't be more than a couple of inches from taking her mouth.

What's taking him so long? It seemed like forever since she'd closed her eyes. She wanted to open them and see if he was still there, but she knew he was. She could feel him, the warmth of his body and the overwhelming presence of man—of Zack—made her skin tingle. Every atom in her body hummed in tune with his. A symphony of rapid breathing, rushing blood, and pounding heartbeats mixed with the special magnetic *something* that drew them together.

Just when she couldn't stand the suspense any longer, his lips touched hers. His mouth moved over hers—warm, soft, and oh-so wonderfully firm. Heat flushed through her and coalesced low in her belly. She shuddered as his tongue brushed along her lower lip, and she opened her mouth to allow him access. He needed no urging as he tilted his head and his tongue swept inside on a mission to conquer the moist cavern.

Izabel moaned into his mouth, overcome by the sensations he ignited inside her. She pressed her hands to his chest and dipped them inside his shirt to test the warm resilience of his skin. A couple of the buttons popped open and she took advantage of the greater opening. Her nails combed through the soft smattering of chest hair beneath his shirt, and then she flicked a fingernail over his flat nipple until it rose into a small peak. He shivered and moaned, and a thrill shot through her. That she could have such an effect on him filled her with awe.

Oh, this man! she thought, wanting to rip the shirt from his shoulders. Instead, she slowly wrapped her arms around his neck and curled her fingers into the hair at his nape. His neatly trimmed beard tickled her skin and his scent of leather, cedar, and musky man surrounded her. This was exactly what she had dreamed of, only better, but she wanted more. So much more.

One of his large hands gripped her hip, then slid around to her back. He tugged gently and before she knew it, she was on his lap. He wrapped his arms around her, pulling her flush against his body and crushing her breasts against his chest.

A niggle of alarm flashed inside her, but she stifled it. This was what she wanted...right?

No one will love you the way I do... The voice in her head startled her.

Why would Chris' voice pop into her brain now?

She concentrated on Zack and the way he kissed her, the way his hands caressed her back, but it didn't stop the rude interruption of Chris' unwanted voice.

I'll never let you go...

You can never leave me...

You are mine...mine...mine...

Hard arms held her in place, holding her down, forcing her to stay when all she wanted to do was run.

His kiss turned sour and she screamed into his mouth.

She could hear his laugh.

She yanked her face away from the man holding her. "No..." The word started as a whisper, but grew stronger as she repeated it, "No. No, no, no, no. No! Let me go!" She shoved as hard as she could against his chest.

The vise of his arms sprung open, and she fell backward onto the grass and dirt. Skittering away on her hands and feet, she sucked in air as if she'd been deprived of it for too long. She came up short against the sun-bleached trunk of an old fallen tree.

Glancing around with wide, startled eyes, she saw Zack. His shirt hung open, exposing a light dusting of curling hair on his well-developed pecs that meandered down to where she could only too easily guess. His chest rose and fell rapidly and a light flush colored his cheekbones, but it was his expression that hit her the hardest. He stared at her as if she'd grown a second head.

She couldn't blame him for looking at her like that. He had to be thinking she'd lost her mind.

What the hell just happened to me? She'd had bad dreams after her break up with Chris, but not for a long time now, and she had *never* heard his voice in her head.

But she hadn't kissed anyone since she ran away, either.

You're mine, Izabel. You always will be. Chris' words from before she'd left him sent a shiver of fear down her back.

She glanced at Zack's confused glower and wished the solid ground beneath her would turn to quicksand and swallow her whole. How embarrassing!

He stared back at her, breathless. Confusion, frustration, and a little hurt showed in his eyes. "What just happened?"

She groaned inwardly. How could she tell him she'd been thinking of another man especially since Zack had been all she wanted to think about. How could she let Chris ruin the good in her life again? How could she explain what she didn't understand herself?

"I... I don't...really know," she replied and, unable to meet his gaze, her eyes darted everywhere but to him.

"I see," he said before he abruptly got up and began putting what remained of their lunch back into the cooler bag. He didn't look her way again as he stalked to his horse and stuffed the item into his saddlebags.

"Zack," she called, getting to her feet as he returned to grab the colorful blanket from the ground and shook it out before rolling it into a ball. When he turned to look at her, she held in her surprised gasp, because for the first time since she'd met him, his eyes were cold. The teasing warmth that had always twinkled in his eyes was replaced with an icy regard she'd never expected to see from him.

"I didn't mean—"

"I don't want to talk about it," he grumbled, then returned to his horse and shoved the blanket into his saddlebags.

She'd hurt him. She didn't know exactly how, but she'd hurt something deep inside him, and now he had retreated to protect himself.

She struggled to find the right words to let him know he held no blame for her actions. "I'm sorry, Zack. I didn't—"

"Don't worry about it," he muttered as he untied their horses, then crossed to where she stood and quickly looked over the spot he'd just cleaned up. She followed his gaze to find that, aside from a few bent blades of grass, he'd wiped away any indication that they'd been there. For some strange reason, that made her heart hurt.

When she looked up, he met her gaze but turned away. "I shouldn't have kissed you."

"No, Zack, you don't—"

He waved his hand for her to stop. "It's okay, I get it," he said carefully. "You know about my past. Hell, you probably haven't even heard the half of it, because believe me, there's a lot to tell, but..." he glanced at her, "that's not who I am anymore. I don't expect you to believe that, but it's still the truth."

Her heart squeezed a little more tightly with each word, and then it dropped to her toes from the hard look in his eyes.

"I'm sorry." What else could she say? She didn't want to discuss Chris, and she didn't know how to explain to Zack that her reaction had nothing to do with him.

He shrugged and held Summer's reins out to Izabel. "You're not the first woman to backtrack when she discovered the kind of man I was."

She frowned as she took the reins. "But you just said—"

"I know what I said, but the truth doesn't always matter, does it?" He swung up onto his horse's back. "Let's get a move on," he said as he turned the gelding toward the path they'd followed to get to the clearing. "I've still got a lot of work to do, and I need to get to it."

Their ride had been a silent, miserable one. She'd stared at his back and the stiff set of his impossibly broad shoulders the whole way back to the ranch. She repeatedly scoured her mind for a way to explain, but was unable to find any words. It wasn't about his past, but it was far easier—not to mention very cowardly of her—to let him believe that was the issue, rather than expose the pain she'd left behind, which apparently, still affected her choices.

When they reached the barn, he took Summer's reins from her as soon as Izabel had dismounted. "You can head on in," he said without meeting her gaze. "I'll take care of your horse."

"What about yours?"

"Like I said, I've got work to do. We'll be heading out again as soon as Summer's settled."

"I can help you."

His lips bent into a rough form of his normal charming grin, but it never reached his somber eyes. "Not today. You go on in; I'll see you later." With that, he turned and disappeared into the barn, taking Izabel's heart and all her newfound hopes with him.

CHAPTER 13

Izabel took a sip of the lite beer she'd ordered, savoring the cold beverage as it slid down her throat, then placed the brown bottle on the highly polished wooden table. She tapped her foot to the lively two-step rhythm of the country song that filled the open space of Tony's Tavern and Grill. The band was actually quite good, and occasionally, they played more than just country—not that she was complaining. She had more important things on her mind to fill that bill.

It had been two days since she and Zack had picnicked in the hills. Two whole days since she'd seen him and completely embarrassed herself—and inadvertently hurt him in the process. She'd slept little that night, her mind filled with the look on his face when he'd turned those cold amber eyes on her. Pain had wrung her heart every time she remembered his hard tone when he told her that he understood it was his fault, when in reality, it had nothing to do with him.

She had spent the next forty-eight hours evaluating herself and what had happened. The conclusion she'd decided on this morning was fear. Fear of the past and her mistakes; fear of the future and the choices she might make.

Only a small possibility persisted that her past might come back to haunt her, but she was done with the past. She wanted a new future, one with a man who made her feel beautiful and powerful all at once. And Zack was that man.

Though it made her cautious, she didn't hold his past against him. Especially now that she knew there was a reason, something terrible that he had tried to escape with casual affairs and a charming smile. He could've chosen worse ways to drown his sorrows, and she could just let him push her aside. But now that she'd seen the pain behind his façade and the longing he wouldn't admit, she wanted to know why. More than that, she wanted *him*. She wanted his kiss on her lips and his hands on her body, she want the rest of him so close, she couldn't tell where he began and she ended. She wanted Zack, and she was sure he wanted her, too. They had a lot to work through, but it would be worth it—even if he decided their time together would be short-lived. She trusted him. She would take the risk and allow him to help her heal. And maybe she could help him as well.

Izabel looked toward the front door as it swung open, but didn't recognize any of the people who entered. She glanced at her watch, quarter to eleven. She took a worried sip of her beer. *Is he still going to come?*

A man at the end of the bar caught her attention, his eyes narrowed. He pointed in her direction, then said something to his friend beside him that made them both chuckle. The angry frown the second, bigger man threw at her made her breath catch in her throat. She'd seen that look before. All she could do was ignored it and hope the bigot left before she did.

"Ignorant, white fools," she muttered and rolled her eyes as she took another sip of beer. She couldn't change their opinion of her any more than she could change the color of her skin. They weren't worth thinking about, especially with all the new friends who surrounded her.

Apparently, Friday night was a big deal in Meriton. She and Emily had arrived around nine o'clock that evening. They'd met up with a couple of ladies, who'd shown up early to stake out the large booth at the back of the bar beside the dance floor and pool tables—a coveted spot, based on the number of annoyed looks they'd already received.

Kate, a short-haired brunette, with a quick wit and warm charm—and the owner of the bistro where Izabel had first met her with Emmy during their visit a few days before—had simply smiled at the dark until the other person finally turned away. The other new woman, Audrey, was a few years older than Izabel, with long auburn hair and seemed quiet, yet watchful. Despite that, however, she had a friendly smile and an accepting manner when Emmy introduced them. They'd all ordered drinks and a bite to eat while waiting for more friends to arrive.

An hour later, the long, corner booth that lined the back wall, and all the chairs opposite, were filled with men and women who seemed to have known each other for years.

Several firemen had been the next to arrive. Emmy had stiffened with nerves when Aaron walked in, but when it became clear he didn't notice her, she relaxed.

David and Josh—the deputies Izabel had met when they'd shooed the protestors away at the MacEntier Winery—arrived a little later in their plain clothes. She'd noted a silent exchange between Josh and Audrey as the men sat at the far end of the table. Then again, maybe she'd misconstrued the longing in his eyes and the tenseness that had filled the air for the few seconds they'd gazed at each other before saying, "Hello." Maybe it was just her own desire for Zack that had her seeing unrequited love wherever she looked.

Every one of them had smiled warmly and welcomed Izabel into their little group. In fact, she felt closer to these people in less than an hour than she had with most of her so-called friends in Seattle. These people were open and accepting, while those she'd left behind had spent more time looking for the flaws in others to use as weapons than in correcting their own.

Mentally shaking her head, Izabel wondered why she'd accepted those people or stayed in that circle for so long. They'd been Chris' friends, not hers, and they had wasted no time in pledging their allegiance to him when she left—making her out to be the cruel, callous bitch who had broken Chris' heart.

She snorted, too quietly for anyone to hear. "If they only knew..."

"Is everything okay?" Emmy leaned in close to ask over the blare of the music, a concerned frown wrinkling her brow. "You *are* enjoying yourself, right?"

Izabel pushed away her gloomy thoughts, plastered the most eager smile on her face, and nodded. "I sure am."

Emmy grinned. "Good. Just jump into a conversation whenever you like." She waved toward the others at the table before she returned to their group conversation.

Izabel glanced at her watch and then at the front doors. A move she'd made more than a dozen times in the last hour, to no avail.

"I'm sure he'll arrive soon," Audrey said from her other side. The woman had been so quiet for the last thirty minutes—ever since the deputies had arrived—that Izabel had almost forgotten she was there.

Turning to the redhead, Izabel frowned. "Who?"

Audrey smiled a bit self-consciously. "I've seen you watching the front door. It's not hard to guess who you're looking for..." She reached over to pat Izabel's hand. "Don't worry, Zack will be here."

Izabel ducked her head as her cheeks heated. Had she been that obvious?

"I don't think anyone else noticed," Audrey said, drawing Izabel's gaze once more. "Besides, I know what it's like to miss someone." Her eyes drifted down the table to rest on Deputy Josh before snapping back to Izabel and then down to the beer bottle, where her fingers resumed peeling the label.

"Do you...know him well?" Izabel asked hesitantly, afraid of what she would hear.

Audrey grinned and leaned closer. "Zack?"

Izabel nodded.

"Yes, but not in the way you mean."

Izabel frowned. "I don't understand."

"Yes, you do," Audrey said with a knowing look.

Izabel dropped her eyes, embarrassed.

"Unlike so many others around town," Audrey continued, "I never dated Zack, but I've known his older sister and the family for a long time."

Izabel nodded.

"Don't let his reputation scare you off," Audrey said. "Zack's a good man; it's just taking him a long while to get over what happened. Maybe he's still trying to, I don't know for sure, but I hope he has recovered. He deserves to be happy again, especially after so long."

Izabel's head snapped up halfway through Audrey's short speech, searching her new friend's face for that mysterious bit of knowledge to explain why Zack kept running hot and cold. "What *did* happen?"

Audrey's brows drew together. "Has no one told you? I'd have thought Zack would've explained to his new girlfriend since you weren't here when it happened."

Izabel shook her head. "Oh, I'm not his girlfriend."

"Ah, I see." Audrey nodded as if that explained everything. She must have read something on Izabel's face because she added, "But you want to be."

It was more of a statement than a question, and Izabel looked away, lifting one shoulder in a vague shrug.

"It's sometimes hard to let go of the past." Audrey's voice was soft and gentle, nearly soothing.

Izabel's back straightened in surprise. "How do you know it has anything to do with my past?"

Audrey's fingers paused on the label she had nearly removed from the bottle and tilted her head to stare at Izabel with an intense gaze. "I meant *Zack's* past. Are you running from something, too?"

After a long pause, Izabel met Audrey's gaze. "Aren't we all?"

Audrey nodded, her eyes shifting down the table before going back to peeling the label from her beer bottle. "I suppose we are..."

A commotion at the front of the bar drew everyone's attention as Zack walked in. He went to the bar, leaned toward the blonde woman mixing drinks, and planted a quick kiss on her cheek. The wattage of the bartender's grin could've lit all of Seattle and its surrounding communities for a year. Then the woman's hand slid behind Zack's neck, raked into his wonderfully soft hair before she took his lips in what looked like a lover's kiss.

Izabel fought the unexpected flare of jealousy that burned through her chest. She had no reason to be possessive.

But it was there anyway.

Zack pulled back, looking somewhat startled, but then he laughed and patted the woman's cheek before he turned toward the back of the bar. He made it three long strides before his eyes met Izabel's, and he stopped in his tracks.

Izabel's heart fluttered in expectation, desperately wanting him to come to her. After his two-day absence from the ranch, she couldn't take her eyes off him. He was the cool water that soothed her burning soul, and she couldn't wait to make things right—and to kiss him again.

But instead of strolling to her side of the booth, he went to the other end and took a seat on one of the chairs. He fell into easy conversation with David, Josh, and the others who sat nearby, so obviously not looking her way she wanted to kick him—or kiss him senseless.

Gazing at him, she wondered where he'd been for the last two days. Had he slept in his truck or on the ground beneath the stars somewhere? Because she'd waited up both nights, hoping to hear the sound of his boot heels coming up the stairs, but they never came. Maybe he'd stayed in the barn to get some distance. Or did he go to one of his many women for a soft bed and a warm welcome? Izabel's stomach clenched again.

Why hadn't I thought of that *before?*

He glanced in her direction and met her stare. His eyes were a bit wary, but his lips curved up and he tipped his head in greeting. She returned the gesture, but looked away, trying to think of a reason to approach him. At first, it hadn't seemed as if he wanted her company, but that small smile gave her confidence that he wouldn't be cold toward her.

The last song ended and the band's lead singer announced they were taking a short break before he left the stage. Izabel watched all the dancers exit the dance floor and knew what she needed to do.

At that moment, the bartender made a beeline across the floor with a cold beer in her hand. She went straight to Zack, and with a quick spin and an arm around his neck, the woman planted her butt on his lap and kissed his cheek before handing him his beer. No one around the table seemed to find her behavior unusual, but Izabel glared at the other woman.

What's going on here?

Zack met her dark look and something akin to regret flashed in his eyes before he turned to the woman in his arms and smiled.

"So much for guilt," Izabel grumbled under her breath.

A few minutes later, the band returned and the bartender finally exited Zack's lap and returned to the bar—though not before smacking another messy kiss on his lips.

Izabel wanted to rip the blonde's hair out, which was childish and irrational, but she couldn't deny the intense anger that bristled inside her the moment the other woman had landed in Zack's lap. She told herself to calm down, that Zack didn't know how she felt or what she wanted, nor had he agreed to it.

Well, I'll just have to show him.

"We're going to slow things down a bit now," the band's singer said a couple of songs later, and Izabel knew it was time to act.

She sauntered to the other end of the long booth and stood behind Zack's shoulder as the slow melody began. He looked up at her, a question in his dark eyes.

She held out her hand and gave him her best smile. "Dance with me," she said in a low voice that carried her heart in it. She just prayed he wouldn't reject her.

CHAPTER 14

Zack sensed her approach like the advance of some great and terrible thing about to happen. Her scent of roses and vanilla assaulted his brain before she even reached his end of the booth. He hadn't expected her to come to him, and though her nearness thrilled a part of him, the other part—the one that had kept him away the last two days licking his wounded pride and fortifying his troubled heart—dreaded speaking with her again.

Yet, when he met her eyes over his shoulder, his heart leaped in his chest and warmth washed over his skin.

"Dance with me?" she asked in a low voice that made every nerve in his body twitch and tingle.

He should say no.

He should turn away and let her go.

Instead, he turned toward her, took her hand, and led her onto the dance floor. Taking her in his arms, he made sure to maintain several inches of space between them before he began the slow two-step. Neither of them spoke for the first few bars of the song. He tried to keep from looking into the green jewels of her eyes, but the intensity of her stare enticed him. And once their gazes locked, he couldn't look away.

So many emotions swirled in her eyes. Desire was there, fear and hope too, and something else he couldn't quite name. The fear he didn't like, but the hope and desire were promising.

Still, he reminded himself, *she'd made her feelings all too clear in the mountains the other day.* For her, there was nothing between them except maybe friendship, but for him, their connection had already grown into something deeper, something more...intimate. Luckily for him, Cade and Addie would be home in a day or two, and then he could get back to his old, lonely life without the lush temptation of Izabel accosting him on a daily basis. No more sleeping in haylofts, the back of his truck, or the old hunting cabin up in the hills, which was where he'd gone last night. No, once Izabel left, he could slip between the sheets of his very comfortable bed without the enticement of knowing she was right down the hall.

Somehow, the thought didn't excite him.

Releasing his hold, he spun Izabel under his arm, but when she completed the spin and came back into his hold, she stepped in far closer than he expected. He shifted back a step to put more space between them, but every time he retreated, she would advance. She was so close that the tips of her perky breasts brushed against his chest, sending a riot of sensation pinging through his body.

Her small hand slid up his arm to his neck, and then her fingernails skimmed along his close-trimmed beard. His jaw tightened and the tips of her fingers brushed ever so lightly over his lips. Her touch pinned him in place as if his boots were nailed to the dance floor.

He frowned into the depths of her eyes and she smiled.

"What are you doing?"

"Touching you," she said simply.

"Why?"

She tilted her head. "Because I want to. I wanted to run my fingers through your beard." Her eyes followed her fingertips as they grazed over his jaw before caressing his lips once again. "And to see if your lips were as firm and warm as I remembered." Her gaze snapped to his. "Do you mind?"

He should say yes.

He should drop her hand and leave.

There were a dozen things he should do to put distance between them and protect himself, but he didn't do any of them. Instead, he glanced at her small hand, still tucked into his giant paw, and was struck by the size difference—his large and work-hardened; hers so tiny and soft. He could close his fist and crush the bones of her hand so easily. So much about her was like that—small and delicate, easily hurt or damaged—but she was strong, too. Stronger than she realized, and maybe even stronger than him. After all, she'd left everything she knew to start over somewhere else, stayed with strangers, and faced a long-held fear to please a friend. He couldn't even speak to his family about the mistakes he'd made that could one day affect them all.

Sighing, he looked into her face, and in that moment, pushing Izabel away was the last thing he wanted to do. He shook his head. "No, I don't mind."

She smiled and brushed her fingers over his lips.

Gently, he nipped at her fingers. "Are they what you remembered?" he asked, watching the awed expression that had filled her face.

A small line appeared between her brows as she stared up at him. Then she quickly licked her lips and shook her head. "I'm not sure. I think I need closer inspection."

With that, she released his hand to slide it behind his neck, flattened her body against his, and tugged him down to press her lips to his.

The sudden movement surprised him and for a moment, he didn't respond. Izabel wasn't deterred; she used her hold on him to wiggle closer as her tongue swept along the seam of his mouth. That small movement compelled him into motion.

With a growl of pent-up desire, his arms wrapped around her, crushing her to him. He tilted his head, parted his lips, and took over the kiss. Izabel moaned into his mouth, the small sound of pleasure lighting a fire in his blood. A kiss in a crowded room wouldn't be enough, no matter how hot and satisfying, but that knowledge didn't stop him.

He traced the curve of her hips, inched down to cup her sexy ass in his huge palms—*Soft, so soft and right, just as I'd imagined*—and lifted her off the floor. Izabel didn't complain. Instead, she held on tighter, darted her tongue into his mouth, and challenged him for control.

Oh, God, she's gonna kill me, he thought, wanting nothing more than to take her home to his bed. *Is she ready for that?*

He didn't know, but he couldn't stop. He kissed a line from her lips, across her jaw, and down her neck. With a contented sigh, she tilted her head back to give him more room. Her hands slid into his hair and she moaned when his lips found the sensitive skin beneath her ear.

"Let's get out of here," she murmured between heavy breaths. "Take me home, Zack."

He froze.

He'd heard those words so many times in the past, but this was different. This woman was different. Her obvious vulnerabilities made her different and brought out his protective nature, though that wasn't so unusual in itself. No, it was the power of his need for her—to hold her and keep her safe—that unnerved him. It was the reflection of that same need in her eyes and the sweet taste of her lips that drew him. Something about her he couldn't define heated his blood and captivated his mind to the exclusion of everything else, even self-preservation.

But those same vulnerabilities and her recent rejection was what made him pause. He lifted his head to stare down into her upturned face. She smiled, her eyes liquid emerald pools. All he saw reflected in her expression was a beautiful woman who wanted him as much as he wanted her. No hesitation, no fear. So different from what he'd seen in the clearing two days ago.

Somewhere in the midst of their wild passion on the dance floor, her legs had wrapped around his waist, bringing her core right up against the now-ridged part of him. He could feel the heat of her through the stiff denim of their jeans. She squeezed him with those long legs and leaned into him again.

"I want you, Zack," she whispered against his ear, her warm breath caressing his neck and raising goosebumps over his skin.

He nearly groaned with the explosion of lust her words shot through him. She nibbled on his neck, tempting him further, but he needed to think this through to protect them both. The last thing he wanted was to hurt her, and in the process, injure his own tattered heart.

Making his decision, he regretfully pulled her legs from his hips and lowered her to the ground. Her hands slid to his chest and rested over his thundering heart. She had to feel it and know how much he wanted her. He cradled her face with its questioning eyes in his hands and gently kissed her lips, then rested his forehead against hers. Inhaling her scent, he struggled to get his stampeding lust under control.

When he thought he could speak, he lifted his head and stared into her eyes. "This is not a no," he murmured, "but I need to think on it a bit."

He hated himself for causing the fragile hope to drain from her eyes as she nodded. "Yeah, I understand."

It was then that he realized the music had stopped, the dancers had stepped away to form a small circle in which he and Izabel were the center, and every eye in Tony's Tavern were riveted on them. And most of them were clapping, grinning like the fools they were.

He cursed quietly, then wrapped an arm around Izabel's waist, lifted his chin, and escorted her back to her chair. He then bowed to the crowd and returned to his place as they chuckled and patted him on the shoulder.

He hated their assumptions, hated that they'd witnessed something he'd wanted to be private, and he cursed himself because his damn reputation had struck again.

The music started up once more as he sat and attacked his beer like a man with worries on his mind. Maybe if he drank himself unconscious he could forget everything that had just happened. Forget that Izabel had propositioned him and the intense flare of desire that still throbbed within him.

He glanced down the tables to find Izabel chatting with his sister. She glanced his way and her lips—still red and swollen from his kiss—curved up encouragingly.

He felt himself respond in kind, but he dropped his gaze to the beer in his hand.

"That was a stunning display," Josh said from beside him. "Even for you."

Zack tried to laugh it off, but his chuckle sounded unnatural.

"Ah, I see," Josh said, then lifted his beer from the table and took a quick sip.

Zack narrowed his eyes at his friend. "What?"

"She's different, isn't she?"

He held in a groan. "Am I that obvious?"

"Well," Josh leaned back in his chair, "your interactions with her have certainly changed, and going by the kiss you two just shared, she's just as willing. So, the question is, why are you still here?"

Zack shook his head. "It's complicated."

"No, it's not."

Zack frowned at his friend. "You don't understand the situation, so you don't know that."

"Maybe I understand better than you think." Josh's eyes drifted down to the redhead sitting beside Izabel.

"Maybe you do..." Zack admitted, knowing a little about Josh's feelings for Audrey.

Josh nodded and met his friend's eyes again. "I may not know the whole situation, but I can say from experience... Don't wait, Zack. If she makes you happy, if she's what you want, then go after her."

"I could tell you to take your own advice," Zack grumbled and took another pull of his beer.

"Maybe I will. Maybe I already have." He shrugged. "The point is, running away and hiding won't make the feelings disappear."

At the other end of the tables, Izabel stood. Zack watched as she wove through the crowded dance floor to approach the bar, where she stood, waiting to get the bartender's attention.

"You're right," he told his friend as he turned back to his beer.

Josh grinned. "I know."

"She's different, special, but she deserves better than me."

"Zack," Josh said, slapping a hand on his shoulder, "that is up to *her*. If she's willing to look past your history—and I know that's what you want—then let her make that decision."

"How'd you get so smart?" He was only half kidding.

Josh laughed. "The military taught me more than just how to be a good Marine. Now," he got to his feet and placed a hand on Zack's shoulder, "it's time to take my own advice." He turned and sauntered down to where Audrey sat.

Zack chuckled as his eyes drifted back to where Izabel stood at the bar. He sipped his beer and waited. One of the men at the end of the bar spoke to her. She gave him a polite smile and replied.

Zack turned away as his hand tightened on the beer bottle, his stomach burning. Why did such an innocuous exchange fill him with such jealousy?

Because you want her to be yours.

He nodded to himself. Yes, he did, and it was time he did something about it.

Chapter 15

Izabel tapped her fingernail against the bar's smooth, well-polished wood. She didn't notice that it kept time with the fast beat of the band playing on the small stage behind her; all she knew was that she was getting tired of waiting to order the shot of bourbon she wanted so badly. She'd tried to find an opening closer to the center and the single bartender, but there had been too many people. Now, she stood at the end of the bar, close to the two men who'd stared at her earlier, waiting for the male bartender to look her way. He seemed to be in a deep discussion with two young women at the other end of the bar and had not bothered to look back at his other patrons.

There was no sign of the blonde bartender who'd kissed Zack earlier. Maybe she'd gone to get something from the supply room or had taken a break, but either way, Izabel was glad not to see her at the bar. The last thing she needed was to view the woman up close, especially after Zack's refusal to leave with her after that soul-melting kiss. Her knees were still a bit wobbly from that, but she couldn't blame him. After what had happened the last time they kissed, he had every reason to be wary. She just hoped he gave her the opportunity to make it up to him.

"You're not from around here, are you?"

Izabel jumped at the loud shout near her ear and glanced over at the larger of the two men who'd stared at her earlier. His friend peeked around the big man's shoulder, with oddly smug grin on his long face. She'd felt their eyes on her the moment she'd approached the bar, but since they hadn't done or said anything, so she'd just ignored them and their stares. Engaging them could only lead to all kinds of problems, but now, social graces required her to reply, especially since outright ignoring them could cause a lot more trouble.

She gave them a stiff smile. "No, I'm not." She looked back toward the bartender, but he still hadn't moved.

"Where're you from?" the big man asked.

"Seattle."

"No." He leaned toward her, encroaching on her space. "Where are you from *originally*?"

She stood her ground and kept her smile polite, but inside, she seethed with anger and humiliation. Why were some people like this? What made them hate her just because of the color of her skin?

She knew the answers, but that didn't make the situation any easier to face.

"Seattle," she repeated.

He stood and moved closer. "You're a pretty little thing, aren't you?"

That didn't seem to need a reply. Instead, she called to the bartender, who still didn't hear her.

A large palm slapped her butt cheek and squeezed. She smacked at his hand on her rear and tried to slide away from him. In response, he stood, blocked her retreat with a hand on the bar behind her, and pressed in closer, blocking out the dance floor and everyone she knew.

"That MacEntier playboy may not want to plow through you, but I'd be happy to spread your *beaner* legs."

Stunned by his audacity, she gasped at the racial slur and stared up at the barrel-chested man. Then she looked around, hoping someone nearby had overheard or seen her distress. But the loud music muted his words to all but her ears, and everyone else was caught up in their own Friday night endeavors.

The big man's friend sidled up beside them, closing her in on all three sides while the edge of the bar pressed into her back.

"What a kind offer," she said, her voice dripping with sarcasm, "but I'm afraid I'll have to decline."

"Ah, come on, *chica*," the second man drawled. "Don't be like that. A sexy little *jalapeno* like you might just like it." His hand cupped her breast.

Rage burned through her as she knocked the man's hand from her body and pushed the bigger man back a step. She wanted to scream at them to leave her alone, to beat them both with her fists, to inform them of their ignorance because she wasn't even Mexican, but it wouldn't do any good, nor did it matter. They had their preconceived notions about Latino people—and most likely, other dark-skinned cultures as well—and nothing she said would change any of it. Still, experience told her to tread carefully.

"I said no!" she shouted in their faces to emphasize her meaning, but they didn't seem to care. Instead, they both chuckled.

The big man gave her a nasty grin and pushed his hand into her hair. "You don't have—"

"Is there a problem here?"

Izabel's knees nearly buckled at the sound of Zack's deep voice. Her eyes slid closed and she sent up a prayer of thanks.

"Izabel?"

She opened her eyes and met his gaze from beside the big man who held her in.

"Fuck off, MacEntier," the big man growled. "You didn't want her."

Zack cocked his head and glared at the other man. "Who said that?"

He reached over and gripped the big man's wrist, and Izabel didn't miss the wince of pain that twisted her attacker's face.

"Because I certainly never did," Zack continued as he carefully removed the other man's hand from her hair and pushed him back. Then he dropped his arm over her shoulders and tucked her safely against his side. "In fact, we have a standing date for tonight, don't we, darlin'?"

Izabel knew he was speaking to her, but his dark eyes were staring daggers at the other men.

"T-That's right," she stuttered, wrapping her arm around his waist and clinging to him like a lifeline in the ocean.

"You little *greaser* bitch," the big man shouted, looming forward as if he would grab her. But before she knew what he was about to do, Zack had pushed her behind him, blocking her from an attack with his body.

"You will not touch her or speak to her that way." Zack's voice sounded strained and harsher than normal.

"I'll speak to her or any other *berry picker* however I like," the big man shouted.

"No, you won't," Zack replied. "In fact, you're going to apologize to her and then leave."

"I'm not apologizing to that little *border bunny,* and you can't make me!"

Everything went suddenly still and heaviness seemed to fill the air. Izabel could feel the tension in Zack's body through her hand, resting on his back. His shoulders stiffened and his hands had fisted at his sides. The big man was about the same height as Zack and the leaner man was only a few inches shorter. She doubted the lean man would stay out of a fight if fists started flying, and that meant Zack was outnumbered.

She didn't want Zack to do this. Didn't want him to get hurt because of her, but she didn't know how to stop it.

"The hell I can't," Zack bit out to the man's challenge, his tone low and dangerous.

It hit her then that the bar had gone silent. No loud music or chatter filled the space. All she heard was her own anxious breathing and then the movement of booted footsteps coming from behind her. She glanced over her shoulder and saw Josh approach, his firm deputy's face fixed in place. He gave her a comforting smile, then stepped between the two men facing off against each other.

Izabel moved behind Josh and watched with her heart in her throat.

"That's enough, Zack. You've made your point."

"He put his hands on Izabel," Zack said, not taking his stony eyes from the big man. "He assaulted her."

"Is that so?" Josh glanced at Izabel, who nodded as David elbowed his way to their side to back up Josh.

"Stay right there," Josh said to the two strangers before he pulled Izabel a few steps away from the men and the crowd, blocking her from the other men with his broad shoulders and greater height.

"Do you want to press charges?" he asked her in a private whisper.

She looked up and shook her head. "I just want this over," she said, mimicking his quiet undertone, "and those men gone."

"You're sure?"

She nodded.

"Okay," he said, "but follow my lead, all right? Don't interrupt."

After another nod from Izabel, Josh turned back to the men. "What do you have to say for yourself, Mr. Greer?"

Greer pushed his chest out as his face turned red with anger. "She's lying. The little bitch came on to me."

"You motherf—" Zack lifted his fists, looking like a madman about to rip his opponent apart with his bare hands.

Josh stopped him with a muscled arm across his chest, while David stepped between them and shoved Greer back a couple of steps.

"Zack, let us handle this," Josh said and turned. "Mr. Greer, you will apologize to the lady." Greer started to argue, but Josh shook his head. "Apologize to the lady, and I won't arrest you right now for assault."

"You're taking their word over ours?" Greer indicated himself and his lean friend.

Josh's lips thinned and he gave Greer a pointed look. "You forget who you're talking to. I've seen this behavior from you before, or something very similar. Remember?"

All the bluster drained from Greer's posture and he looked away. "Come on, Schiff," he said to his lean friend as Greer pushed him toward the door. "Let's get out of this shithole"

"Hold on a sec," Josh said, grabbing Greer's bicep to keep him from slipping away. "Apologize first, then you can leave."

Izabel shook her head. She didn't care about a meaningless apology; she just wanted the revolting man and his equally disgusting friend to leave—but she held her tongue as Josh had asked.

Greer glared at Josh for a long moment, measuring the sizable deputy, then he shifted his horrid gaze to her. There was no contrition in his eyes, no repentance on his face, only anger and hatred and a weak promise of retribution. "Apologies, *senroita*," he said in a barely concealed snarky tone. "It won't happen again." He turned to Josh. "Good enough for you?"

Josh glanced at David, who nodded.

He crossed his brawny arms over his chest. "Now apologize to Mr. MacEntier."

"Why him?" Greer asked, affronted.

"Because I said so."

Greer glared but relented under Josh's unblinking stare. "Sorry," he blurted out. "Can we go now?"

Josh nodded. "But remember," he said and Izabel heard the steel in his gravelly voice, "the next time you do something stupid, like assault another woman or start a fight, it will be jail time for you *and* your friend, whether the other party wants to press charges or not."

Greer narrowed his eyes at Josh but quickly lowered them, and then the two men hurriedly shuffled out the door.

"All right, everyone," Dave shouted and waved to the assembled crowd, "the excitement's over. Go back to your tables and enjoy yourselves." The people began to move away and a low buzz of muttered conversation filled the room.

"You didn't have to do that," Izabel murmured to Josh once the men were gone.

"He deserves worse," Josh turned toward her, "but I think you did the right thing. Greer's a bully, and you don't need him singling you out when you're all alone—as he's been known to do when someone goes against him. This way, at least he's just pissed at me for forcing him into an apology."

"Would you really have arrested him?"

"No. You didn't want to press charges and I didn't see anything. We didn't have anything to arrest him for..." Josh grinned, "but *Greer* didn't know that."

Izabel chuckled. "Well, thank you for your help and David's, too."

"I tell him, but it's not me or David you should thank." He tilted his head toward Zack, who hadn't moved from where he'd faced Greer. Zack stood like a statue, his head down, his eyes closed, hands fisted at his sides, only his chest moved with each intake of air. "I pushed the apology for Zack's sake as well as yours."

She touched Josh's arm. "I know, and thank you, again."

Josh covered her hand and gave it a little squeeze. "Go easy on him," he whispered. "I've never seen him like this."

Her eyes switched to Zack and all awareness of Josh or anyone else disappeared.

Zack had defended her. Protected her with his body. Had demanded an apology for her humiliation. It didn't matter that the words Greer spoke hadn't been real. This man beside her had gone to battle for her and had been willing to do more. That had to mean something. Right?

She reached out and eased his closed fist open. His hands, like hers, trembled from the tension and rush of unspent adrenaline. She felt a little weak and unsteady as she looked up to find his soulful brown eyes staring down at her.

"Are you all right?" he asked in a husky voice.

"Yes, thanks to you. Are *you* all right? I was afraid you might..." She dropped her chin to hide the sudden burn of tears that filled her eyes.

"Zack?" a woman called from the bar, and from the corner of her eye, Izabel saw the blonde bartender was back. She held a small knife in her hand and a pile of cut limes lay on a cutting board on the bar. "You need a drink?" Her blue eyes were bright and warm as she looked at him.

A flash of anger straightened Izabel's spine. *Can't everyone just leave us alone for one minute?* Then the whirl of fury faded as quickly as it came. *He's not mine...yet.*

Zack's head turned to the pretty bartender and in an emotionless tone, he replied, "No."

A frown wrinkled the bartender's brow and her caustic gaze cut to Izabel for a brief, icy moment. Her hand visibly tightened on the knife before she spun away to chat up another man at the bar.

Zack tucked a curled knuckle under Izabel's chin, lifting her face to his. When she met his warm whiskey eyes, her whole body began to shake.

"I'm okay," he said, wiping away tears with his thumb that Izabel hadn't known she'd shed. Then he cupped her cheek in his palm. "What do you need?"

"You," she whispered, and her eyes widened. She hadn't meant to say that out loud, hadn't even realized she'd been thinking it.

He smiled and his dimples winked at her. "You have me, sweetheart. What else do you need right now? A drink, some food, water, what?"

She shook her head. "Bathroom. I...I want to use the bathroom and then get out of here." She hated how shaky she sounded, but she couldn't stop that any more than the trembling in her body.

"All right, sweetheart." Zack wrapped his arm around her waist and the band started another song behind them. "Let's get you to the restroom."

* * *

Izabel splashed water on her face and tried to get herself under control. Her hands still shook, and she wasn't sure if her legs would hold her long enough to reach the front door. But, aside from a few initial tears, she refused to breakdown in front of everyone at the bar.

Emmy had rushed in to check on her, shooing everyone else out in the process, and even now, she stood beside her at the sink, rubbing Izabel's back consolingly.

"Most of the people around here aren't like those jerks," she said for the second time since Izabel had quickly explained what had happened. "Please don't let them ruin our town for you."

A corner of Izabel's mouth lifted and she nodded. "I won't. It's not the first time I've experienced racism or sexual harassment, and it probably won't be the last." While her voice was still a little shaky, the words had all been true.

"I don't get it," Emmy said, stepping over to a stall to gather a wad of toilet paper. "Here," she held out the handful of paper, "you have mascara under your eyes."

Izabel took the tissue gratefully and began cleaning her face. She looked at her friend through the mirror and saw Emmy appeared deep in thought.

"What?"

Emmy met her gaze with a frown.

"What don't you get?" she clarified.

"Oh." Emmy shook her head. "I was just wondering how people can be like that. Why do they think they're better than you? Or anyone, for that matter."

"I don't know," Izabel said, staring at her naked face in the mirror, not wanting to get into the politics that promoted hate or the history of intolerance and misogyny within the United States, not to mention the rest of the world.

"But I'm glad to have you and your family on my side."

Having wiped away most of her makeup, she wadded up the messy tissue and tossed it into the trash before she turned to face her friend.

A grin split Emmy's face. "Zack was kind of magnificent, wasn't he? I've never seen him so angry over a woman. Protective of her, yes, but never enraged enough to beat another man to a pulp...but that's how he looked defending you."

"He was wonderful, coming to my aid like that. But I have to admit, all that raw male anger built up inside him was a bit frightening, too."

Emmy grabbed her hand and held it between both of hers, her eyes full of worry and earnestness. "Oh, Izzy, he'd never hurt you. He's a big guy and protective of those he cares about, but Zack would never raise a hand to a woman. You don't need to fear him."

"I don't," Izabel said and meant it. "It was just the situation, and I'm still a little rattled by the whole thing."

"Well, then" Emmy patted her hand and led her to the door, "just relax and let Zack take you home. I know my brother; he'll take care of you and you'll be safer than in your mother's arms. All right?"

Izabel nodded, but tremors still shivered through her. She didn't think it would stop until she got away from the bar.

Emmy pulled open the door and Izabel followed her out into the hall. Zack pushed away from the opposite wall, his worried gaze locked on her as he stepped forward. "Everything okay?"

Izabel nodded.

"Take her home, Zack," Emmy said. "She needs to be warm and cozy and safe."

"I can do that," he said as if he'd just been waiting for direction on how to help. He handed Izabel her purse he must have collected from the table, and then placed his arm securely around her. Without realizing it, Izabel leaned into him, needing his warmth and strength...needing him.

Emmy leaned in close to whisper, "Remember what I said... Just relax."

"She'll be fine, Emmy.." Zack led Izabel to the front door and out into the parking lot, but called over his shoulder to his sister, "Say our goodbyes to everyone."

The cool night air splashed against Izabel's face as they stepped outside. Overhead, she saw a smattering of stars twinkling between the gathering clouds, but the moon was nowhere in sight. She could smell moisture in the air and suspected it would sprinkle before the night was through. Her gaze darted around the parking lot, expecting to find her attackers waiting for them. But no one jumped out of the darkness as they meandered through the rows of parked cars the only people in sight were in the cab of a truck near the door, too wrapped around each other to notice her and Zack leaving.

The wind blew gently and the slight chill crept beneath her collar, making her shiver.

"Are you cold?" Zack asked as they strolled toward his truck in a shadowy corner of the lot.

"A little," she replied, "but it's getting better with your arm around me."

His white teeth flashed in the darkness.

"I like it when you hold me," she admitted, and he hugged her a little closer.

"I like it, too."

They reached his truck and she stopped by the passenger door and turned to face him. Tilting her head all the way back, she met his gaze.

What was it about him that seemed to reach inside her like a soothing balm? That touched her heart in ways no one ever had?

"Zack, I..." The backs of his fingers brushed down her cheek and her words stuck in her throat.

"Yes?" he asked, bracing his hands against the truck on either side of her.

"I need to talk to..." The sentence sputtered out when his brows drew together and his eyes dropped to his hand near her shoulder.

He cursed and stepped back.

"What's wrong?" she asked, looking around for what had caused his reaction as her limbs began to shake.

He reached into his back pocket and pulled out his phone. Turning it on, he angled it to illuminate the side of his truck as he walked from the rear bumper to the front fender, where he hissed in a breath as he leaned around the front. "Oh, no..."

"Zack?" The tremors wracking her knees grew stronger.

He held up one finger in a signal to wait. "Just one more second." He dashed to the other side of the truck, snapped on his phone, and another more vicious curse echoed through the night.

"What is it?" she demanded, wrapping her arms around herself, trying to keep her anxiety at bay. "What's going on?"

He came back to her side and pulled her into his arms. "I need to go back inside for a minute," he said as she huddled against his chest. "Josh and Dave need to see this."

"Why?"

Straightening, but not letting her go, he pulled out his phone and pointed it at the side of his truck. "Someone keyed my truck," he said, shifting the light so she could see the long line gouged in the paint. "And both tires on the other side are flat."

Izabel's eyes widened and she glanced behind her, huddling a little closer to Zack. "Do you think those men did it?" Her gaze swung back to Zack's. "Did they retaliate because you helped me?"

Zack shook his head as he did a quick search of the area. "I don't know them, so I don't know how they would know my truck. But I am going to report it and have them checked out anyway."

Putting his words into action, he turned on his phone and dialed his friend again. He lifted the phone to his ear, then wrapped his arm around her, pulling her against his chest.

Izabel sighed as she rested her head on his chest and let the strong, steady beat of his heart soothe her nerves. *Well,* she thought, *at least I'm in his arms again.* She smiled to herself and listened as Zack told his friend to come outside.

It was going to be a long night.

CHAPTER 16

Half an hour and several questions later, Izabel rested her head against the truck's passenger seat and sighed. Her eyes burned with exhaustion and her limbs felt thick and heavy. After everything that had happened tonight, she was thankful to finally be leaving the town behind them. Even more so to be riding in a truck with Zack behind the wheel.

Josh and Dave had come out to inspect the damage after Zack's call. Since both of them had been drinking, Josh called another deputy to take the report. He'd snapped a few photos and told Zack he'd get more pictures in the morning.

"In the meantime," Josh said with a grim grin as the first drops of rain began to fall, "you can take my truck." He tossed the keys at Zack, who caught them one-handed.

"You don't need it?"

Josh shrugged. "I have another vehicle at home, and Dave can give me a ride later tonight. Just keep it until you can get yours back on the road."

When they'd left a short time later, Izabel had said a little prayer of thanks and glanced back at the tavern as Zack backed the truck out of its spot. The blonde bartender from earlier was standing at the tavern's entry, wiping her hands on a white bar towel, and glaring at Izabel as the truck pulled away.

Izabel was too tired to consider the woman's expression. Instead, she turned toward the windshield, put the woman and the whole incident out of her mind, and tried to relax.

Now she watched the yellow lines zip by as they made their way home, her senses lulled by the rhythmic *whisk* and *thump* of the windshield wipers scraping away the sudden rainfall. Zack had blanketed her with a farm jacket he'd pulled from his truck before they left. It smelled like him and that, along with its warmth and the truck's heater, had helped to ease her shivers.

Her first inclination had been to slide across the bench seat and snuggle up to Zack's side, but the gearshift sticking out of the floor had changed her mind. It would be awkward for him and her both if she had scooted over and allowed her legs to bracket the long, bent metal rod. Instead, she'd slouched in the seat and concentrated on the scent of his jacket.

They'd driven several miles out of town when Zack cleared his throat. "You wanted to talk about something earlier. You want to tell me what?"

She glanced at him in surprise and looked away. "I..." she started, but the words died out. "Pull over."

"What?" He glanced at her. "You said you wanted to get home."

"I do," Izabel replied, "but this isn't the kind of conversation I want to have while you're driving."

"But you're okay with us sitting in the truck on the side of a deserted road in the middle of the night?"

She glanced out the window at the passing terrain and the stygian darkness that surrounded the few and far between streetlamps they passed. "Well…" She dragged out the word with uncertainty. "The privacy is good, but…"

"Okay, then." He flicked on the turn signal and took a quick turn onto a narrow, overgrown dirt drive. They had almost been to their turn onto the MacEntier's long gravel driveway, but now Zack seemed to be making his own trail straight into the forest beside the road.

Izabel sat up as a shot of wariness zapped through her. "Where are we going?"

"Somewhere *private*," he said without taking his eyes off the road, "where we can talk."

"In the woods?" She eyed the uneven road as it angled into the hills and under the trees' thick boughs. "Should I be worried?" Her lips quirked at her joke, but the cautious part of her wanted to know.

"I have a small cabin on the back side of our property," Zack said as he maneuvered the truck over several deep potholes. "I'd planned to build a house there one day, but all I've got right now is a simple place to go when I need to be alone."

"Where you take your women, you mean," she said, teasing him.

Zack glanced over at her, his face stony. "I've never brought a woman out here, Izabel. You're the first."

Her eyes widened. "Really?"

"Yes," he grumbled as he downshifted and the truck crawled over a steep rut in the road.

Izabel's heart thudded in her chest. They were going somewhere private where she would be alone with this man who made her body sing with a tender look or soft touch. What if he kissed her again? What would happen when there were no distractions to stop them?

But then again, after what she had to say, it may not even be an issue.

* * *

Twenty more minutes and a lot of bumps later, Zack maneuvered the truck through the thick layer of trees and into a clearing. The rains had ceased for the time being and the clouds had scattered, but Izabel couldn't see much in the darkness, except that the ground in front of them leveled out and the headlights revealed a small, single-story log cabin ahead. It looked as if it had been there for decades. The clear-stained, wooden walls were sun-faded and ugly black strips of mildew flowed down the corners from damp weather and little cleaning. There was one huge window in the front—shrouded by inside curtains—and a covered deck that ran the length of the building. To the right of the windows, a weathered-looking front door stood closed. No light came from inside the building, and Izabel feared what kind of a mess she'd find inside. From the look of the outside, she pictured a dingy, cramped, cluttered disaster waiting just behind the front door.

She couldn't tell how big it was in the dark, but she had misgivings about stepping inside to find out.

"Well, we're here," Zack said as he opened the truck door and slid from the seat, leaving the key in the ignition.

"I can see that," Izabel murmured, though she tried to keep her reservations to herself.

Zack rested an arm against the truck's roof and ducked his head until he looked in at her. His eyes danced with mirth in the cab's overhead light. "I know it's not much to look at from the outside, but the inside is clean."

He must have heard the doubt in her comment. She cleared her throat. "I'm sure it's fine."

She opened her door and dropped to the muddy driveway. Off to the side of the cabin, she could just make out the shadowed shape of tall trees that seemed to circle the back of the cabin and she heard the sound of water gurgling over rocks from somewhere behind them.

Zack's truck door closed with a *bang* that made her jump, but she quickly recovered and followed his example. Instantly, they were thrust into total darkness, but strangely, she wasn't afraid. She knew Zack was close and that he would take care of her.

Closing her eyes, she leaned against the side of the truck and sighed. This was not how she'd planned for this night to go.

Why didn't I just tell him to go home? She shook her head. No, that wouldn't have worked. She didn't want to have this conversation at all, especially not somewhere anyone else might overhear. But if she wanted something with Zack, then she needed to explain why she'd pushed him away.

Still resting against the truck, she opened her eyes and gasped. The velvety black sky glittered and twinkled among the dissipating clouds with an almost magical beauty.

"Is something wrong?" Zack asked from the other side of the vehicle, worry in his tone.

She shook her head, her eyes glued to the gorgeous, star-filled sky, but then realized he couldn't see her.

"No, nothing's wrong," she said, a touch of awe filling her voice. "I've just never seen so many stars before."

She heard his boots crunch over the ground as he rounded the truck. He touched her shoulder briefly before he leaned his back against the truck next to her, close enough that the heat from his body warmed her side.

"Yeah," he crooned, and Izabel heard the smile in his voice. "It's beautiful. Just wait until all the clouds are gone. You'll never see anything like it in the city. Too much light pollution."

She nodded, but didn't speak.

Suddenly, there was a rasping *click* and a small flare of light illuminated a tiny space before them. When Izabel looked, she found a lit lighter in Zack's big hand.

"I don't have a lantern out here, so this'll have to do for now." He waved an arm toward the grungy cabin. "Shall we go in and have that conversation?"

Izabel nodded and headed for the front door.

Thankfully, her first impression of the place had been incorrect. While the outside looked like a dump, the inside was a clean and cozy space, filled with small tokens that made her think of the tall, broad-shouldered man behind her.

Directly across from the enormous front window sat a long, comfy-looking, corner couch with well-padded seats and a couple of throw pillows. A large, rectangular rug in antique reds and browns with a large bear printed in the center covered the floor. Above them, roughhewn logs spaced evenly apart made the ribs of the ceiling, which angled downward from a high center peak, giving the whole cabin an airy quality. Sheetrock had been nailed up between them to hide the insulation and a thin coating of off-white paint gave it an old-timey feel that Izabel thought fit Zack perfectly. A not-quite-translucent curtain blocked off what looked to be a bedroom from the front room, and behind the couch was a small kitchen.

Overall, the interior was homey—a place to sit and relax while staring out at the landscape. The night hid whatever that vision was, but Izabel pictured hills and trees and a river in the distance. She imagined deer roaming through a wide, grassy front yard, or maybe a bear scurrying through the river, headed for some unknown destination while a bald eagle soared in a deep blue sky.

"I'll get a fire started in the stove," Zack said as he closed the door behind him and headed for the kitchen. "Make yourself comfortable. I'll be back in a minute."

Izabel smiled at him and went to sit on the overstuffed couch. To say she was surprised by the cleanliness of the interior would've been an understatement, but that seemed to be the norm with this man. So much about him was not what she expected, and all of that was good.

Zack returned to the front room a few minutes later. "I don't have a lot stored here—a few beers and some crackers or chips—but if you want something...?"

She shook her head. "I ate at the bar. Maybe some water though."

He smiled. "Coming right up."

He returned with the glass a moment later and then settled in beside her. She took a drink and set the glass aside as, turning to face her, Zack laid his arm across the back of the couch.

"So," he said slowly, giving her his undivided attention, "what did you want to talk about?"

Izabel twisted her hands in her lap as nervousness tightened her muscles and a rock of uncertainty dropped into her stomach. She opened her mouth to speak, but nothing came out except a small squeak in the back of her tight throat. Her eyes widened and flew to his face, expecting to see disdain and dismissal, but instead, she saw the same patience in his warm amber eyes as she had from the moment she'd met him.

The corner of his mouth curled up in a sideways grin and he reached over to touch her shoulder. "Hey, sweetheart, take your time. I'm not going anywhere."

She should've expected he would know exactly what to say to calm her down. What she hadn't anticipated was the rush of tears that filled her eyes.

"Hey," he crooned again as he scooted closer and pulled her into his arms. "Hey, it's okay." He smoothed her long curly hair from her face and soothed the fear that had suddenly sprung up within her. Shivers wracked her body and she struggled to get control of herself.

What is wrong with me? This wasn't like her. She'd learned early to hide feelings of hurt and vulnerability, but something about this man and his easy manner had opened her heart—the same way Addie had when they first met.

It took a minute or two, but eventually, Izabel ceased her tears and sat back to face him.

"I'm sorry," she said as she wiped her face with shaky fingers. "I'm not usually so emotional."

"It's not a problem," Zack replied as he tucked a stray curl behind her ear. "I don't mind. So take your time; I have all night."

She stared at him, once again stunned by his generosity. "You're so different than what I thought you'd be..."

He chuckled. "And what did you think I'd be?"

She shook her head. "I'm not sure, really. Overbearing? Demanding? Something other than warm and patient and kind."

"So you thought I was a jerk," Zach said with a quirk on his lips.

She gave him a watery smile. "I suppose…but that's not what you are."

A twinkle of mischief danced in his eyes. "Good to know."

Great, now he's laughing at me. She inhaled and let the breath out slowly. "This is not going the way I'd planned. Not that I had actually planned it, but it wouldn't have been this way if I had." She closed her eyes, groaned at her rambling, and then let out a sigh.

One of his large hands closed around hers and rested on her thigh. "You're doing fine. Why don't you start by telling me if you're okay? After everything that happened at the bar…I was worried."

She met his concerned expression. "I'm okay. It was just a little…shocking, I guess. But not anything I hadn't heard before."

His brows drew together and anger flashed in his eyes. "I'm sorry to hear you've had to deal with that crap before. I wouldn't have allowed it if I'd gotten there sooner."

"You were there soon enough," she told him with a little grin. "Thank you for that, by the way."

"No problem." He lightly squeezed her hand and then released her. "I'm happy to come to your rescue anytime."

The smile she gave him was shy and grateful. Then she took another deep breath and released it slowly. "As much as I appreciate what you did for me tonight, that's not what I wanted to talk about."

"Okay, then what did you want to talk about?"

"The kiss..."

He grinned. "I was wondering about that myself. It was pretty damn hot and not something I've ever done before."

She tilted her head, confused. He'd kissed other women, so why would he say he'd never done it before?

He must have read the puzzlement on her face because he hurried to clarify, "I meant on the dance floor. I've never gotten that hot and heavy with anyone in public before...not that I'm complaining. It was fantastic, but a little confusing after the other day."

She nodded in understanding. "I know. That's what I wanted to talk to you about."

"Okay," he said, settling against the couch back, his arms crossed over his chest and wariness in his eyes. "Go ahead. I'm all ears."

Chapter 17

Izabel's gaze dropped and she wrung her hands in her lap once more. It took all of Zack's willpower to keep from pulling her into his arms again. All he wanted was to console her, to see her smile, to wipe that haunted look from her eyes forever, but he knew this was important. Whatever she needed to say had to come out. Plus, he sensed the change in her that he'd been waiting for about to occur. So he sat back—every muscle tense as uncertainty and his protective nature wound him up—and listened to her every word.

She took a deep breath and began.

"I am a Latina. I was born in Seattle to Brazilian parents. My dad was half-white and half-black, and my mother a full-blooded *Brasileira.* We often visited family in Brazil when I was young, and we lived with them while we were there. So you will understand when I say that I spent a good part of my life surrounded by the Brazilian ethos—their belief structure, art, ethnicity, religion, traditions, everything." She looked up at him briefly before she focused on her twisting hands. "I tell you this as a precursor to explain…" she shrugged, "who I am, in the hopes that my mistakes are a little more understandable."

She paused to look at him and he nodded. Her chin dropped and her fingers fiddled with a corner of her shirt.

"The Brazilian culture is still very male-dominated and *machismo.*" The last word left her lips filled with derision. "It is a more common attitude there than it is in the States now. The man is the one to make the decisions—at least, that's how it was in my house—and my father was very domineering. Thinking back, he rarely had much of anything nice to say to me or my mother. I tried to ignore him, but it was hard not to take his hurtful words to heart."

She looked up and Zack's heart twisted at the sadness and vulnerability he saw in her lovely emerald eyes.

"Sometimes words leave deeper scars than fists," she said quietly and then shrugged, her eyes sliding away from Zack once more. "I learned to hide my feelings so he wouldn't see how much it hurt when he told me I was fat, or that women weren't supposed to use power tools, or that I couldn't beat him at strategy games because I couldn't think like a boy. Things only got worse once I reached my teen years."

"That must have been...very difficult," Zack said and a strong urge swelled within him to hunt her father down and aggressively explain a few things to him about how he should treat his daughter.

She nodded. "It was, and his abuse went on for many years. Until, one day, my mother decided she'd had enough."

"Why did she stay so long?" he asked, not wanting to interrupt but curious about the answer.

Izabel canted her head, but she didn't meet his gaze. "Brazil has a very family-oriented social culture. Extended families often lived together to help with the rent and other bills. Being loyal to the family is paramount, and the father was always the head of the *familia*."

She looked up and he nodded, wondering if her father ever realized the damage he had done to his only child.

Izabel looked away and sighed before she continued, "My mother never really told me what made her decide to leave. Maybe it was because of how he treated her, or how he ran me down, or the strength and supposed equality for females she found in the American culture. Whatever the reason, she divorced him—which was unheard of in his family. It had been a blow to his pride, and he didn't speak to either of us for years."

"But you've talked to him, haven't you?" Zack didn't know how he knew that, but he was sure of her answer.

She nodded and he tried to hold back a groan. Sometimes being right sucked.

"He's gotten better," she said, "and I don't let him speak badly to me or about my mom. But he's still my dad, and I want to know him."

"Nothing wrong with that, especially if you stand up to him."

She gave Zack a quick, shy smile and then focused on her lap again. "My mom and I lived on our own for a couple of years after the divorce, until I left for college. She didn't like being alone so much, and I had no desire to move in with either of my parents again, so she moved back to Brazil."

"You must miss her," Zack said quietly, still fighting the impulse to hold her, to protect her from what he felt coming with her next words.

She shrugged. "I do miss her, but I chat with her as often as I can. Her nagging has only increased over the last few years, so I've been avoiding her calls."

Zack frowned. "Why?"

"She knew something was wrong," Izabel said sadly, almost defeated. "I think she knew it all along..."

"And what was that?"

Izabel's shoulders sagged as if the weight of the world had just landed upon them. "His name was Chris Richards."

Zack's heart lurched and his stomach twisted into a knot. He'd been afraid of that—that another man had hurt her somehow. Part of him wanted to tell her to stop. He didn't want to hear about her relationship with some other guy, didn't want to suffer the jealousy that would burn through his veins or suffer the anger that would have no outlet. But the bigger part of him—the one that longed to have her in his arms again, to press his lips to hers and feel her respond—needed to know what had happened. Maybe then, he could make it better and help her to heal.

"Looking back now, I don't know why I didn't see the similarities. Maybe I was looking for someone like my dad—someone whose attitude and beliefs felt...familiar."

"Was he also from Brazil?"

She shook her head. "No, he was born and raised in Seattle, but he was every bit as controlling and condescending as my father had ever been at his worst. He was just more…subtle, and at the time, I was too young and stupid to realize it."

Izabel fell silent, clearly thinking over the past, and Zack's hands curled into fists that he hid beneath his arms as he crossed them over his chest. He hated hearing this, and even more, he hated that she'd been hurt. Hated that the fury tingling along his spine had nowhere to go. His heart hammered against his ribs and he wished vainly wished for something or someone he could tear apart.

How could anyone treat this beautiful, strong, intelligent woman so badly? What had she needed to do to regain that strength to stand on her own? Awe filled Zack's chest, mixed with a hearty dose of pride. She was amazing, and she didn't even know it.

"I really did think Chris loved me," Izabel began again. "At least, I did at first. But then he started belittling me and my work, telling me to let him take care of everything and to not worry myself over anything." Her hands balled into tiny fists and she slammed them against her thighs as her chin lifted stubbornly. "But I liked my job, my career, and I was very good at it, no matter what he said. I would've gotten that last promotion if he hadn't sabotaged me."

"You two worked together?"

She nodded, some of the fight draining from her again. "We'd partnered on several projects, but eventually, I put a stop to that."

"Eventually?"

"Yeah. The changes in his behavior and attitude had happened slowly. So much so that it took me years to realize what he was doing. When it finally became clear that he wanted me to quit and just stay home for *him*, I was no longer sure he was the man I wanted in my life." Her jaw tightened as she stared at some point across the room.

"When the boss unveiled a new project and promised a promotion to whoever came up with the best marketing strategy, I told Chris I wanted to work on it alone. He didn't like it, but he didn't have a choice. I kept my ideas to myself, but he found the portfolio with all my notes and sketches. He stole them and when I found out, he made sure no one would believe me—made me out to be some kind of unstable lunatic he had to struggle to keep sane."

"The bastard," Zack growled, and Izabel gave him a tight smile of gratitude.

"I went to my boss and tried to explain what had happened. I don't know if he really believed me, but it didn't matter because he did nothing." Her hands curled up tightly in her lap and she pounded them against her thighs. "Chris got the promotion with *my* ideas. And when I confronted him, he told me he did it for my own good!" Her voice had increased in pitch as she spoke until the last words came out as almost a squeal.

"What an asshole," Zack muttered, but she didn't seem to hear him.

"We tried to talk it through. I don't know why I'd even agreed to do that much, but when I caught him with another woman two days later, that was the bitter end of it." She shook her head and a snort escaped her lips. "Chris had always said no one would love me the way he did," she continued, her voice shaking with every word. "That if I tried to leave, he'd find me and never let me go. Even with another woman in his bed, he still claimed I was his and that I could never leave him."

"He threatened you?"

She nodded and new tears streamed down her face. "They were always hidden in pretty words, but they were threats. All of them."

Zack had reached the end of his restraint. He pulled her into his arms, shifting their bodies until she sat in his lap with her face tucked against his neck while she cried, as if her heart had broken all over again.

Zack's heart sank into his boots at her evident sorrow, and his stomach roiled with feelings of inadequacy. What could he offer a woman like her? She was so damn remarkable, had overcome so much, and he still wallowed in a decade-old grief that had done nothing but win him a moniker he now despised.

He wanted to shout that her ex wasn't a good man, wasn't a man at all, but rather a selfish, power-hungry child who didn't deserve a wonderful woman like her. If he thought he could run Chris Richards down further in her eyes, he would've ranted all night. But that wasn't what she needed, nor did she need to deal with the jealousy that raged through him. Izabel deserved better than that. Better than his petty insecurities, better than anything that other man ever gave her. She deserved the world, and Zack wanted to give that to her and more.

Minutes passed as he held her against him, rocking her gently, murmuring words of comfort, and kissing the top of her head. Soon, her tears dried up and she hiccupped against his neck.

She inhaled, then cleared her throat. "I've never told anyone all of that before. I'm sorry I kind of lost it."

"No problem," he said, still rocking her and holding her close. "You can cry on my shoulder anytime."

A shaky laugh spilled from her, but her short reply was heartfelt, "Thanks."

He responded with a hug and a chaste kiss to her forehead. "Thank *you* for trusting me."

They stayed that way for a few minutes, the silence heavy but not uncomfortable.

"When we kissed up in the hills the other day," she said quietly as she sat back and looked into his eyes, "I didn't push you away because I didn't want you. The memories came back, and I panicked. Do you see now? It wasn't your fault; it was mine."

Something inside Zack seemed to shift and fall into place, as if it had been waiting for someone to give it a little shove to make him feel whole again.

Sadness welled within him and an urge to bare his soul to her struck hard, slamming into his chest like a two-ton bull. He wasn't ready for that—had never believed he would ever be—but something about Izabel made him want to share the pain he'd carried for so long. Still, he held back. He would be here for her tonight, and tomorrow, if he still felt the same, he would tell her how he became Meriton's Casanova Cowboy.

He must've waited too long to speak as he stared into her beautiful eyes—feeling so damn thankful she had come to Montana and ended up here with him—because her delicate brows lowered and she searched his face nervously.

"You do believe me, don't you?"

The smile that stretched his lips felt as if it reached from ear to ear. "Yes, I believe you, sweetheart." He chuckled as he brushed her bouncy curls from her face, running his fingers through the softness. "It makes me happy to know you wanted me."

She tilted her head and returned his smile. "And why is that?"

"Because I wanted you, too... I still do."

With that, he bent his head and took her mouth with his.

* * *

Izabel held her breath, but once his lips touched hers, it was as if the warmth of life flowed into her. He filled her lungs, her senses, her heart—and her body responded. Something clenched deep inside her and her nipples tightened inside her bra. The sensitive buds sent little shots of lust through her every time they scrapped against the material that held them. She wanted to dive in, kiss and lick and nibble every inch of this man, but she also wanted to make their time together last.

She ran her fingers along his jaw, then raked them into the short, crisp hair at his nape. The last thing she wanted was for him to stop.

She was afraid of hearing Chris's voice in her head again, but this time, when Zack's tongue traced her lower lip and she opened her mouth to him, her mind went blank. No, not blank... Her mind filled with thoughts, and scents, and images of this man, of Zack. She welcomed the hungry nature of his kiss and the hard strength of his body, and she wanted more.

Without breaking the kiss, she slid her hands down his chisel chest and tugged at the navy material of his T-shirt until it came free from the waistband of his jeans. Greedily, she slipped one hand inside and she groaned at the hard heat that flexed beneath her fingers. Needing to touch him, to see him, Izabel sat back and jerk the rest of his shirt from his jeans. Frantically, she pulled and pushed it upward until Zack lifted his arms and allowed her to haul the shirt over his head.

She couldn't seem to catch her breath. The masculine beauty she'd unveiled sucked it all from her chest as her eyes took in every work-hardened crest and valley of his well-built body. The breadth of his shoulders, the thick layers of muscle that made them and his brawny arms bulge and flex when he moved. The perfect plane of his pecs and the ridges of his belly. Her nails rasped over the dusting of dark, curling hair on his chest, her fingers following its path as it narrowed into a line that disappeared under his jeans.

"Izabel?"

She looked up, startled by the strangled sound of his voice. His cheeks were flushed as his breath heaved in through parted lips, and his soulful whiskey eyes were hooded and full of passion as he stared back at her.

"You are gorgeous, Zack."

He smiled, but when she swiveled and got to her feet, apprehension filled his face. "What are you doing?"

Reaching for the closure of her jeans, her mouth curled suggestively as she popped the button and slowly lowered the zipper.

Zack's lips tipped up at the corners and appreciation washed over his expression.

Once she'd shed the jeans, Izabel crawled back onto his lap, but straddled his legs this time.

"Did you think I was going to leave?" she asked, flicking her nails over his nipples. Her grin grew when he sucked in a breath and his eyelids closed briefly. When they opened, he cupped her butt cheeks in each of his huge hands and drew her against the large bulge in his jeans.

"I thought so, yes." He ducked his head and his lips found her neck. "I thought you might leave me with this," he said as he lifted his hips and pressed himself against her core.

She moaned as he nibbled the tender column of her throat, drawing gasps of pleasure from her. When he found a sensitive spot at the base of her neck, a sharp pang of desire shot through her belly. Lust electrified her, zapping along nerve endings and driving her need for him...for Zack.

"What do you want, Izabel?" His voice sounded rough against her skin. "Tell me what you need."

"You, Zack. I need you," she gasped. "I want to see you. I want to feel your skin on mine. I want you to make love to me. Right now!" She reached for her blouse and quickly unbuttoned the first two buttons, but frustrated with how long it took, she reached down and yanked it over her head.

Zack's passion-filled eyes had followed her movement, but now she sat back and watched as his gaze devoured her. From the disarray of her curly hair to her small breasts and down to the plain white bikini underwear she wore, he soaked it all in as his chest rose with each rapid breath. Slowly, almost reverently, he traced the gentle swell of her breasts above the lace edge of her bra with his fingertips. The touch sent a shiver through her body as need pulsed hot and wet between her thighs.

"Oh, God, Zack," she cried, the ache from his simple touch so acute, she had to grip his shoulders to keep from tumbling to the ground. Her head dropped back onto her neck and she sighed. "What you do to me..."

"Tell me, goddess," he said with a throaty growl as his hands bracketed her face and pulled her in for another soul-melting kiss.

"You've lit a fire inside me," she said when he let her up for air. "You give me strength when I feel week. You make me feel strong and beautiful and wanted. You make me want...more."

He rested his forehead against hers. "You're all those things, sweetheart, all on your own. You don't need me."

She shook her head, but she couldn't speak. Her eyes burned, and her throat ached with need and the sweet emotions that swelled within her. He kissed her again, slow and sensual, and the throb between her thighs increased.

His hands slipped down her neck, tugging her bra straps over her shoulders before his nimble fingers deftly released the back hooks. She grabbed the undergarment when it fell and tossed it aside.

His eyes lit on her dusky breasts, the dark rose nipples already hard and sensitive, waiting for his touch. But all he did was stare as if stunned.

"Are you all right?" she asked with a little chuckle.

He looked up into her eyes with something akin to awe in his gaze. "You're so beautiful," he whispered and cupped her small breast. He played with her nipple and watched as she wiggled on his lap—wanting his mouth on her skin, wanting him closer, wanting him inside her.

"Are you playing with me?" Somehow, and despite all the walls she'd thrown up, the fear had snuck inside her.

"Never," he said as he pulled her to him and took her nipple into his mouth. Heat washed through her body as he suckled and nibbled at her breast until she thought she would scream with pent-up passion. Then he moved to the other, performing the same techniques with his mouth while his hand kept the other tip hard and craving the return of his moist heat.

She clung to him, writhing with every nip of his teeth and each tender lave of his tongue.

Suddenly, his arms tightened and before she knew what was happening, he lifted them both off the couch and turned to lay her on her back. He knelt over her, kissing her breasts and then the soft valley between them as he slowly made his way to her belly. He left a deliberate trail of kisses along the edge of her underwear. She squirmed as his big hands slid along her legs, up her thighs to her aching center—the place that longed for his touch, his invasion, his desire. His fingers slipped inside her panties, combed through her curls, and then his thumb slid over her. She jumped when his appendage collided with the swollen heat at the apex of her legs, the sensation so intense she gasped.

"More," she cried. "I want more!"

"As you wish," he murmured as he placed an open-mouthed kiss against her hip. The next instant, he tugged her panties down her long legs and spread her wide. His eyes burned as he looked down at her, and Izabel had a sudden urge to hide from him. She lifted her hands and tried to close her legs, but he shook his head.

"No, goddess. Don't hide from me. You are too beautiful for that. Let me look and bask in your glory."

She laughed at his outrageousness, but his words and the adoring expression on his face calmed her. He made her *feel* like a goddess.

When she ceased and simply laid still, allowing him to look, he grinned and then slowly lowered his head between her thighs.

Izabel inhaled deeply, anxiously, expectantly. It had been so long since she'd allowed anyone to touch her like this. Of course, she'd had other lovers in the past, but none had ever touched her or stirred her emotions the way this man did.

When his soft kiss brushed against her swollen nub, her hips lifted toward his mouth in unconscious supplication. He blew against her heated skin and goosebumps rose all over her body. The knots of desire low in her belly swelled and tightened, tugging at the over-sensitive area between her legs. His tongue prodded at her folds and then pressed into her, licking upward with the flat of his tongue.

She grasped his head, her fingers curling into his hair, unwilling to let him go. He chuckled against her core, the vibration seeping through her skin, turning up the heat inside her. Then he sucked her into his mouth and she lost all sense of her surroundings. The only things that existed were her and the man taking her to the edge of heaven.

She had no idea how long he held her there, licking and sucking, sliding one finger, then two, in and out of her until she felt wild with need. Begging for release, for more of him, for *all* of him, but he took his time pleasuring her. It could have been minutes or hours, but Izabel didn't care. All that mattered was Zack.

He hummed against her heated flesh and her fingers tightened in his hair. In the next moment, everything he'd built up and banked inside her—every tense ball of need, every tight knot of desire—exploded at once. Her hips lifted off the couch and he gripped her butt to hold her there. His mouth and fingers kept plying her, bringing her to the pinnacle again moments later, and then he helped her ride the undulating waves of her orgasms with knowledgeable precision as she slowly drifted back to earth.

Unhurriedly, he kissed his way up her body and found her mouth once more. Slow and sensuous would describe the gentle brush of his lips against hers. Then, with his arms braced on either side of her, he pushed himself up to smile seductively into her eyes.

She looked up at him, her breath still wheezing through her open lips. The look in his eyes stirred her body and her heart.

Oh, this man is dangerous for me... But she couldn't make herself regret what they'd done nor was she about to back out now. Though she would need to be careful of her already tender heart. *Remember, he doesn't do long-term. This is just for fun, nothing more.*

But he also said that wasn't who he is anymore...

She shoved the voice of niggling doubt out of her head and smiled at the gorgeous man hovering over her.

"That was…amazing," she said as she brushed her hands over his chest. "But I hope that's not the end of it."

Zack chuckled, then kissed her. "No way," he said, and then got to his feet to strip off his boots and jeans.

Izabel watched with rapt attention, biting her lower lip as Zack pushed his underwear down his legs, then stood before her in all his naked, Adonis-like glory. Every hard line appeared to be chiseled to perfection. From his wide shoulders and chest to his trim waist and long, powerful legs, he was everything she'd ever dreamed of in a man and more. Even the most male part of him—thick and long, ready and waiting...for her—looked as if it belonged on a god.

Mesmerized, she reached out and took him in her hand. His flesh was hot and hard, but so velvety to the touch. He inhaled sharply, but didn't try to stop her. She smiled as she stroked him, thrilled by the tiny muscle spasms that twitched in his belly and thighs. She couldn't wait to cradle his hips between her thighs, to feel him inside her.

She looked up and found him watching her. His dark eyes burned with desire and were filled with a promise she couldn't wait to accept.

She laid back on the couch, her fingers lingering on his shaft before she twirled them around the head and released him, and he moaned.

"Come here," she said in a low, throaty voice, and she didn't have to say it twice.

Zack crawled onto the couch and settled himself between her legs, but held his body above hers as he looked down into her face. Izabel couldn't look away from the multitude of emotions that churned in his eyes. It felt as if he saw straight past the shell she showed the world and into her heart, her soul. Tenderness and affection filled his gaze, but she read a touch of fear and insecurity there, too.

Why would he feel uncertain? she wondered, but she refused to let him pull away. Not that he tried to, but she figured a little more incentive wouldn't hurt, either.

"I want you, Zack," she said softly, placing her hand on his bearded cheek. "Please don't tease me."

He shook his head. "No, sweetheart. I'd never do that to you, but I don't want to scare you, either."

"You won't. I'm not afraid of you. Please, Zack. Don't hold back."

His expression shifted slightly, and then he smiled. "As you wish, my goddess." As he lowered his head and kissed her, his hips gently rolled forward, prodding at her until he found her entrance. Slowly, he pushed in, only an inch or two, then stopped when she moaned. His lips never left hers. She could feel him trembling with the effort it took to hold himself over her, keeping himself still while she adjusted to his size.

She wanted to tell him to let go, but something kept her silent. No one had ever taken such care with her before, and she wanted to cherish it and him.

Her hands slid over his arms, the muscles rock-hard and twitching ever so slightly. She let her fingers trace down his sides to his buttocks, where she gripped him and pulled, hoping to encourage him to fill her completely. Her hips pressed upward, and he chuckled against her lips. He broke the kiss and rested his forehead against hers. "You're making it difficult for me to make this good for you," he rasped against her lips.

She cupped his face in her hands as her hips pressed upward again. "You've already made this more memorable than you could ever know, Zack. I want to be as memorable to you, too."

He grunted a short laugh. "Sweetie, if you make this anymore memorable, you might just kill me."

"That's not funny."

"It wasn't meant to be."

"I want you..." she murmured, kissing him softly. "I want all of you." Another kiss. "Now."

"As you wish," he whispered, then slanted his head to capture her mouth, taking over as his hips slammed home.

Izabel gasped at the sudden movement, but a heartbeat later, she responded in kind. She met every thrust with one of her own. Her body arched into his, wanting more contact, more friction, more of him against her bare flesh. No thoughts crossed her mind, no worries about her past or future. Nothing mattered but this moment and the man in her arms, driving her higher with each plunge as his large body moved in time with hers.

Once more, time seemed to stand still as he took her to the edge. She tucked her face into his neck and huffed out soft moans of pleasure that seemed to encourage him further. His movements increased in speed and vigor as his arms crushed her against his chest.

Too soon, her head dropped back and his name fell from her lips in a cry of joyous release. A moment later, he groaned as he surged into her deeply one last time, then shuddered as she felt the fountain of his warmth spread within her. It was then that she realized what they'd done and the consequences that might follow their unprotected act. But she'd think about that later.

Zack's body collapsed over hers, flattening her into the cushions. She loved having him like this—his big body sprawled over hers. Somehow, it made her feel safe, protected, and...loved. But she wouldn't be so foolish to believe the last—he'd need to be the one to step over that line first. She wouldn't scare him away by making too much out of their little tryst.

"Are you all right?" he asked, his voice muffled by her hair and the couch before he pushed back. "Am I crushing you?"

"Yes," she smiled and tightened her arms around him when he began to move away, "but in a good way."

He returned her grin, then easily maneuvered them until he lay flat on his back and she was sprawled over his chest, her legs still embracing his body.

"So you enjoyed yourself?" he asked once he tucked one arm behind his head and they were both settled again.

She layered her hands on his chest and propped her chin on them. "You know I did. How about you?"

"I'm still breathing," he joked, "so it was good."

She frowned. "Just good?" Pushing out her lower lip, she gave him a pout of faux disappointment.

He laughed and then grew a bit more serious as he brushed a curl from her cheek and cupped her face. "It was great, fantastic, totally blew my mind."

"Don't tease," she said, moving to sit up, but his arms suddenly wrapped around her and drew her back down.

"I'm not teasing," he said with a somber look on his face. "You are an amazing woman, Izabel. In every way." He stroked her cheek. "I am touched that you would give yourself to me, and I am more honored than you can ever know. I will never forget this night...or you."

Warmth flushed through her and she was certain her cheeks were as dusky-red as a new rose. "That was the most beautiful thing anyone has ever said to me."

One side of his mouth drew up and he traced a finger over her lower lip. "You should've heard things like that long before now," he told her, lifting his head to take her mouth in a long, lingering kiss.

She sighed when the kiss ended. Her eyes opened to meet his and something surprising flashed in the depths of his whiskey eyes, but it disappeared so fast she thought she'd imagined it.

Mentally shaking her head, she slid her body purposely against his and he groaned.

"In that case...I'd love to hear your body tell me more." She wiggled her hips against his growing length.

He gipped her butt and held her against him. "Your wish is my command, goddess." He made to sit up, but she placed a hand over his heart and he stilled.

"I'm not commanding," she said with a solemn look. "I would never demand that from you."

"I know," he said with a grin, "but it's fun to pretend, goddess." With that, he kissed her hard and long, and then spent the rest of the night showing her exactly how much fun his imagination could be.

CHAPTER 18

Warmth, comfort, and satisfaction surrounded Izabel as she slowly woke from a deep slumber. Rolling onto her back, with her eyes still closed, she stretched languorously as a happy smile curled her lips. Once she got past the uncomfortable explanation for her previous behavior, her night with Zach had been everything she had hoped it would be. Not only was he the most skillful lover she'd ever had, but he was also exceptionally tender, which had only strengthened the growing bond between them. More than just that certain something that zinged to life whenever they touched, their undeniable attraction—which had started when they first locked eyes at the wedding—had been reinforced by everything they'd done last night. Wonderful, glorious, or special didn't even begin to explain how her time with Zack had felt.

Sometime during the night, he had kissed her, cradled her in his arms, and carried her to the bed, where they'd enjoyed a few more rounds of delicious lovemaking. Despite their lack of caution, she couldn't bring herself to worry overmuch. They needed to talk about it and any possible consequences, but in the frenzy of the burning need they'd both surrendered to, it had slipped their minds. Normally she was much more careful about using protection, and she couldn't figure out why she'd been so lax with Zack.

She had no idea what time it was now, but even with her eyes closed, it was clear that bright sunlight filtered into the small cabin through the huge front window. The rich aroma of coffee tickled her nose, and she slowly opened her eyes as she rolled onto her side.

Zach stood in the kitchen, wearing the same jeans and T-shirt from the night before.

Too bad, she thought, having looked forward to seeing his gorgeous nakedness one more time, but still pleased to find him there. For a moment, she simply stared, taking in every chiseled line of his large frame, completely enjoying the view.

He shuffled around the small room as if comfortable with it, clearly doing his best to keep from waking her. He appeared to be cooking at the huge stove near the back wall.

How could she have ever thought him anything but beautiful? He had a ruggedness about him, yes, but there was a sweet gentleness to him that she found utterly appealing. He was funny and kind, and she was already feeling things she knew she shouldn't.

Just then, he turned to look at her and grinned. "Good morning, sunshine."

"Morning," she said as she held the sheet against her chest and sat up. "What are you doing?"

"I thought you might be hungry," he said, giving her a lusty look that hinted at what *he* hungered for.

She giggled. "I thought you didn't have anything here?"

"I didn't." He shrugged. "So I ran over to the house to grab some food for us."

She frowned and tried not to roll her eyes. *Great! Now his whole family knows we've slept together.*

He must have read her thoughts because he quickly removed the pan with their partially cooked breakfast from the heat and came to the bed. He sat, pushed her errant curls back over her shoulder, and cupped her cheek before he kissed her gently.

"Don't worry," he said as he pressed his forehead to hers. "It was very early and no one saw me. Our secret is still safe."

His kindness and care for her and her reputation made her feel more than a little guilty. She wasn't ashamed of what they'd done; she just didn't want to broadcast it to everybody in town quite yet. It was private, between just the two of them, and she'd like it to stay that way for now.

"Thank you," she said. "I appreciate your discretion."

He smiled at her and got up to finish cooking.

"Most people in this town may think I'm a playboy," he said as he set the pan back on the stove and picked up a spatula, "but I know how to take care of a lady. My mama taught me right." He flashed his brilliantly charming grin, dimples and all. "Besides, my sisters would never let me hear the end of it if I didn't do right by the lady I'm with. And I'd never cross either of them...they're scary." He gave a theatrical shiver and Izabel laughed.

"Oh, yes," Izabel said, still chuckling, "I can see what a tyrant Emmy is. Grace, being the oldest, must be worse."

He rolled his eyes dramatically. "Oh, you have no idea."

She laughed again and his eyes twinkled with mirth and happiness.

"Why don't you get dressed," he said as he deftly scrapped scrambled eggs onto two plates and set the pan in the sink. "Breakfast is about ready."

Seeing that he was busy, Izabel wrapped the sheet around her body and went to the front room to search for her scattered clothes.

She glanced out the huge front window as she wiggled into her jeans while trying not to flash anyone who might be outside watching. She chuckled to herself as she pulled her shirt over her head. *Do you see anyone out there? Relax, you're in the middle of nowhere.*

Still, she couldn't shake the feeling of eyes studying her every movement. There were so many places to hide in those trees and shrubs beyond the river, but she pushed all that aside, refusing to let it ruin her morning or the beauty of the area.

The view was every bit as gorgeous as she'd imagined it would be the night before. The small front yard, still a little damp from the rain the night before, bracketed by an assortment of tall trees, opened to a wide valley with tall, sun-tanned grasses and wildflowers. A rapidly flowing river cut through the lovely view and disappeared around a hill farther down the vale, and she could swear she saw an eagle floating through the sky.

A smile tugged at her lips as her imagination went wild.

She could see herself living here, drinking tea, reading a book, or just watching the wildlife as the sun went down. A pang of something hit her heart at the thought. The idea of living here seemed like the ultimate in relaxation. She knew it would also be a lot of work, but it would be worth it to have this view to come home to—and maybe even the man in the other room, too.

She shook off those thoughts. *He doesn't do long-term,* she reminded herself as she picked up her underthings and stuffed them into her back pocket.

"Come and get it," Zack called from the kitchen.

Grinning, she hurried around the couch to the other room. They sat at the small table in the kitchen, and after a quick blessing, they dug in to the simple meal he'd prepared.

"You're not a bad cook," she said as she set down her fork and used a paper towel to wipe her mouth.

He raised his eyebrows. "You're surprised by this?"

She tilted her head and pretended to consider his question before her lips turned up teasingly. "No, not really. You seem very self-sufficient."

"I am," he said, wiggling his eyebrows. "I'm creative, too."

His subtle reminder of their bed-play from the night before sent a wave of warmth through her. Her face warmed as certain areas of her body tingled with the memory of his kisses, but she met his gaze evenly.

"Yes, you are that, too." Hiding her smile as she stood, she ignored his roar of laughter as she collected the empty dishes and took them to the sink to wash.

"You are such a remarkable woman, Izabel," Zack said as he came to the sink and started drying the washed dishes with a clean towel. "I'm going to miss having you around all the time."

Izabel froze. "What do you mean?"

He glanced at her and frowned. "Well, Addie and Cade will be back either today or tomorrow. I thought you'd be moving to their place once they got home."

"Oh," Izabel muttered as she picked up the last coffee mug and scrubbed it clean. "Of course... I'd forgotten."

She was excited to see Addie, to sit and talk and learn about everything that had happened since they lost touch. But the thought of leaving Zack tightened her chest as a heavy weight settled in her gut.

"Wow," Zack joked as he placed a dried plate in the cupboard. "I must be better than I thought to wipe Addie from your mind."

"Don't flatter yourself too much," Izabel said with a teasing smile. "I'm a little tired this morning and the coffee hasn't kicked in yet."

"Sure... Whatever you say, sweetheart," he said with a knowing smirk.

Done with the dishes, she drained the sink, wiped everything down, and wrung out the washcloth she'd used. When she turned to him, he'd already hung the towel up on a hook by the stove and stood, arms crossed, leaning back against the counter, watching her.

She lifted an eyebrow. "Is something wrong?"

He tilted his head. "That depends."

"On what?"

He dropped his arms to his sides, pushed off the counter, and slowly sauntered over to where she stood. Eyes locked on hers, he stared down at her for a long moment before his hand slipped around her neck and he lowered his head.

Firm, dry lips pressed against hers and she closed her eyes, her whole body loosening as if releasing a deep sigh. One slow brush of his mouth, then two, and she lifted her arms to wrap them around his neck, clinging to him and kissing him back. She opened her mouth, surrendering to whatever he wished to do. His tongue dashed inside, savoring every corner as it dueled with hers. He tasted like bacon and black coffee, and she loved it. She lifted her leg to his hip, his big hand sliding along her thigh.

Maybe I should've waited to get dressed, she thought with a grin.

He released her leg and pulled back. Breathing hard and fast, he rested his forehead against hers and sighed. "You are *so* tempting," he said before stepping back. "But if we keep doing that, we won't be leaving here today."

Izabel smiled. "I'm not sure I would mind that outcome."

His brows rose in surprise. "I've corrupted you," he said with a merry glint in his eyes.

"Maybe a little," she answered, "but I'm not complaining."

He groaned, though a grin lit up his face. "If I didn't have a ton of work to do, I'd test that assertion."

"What do you need to do?" she asked, following him to the bed to help arrange the blankets into a semblance of neat and tidy.

"Rancher stuff," he said, but his tone was lighthearted.

Izabel chuckled. "And then?"

"I've got to go over to the winery. They're almost done with the final touches, and I need to do an inspection and make plans to start moving our inventory there. I also need to set up some interviews."

"You haven't hired anyone yet?" she asked, surprised.

He shook his head. "We've had so many setbacks, and I didn't want to get anyone's hopes up too soon. I have a manager lined up who will do most of the actual interviews, but I have a lot of other things to do yet. Hopefully, this time, we'll get to open the place and start making some money."

"It might take a while to make a profit," Izabel said quietly. While working at the marketing firm in Seattle, she'd seen several wineries end up closing before they ever even got off the ground. She thought Zack's endeavor had all kinds of potential, and she had told him so.

"Well, I hope you're right." He tossed the pillows to the head of the bed. "I know it might take some time, but we could use some income diversity, and as long as it makes enough to put money back into it and stay open, I'll be happy for now." He glanced around the cabin as he brushed his hands on his jeans. "Do you need to use the restroom before we go?"

She shook her head. "I'm good."

He nodded and, with a hand on her back, he guided her to the front door and out onto the deck. "Why don't you head out to the truck," he said as he closed the door and ambled toward the side of the cabin.

"Where are you going?"

He glanced over his shoulder, then turned when he reached the corner of the cabin. "To use the *facilities* out back."

She frowned, but the look he gave her—not to mention the little potty dance he did where he stood—brought understanding. "Oh, okay." She chuckled as she stepped into the front yard. "I think I'll just run down to the river for a minute or two."

"I'll meet you there," he rushed, then disappeared behind the building.

Shaking her head and laughing softly, Izabel strolled down to the river, the ground just a little damp in places from the evening rain. The warmth of the sun, though, would dry it all in no time.

This place is wonderful, she thought as she tossed a small stone into the bubbling surface of the water. She'd never been around so much open space or so many huge trees, and it was so quiet. Not much else could be heard aside from the river and the occasional breeze that made the tall grass and trees murmur and sing. *Maybe we could do some skinny-dipping the next time we come here,* she thought. A grin tugged at her lips as an image of Zack, naked as a babe, splashing through the shallows came to mind.

Staring at the river's sun-reflected surface, that odd sense of being watched suddenly struck her again. She looked up at the meadow beyond the river, at the huge trees farther out and all the shadowed areas, and shivered. Maybe someone *was* out there.

Just then, Zack's arms wrapped around her waist from behind and he leaned over her to place a kiss on her neck. She'd gasped at his first touch—having psyched herself out about a watcher lurking in the woods—but then she relaxed into his hold and moaned happily. "That feels nice."

"You like that, do you?" he asked against her skin.

"Absolutely."

"Well, in that case…"

Before she knew what he was doing, he'd spun her around to face him, hauled her up against him, and proceeded to kiss her thoroughly. She was panting when he finally pulled back.

"We will definitely need to come back here soon," he murmured, his voice low and husky. "In fact, I vote we stay another day."

She pushed against his chest. "As much as I'd love to spend another day with you, you know we can't."

He took a step back as his smile faded into a little boy pout. "Yeah, I know."

"But I agree, we need to come back…very soon."

Zack's face lit up and he reached for her. "As you wish, godde—"

Izabel heard something buzz as it passed her ear, she felt a breath of air against her cheek, and something tugged a few strands of her hair forward.

Then he cried out and Zack's happy face crumpled into a grimace of pain. A loud *crack* echoed through the air, bouncing around the valley, making it hard to determine where it originated.

Zack stumbled away from her and with a harsh curse, he crashed onto the grass. Izabel followed him, crouching beside him to help if she could. He was holding his left arm, but she didn't know why, not until he turned and saw her beside him.

"Get down," he growled as he released his arm and pulled her down beside him. She barely registered the dampness of the grass as she dropped to the ground, because of the red stain running down his left arm, saturating his right hand.

Blood. He's bleeding…!

"What happened?" she asked as Zack positioned his body to protect hers and, using his good arm, maneuvered his T-shirt over his head and down his bloody arm.

"Someone's shooting at us," he replied, his eyes focused on the valley and trees beyond the river.

"Shooting?"

"Yes."

"Why would anyone be shooting at you?"

His gaze snapped to hers as he wrapped his shirt around the wound. "What makes you think they're shooting at *me*?"

"Because…" She glanced at his arm, taking the ends of his shirt from his fumbling hand and pulling the knot tight to stem the bleeding. With the knot tight, she dropped her hands and returned her gaze to his face, one brow raised in question.

"Thanks," he said, even as he shook his head. "Shooting me may just mean they're a terrible shot. I think it's more likely someone followed you here for revenge."

Izabel frowned. "Who?" She paused, but he didn't take his eyes off the valley. Then it hit her. "*Chris*? You think Chris did this?"

"It would make sense, considering your situation. Especially after that very public kiss last night and the fact that you're here with me now."

She shook her head, unable to imagine Chris Richards firing a gun, even if he was upset about her involvement with Zack. She just couldn't picture it.

"What about those guys at the bar last night?" she asked. "They have a problem with both of us. It could be them."

Zack's lips thinned, a tight nod his only reply.

"What do we do now?" she asked, unwilling to argue about it further while they lay on the ground, Zack bleeding, with the potential of them still being in danger.

"We get out of here," he said.

"Do you have your phone on you?" she asked. "We could call for help."

"No, I left it in the truck last night, but it wouldn't matter anyway."

"Why not?"

He glanced at her briefly before studying the area again. "There's no service out here." He muttered a curse, his eyes rapidly searching their surroundings before he fell quiet for a couple of minutes while he examined the area more closely. Then he turned back to the valley for several more minutes, his body tense as he lay over her.

"Well," he said quietly, "either they can't hit us from where they were and are now repositioning, or…"

"Or?"

He looked her in the eye. "Or they stopped." He turned back to the open area across the river. "I don't see any unnatural movement…so I'm going to assume they've stopped."

"Okay," Izabel replied, not understanding any of this, "so they've stopped. What does that mean for us?"

"Well, if they left," Zack said, rolling to get his feet under him while staying as low as possible, "then it means we're safe."

Her fingers tightened on his shirt as he moved. She didn't want him to stand and get shot again, possibly fatally this time. "And if they haven't left...?"

He grinned at her as he deftly untangled her fingers from his clothes. "Then I'll probably get shot again," he said in a rush as he rose to his full height.

"No!" Izabel scrambled to her feet, meaning to stand between him and the next bullet she felt certain would be meant for him.

But as she clumsily stumbled over her feet and finally stood, he pushed her back and held her behind him.

"Zack," she whispered, "I don't think I'm the target."

He didn't reply.

Still, she fought to get around him, unwilling to let him take all the risk. It seemed like forever ago that she shouted at him and tried to push her way forward, when, suddenly, she broke through. She turned to him and pounded on his chest to punctuate her words. "Damn it, Zack! Don't you ever do something so stupid again! Do you hear me?"

He captured her wrists in his hands and looked down at her. "Hush, now, sweetheart," he said gently. "Do you hear that?"

She stopped to listen, but after several seconds, her brows drew down and she scowled. "I don't hear anything," she railed as she tried to pull free from his grip.

He grinned. "Exactly."

That made her pause. He was right. No additional loud cracking sounds filled the air and enough time had passed since he'd stood that if they were going to fire at him, they would have done so by now. Maybe it had just been a warning. *Yeah, but a warning for what?*

"Let's get back to the truck so we can get out of here, and I can call Josh," he said, pulling her along with him while his eyes continued to pan the valley.

She followed him without resistance and when they reached the vehicle, they both quickly climbed inside.

Zack grabbed his phone off the dash, only to toss it back a moment later.

Panic still raced through her and it was all she could do to keep from shouting in fear. "No signal?"

"Nope."

"Can we get out of here then? We can call from the road or the house, whichever gets us a signal first."

He glanced out the back window and then at her. "You're right." With that, he turned the key and put the truck into gear. He looked over at her. "Hold on," he said, and then stomped on the accelerator.

The engine revved and Izabel smacked into the dash as the truck rushed backward, only to skid through the damp earth to an abrupt stop. Zack shifted and Izabel slid back in her seat as the truck's tires spun in the mud briefly, before they caught and the truck accelerated down the rough path into the trees. Zack didn't slow down as much as he had last night for the large ruts and holes; instead, he seemed to drift the truck through them, and Izabel prayed he wouldn't get them stuck out in the woods. He was smart and she trusted he could handle himself and the truck with ease. If anyone would get them to safety, it was Zack MacEntier.

Chapter 19

The tires squealed in protest as Zack turned onto the dry, paved state route that would take them home. They skidded a bit, but—as she'd expected, and even with only one hand to steer—Zack never once lost control. He'd glanced at her several times as they'd bounced over the uneven forest road—his eyes alert, though slightly dilated and tight with pain—and each time his expression had been apologetic. She'd smiled at him every time, instinctively knowing he needed the encouragement. After all, even with all the agony he must be in, she had no doubt he was worried about her.

He seemed to breathe a little easier when they'd finally reached the pavement and his attitude calmed her scattered nerves. They turned onto the MacEntier drive a short few minutes later, and then he looked at her sharply, as if something terrible had just occurred to him. "Are you all right?" he asked, worry and pain making his words curt as he visually search her body. "Are you hurt anywhere? Did the bullet hit you?"

She shook her head. "No, I'm fine, but you should see a doctor."

He clenched his jaw and glanced down at his arm. She couldn't see it from the passenger seat, but she knew by the tense lines around his mouth—and how he was now sweating profusely—that the pain had increased.

"It's not bad," he muttered, turning back to the road. "I'll clean it and wrap it up once we get back to the house."

"You were shot, Zack!"

He glanced at her. "It's just a scratch, sweetheart. Barely enough of one to even leave a scar." His lips curled into a cocky grin. "Should be kind of sexy, don't you think?"

Izabel's mouth dropped open. "Are you crazy?"

He laughed but grimaced as he pulled his arm into his lap. "Nah, like I said, it's not bad. I've done worse to myself putting up fences. Don't worry so much. I'll be fine."

"You better be," she said and reached over to pat his thigh. It seemed a little silly, but she needed to touch him. "I'd still feel better if you at least had your sister or some other medical professional look at it."

"Emmy will fuss too much." The look she gave him made him sigh. "All right. I have a firefighter friend who's also a paramedic. Will that satisfy you?"

"Yes," she said as they turned into the yard and parked near the house. "It would at least make me *feel* a lot better, but if he says you need to go to a doctor, then you *go* to the doctor."

He nodded, then turned the key and sat with his eyes closed for a moment. Then he sighed and turned his head toward her. "I'll call him right after we notify the police. Right now, though," he swayed slightly, "I think I might need a little help getting inside."

Izabel's chest constricted when she saw the amount of blood running down his arm from beneath the makeshift T-shirt tourniquet, but she immediately jumped into action.

"Stay right there," she said as she quickly exited the truck and ran around to his side, calling for his sister or one of his parents to help. Carefully, she opened his door and allowed him to slide off the seat. He'd waved off her assistance and seemed well enough on his own at first, but after the first step, his knees buckled and he nearly collapsed to the ground.

"Here," she said as she wrapped her arm around his waist. "Put your good arm over my shoulders."

The house's front door opened and Janice stepped out. "What's going—Oh, my goodness. Zack!" She rushed over to help support him as best she could. "Baby, what happened?"

"I'll be okay, Mom."

"Is Emmy home?" Izabel asked, hoping the nurse would be available to assist her brother.

"No," Janice replied and Izabel's hopes evaporated. "She had a shift today. I'm the only one here."

They struggled under Zack's much greater weight as they crossed the deck and stumbled into the house. They'd almost made it to the living room sofa when he suddenly stopped.

"I think I'm going to be sick..." he said, his words slightly slurred. He swayed heavily and it was all the two women could do to keep him upright. Then his eyes rolled upward and his legs gave out, dropping him to the floor and taking them with him.

Janice got to her feet first as Izabel tried to roll Zack onto his back.

"Get some towels from the bathroom," Janice said, pointing across the room. "Put some pressure on it and I'll call for help."

"Zack said he has a friend who's a paramedic?"

"Yes," Janice said as she headed for the kitchen to get her phone, "I know Aaron. I'll call him, too."

* * *

Lightning flashed outside the large window to the right of Zack's propped-up hospital bed. He blinked slowly a few times to clear the bright image from his vision and counted the seconds while listening for the crash of thunder to follow. It had been booming out there for almost an hour and it seemed to be moving farther away after each crash of thunder, but from what he'd seen from the window, not a single drop of rain had actually fallen yet. That was unfortunate, considering the relatively dry spring they'd had this year, not to mention the increased summer temperatures. He'd been hoping the tiny bit of rainfall they had a few days ago was a sign of changing weather. They could use a good drenching to keep the threat of wildfires to a minimum. Unfortunately, this storm wouldn't give them any relief. Instead, it might strike the spark that started a fire somewhere in the hills, which could devastate everything for miles.

He sighed and turned his head to look out the window. He hated hospitals and especially hated being forced to sit idle when he had work to do at the ranch. Even if his father, sister, and neighbors had volunteered to assist with the chores while he was laid up, just thinking about it all made his muscles twitch with the desire to leave this place.

When he'd first opened his eyes four days ago, Zack had no idea where he was. The last thing he remembered was seeing Izabel's worried face as Aaron and an EMT loaded Zack into the ambulance. Since then, he'd had surgery to repair the damage in his arm caused by the hollow-point bullet, as well as to close the entry and exit wounds.

The doctor had told Zack he'd been lucky. The caliber the shooter had used was so small, it had missed his humerus and exited without causing any major destruction. Luckily again, the concussive force of the bullet hadn't broken his arm, which would've left him in severe pain and in an awkward cast for several months. As it was, despite its small size, the jagged, blossomed-head of the bullet had caused enough damage to the muscle that he'd need physical therapy to get his arm back into shape again.

He looked down at the sling that held his injured arm and wiggled his fingers. His eyes squeezed closed on a wince and his teeth ground against the blooming pain.

At least the arm was still usable, but it hurt like hell when he moved it too far in *any* direction. He cursed under his breath. He hated being an invalid.

It could've been so much worse, though.

He had thanked God several times since awakening from surgery that afternoon for his good fortune. He would've gladly taken a graver injury to spare Izabel any harm. Thankfully, though, that hadn't been necessary.

Izabel and the rest of his family had been there waiting for him when he'd awakened after surgery—all of them teary-eyed and smiling to see him conscious again. They'd hugged him, shook and held his hand, and talked so long, he'd almost fallen asleep while they were still there.

Finally, Emmy shooed everyone out, saying they could come again tomorrow, but he'd asked Izabel to stay. He hadn't missed the red puffiness around her eyes or how quiet she seemed, and he wanted a quick word to reassure himself she was okay.

"Hi," he'd said, his voice raspy, once the door had closed behind the others.

She smiled and reached for the cup of water with a straw, somehow knowing his throat was dry. "Hi, yourself," she said, holding the cup so he could sip from the straw. When he finished, she set it aside where he could reach it later, and turned back to him.

"You look a little worn out," he said.

"So do you," she answered as she took his hand. "Are you doing all right? Do you have enough pain meds?"

He nodded and winced. "Yeah, it might still hurt, but too much of those meds and I sleep all the time."

"Maybe that's the point?"

He tilted his head. "Maybe."

She nodded and looked down at their joined hands.

"Izabel," he said, squeezing her fingers gently. "Everything *is* okay. You know that, right?"

She inhaled, but he heard the soft sob she tried to hide.

"Hey," he said, pulling her a little closer so he could cradle her cheek in his good hand and brush away the tears with his thumb. "Why are you crying?"

She shook her head, sniffed, and then inhaled deeply, obviously struggling to control herself. "I haven't slept much lately...and I've turned into a whimpering faucet." She met his gaze. "You could've died out there, Zack."

"Oh, baby," he crooned and encouraged her to sit on the bed where he could clasp her against him. "But I didn't die. We both got home alive."

"I know," she said, her voice low and sad, "but it—"

"Stop," he said, pushing her up and turning her to face him. "Just stop and listen to me. We are fine. *I am fine.* I will not let some lunatic change my life, and I don't want that for you, either. We're safe. The sheriff's deputies have been out there to poke around, and I'm sure they've found clues to help figure this all out. We *will* figure it out."

She nodded but didn't speak.

He tucked a stray curl behind her ear and smiled. "I don't want anything to diminish what happened between us at the cabin."

Her lips curled upward and her cheeks turned rosy. "Me, either."

"Then stop fretting over what might have been and be happy for what we have."

He'd been able to coax more smiles and a few giggles from her that day. They'd even discussed going back to the cabin again. After all, it's not like they could do much together under his parents' roof, and Izabel had seemed more than eager despite the traumatic event they'd experienced. When he'd finally kissed her goodbye, warmth and emotion had welled up inside him, making him wish they could go somewhere private, but that wasn't possible. He'd just kissed her slow and deep, then told her to come back again the next day, which she had—and every day since. Yesterday, she'd brought him the clothes he now wore in preparation for his discharge today. In fact, she should be arriving at any moment to finally take him home.

He brushed his hand along his jeans-clad thigh, anxious to be out of here and to talk with Josh to see what they'd found so far. Izabel had accused Zack of being very cavalier about the whole getting-shot-at thing, but that was far from the truth. The pain in his arm reminded him *often* of just how lucky they'd been, but he didn't want Izabel to dwell on it. She had enough bad in her life so far, and he just wanted her to smile, laugh, and enjoy life. Fretting over something neither of them had any control over was pointless and depressing. That didn't mean he didn't take it seriously, though, or that he wasn't afraid. Hell, he could spend days worrying about how Izzy could've been the one bleeding and possibly dying on the ground that day, but he'd cut those thoughts off. He wouldn't be any good to her if he was lost in his own dark world of apprehension.

Familiar voices came from the hall and suddenly, his heart swelled to bursting and an electric heat stronger than the storm outside swept through his body. A few seconds later, Izabel entered with a smile so bright it could rival the sun—or at least, it seemed that way to him. He swung his booted feet off the bed, prepared to haul her against him and plant a big I-missed-you kiss on her luscious lips. The arrival of two more people behind her, one pushing a wheelchair, stopped him.

The flying high feeling that had struck him just before Izabel entered deflated quickly. Not that he wasn't happy to see Cade Brody and his new wife Addie; he just knew Izabel wouldn't want to make a scene. He'd have to wait until they were alone before he could kiss her again.

"Hey, you big oaf," Cade said as he approached, parking the wheelchair he pushed off to the side. "Heard you got shot." He grinned and held out his hand, which Zack took good-naturedly.

"Yeah," he said. "I don't recommend it."

Cade leaned in and loud-whispered, "You know chicks dig scars though, right?"

Zack grinned, his eyes flicking over to Izabel for an I-told-you-so smirk.

Cade chuckled along with Zack and released his hand.

Addie smacked her husband's arm as she stepped around him, scowling as she did. "Be nice, Cade," she said, then turned a wide smile on Zack. "I'm so glad to see you still breathing, Zack." She leaned forward and kissed his cheek.

Zack glance up at his friend, a look of triumph in his eyes and he was rewarded with Cade's dark scowl. He stifled the chuckle that tickled his throat, but he couldn't suppress the grin. Cade was very protective of his new wife—possessive too from the look on his face.

"Hi, Addie," Zack replied. "I hope this jerk's been taking good care of you." He nodded at Cade. It wasn't really a question, though. Zack understood exactly how much Addie meant to Cade, and how she'd bridged the gap between Cade and his brother Cord.

Addie looked up at her husband with love shining in her eyes. "He's been wonderful, of course." She turned her happy grin on Zack, who noted something about her had changed. It wasn't physical, like a haircut or lipstick color, but something...

"You look different," Zack said without thinking, then realized how that might have sounded and tried to recover. "Not that you look bad or anything; you're as pretty as ever, but something..."

Izabel laughed right along with Addie and Cade, but none of them said a word.

"What?" He examined their smiling faces, wondering what he was missing.

"Shall we tell him?" Addie asked, her eyes twinkling with mischief as she glanced at her husband.

"It's up to you, sweetie," Cade replied, looking far too proud to not be hiding something big.

Then it hit Zack like a Mac truck. "You're pregnant! Aren't you?"

Addie nodded, her already broad grin spreading from ear to ear.

He looked at Cade and saw the excitement that glittered in his blue gaze. Zack knew Cade had wanted a big family—that Cord had wanted the same thing—but he hadn't expected these two to start so soon.

"Well, congratulations!" Zack said, pushing to his feet and offering his hand to Cade once more. "Couldn't let Cordell show you up, huh? You just had to make a friend for little Bethany." He laughed with his friend as they embraced in a brotherly hug. He winced a bit and Cade pulled back.

"Sorry, old man," Cade teased, but then turned serious. "I didn't mean to hurt you."

Zack waved him off. "Don't worry about it." He turned to Izabel and held out his hand. "Shall we get out of here?"

Izabel glanced at the chair and Zack knew he'd be in for an argument if he refused to let them wheel him out. He grinned and went over to the conveyance and sat down. Holding out his hand again, he asked, "You ready?"

Izabel took his hand. "Yes."

"Great," Cade said as they exited the room. "I'm driving."

Zack groaned but grinned as Cade pushed Zack down the hall to the elevators.

"So, do you have names picked out yet?" he asked as they waited for the lift to arrive.

The newlyweds glanced at each other, and Addie answered, "We're still deciding..."

When the doors slid open, they entered the elevator, and Izabel pressed the button for the first floor. She released his hand to wrap her arm around his neck and squeezed him gently.

Suddenly, another image of Izabel filled his mind. Her wildly curling hair fluttering with a gentle breeze as she stood by the river near his cabin. Her eyes were soft and loving as she looked at him, her belly full and round with his child.

He blinked, surprised by the vision and the strength of the emotions it stirred within him. There had been a time that he'd wanted a family, but it had died long ago—before the Casanova Cowboy had been born. He hadn't looked back at those old dreams since. The nickname hadn't bothered him as a younger man, but in recent years, it had started to chafe and had become unbearable. Especially now that he realized he wanted that other life he'd once envisioned—and he wanted it with Izabel.

But would she accept him as more than just a friend? More than a friend with no-strings-benefits? Or was what happened between them a one-night fling? Does she see him as a man she could trust and love, or as the Casanova he'd been christened?

How does a man go about asking the woman he loves to ignore everything she'd heard about him—and everything she had yet to hear—and to trust him with her recently splintered heart?

They exited the elevator and headed for the front doors where he refused to let them wheel him any farther.

"I can walk the rest of the way," he said as he got to his feet and was a little surprised that no one argued with him. Thankful for their agreement—or at least, their silence—he draped his good arm around Izabel's shoulders before heading outside.

The ground was still dry when they crossed the parking lot to Cade's truck, and Zack noticed the lightning had dwindled to a slight crack in the distance. But Zack was still stunned by his previous thoughts and couldn't help but glance down at Izabel.

Am I in love with her? he wondered as she smiled at him and his heart clenched. He didn't know. It had been so long since he'd allowed anyone inside the walls he'd created to protect the ruins of his heart. Had the fractured pieces mended themselves when he wasn't paying attention? Or had Izabel been the catalyst that put them back together?

He shook his head. It didn't matter what caused him to feel these types of emotions again. Maybe it was just the right time and Izabel was the right girl. Whatever the reason, he wanted more than just one night with her, and he planned to make sure he got it.

CHAPTER 20

Zack whistled softly as he ambled through the parking lot at Tony's Tavern where he'd stopped for a quick lunch. The sun was high amid the cotton candy clouds, which contrasted beautifully against the big indigo sky. The heat that had been hammering the area all summer had abated today, and the gentle breeze brought just a touch of coolness. It lifted his spirits a bit not to be beaten down by high temperatures, and he'd been happy to head into town to pick up a few things at the hardware store they'd needed at the winery earlier that morning.

He glanced at the sky again. "Some rain would be appreciated," he murmured to whatever deity might hear him.

As he approached his truck—which Josh and Aaron had delivered to Zack's ranch when they came to visit on his second day back home—his eye followed the long scratch in the paint that the rig had mysteriously acquired the last time he'd been to the popular bar. Ignoring the irritation that pricked him at the undeserved vandalism of his property, he stopped beside the vehicle, squeezed his eyes shut, and lifted his face to the sun, saying a little prayer of thanks for good friends he could rely on.

He was not going to let the past bother him today. He had a lot of work to do, and he'd rather spend it not worrying about the past or the future. Even if his burdens pressed him from all sides, threatening to drag him into a pit of poverty and despair, but today, he stubbornly refused to listen.

Despite his disability, he had pushed himself to keep moving, because after a few days of bedrest—rest he badly needed, but grudgingly accepted—desperation to be outside, to feel the sun and wind on his skin had pushed him out of bed. His recovery wasn't even close to one hundred percent yet, but when he'd awakened yesterday—only five days since he'd returned home—he couldn't stand one more day in bed. So he'd gotten dressed and—after a short argument with his family, which he'd won—headed outside, where he quickly discovered he could still do many of his old tasks around the ranch, and then insisted on relieving Emmy and their father of them. Though he still needed a lot of rest, it was better than being a prisoner in his room for twenty-four hours a day.

Plus, he hoped to see Izabel again as soon as possible. After she and his friends had driven him home from the hospital, Izabel had visited him daily, though he was often asleep and didn't get to speak with her. They talked a few times on the phone, but since she'd moved in with Addie at the Brody's ranch while he'd been in the hospital, he didn't see her nearly enough. For the most part, they had good conversations, though part of him felt betrayed by her departure—and he'd struggled to get past his hurt feelings. After all, that had been her plan, and he had no right to be upset that she did exactly what she'd said she would. Had he thought she would change her mind?

He dropped his chin to his chest, still squeezing his eyes closed.

Maybe I'd hoped she would.

Pushing down the ache that rose in his throat, he shoved away from his truck, lifted his eyes, and opened the door. With his arm in a sling that was tightly wrapped against his body, he awkwardly climbed into the cab, careful not to bump his left arm, and plopped into the seat with a sigh of contentment. Tony's food was quite good and had his stomach feeling pleasantly satiated, but he had no time to linger. They needed the parts he'd picked up at the hardware store, and he'd been gone too long already.

Leaning forward, he pushed the key into the ignition, but then stopped when his eyes caught a glimpse of something white tucked under one of his windshield wipers. He tilted his head as a corner of the paper fluttered with the wind.

What the heck is that? he wondered, still staring at it through the windshield.

"And more importantly..." he muttered as he pushed open his door and stood on the edge of the floorboards to reach for the folded scrap of paper, "how long have you been there?"

He snatched the paper from under the wiper and glanced around the parking lot. He didn't see anything out of the ordinary, so he searched the nearby businesses, then the buildings across the road.

When he still found nothing, he dropped back into the driver's seat and groaned at the shot of pain that lanced through his injured arm. The damn thing was healing nicely, and he would return to the doctor at the end of the week to verify that, but it still ached terribly. The agony when he'd bumped it at the barn yesterday nearly dropped him to his knees.

He took a moment to sit back and breathe, waiting for the shock of pain to dissipate. Once it had, he forced himself to inhale deeply one more time before he opened his eyes, pulled the driver's door closed, and then lowered his eyes to the paper.

He frowned. *Who would leave a note on my truck?*

With another quick glance around the area, he flipped open the paper and read what looked like a hastily penned note.

> *My Big Teddy Bear ~*
> *I know we can't be together right now, but when the time is right, trust me, I'll take care of everything. Nothing and no one will keep us apart.*
> *I just hope you have learned your lesson.*
> *All my love,*
> *Your Sweetheart*

He frowned. "What the...?" His eyes snapped up and once again, he took in his surroundings before he turned back to the note in his lap.

My Big Teddy Bear? No one called him that. Then again... *Maybe Izabel gave me a silly new nickname just to mess with me.* He grinned at the thought, but it quickly fell away. Nothing about this seemed like something Izabel would write or do. Besides, if she wrote it, why wouldn't she sign her name? And why would she leave a note and not wait or come looking for him?

And what's this bit about learning my lesson? It almost sounded like a threat. He glanced at his arm. *Or maybe a reminder of a past lesson.* Could this note be from the person who shot at them out by his cabin? And if so, why did they do it? What did they hope to gain? Were they trying to frighten him?

He scoffed at that. He didn't frighten easily, and this wasn't the way to go about it in any case. If they'd threatened his family, friends, or Izabel...? Now that would've really scared him. But this note was aimed at him, as surely as the bullet that pierced his arm had been.

The fine little hairs on the back of his neck stood up and he lifted his head.

Someone was watching him; he felt it. He eyed every corner, every shadow, looking for whoever had their eyes on him, but again, he saw nothing.

He glanced over at Tony's Tavern and saw the blonde bartender passing by the front windows on her way back from serving one of the other patrons. He couldn't remember her name, but she'd been all smiles when he'd entered earlier. She'd glanced at his injured arm and fussed over it a bit, but there'd been no hot kisses today—not like the other night. Still, she'd treated him sweetly, teasing and flirting, just like before. Nothing new there. Lots of women flirted with him, even when he wasn't interested.

Could one of them be the shooter? He shook his head. No, he endeavored to never let a woman feel jilted when she showed interest in him, so that couldn't be right. Maybe it was a boyfriend who saw him as competition for his woman's attention? That seemed to make more sense, but he hadn't been messing around with any woman except Izabel—and hadn't for a long time. So a jealous boyfriend didn't seem to fit, either. Unless Izabel's ex-boyfriend had suddenly shown up in town, though he doubted that was the case.

Who could it be? And were they still a threat? If so, he'd need to keep his distance from Izabel. His heart sunk at the thought of having to wait to hold her close again, but the last thing he wanted was to put her in more danger. Just the thought of it sent a shock of dread down his spine.

Straightening in the seat, he shoved the note into his shirt pocket and leaned forward to start the truck. He'd need to let the sheriff know about this new development before he headed back to the winery. It might be nothing, but he wasn't about to risk his family or Izabel by ignoring it. He'd rather be shot again than see any of the people he cared about get hurt because of him.

CHAPTER 21

Izabel closed her eyes and tilted her face to where the sun shined down on her from high in the clear blue sky. She let her body sway with the rocking motion of her horse as he carefully picked his way down the narrow path she and Addie took into the tree-dappled valley beyond. A warm breeze swept up the rocky side of the ridge where they rode, and Izabel smiled as it caressed her cheeks, loving the sense of freedom she experienced when riding—and wished the rest of her life felt as calm and soothing.

Just over two weeks had passed since they'd driven Zack home from the hospital. He was doing well and would be starting physical therapy in a few weeks, but it would be a while before he'd be completely free of the sling that held his arm against his chest. That didn't slow him down, though. He insisted on doing the chores he could perform unaided, and then he spent a lot of time at the winery, formulating their final plans and details for the fast-approaching opening day—which had been scheduled for mid-August, eight days after the start of the state fair. Izabel looked forward to both with great expectation.

Zack, however, didn't seem overly excited about the fair or the winery's opening. The closer the time came, the grouchier he seemed to get and the less she saw of him. Izabel had assumed that not only was his health less than it had been, but that he was buried in work and preparations for the winery—the short phone calls they'd shared lately indicated as much. But even she hadn't been immune to his increasingly shorter temper. During one conversation a couple of days ago, she'd offered to help him with the winery, but he'd instantly shut her down.

"I've got it under control," he'd said before she even got a chance to explain what she could've helped him with. She knew how to promote a business, how to bring in customers—both locals and tourists—but he hadn't wanted to hear any of it. The whole incident had been so unlike the gentle man she'd come to know, and she'd begun to worry that all the stress was too much for one person, especially considering what he'd suffered recently.

She spoke to him again after his thoughtless dismissal of her assistance, and everything had seemed...fine, but she hadn't yet broached the topic of his attitude, afraid it might spark a very real argument she didn't want to have.

On top of that, Zack still seemed annoyed that she'd moved to the Brodys' house while he was in the hospital. She'd explained that she didn't want to impose on his family and how they could still see each other whenever they wanted, and he'd grudgingly agreed, but there was still something that had wedged its way between them—something Izabel didn't understand and wasn't sure how to deal with it.

What was worse, was that she had begun to feel how she had when Chris dismissed her ideas and became angry when she didn't act or say what he wanted to hear. Though she didn't want to believe it, she feared this new Zack had fooled her the same way Chris once had and that all she'd shared with him had been as much of a fake fairytale as Chris Richards had been.

"Are you a sun worshiper now?" Addie called over her shoulder, disrupting Izabel's dark thoughts.

Izabel opened her eyes and grinned at her friend's mischievous expression. "No," she replied, "just soaking up the vitamin D."

"We'll make a country girl out of you yet." Addie chuckled as she reached the bottom of the path and stopped to wait for Izabel.

"I don't know about that," Izabel replied as she urged her horse down the path. "But I could certainly get used to this."

Addie's face lit up at her comment, and she returned her friend's infectious grin.

They'd been on four of these long rides since Addie had returned, and Izabel wanted to kick herself for not going with her friend when they were younger.

Their time together over the last couple of weeks had been medicinal. Izabel had explained about Chris and why she'd disappeared the way she had. It had been a hard conversation, full of heartache and tears, but they'd gotten through it. Since then, it seemed like they'd grown even closer than they'd once been, and Izabel thanked the fates every day that Addie had such a sweet-tempered disposition. There'd been no accusations, no angry recriminations, only reignited friendship and love.

"Are you excited about dinner tomorrow night?" Addie asked as Izabel's horse stopped beside Addie's.

"I am, yes. Zack..." She tilted her head back and forth as if weighing her words. "Well, I'm not sure if he is or not."

"Is he still peeved about missing the county fair last month?"

Zack had just come home from the hospital during the four days that the fair had been in full swing. The doctor had told him to stay in bed and rest, and in truth, he'd been too exhausted to go, but that hadn't meant he wasn't discouraged. Still, he'd insisted she go with his friends anyway.

"I don't want you to miss one of the best things about small towns," he'd told her over the phone.

"I've been to fairs before; I don't need to go to this one." She had tried to argue, to say that she'd rather be with him, but he'd been so adamant that she finally agreed to go without him. She had a good time at the fair with his friends, Emmy, and her friends too, but Zack had weighed heavily on Izabel's mind the whole time.

Maybe all that accounted for some of his grouchy behavior, but Izabel sensed it was more than just missing the fair or her attending without him.

"I'm not sure," Izabel said in answer to Addie's question about Zack and the fair. "I don't think so, but *something* is off with him."

Addie cast a worried frown her way. "Why do you say that?"

"I don't know," she answered truthfully. "He seems...tense and distant, like he's trying to pull away."

Which scared her silly and filled her head with too many questions she couldn't answer. Had he already grown tired of her? Did he actually regret what had happened between them? Was their night together the only one she would get?

Those were only a few of the questions that troubled her mind. She hoped none were true—that what she'd felt with Zack that night had been the same for him—but his aloof attitude seemed to say otherwise.

"Well," Addie said as they began riding again, "he was just shot. Maybe he's got some PTSD. I know I had some trouble with it after I was attacked."

One of the long conversations they'd had last week involved how Addie and Cade had met. How she had stupidly pushed him away, only to be attacked shortly after. Thankfully, he came back and saved Addie's life, only to almost lose his own.

"Maybe," Izabel replied. "He did talk to a psychologist while he was in the hospital. They told him to contact them if he had any trouble."

"Maybe you should do it for him."

Izabel's face heated and guilt banded her heart in a tight knot. "I did," she said quietly, "and he wasn't too happy about it. We had our first fight over that."

"Hmm, that doesn't sound like the Zack we all know and love."

"I know. It was odd… He apologized later, though."

"What was his excuse?"

"He said he'd been stressed over some details with the winery and that he shouldn't have taken it out on me." She didn't tell Addie that she wasn't sure she believed him—not about the apology, she knew he'd meant that, but she felt something more than the winery was at fault.

"Well," Addie said with a shrug, "maybe that's all it was. Did he agree to talk to a doctor?"

"He said he'd think about it."

Addie shook her head and sighed. "Men are so frustrating sometimes."

"Yeah." Izabel chuckled in wholehearted agreement.

She'd been honest with Addie about her relationship with Zack. She knew she could trust her old friend to keep the details to herself. Besides, she needed someone to talk through her thoughts and feeling with, and Addie knew about Zack's past—though she didn't know what had happened to change him so many years ago. But she had been able to confirm what Izabel already knew, that Zack was a good man. Addie had also encouraged her to be patient with him, which was exactly what Izabel was trying to do.

The horses slowly made their way through the shade beneath a group of evergreen trees while the soft breeze shifted the air around them, ruffling the women's hair.

"Do you think he's already…moving on?" Izabel asked a few minutes later when they stopped at a creek to water the horses.

Addie turned to her slowly, her eyebrows raised. "Do you?"

Izabel sighed. "I don't know."

"Maybe you should ask him?"

She shrugged. "Maybe."

"Why do you even think that?" Addie asked as she swung down from her mount and began checking her saddle's girth.

Following Addie's lead, Izabel did the same, thinking through her reply.

"I know he was a lady's man in the past," Izabel said, "that he's a shameless flirt and has dated more than his fair share of women. I also know he doesn't do long-term. Even if he doesn't want to be that man anymore, he doesn't do anything to change anyone's mind, either." As she spoke, Izabel loosened the girth and tugged on the thick strap to tighten it, releasing a little of her frustration at the same time. "I mean, you should've seen the way he carried on with the bartender at Tony's Tavern the night before he got shot. She was all over him, and he didn't discourage any of it."

"That bothered you?" Addie asked, done with fixing her saddle.

"Well…yeah, it bothered me."

"Even if he didn't know you were interested in him at the time?"

Izabel rolled her flattened lips between her teeth. "Yes, well, I know that, but it was still…annoying."

Addie chuckled and led her horse to a shady spot by the trees, letting her horse graze on the long grass nearby as she sat and leaned back against a tree.

"Zack's a popular guy, but he's also a pretty simple guy," Addie said as Izabel joined her in the shade, "at least as far as his wants and needs go. He may not like the reputation he's fashioned for himself or the nickname he was given, and he may be a flirt, and yes, women do love him, but he's also a loyal, honest, caring man who would do almost anything for the people he cares about." She waved her hand when Izabel opened her mouth to respond. "I know you know these things in your head, but what do you feel in your heart? Do you love him?"

"I don't know. I don't know if I trust myself or my judgment anymore when it comes to men."

"After Chris, you mean?"

Izabel nodded.

"Well, I *can* tell you, Zack cares about you."

"You don't know that," Izabel snapped.

Addie nodded. "Yes, I do. It's obvious. I've seen it in how he looks at you. He cares, Izzy. So why would you think he's pulling away?"

"Because he *is*." Isabel hated the whiny tone of her voice, but she couldn't help it. "He's been so distant lately and it's not getting better. He's grumpy and short-tempered. He even snapped at me the other day." She explained about her offer of assistance that he cut short. "Why would he resist my help if he wanted me around? I'm a professional, Addie. Most people would grab my offer with both hands and squeeze me for every penny they could get with my skills."

"Maybe he just needs a little time," Addie offered, patting her friend's leg. "He's got a lot going on and he's about to have a lot more."

Izabel snapped her gaze to Addie. "What do you mean, more?"

Addie dropped her chin and sighed. "I shouldn't have said that."

"Why?"

"Cade and Cord have some plans they want to include Zack in," Addie said, then shook her head and held out her palm to waylay Izabel's obvious questions. "That's all I can say, and please, don't mention it to Zack. It's supposed to be a surprise. I believe they planned to ask you about it as well—to take advantage of those skills you mentioned." She grinned. "I think you'll love it, and we hope he will, too."

Izabel pressed her lips together, but nodded, knowing she wouldn't get anything further from her friend on that topic.

"Looks like another storm's coming in," Addie said as she stared out at the purple-gray clouds rolling over the foothills to the north and coming their way.

Izabel followed her gaze as a long, thin flash of light broke from the bruised-looking clouds. It reached down toward the tall trees, illuminating the spiky tops of evergreens for a second before the deep shadows returned.

"Great," Addie said after the flicker they'd just witnessed, "another lightning storm. I hope there's at least some rain with it this time."

"Is it a problem?"

Addie sighed. "I only know what I've been told, but both Cade and Cord worry about them and the risk of fire they bring. Their firemen friends have delighted in frightening me with stories about wildland fires they've worked around here." She turned to look at Izabel, a sober expression in her soft brown gaze. "It's terrifying what can happen out there—how much land and how many homes can be destroyed, and the lives that can be lost. I don't want to ever experience one myself, but from what I understand, it's a good possibility, what with the storms and the tourists and campers all around here. Not to mention, it's been a dry year so far and the boys are all volunteers with the forest service."

Izabel's eyes widened. "The boys? You mean, Cade and Cord would be out in fire?"

Addie nodded. "Zack too, if he's not still laid up, though they'd only be in a clean-up crew and only if it came close to town or homes in this area."

Izabel made a commiserating face before she turned to frown at the dark clouds in the distance. She imagined a line of red, orange, and yellow licking up the dried bark of every tree in sight, their pitch snapping and popping as it cooked inside their rough brown skin. The leaves and pine needles turning orange and swaying with the waves of heat a fire that size would create. If the wind kicked up, the whole valley they sat in would be consumed in an afternoon, and Zack would be out in the middle of it all.

"What a terrible thought," she murmured as a shiver rocked her.

"I know," Addie replied as she stood. "But whether or not there's rain to go with those flashes," Addie paused to mount her horse and then tilted her head to indicate the storm clouds, "we should get back."

Izabel nodded and followed Addie's example, and they started making their way back to the Brody ranch. Her friend's fear of a wildfire stayed with Izabel the whole way, and she wondered if Zack would worry over her if a fire did come. She'd certainly be concerned about him, especially if he had to go out in it to help.

What would she do if anything happened to him? *God forbid he gets hurt or burned.* She winced at the thought. It was better to hope for rain than to consider what might happen to Zack in a fire. But whatever happened later, she still had a lot to work out with him. All she had to do was find the courage to do it first.

CHAPTER 22

The walls in his best friends' dining room seemed to close in on Zack as he shifted in his chair, causing multiple loud squeaks to fill the otherwise peaceful room. Knife and fork held clumsily in hand—due to the sling on his arm—to cut his steak, Zack paused and stared fixedly at his plate, refusing to look up.

"Don't mind the chairs," Addie said from the other side of the table, and he could hear the smile in her voice. "They're old and...unique."

Zack nodded and went back to cutting his steak, his chair once again protesting loudly.

"I think the word you were looking for was 'creaky,'" Cade joked from one end of the table.

The others laughed softly and Zack smiled. He'd eaten at this table many times over the years but had never noticed how much noise the chairs made until today.

Quiet blanketed the room once again, the only sounds were of their utensils, tapping and sliding on porcelain plates, muted by the tension in the air.

Guilt squeezed Zack's chest; he knew the depressed mood was his fault. He'd been less than talkative since arriving, but he couldn't help it. Izabel's presence had stolen his words. Every inch of him was finely attuned to her as she sat quietly across from him. She hadn't said anything other than hello, but the sound of her soft voice had struck him like a bolt of lightning, and he feared if he looked at her, if he spoke to her, he'd never stop.

The problem was, he wanted to cast his eyes upon her. He wanted a lot more than that, but things had changed.

The last couple of weeks had been rougher than he'd expected. His failures had brought home to him, once again, that he had nothing to offer a woman as a man or a partner. Not only that, but financially, he was about to fall on his metaphorical ass.

The winery was almost finished, but he'd run out of money. He'd even gone to the bank for a loan, using his tiny cabin and the small corner of land his parents had gifted him on his twenty-fifth birthday as collateral. Unfortunately, because he'd never bothered to change the title—pure stupid laziness on his part—his parents were still listed as the owners, which meant he would need their signatures for the loan. Letting them know about his dire straits so they could worry about his future and their own was the last thing he wanted. So he'd left the bank, his mind reeling as he tried to think of some way to raise a little money without letting his family know what a failure he'd become.

He sawed at his steak, trying not to shake the table or his creaky chair as he attempted to tamp down his internal panic.

His truck—the only thing that was really his—wouldn't get him much. Even with the replaced tires after the incident at Tony's Tavern, it was too old to gain him what he needed. Besides, he needed it for the ranch.

Only one other thing—kept in a small, dirty velvet box in his truck—could give him a little breathing room, but after all the years of holding on to it and the memories it carried, he was loath to let it go. Every time he considered it, the guilt stabbed like a jagged knife straight through his heart.

He glanced at Izabel through lowered lashes. *Maybe it's time to let it all go.*

Zack tucked his final piece of the wonderfully tender steak Cord had grilled for their meal into his mouth and chewed purposefully, concentrating on the flavor and not grinding it to dust with his teeth.

Not only had he hit the proverbial financial wall, but there was also that damn enigmatic note on his windshield several days ago. No other notes had shown up since, but the threat he'd detected in the words had been real and had him constantly looking over his shoulder. He'd vowed then and there to keep his distance from Izabel to protect her from the danger it might represent, but now his humiliation over the winery caused him to growl and cower like a dog in her presence. She'd tried to help him in several ways—they'd even argued about her poking into his private business—but underneath his sudden anger, he hadn't blamed her. He'd been proud and flattered that she cared enough to speak to his doctor about getting him some help. Unfortunately, that warm feeling of being cared about came a little too late, and he'd said some things he didn't mean.

"I ran into Aaron Monroe in town today," Cord said into the empty void of conversation. "He said the department was put on alert."

That got Zack's full attention, and his gaze snapped over to where Cord sat at the opposite end of the table from his brother.

"Alert?" he asked, and gulped from his water glass to clear his overly tight throat. "Was it the storms or a tourist?"

Cord nodded as he swallowed a sip of coffee. "They think a lightning strike started it. The fire's still several miles out," he waved his hand in a northwesterly direction, "and right now, it's not moving this way."

"Yeah," Cade replied grimly as he pulled his coffee cup forward, "but we all know how quickly that can change..."

Zack sighed and nodded, as did Cord.

"Do they know how bad it is right now?" Addie asked.

Cade reached for her hand and gave it a squeeze. "Bad enough to put our town firefighters on alert."

"And that's really bad, right?" Izabel asked quietly, and all three men nodded.

Zack met her worried gaze for a moment. Wanting to ease her concern, he gave her a reassuring grin before turning to Cord. "Will they be calling the volunteers?"

Cord shook his head. "Aaron didn't know, but I imagine if it gets big enough, they will."

"We've already made plans with Joe to get the cattle moved and everyone out of the way if we need to," Cade added.

Zack nodded. "Any chance we could jump on that bandwagon, too?" His family's ranch didn't have as many animals as the Brody's, or as many workers, but Joe Baker was a skilled ranch foreman and could easily sort them all out if needed.

Cade grinned. "Already done. That was one of the things we wanted to talk to you about."

Zack's eyebrows went up as gratitude filled his chest. "Much appreciated," he said as he pushed his empty plate away and stood to fill a coffee cup from the pot on the sideboard. When no one else wanted a cup filled, he sat down and let his gaze sweep his friends' faces—being careful not to settle on Izabel. He knew there was more, so he tried to sound casual when he asked, "And what's the other thing?"

Cord smiled and stood. "Let's go to the office and we'll tell you all about it."

"We'll clear the table and join you shortly," Addie said as she and Izabel began stacking dishes.

Zack slowly followed his friends down a short hall in their redesigned old home to what used to be the master bedroom, which had been converted into a large office the twins shared.

By the brothers' attitudes, Zack knew something big was coming. He wasn't sure if it was good or bad, but a huge rock had settled in his belly. An itch of nervousness tickled his spine as he sat in one of the cushy brown leather chairs and set his coffee on the small table beside it. Cade took the matching chair to Zack's left, and Cord sat behind their father's old, large, elaborately carved desk facing them.

"We have a business proposition for you," Cade said without preamble.

Zack's heart dropped to his feet. He'd love to work with these two, but he was already overdrawn and stretched to the breaking point—not only with finances, but with his time and sanity as well. Still, because they'd been talking about running a business together since they were kids, it would seem odd if he didn't at least ask about it.

"What kind of business proposition?"

"We want to create a vacation spot for folks who want a little taste of country or ranch life in Montana."

Zack frowned. "Aren't there a bunch of those all over this state already?"

A slow smile curved Cord's mouth, and he tapped one of the half-dozen folders full of papers on his desk. "Yes, there are a few, but this is a little different."

"How so?"

Cord exchanged a knowing look with his brother that seemed all too smug to Zack's narrowed eyes. *What are they up to?*

"Well," Cord began as he lounged in his chair and folded his hands in his lap as if about to explain the meaning of life, "we want to expand our income options and appeal to a larger pool of clientele."

"Okay, and how do you plan to do that?"

"First off, we'll be working with the forest service to run hunting and fishing tours both on our land and theirs. We'd offer private cabins, an area for glamping, a restaurant, and a winery for our customers. We'd have individual and group riding lessons and tours, plus a number of other options as well."

"And," Cade added, drawing out the word, "because of the assault at her old place and the trouble she had recovering from the incident, Addie convinced us to include an area for trauma patients to work with the horses—like she did when we moved here—but that'll come about a little later."

"Interesting," Zack said. "I assume the winery you're talking about is mine, but what the hell is *glamping?*"

"Of course, we're talking about your winery," Cade said, leaning over to slap Zack's shoulder, saw the sling that still held his arm, and sat back again. "And don't worry about glamping; you'll know what it is soon enough."

"What about the protesters?" Zack asked, though he hadn't seen any of them for over a week.

"What protestors?" Cade asked. "You mean the ones who trashed the winery last winter and have been buzzing around all the ranches near here lately?"

Cord shook his head. "We don't *know* if they vandalized the winery last winter, though they did make a real nuisance of themselves otherwise, yes. But they seem to have disappeared, which is very convenient for us."

"Yeah, convenient," Zack grumbled. "What if they come back?"

"We'll deal with them, but until they do, we'll just move forward with our plans."

"And what would be your plans?" Zack asked slowly.

"Well, we'd like you to oversee the backcountry tours for hunting and fishing," Cord said, "as well as the riding lessons and the animals."

"Me? Why?"

"You know those trails as well or better than Cade and I do," Cord replied. "And you're great with animals and people."

"Sounds like you want me to do all the work," Zack grumbled. Not that he disliked the idea; it was just that he wasn't in a position to accept it.

"Not *all* the work," Cade joked. "Cord and I will pull our weight, too. At least until we learn all your secrets." He wiggled his brows and Zack rolled his eyes.

"Cade has it half right," Cord said with an admonishing glance at his twin brother. "We could learn a lot from each other, but Cade and I will have work to do, too. We're not completely useless when it comes to ranching and relaxing." He grinned. "Plus, we're willing to be the bank for this project."

Zack's brows drew down. "What do you mean, you'll 'be the bank?'"

Cord tilted his head. "We know you've got your hands full with the winery right now. If you need it, we can help get it set up and ready for customers, as well as finance the client cabins on both of our properties. We are even willing to cover the cost of enlarging the restaurant section of the winery in a year or two, or maybe build a separate one if that would be a better option."

Dumbfounded, Zack stared at his friends. *Do they really have that much money?*

They obviously had no idea the extent of his financial issues, so he shouldn't be angry with them for suggesting this huge undertaking.

But regardless, he was.

"It's a great offer," Izabel said as she and Addie walked in the door. "It could do a lot for both ranches, including providing several sources of income beyond ranching, and more jobs for locals."

Zack tossed her a dark look as she sat in a chair by the window and Addie settled in Cade's lap, but concentrated on the brothers. Izabel raised her eyebrows at him as if to ask, 'What's wrong with that?'

"What brought this idea on?" he asked, as if he didn't know Izabel had something to do with it.

Cord fiddled with the papers on his desktop. "It's something I've been thinking about for a while now," he said. "With Cade back home where he belongs, it seemed more realistic, and since we'd all talked about it for years, I thought now would be a good time. Addie suggested that I run it by Izabel because of her marketing experience, and she approved."

He flashed a smile at Izabel, who returned it.

"It *is* a good concept," Izabel said again, "and I've got lots of ideas on how to make it grow."

Cord's smile widened. "With her help, we've been able to map out the plan for the next three to five years. If we get started right away, we should be able to have customers coming in by next spring. It'll be a boost to us and the town, and as Izzy said, will diversify our income so we're not so dependent on the weather and cattle."

As Cord spoke, Zack felt his insides twist painfully and he gripped the arms of the chair so hard his knuckles turned white.

"On top of all that," Cade added, oblivious to Zack's discomfort, "we know we can trust you as a partner."

"I'm not so sure," Zack muttered darkly.

Cade frowned, but Zack didn't let him speak.

"It sounds great, guys, but I don't think I can join you this time."

Cord's shoulder slumped but his blue eyes turned sharp. "Why not? You always wanted this as much as we did."

Zack shrugged. "I know, but I've got a lot on my plate right now. I can't really afford to add any more."

"Is this about the winery?" Izabel asked, and Zack toss a glare at her.

"Among other things..." he replied grimly.

"We can help with the winery," Cade offered hopefully.

"Yes," Cord added, "we're in a position to help you with whatever you need, Zack. If you're low on funds, we can loan you the money, and you can pay it back when this endeavor begins to pay off."

Zack started shaking his head before Cord even finished. "I can't have you paying my bills. I won't take advantage of you that way."

"You wouldn't be," Cord replied. "It's a business deal, and we can work it any way you like."

"And you'd be paying us back, Zack," Cade said, his tone more serious than it had been. "It's not charity."

Zack shook his head and glanced at Izabel. "I told you to leave this alone."

Her eyes widened. "They came to me. It wasn't my idea, but it *is* a good one."

"You think I don't know that!" Zack shouted and felt like a brute when she flinched.

Grief and embarrassment weighed on his heart, making his chest ache. He pushed to his feet and went to the door where he stopped and looked back. He wanted to join them in this wonderful challenge, but how could he? He'd be dead weight to their plans, and he couldn't risk dragging them all down with him or endangering them. As far as he knew, he was already a danger to their well-being by just associating with them.

He glanced at Izabel briefly but the sadness and confusion on her face only twisted the knife deeper. *Will I lose her, too?* He shoved the thought away.

He turned to Cord. "I'm sorry," he said lamely, "but I can't be a part of this. I wish you all luck, though, and I hope it works out well."

His feet were like lead weights dragging across the hardwood floor as he made his way to the front door. His cheeks burned from the astonished looks on all their faces as he walked away.

Footsteps hurried after him but stopped before leaving the room.

"Let him go." Cord's soft tones barely reached his ears.

"But there's something wrong..." Izabel's sweet voice was just a little louder.

"Yes," Cade's reply was hard, "but he wants to work it out on his own."

Zack sighed as he pulled the door closed behind him.

Cade was right; Zack needed to work this out on his own. But was it pride or mortification that made him refuse to take their money?

Why did I turn them down? he wondered as he hurried to his truck and climbed inside.

Izabel's pained gaze flashed in his mind and he slammed his fist on the steering wheel.

Pride did it. Of, course it was pride. He'd turned down his best opportunity to resolve his financial troubles and live a dream they'd shared for decades because he didn't want to look weak in front of a woman. A woman he wanted more than anything to hold in his arms and kiss again, to take care of as his own. He hadn't felt that way in years, but he couldn't deny it was there. Instead, he'd acted like a petulant child throwing a tantrum.

Maybe he was ignorant. Maybe that's why the one risky endeavor he'd attempted seemed beyond his ability to complete.

The disappointment on his friends' faces was another wound that made his ribs squeeze.

He lifted his head and looked at the Brody's big house.

I should go back in, he thought, but something inside wouldn't let him. He needed to think, to get away from the distractions and consider his minimal options carefully. Once he did that, and if the Brodys' plans still seemed like an answer to his prayers, then maybe he'd come back and actually discuss it with the brothers...alone.

He caught movement from one of the windows and focused on it. Izabel stood there, staring back at him with concern painted all over her face.

His stomach clenched and a need to run took hold of his senses as he started the truck and backed out of his parking spot. He couldn't think straight with her around, and he didn't want her to know the truth behind his childish behavior or the fear for all of them that had his heart hammering in his throat.

If he wanted to see her again, however, he'd have to tell her *something,* eventually. He'd need to tell them all about the threatening note and his financial troubles.

Just not now.

Stepping on the gas, Zack left in a cloud of dust, promising himself he'd find a way out of this mess...it would just take a little while.

CHAPTER 23

Izabel wiped the sweat from her forehead with the back of her hand as she, Addie, and Emmy meandered down the sidewalk in town, chatting and giggling at their silliness. It was past noon and the temperature had soared into the high nineties, but despite the low humidity of the air, Izabel felt like a damp, limp rag. Her shirt seemed to be glued to her back, the little tendrils of hair that had escaped her bushy ponytail were stuck to her neck, and drops of sweat kept dribbling between her breasts. All of it made her itchy and uncomfortable, but the company helped take her mind off the irritations hounding her in the heat.

Only two weeks remained before the winery's opening day, and less than eight days before the start of the state fair. She'd started working with the Brodys on their new business venture, and already had several magazines and other venues—including a small booth at the upcoming fair—interested in advertising the business. The idea practically sold itself, which hadn't surprised her. Cowboys and their lifestyle carried a mystique about them. The chance to spend time on a ranch or in the country, seeing the men and their work up close, was an infectious curiosity. Now, if she could just find some cowgirls to hire that would even out the interest.

The twins claimed that Zack would come around and join them in their business venture, but Izabel wasn't so sure. Something was wrong. It definitely had to do with the winery and she had her suspicions about what, but she knew he would never tell her. The man was sweet and easy-going most of the time, but he was still a man with a man's pride.

While they strolled down the road, Emmy recited a surprisingly happy story about the recovery of a burn victim from the ER where she worked. Izabel only half-listened as she wondered how Zack was doing. Had he dove into advertising for the winery yet, looked at the type of clientele he wanted to attract, or started planning the marketing tactics he wanted to use? She doubted it, which was why she had pulled a few strings with some of her contacts in Seattle and elsewhere to drum up a little free advertising for him.

"My goodness," Addie complained as she tugged at her shirt, "I'm going to *melt* in this heat."

"Me, too," Izabel replied, fanning her face with her free hand and putting her thoughts about Zack aside for a moment. "Will it be like this the rest of the summer?"

Addie's eyes rounded and she gave Izabel a dramatic nod.

"Oh, you two need to toughen up a little," Emmy said exasperatedly as she tugged a strand of hair that had come loose from her braid off of her neck, otherwise seemingly unaffected by the heat.

Izabel suspected it was an act to tease the non-natives—namely her and Addie.

Emmy flicked the curled brim of her straw cowboy hat. "Y'all should've worn a hat."

Addie groaned. "I'd thought about it, but Cade's taking me out tonight and I didn't want to have hat hair."

"I've got to get me one," Izabel mumbled, eyeing the shade the hat's brim provided Emmy's head and shoulders.

"There's a shop a couple of streets over," Emmy said to Izabel. "We can stop in before we leave to find one for you." She tilted her head. "With your exotic beauty, I think you'll look great as a cowgirl."

Izabel rolled her eyes. "I've got a long way to go before becoming a cowgirl."

"Maybe," Emmy said with a grin, "but it doesn't hurt to look the part first." She winked and Addie giggled.

"Yeah," Addie joined in on the gentle teasing, "you'll turn all the cowboys' heads with your lean figure and those gorgeous green eyes."

Izabel's face grew hotter as an image of Zack, looking at her with his smoldering amber gaze, popped into her head. She bumped Addie with her hip. "Stop it, you." She smiled to take the sting out of her words, and Addie laughed again as they continued down the sidewalk.

"Why don't we drop in on Kate at the bistro so y'all can cool off a bit?"

Emmy suggested.

"Yes!" Addie and Izabel replied in unison, then they turned and headed toward Kate's shop.

As they waited at the corner to cross the street behind a small group of happy tourists, Emmy whistled appreciatively at a new, glossy-white Mercedes as it approached the corner where they stood. Though splattered with dried mud, its sparkling aluminum wheels and shiny chrome accents flashed in the brilliant sunshine. "Now, that is a *totally* impractical vehicle for Montana."

"Very," Addie agreed. "It's pretty, though. I'll bet it's a tourist. I can't see anyone spending that kind of money and then letting it stay all dirty like that."

Izabel bent her knees a bit to hide behind two tall men in front of them, while at the same time, she strained to see who drove the car. She didn't know what it was about the Mercedes that filled her with such dread, but it seemed to come in ever-increasing waves as the vehicle drew closer.

Thanks to the darkly tinted windows, all she could tell was that a man drove the car. No other characteristics were evident through the opacity of the tinted windows.

Sprays of mud, that had long since dried, speckled the whole side of the car and tires, indicating that whoever the driver was had been around town since the last rain. From what Izabel could remember, that was a few weeks ago.

Just before Zack had been shot! Her breath stopped and twisted in her throat. *It can't be him,* she thought, a little stream of panic flooding her chest. *There's no way Chris would come after me, and there's even less chance that he'd shoot at someone... Right?*

She stifled the moan that threatened to escape her throat and tried to get control of her suddenly trembling body. Chris had never been the 'grab a gun and shoot your opponent' kind of guy—he'd always looked for other, more political ways to ruin an adversary's life. But if he was actually here... She no longer had any idea what he would do.

The car drove passed without any hesitation, as if the driver hadn't found what he'd been looking for.

If he had *been looking...* Izabel inhaled deeply as relief surged through her. Maybe she was wrong. Even if it *was* the kind of vehicle Chris would rent—even in Montana—that didn't mean it was him.

Yet she couldn't deny the sense of unease that had stolen over her at the sight of the shiny car or the remaining tingle of worry that tickled her spine.

As the Mercedes disappeared around the corner, Izabel's gaze swept over the few people across the street. A woman's blonde ponytail caught Izabel's eye and she focused on the woman's plain, unmade-up face. The other woman looked familiar, but it took Izabel a moment to realize that she'd seen this woman before—she was the bartender the night Izabel had kissed Zack on the tavern's dance floor.

The other woman seemed to be glaring directly at Izabel. Why exactly, Izabel could only guess—not that she really cared, but it was unnerving all the same.

The whole staring match lasted only a few seconds before the woman rounded the corner out of sight, but Izabel's sense of alarm remained.

"You know," Emmy said close to Izabel's ear and, due to her heightened state of alarm, Izabel jumped at the sudden sound. Both of her friends frowned at her, clearly wondering what was wrong, but Izabel grinned to hide her discomfort as they crossed the street and headed down the sidewalk.

Emmy shook her head and continued, "Zack is miserable without you. He's been moping around the ranch like a bear with a sore paw."

"I'm miserable without him, too," Izabel replied, and Addie gave her a sad smile.

"Why don't you come over tonight?" Emmy suggested. "We could have dinner; I'll make an excuse to leave you two alone, and then you could talk."

Izabel shook her head. She wanted nothing more than to talk to Zack about what had happened after dinner with the Brodys last week, but she was giving him space to work it out for himself, just as Cade and Cord had suggested.

"I know he's been grumpy," Emmy said, "even before your...disagreement, falling out... What *was* it, exactly?"

Izabel exchanged a glance with Addie and they both shrugged.

"The boys wanted to include him in a business deal," Addie explained. "He didn't seem happy about it."

"He's pretty stressed over the winery and all the problems it's had," Emmy said. "I wouldn't be surprised if he's low on funds."

"We could help him with that," Addie said. "In fact, we offered to, but he turned it down."

Emmy's lips thinned with irritation. "Men... Too damn proud."

"I think it's more than that," Izabel said.

Emmy glanced at her. "Like what?"

"I'm not sure, but whatever it is, it's been bothering him for a long time."

It was Addie and Emmy's turn to exchange a glance.

"What?" Izabel asked.

Addie shook her head. "I don't know the details, and I'm sure Emmy won't elaborate, but he's had some hard times in his life."

"So I keep hearing," Izabel grumbled, then another thought came to her. "What about the protestors and all the trouble they caused? Are they back again now? I hadn't noticed..."

Emmy shook her head. "I haven't seen or heard anything from them in weeks. It's like they just disappeared."

"Weird..." Izabel murmured as they reached the door to Kate's bistro. It opened just before Addie reached for the handle and out stepped the man of the hour, causing every worry in Izabel's head to burn to dust.

"Zack," Emmy said a little startled. "I didn't know you were in town today."

His dark eyes scanned over the women's faces and stopped on Izabel before he spoke. "I had to pick up some things," he said, his eyes never leaving Izabel's face, "and I have a meeting with the sheriff a little later."

"Why? Did something else happen?" Emmy asked worriedly.

"No," Zack replied, finally turning to his sister. "He just wants to go over the complaints and update me on the investigation of the winery break-in. We've done this a few times over the last year. Not much seems to have come up, though."

"Too bad," Emmy said. "I was just telling the ladies that I haven't seen the protestors for quite a while."

"Me either, and good riddance. It'll be too soon if I never see them again." Zack turned to Izabel. "If you ladies don't mind, I'd like to speak with Izzy for a moment."

Izabel's face flushed. Since the moment he'd appeared, she hadn't been able to take her eyes off him. It was as if she'd been dying of thirst and he was just the tall drink of water she needed. But the moment his eyes fell on her the second time, a buzz of excitement had fluttered in her belly, and with his words, it raced outward into her arms and legs making her body tingle.

"Sure," Emmy said as she winked at Izabel. "We'll be inside."

With that, she and Addie went into the bistro, leaving Izabel alone with Zack.

Suddenly feeling shy, Izabel looked around, unable to meet his eyes. He shifted his feet as he stared at the ground, the cup of coffee he'd just purchased dangled loosely from his fingertips at his side.

"I wanted to apologize for last week at dinner," he said quietly and she looked up at his face. Color had stained his cheekbones, and upon closer inspection, she noted he looked tired and a little...sad. "I haven't been myself lately, and you seem to get the brunt of it when it has nothing to do with you." He looked up, and Izabel's heart twisted at the pain she read in his eyes. "I'm really sorry, Izabel. I've already spoken to Cade and Cord, but I wasn't sure how to make things right with you...again."

Izabel smiled and reached for his free hand to twine her fingers with his. "I think you're doing just fine."

A slow grin curled his lips and the lines of tension around his mouth and eyes seemed to ease. "Thank you. Your kindness means a lot to me."

"And your ability to accept your mistakes and try to rectify them means everything to me. I just wish you'd trust me enough to tell me what's causing you so much grief."

He lowered his gaze to their clasped hands as his ears turned red with what she suspected was embarrassment. She wanted to push the issue, to find out what had held him back and upset him so much last week, but she needed to wait for him to tell her.

"Would you have dinner with me tomorrow night?" he asked, meeting her eyes again.

"Absolutely." She grinned. "I've been dying to spend time with you."

"Me, too."

They stood staring at each other as the bistro clients periodically entered and exited through the door beside them—though neither of them noticed.

"I'd really like to kiss you right now, but..." He glanced around at the cars and people around them.

"I'd love that too, but I agree, it's a little too...public."

"Yes," he said, his voice low and sultry as his eyes gleamed at her, "especially for the kind of kiss I'd like to give you."

Izabel's body flooded with heat and her eyes widened. "I'll see you tomorrow night," she said, her voice a little unstable. "Can we talk about it more then? Maybe just…skip the talk and get right to the kiss?"

Man, I am such a hussy. But she couldn't help it, this man melted her heart and made her sweat faster than the hot August sun.

His smile broadened and he gently squeezed her fingers before releasing her hand. "Yes, we will." Then he nodded at her and turned to amble down the sidewalk.

She bit her lip as she watched him go, loving the loose way his long-legged body ambled down the sidewalk, and remembering all that hard muscle and heat as he had moved over her that night at the cabin.

Someone knocked on the bistro's window, snapping Izabel out of her revelry. When she looked, she saw Addie and Emmy smiling like idiots, waving for her to come inside.

She glanced down the street just in time to see Zack turn the corner and sighed. Tomorrow night couldn't come fast enough.

Going to the door, she pulled it open and paused as a cool blast of air washed over her from inside. Might as well enjoy it for a moment, because the minute she sat at the table with her friends, they'd have her blushing with all their questions, suggestions, and meaningful looks.

Still, even with their embarrassing comments and the possibility that Chris Richards might be in town, the happiness inside her would not abate. She was going on a date with Zack tomorrow, and she couldn't be happier.

* * *

His meeting at the sheriff's office took a little longer than Zack had expected, though they had about as much new information about the incident and who was at fault for the damage at the winery as he'd thought. Which was to say, none. Every lead they'd followed led nowhere, and they had just asked him in to let him know that the case would stay open but would no longer be worked unless additional evidence arose.

Of course, he'd been angry about that, but no amount of cajoling or arguing had changed the sheriff's mind.

It had been dinnertime when he left the sheriff's office and decided to grab something to eat at Betsy's Diner. The food wasn't as good as anything homemade, but it was close enough.

Now, sitting in a comfortable booth and sipping coffee after finishing his meal, Zack grinned as a couple of his friends entered the diner's front door. The place had been packed since Zack arrived and still was, which left the two firefighters without a place to sit. Even the front counter was filled with people.

Before they could leave, Zack waved them over to his table. Since he'd be leaving shortly, they could take his booth. Besides, he wanted to ask about the smoke he'd smelled in the air earlier.

"Hey man," Aaron said as he slid onto the seat opposite Zack. "Glad you're here to share your table."

"No problem," Zack said as he nodded to Hawk, the normally quieter of the two firefighters. "I'm glad to be of service."

"Howdy, Zack," Hawk murmured as he sat next to Aaron.

"What are you guys up to tonight?" Zack asked.

The other men exchanged a look that spoke volumes of something Zack didn't understand.

"It's Johnny's night to cook at the station," Aaron replied when he saw the confusion on Zack's face, then shivered dramatically.

"Ah, I see," Zack said. "So he's still struggling in the kitchen, I take it."

Everyone in their friend circle knew that Big John Devereux's strength lay in his huge, muscular body and not in his culinary talents. The tall man from Puerto Rico via Louisiana had been endeavoring to improve his skills over the last year, but apparently, he hadn't quite accomplished his goal as of yet.

"That would be a *big* no," Aaron answered.

"That's not entirely true," Hawk offered in a low voice. "That frickin' chicken thing with mushrooms and champagne sauce he made last week wasn't bad."

Aaron chuckled. "I think you mean, chicken fricassee, and yeah, that wasn't bad." He turned to Zack with a shrug. "So I guess you could say he's improving, but he's sure taking his time with it."

"What's on the menu tonight?"

Hawk leaned forward, one lip curled in distaste. "Some kind of Cuban liver and onions."

Aaron groaned and made a face that clearly stated his opinion on the meal.

"Liver's supposed to be good for you," Zack said with mock solemnity. "It's chock-full of vitamins and minerals that every growing boy needs."

"Yuck!" Aaron said, disgust evident on his face and in his voice. "In my humble opinion, a meal should *taste* good, as well as be good for you."

Hawk nodded in agreement, his face a study of absolute seriousness.

Zack laughed. "I can't argue there. I hate the stuff, too."

"Well then," Aaron said, "now you know why we're here."

Choking back another chuckle, Zack sipped his coffee, waiting while his friends looked over the menu and placed their orders.

"So what's the deal with the smoke and ash in the air?" Zack asked once the waitress left the table. "Did something happen with that fire you told Cord about or is it a new one?" He hadn't had time to check the news over the last few days, so he figured these guys could update him.

Hawk nodded, but he let Aaron do the talking.

"Yeah, that one northwest of us flared up last night with some winds that came down from Canada. With all the heat we've had this summer and so little rain…" he shook his head, "it spread to almost double its size in minutes."

A frown drew Zack's brows together. "Is the town in danger? Are we?"

Aaron shook his head. "No, no. The department's still on alert, but it's not a town emergency…yet"

"Right, don't get too comfy though," Hawk added. "It's not out of control, but another night like the last one might be enough to push it into an enormous rager that could take out this entire town and everyone in it."

Aaron and Zack stared at their friend in stunned silence. Not that they didn't know what could happen, but they were shocked the usually reserved Hawk would say something so dark.

"I'm sure we'd get everyone out of here before that happened," Aaron said, glancing at Zack.

"Yeah," Zack agreed, though his stomach had tied itself in a knot. "The Brodys and I already have a plan in place."

"Well, you're ahead of some," Hawk replied and then stared down at his folded hands on the table.

"Did any more fires flare up elsewhere?" Zack asked as he set his empty mug aside, preparing to leave.

"Yeah, a couple," Aaron said, "They're farther away, but they're adding to the smoky haze we saw today. Don't be surprised if you see ash on your truck in the morning."

Zack shook his head and stood. "Great. Thanks for the uplifting news."

Aaron grinned. "Anytime, man."

"See you." Zack nodded to both men as he left the table and went to the counter to pay for his meal.

Once outside, and momentarily forgetting about the low quality of the air, Zack took a deep breath and coughed. The smell of smoke was heavy and a flicker of worry increase the weight of responsibility he'd been carrying. He'd need to keep a better eye on the news. Headed for his truck, he made a mental note to check with the Brodys to see if they were paying more attention to what was going on in the world than he was.

As Zack strolled around to the back of the building where he'd parked his truck, he flicked through the keys on his keyring to find the correct one. Once again, he was reminded that he needed to sort out the ones he didn't use anymore. He'd just found the right key when something hit him from out of the dark, taking him off his feet and slamming him into the diner's concrete wall. It felt like being tackled by a three-hundred-pound linebacker. Pure agony shot through his injured arm when it was crushed between the wall and his ribs. The man who'd thrown himself at Zack stepped back as his victim crumpled to his knees, cradling his sore arm against his chest and moaning in pain.

Zack silently prayed the wound had healed enough not to have opened again.

"Not such a big man now, are you?" a familiar voice taunted from behind Zack.

Rotating his body, Zack glanced over his good shoulder, but only got a brief glimpse of a tall man with a bushy beard before the man's fist caught him high on the cheek and spun Zack back into the wall. Stars danced behind his eyelids and he blinked, trying to clear them because he knew he was in trouble.

The area wasn't well-lit, but Zack didn't need another look. He knew the other man; he recognized the protestor who'd kept trying to bait Zack into a fight—and it looked like he had finally gotten what he wanted. Unfortunately, Zack was far from a hundred percent, physically. His injured arm throbbed, and he could feel his cheek and eye starting to swell from the punch to his face, but he wasn't going to just lay down and take what this man wanted to hand out.

"What do you want?" he asked as he pushed himself to his feet.

The other man punched him again, low in the back, and Zack fell against the wall.

"I warned you..." the man said, ranting like a lunatic. "This is what you get for treating her like a *whore*."

Zack clenched his teeth at the new wave of pain. He inhaled and prayed the asshole wouldn't hit him again or at least, not right away.

Maybe if I keep him ranting…

Quickly rolling his body along the wall, Zack turned to face his attacker. "What the hell are you talking about?"

"You know exactly what I'm talking about, you bastard!" the man shouted, taking another wild swing.

Zack had just enough warning to block the blow aimed at his belly. Not that it didn't hurt, anyway.

"You treat women like shit," the man said, landing a couple of body blows. "She deserves better…better than you, that's for sure. It's time someone taught you a lesson."

"Hey!" another man screamed from the front of the diner.

Eyes closing, Zack breathed a sigh of relief when he recognized Aaron's voice, but then wondered if he'd misheard. *I just left Aaron inside,* his muddled mind thought. *Why would he be out here?*

"Get away from him," Aaron shouted and Zack turned to see the outline of his friend's broad shoulders coming toward them.

The other man's head had snapped to his left and he moved as if to run away, but Zack stopped him with his foot. The man stumbled over Zack's outstretched leg and sprawled on the ground. He fumbled getting to his feet, which gave Aaron just enough time to jump onto the man's back and subdue him.

Hawk showed up a moment later. "You okay?" he asked Zack, who nodded.

"Who's this guy?" Aaron asked as he held the man's arms behind his back while the stranger squirmed on the ground.

"One of the protestors," Zack muttered. "Guess they didn't all leave."

"Hold still!" Aaron shouted at the prone man lying beneath his knee, which was planted between the man's shoulder blades. "Did you call the sheriff?" Aaron looked up at Hawk.

Zack suddenly realized why Aaron had come after him. He'd forgotten his phone on the table inside.

Hawk nodded at Aaron's question. "A deputy should be here any minute."

"You brought my cell phone out?" Zack asked, sounding a little dazed, even to himself.

Aaron flashed his too-charming grin. "Good thing you were forgetful tonight."

"Yeah, I guess so." Zack sighed as he slid down the wall until his ass hit the ground.

"What'd he want?" Hawk asked, nodding to the protester who'd started squirming again.

"Don't know for sure," Zack replied.

A car skidded to a stop on the road beside the diner. The deputy flicked on his lights and jumped out of his car. "What's happening, boys? Someone called in a fight?"

"Yeah," Aaron said as he hauled the protestor up by one of his arms. "This guy jumped my friend."

* * *

It was nearly two hours later before Zack was able to get in his truck and drive home. The throbbing in his arm had lessened some, but it still ached from being body-slammed against the brick wall. Luckily, when he'd undressed for a shower, he'd found that the wound had not reopened. One glance in the mirror, however, showed he'd not only have a bruise on his cheek where the man had punched him, but his eye looked as if it would be well-blackened with more bruising by morning.

Now, as he finally crawled into bed and pulled the sheet to his waist, his mind once again turned over the events at the diner.

"What *had* he been ranting about?" Zack muttered into the darkness as he tucked his right hand beneath his head. The man had said something about 'treating her like a whore.' That bothered him more than he wanted to think about because he prided himself on never being *that guy*. Not only would his mother hound him exhaustively for the rest of his life if he ever treated any woman as something less than an equal, but he had no doubt his two older sisters would threaten bodily harm as well—and his father wouldn't be pleased, either. He loved them all too much to embarrass any of his family by acting that way, so the comment didn't make sense to him. He enjoyed women but had too much respect for most to even consider making one a plaything for his pleasure.

"She deserves better..." the other man had said, but he'd never said who *she* was. He'd also said, "It's time someone taught you a lesson."

"I suppose he was the one to teach me a lesson," Zack said to himself, "but who was the *she* he'd mentioned?"

That he knew of, only two women had ever bad-mouthed him, but even they never hinted at being 'treated like a whore.' Mostly, they thought he was screwed up, unreliable, and would never have a lasting relationship with anyone. He didn't wholly disagree with that assessment, but he had changed quite a bit since they'd known him.

A chill suddenly swept over him and a rock of dread dropped into his belly. *Could he have meant Izabel?*

He shook his head. Not the way she smiled at him that afternoon, with her green eyes sparkling and her fingers entwined with his. No way would Izabel have said that.

He inhaled sharply as another dark thought struck him. *Could the protester be the man she'd left behind in Seattle?*

He shook his head again. No, she would've said something when she saw him at the winery protest right after she arrived.

"But who else could he have meant?" Zack grumbled. He turned onto his side and tried not to think any further along those lines. Izabel was meeting him for dinner tomorrow, and he intended she understood exactly how sorry he was for ghosting her the way he had this last week—he'd *show* her...if she'd let him.

Besides, he told himself, *the shooting and what happened tonight doesn't really matter anymore.* The protester had been a troublemaker and, apparently, the mystery of who had been responsible for shooting him had been solved. Now the man was in jail and wouldn't see a judge for several days. Zack had nothing to worry about except making up with Izabel.

He smiled as he closed his eyes, and with thoughts of Izabel's warm kisses, he drifted off to sleep.

CHAPTER 24

Nerves zinged and fluttered around inside Izabel all day. She'd been so anxious to see Zack tonight that she'd barely gotten any work done on the winery opening—though she'd already done enough to ensure a large turnout for opening weekend in two weeks' time.

She loved doing this—helping people, helping her friends realize a dream. What she really hated was the large black and purplish bruise darkening Zack's right eye when he'd arrived at the Brodys' front door to pick her up for their dinner date.

"Oh, my..." she'd said as she reached up to touch his cheek and dread mixed with remorse wrapped around her chest. "What happened to your face? Does it hurt badly?"

He shook his head and explained the incident that had occurred the night before. Her first thought had been that Chris Richards was to blame, and her guilt for not mentioning his presence to anyone grew even heavier. She tried once again to envision the scene but struggled to do so. She wouldn't have expected Chris to be so physical in his violence, but who else would do such a thing?

"No big deal," Zack had replied as he pulled her hand away from his face and led her to his truck. "I barely feel it; believe me, I've had worse. Luckily, I forgot my phone and Aaron came looking for me. I'm not sure the guy would've been arrested if he hadn't."

Thankfully, Zack filled in more details on the situation as he assisted her into the truck and then hurried to slide in beside her.

"You even know the guy," Zack continued with a sardonic chuckle as he pushed the key into the ignition and started his truck.

Izabel's stomach turned to ice and she fumbled over words in her head, unable to form even one simple question as she stared over at him. He didn't seem to notice as he shifted the truck into gear and headed down the road.

Zack glanced over at her as he drove. "You remember the big protester with the beard? The one who tried to start a fight with me when we went to the winery the first time?"

Shoulders sagging in relief, Izabel had nodded.

"Well, he throws a mean punch."

"*He's* the one who attacked you?"

"Yep," Zack had said as they sped down the road to town. He shrugged and gave her a mischievous smile that made her heart speed up. "I guess he really doesn't like me."

"And he hasn't said anything as to why?"

Zack shook his head. "No, not really. He shouted a bunch of crap at me while he was kicking my ass, but nothing that made sense."

Izabel had sighed, thankful the incident hadn't been worse, and that her ex-boyfriend hadn't been involved. Maybe her imagination really had gotten the better of her when she saw that car yesterday.

The rest of the drive to town had been filled with pleasant conversation about the ranch and the Brodys' plans. After speaking with Cord and Cade a few days before, Zack was on board with everything they'd suggested, and Izabel had been more than excited to tell him everything she had planned.

"Wow, you really do know your stuff," he'd said. "We'd better do a little more planning for opening weekend." He'd smiled at her with so much pride and affection that her heart flipped in her chest. Still, there was a tension in his shoulders that said—more than his words had—just how much this project weighed on him. She knew he had no more money, that he would need to borrow quite a lot from his friends to finish the winery and prepare for the big opening, as well as pay his new staff and the ranch mortgage, but she was good at what she did, and she intended to ensure their success, especially Zack's.

A short time later, they'd found a booth at Betsy's Diner, ordered their meal, and ate while they continued the business conversation, and Zack took every opportunity to flirt.

Izabel decided she really liked the diner. The comfortable lighting, photographs of landscapes from in and around Meriton, and the old-fashioned tablecloths with depictions of farm animals and country life gave the place a homey feel she truly enjoyed. That was, until Zack set his credit card on the table beside their dinner bill.

Izabel frowned. "You know, after everything you and your family have done for me, I should be paying for dinner."

He shook his head. "Oh, no. My momma would give me a serious tongue-lashing if I ever let a woman pay for a dinner date, especially when I invited her."

Her cheeks warmed at the implication and she smile at him. "That's sweet, but a little antiquated, don't you think?"

"Maybe," he replied with a shrug, "but that's how I was raised, and I'm not changing now. Besides, I want to take care of it tonight. Will you let me do that and just say thank you?"

She chuckled. "I can do that, but tell me something in return."

His eyebrows rose and curiosity sparked in his warm brown eyes. "What do you want to know?"

"Why *did* you invite me to dinner tonight?"

Looking down at the table, he lifted his shoulder in a casual shrug and then slouched back in his seat. "Do I need another reason beyond wanting to spend time with you?"

"No... I suppose not."

"Then why ask?"

She tilted her head. "You seem nervous."

He glanced at her with that sideways grin of his and her heart fluttered in her chest. "That obvious, huh?"

"A little," she replied. "I get the feeling there's more to this dinner than just *spending time*."

He sighed. "You're right; there is." He paused and they both fell silent as the waitress approached to take his card and the bill to the register. As soon as she was out of earshot, Zack pushed the napkin he'd been fiddling with away and met Izabel's gaze. "I guess I'm trying to make up for my bad behavior toward you lately."

"You already apologized for that."

He nodded. "I know, but it seemed…inadequate."

Wanting to relieve the shadow of doubt she'd seen in his eyes, she reached across the table to squeeze his fingers. "I've already forgiven you and moved on, and you should do the same. The last thing I want is for you to keep punishing yourself over something that's been resolved."

He inhaled and shook his head as he released his breath in a rush. "But it's not."

Her brows drew down in confusion. "What do you mean?"

He opened his mouth as if to speak, but then dropped his gaze and shook his head, obviously having an internal debate.

"Zack?"

He sighed, but then sat forward and straightened his shoulders. When he met her eyes again, he looked determined. "What has my sister told you about me? About my past?"

"Emmy?" Izabel shrugged. "She didn't say much, just that you're a good man who's had some hard times in his life."

His eyebrows shot up and bewilderment filled his whiskey-colored eyes. "That's it? She didn't give any other details about my 'hard times?'"

Izabel paused, quickly thinking back on the conversations she'd had with his sister, and then shook her head. "Nope. Aside from her teasing and an occasional snide comment about brothers being a pain, that was all she said."

"What about any of the other ladies you've met here? Did they tell you anything?"

"No, everyone pretty much said the same thing as your sister," Izabel replied. "I was nosy and asked what had happened, but they all said to ask you."

An astonished chuckle slipped through his lips. "I've got to say, I'm surprised…and grateful for their discretion."

Izabel stared at him, uncertain of what to say. What could be so bad that a whole circle of friends had to protect him from the past?

"Did you…hurt someone?" She almost said 'kill' instead of 'hurt,' but she couldn't force it out. She couldn't believe Zack would purposely hurt anyone.

His eyes snapped to her face but then he suddenly glanced around before he shook his head, not looking at her. "It's not like that..." he said slowly. "Not the way *you* mean, anyway."

"Then what is it that you've been carrying around for so long? You can trust me, Zack. I won't tell anyone. Just talk to me."

That brought his eyes back to hers. His face softened into the sweet, yet slightly mischievous, grin that always made her heart beat faster.

"I know that, sweetheart," he said softly as he reached across the table and held his hand out for her to take. She slid her fingers over his much larger hand and smiled. She loved his hands—his long fingers and calloused palms, warm and strong and solid...just like Zack.

"Look, Izabel," he said, leaning over the table a little, "I like you…I like you a lot. I don't want there to be any confusion about that."

Warmth filled her chest. *Could he mean...?*

No, he doesn't do long-term. That reminder dissolved the pleasant feeling inside her and sent her heart crashing to her toes. Their tryst was just for fun. She couldn't let her heart get any more involved. Even as it was now, losing him would be painful, and the last thing she needed was to get in deeper and make it worse. He was used to this life—adept at loving and leaving with little heartache—but she wasn't and she wouldn't allow herself to become just another one of his conquests. She wanted more, but she was unsure if he'd be the one to give it to her. So far, all he'd shown was an attraction to her body. He did seem to enjoy her company, but there hadn't been any talk about a future for them together.

Her chest tightened and a coldness enveloped her as fear and self-preservation induced her response.

Izabel chuckled. "You *like* me? You mean, like all your *other* women?"

The smile fell from his lips and his eyes turned hard. "Is that what you think? That the man you've been with isn't the real me, but, instead, that damn Casanova everyone has labeled me as? That I'm just playing around with you until the next woman comes along?"

Izabel's stomach twisted and she winced at the pain she read in his eyes. Was she wrong? Was he trying to tell her he wanted more, too?

The silence between them lengthened as the waitress returned with Zack's credit card and a pen to sign the bill for their dinner. When the waitress wished them a good evening and left them alone, Izabel reached across the table, hoping he would give her his hand again. When he didn't, she just pressed her palms against the cool, smooth surface and focused all her attention on him.

"Please, Zack, don't pull away. I didn't mean that the way it sounded. I'm just feeling a little insecure and only teasing you a bit, but I can see now that this isn't the right time."

He wouldn't meet her eyes. "No, it's not."

"May we try that again?" she asked quietly.

Locking his gaze on her, he stared at her hard and she prayed her stupid fears and loose lips hadn't just messed up a good thing.

"Okay," he said and a small grin curled up the corners of his mouth.

Relief relaxed her muscles. "Okay. So, you said something about liking me?"

"Yes, I like you," he said, "a lot, and no, it's not the same as with anyone else."

Her answering smile felt a mile wide. "I like you too, Zack."

His grin broadened and he reached for her hand again. "I'm glad to hear that."

"I'm sorry if I hurt you," she murmured. "That's the last thing I want to do."

"Don't worry about it," he said, still smiling. "I've just grown a little over-sensitive about my past, though I should've expected something like that after all the things I've done."

She shook her head. "No, I was wrong. I'm just...a little afraid. But I won't let it happen again."

"I appreciate that," he said with a look that told her he understood her fear all too well, and then fell silent for a few moments.

He sobered a bit, staring at their joined hands as his thumb gently drew small circles on the back of her hand, sending shots of awareness through her body. Warmth and a growing tension swirled inside her, slowly making its way outward from her belly. Her breasts tingled with anticipation and another kind of heat began to build between her thighs.

"I'd like to get to know you better..." he said, his voice low and a little husky.

"Are you sure that's what you want?" she asked. "I'm not really a fling kind of girl, you know."

"Yes, I know."

"And you still want to take this to the next step?"

He nodded.

"You know that means a long-term commitment to one woman. To *me*."

"Yes, I know. I don't want any other woman, Izabel. I just want to be with you." His eyes bored into hers and the blaze of affection staring back at her was almost overwhelming.

"For how long?" she murmured as hope that she understood him correctly lodged in her throat.

"For as long as you'll have me."

The burn of tears filled her eyes and she struggled not to let them fall. "Oh, Zack..." She didn't know if she could squeak out another word through the thick emotion in her throat, so instead, she squeezed his hand.

Zack grinned. "Do you want to get out of here? Somewhere we can be alone and talk? I have a lot to share with you."

She smiled and nodded enthusiastically.

Something clouded his face and Izabel frowned.

"The only place we can be alone is at the cabin," he said, clearly concerned about her reaction to going back there.

Her stomach curled in on itself and her mouth felt suddenly dry, but she wasn't going to let fear sway her. "That's okay," she said, her voice a little raspier than she'd hoped.

"Are you sure?" he asked. "I don't want to take you there if the trauma–"

He halted when she shook her head.

"It's *okay*," she said, emphasizing the last two syllables. "I'm not saying I haven't had nightmares about you being shot—and not in the arm, either—but that place is too beautiful to be ruined by such ugliness. We'll face it and make new, wonderful memories…together."

Zack's smile broadened. "I can do that...but only if you're sure."

"I'm sure," she said, "but there is one thing..."

He frowned and a worried look wrinkled his brow. "And what's that?"

"We need to stop at a store before we go up there," she said in a teasing tone. "We're going to need protection this time." She gave him a pointed look and Zack laughed.

"Don't worry," he said as he patted his jacket pocket, "I've got that covered. I won't let us get carried away this time."

She grinned. "Good...not that the last time was awful or anything."

That comment only made Zack laugh harder. "No, my sweet goddess, it wasn't awful at all."

CHAPTER 25

The drive from the restaurant to the cabin was a silent one, but that didn't stop the electric tension from snapping and crackling between Zack and the gorgeous woman beside him. The sparks of desire that filled the cab were nearly a physical thing, and Zack fought his need to glance Izabel's way every few seconds to see how she handled the situation—because *he* felt totally out of his comfort zone. He wanted her desperately, but it was more than that—more than a need for her body, more than the need to give and receive pleasure. He wanted her smiles and laughter, her sorrows and tears, everything and anything that made her the woman she was. He wanted her in his future, to give this one-of-a-kind woman his heart and to cherish hers forever.

His fingers flexed uneasily on the steering wheel and guilt churned his stomach. Before he reaped any rewards, he needed to come clean, to tell her about his past and bare his wounded soul—to be as brave as she had been when sharing the pain she had overcome.

Just thinking about saying the words out loud caused a sheen of sweat to swath his skin. The rushing thoughts in his head on how to lay himself bare to her made small talk or even flirting difficult. When she'd scooted across the bench seat to rest her head on his shoulder and her little hand on his thigh, the surge of need that assailed him made forming intelligent sentences even harder.

Still, he had relished her closeness as they sped out of town, but he struggled to keep from physically responding to it. She was so damn beautiful—his golden goddess, come to Earth to enrich his life—and she was about to become all his.

Hell, he thought with a crooked grin, *in my mind, she's already mine.*

Thirty-some minutes after leaving the diner—and some speed limit breaking on his part—they pulled up to Zack's small cabin. The sun had already set behind the mountains, but the darkening blue sky had filled with oranges, pinks, and lavenders that stained the thin rows of fluffy clouds overhead.

Zack switched off the engine and, leaving the key in the ignition, he hugged the steering wheel as he looked around the clearing, automatically checking for any possible danger—even though he knew the threat had passed.

Wondering about Izabel's reaction to being back here, he finally allowed himself to glance over and found she was also scoping out the area. She didn't appear nervous exactly, more determined than anything else. Her courage humbled him. Her inner strength brought a smile to his face and pride swelled within his chest. Most of the women he'd cozied up with over the years wouldn't have agreed to come back here, let alone seem undisturbed by returning to the scene of such a traumatic event. She was a wonder of a woman, and he made a mental note to let her know just how wonderful he thought she was every single day.

He took a deep breath and let it go in a huff. "Well, we're here."

She grinned up at him. "It's as beautiful as I remember."

"No residual nervousness or...fear?"

She lifted her trim shoulders in a nonchalant shrug. "A little trepidation, but it'll pass. I want to reclaim this place as our own, Zack, so don't worry about me."

"A goddess in command of herself and her surroundings," he murmured and chuckled when she lowered her eyes demurely, her cheeks darkening with a pink blush, even as a shy grin tugged up her luscious lips. "Stay right here and I'll get the door."

Before he could give in to the temptation to kiss her again, Zack jumped out of the truck and hurried around to open her door. He held out his hand and then helped her down from the cab. Their bodies brushed as she slid off the seat. She looked up at him as her feet settled on the ground, and they stood, staring into each other's eyes, for a long moment where he almost forgot to breathe. His gaze dropped to her lips, and he nearly groaned when the tip of her pink tongue swept over the lush surface. His blood heated while his heart thundered in his chest, and the growing pulse in his jeans echoed in time with the rapid tempo pounding inside him. The repetitive litany in his head beat along with both: *Kiss her. Kiss her. Kiss her, now!* He couldn't deny the command for long. He met her gaze again and the look of trust and desire reflected in those green depths pushed Zack up and over his wall of restraint. Giving in to his body's demands, he lowered his head and kissed her.

Her hands slipped around his neck and into his hair, clutching him to her as she returned his ardor with an equal amount of her own. She slanted her head and he deepened the kiss as his arms pulled her in and tightened around her. He wanted to be closer—to not have any barriers between them, to feel the satiny smoothness of her soft brown skin, to taste its sweetness, and to bring her pleasure in the most intimate of ways. He could easily lose himself in her, forget everything he'd done and all his failures—and he would—but first...he had things to tell her.

Pulling back, he rested his forehead against hers as they tried to catch their breath after the flare of passion had stolen it from them. He bracketed her face with his big hands, nearly engulfing her head, and a sudden sense of protectiveness washed over him. *Such a trim, delicate woman who could so easily be hurt, so easily be lost to me.* The thought wrenched his heart, as if invisible hands had reached inside his chest and twisted it, hard. The pain of it nearly buckled his knees.

No, he thought, *I won't let that happen.*

Zack straightened and met her questioning gaze. Her chest still rose and fell with her heavy breaths and her pulse fluttered wildly beneath his thumbs, but he could not let her beauty and his need distract him. He had something to do.

He took her hand and without another word, led her to the cabin.

Once inside, he took her coat, set it aside with his hat, and steered her to the long couch. An image of how Izabel had looked lying on those cushions—bare, except for her panties, as she reached for him—popped into his head. She'd been so beautiful, so strong, and she'd wanted him—and from every indication, she still did. His cock swelled at that memory, making his jeans even tighter than before—just as knowing she still wanted him brought a sense of wholeness to his heart he hadn't felt in years.

Izabel sat on the couch and he settled in beside her. Still holding her hand, he turned slightly so they faced each other.

"I get the sense there's something more on your mind than an intimate evening alone," Izabel murmured, her gaze intent on his face.

Jitters jumped to life in his stomach, but he refused to be a coward. He nodded. "Yes, I...I need to tell you…about—" His throat closed and the words halted like a radio that had been switched off.

A line of concern appeared between Izabel's brows. "Zack? Are you all right?"

He nodded and tried to swallow the knot of regret and pain that had blocked his throat.

"I'm okay," he said, his voice a low rasp. He'd known this would be hard, but Izabel was worth the heartache that bringing up the past would cause, and he wanted her to understand, to truly know the man she wanted a commitment from. "I guess I'm just a little nervous."

She squeezed his hand and reached up to brush her fingers against his cheek. "No need to be nervous, handsome. I know there's something you're hiding from me. I know it's not good, but if you want to tell me, I want to hear it. Though, I'll wait, if you need me to."

He nodded, understanding what she meant—no more secrets between them, no barriers to keep them apart, nothing he could use to push her away. But only if he was ready.

"I don't want to wait. I need to tell you about...my nickname. About how, and why, the Casanova Cowboy came about," he said quickly before his emotions stopped him.

* * *

Izabel's heart stuttered in her chest. She had wondered about his past—what had caused him so much pain, and why he'd tried to lose himself in women and sex to avoid what he didn't want to think about—and he was going to tell her. On his own, with no prodding from her.

Part of her was proud of him for broaching the difficult topic, but another part feared what he would say. How would it affect them? Would it change how she looked at him? It could, especially if he'd done something so heinous or dishonorable that she couldn't forgive him.

No, she thought, *no matter what he had been, Zack would never purposely hurt someone.* Whatever it was, he hadn't planned it, hadn't intended to cause pain for anyone else. She believed in him, trusted him, and prayed she hadn't been fooled by a man a second time.

"Back in high school," he began, his eyes focused on their clasped hands, "before I became…what I am, I was a very different guy."

Without lifting his head, he glanced at her quickly, and she gave him an encouraging smile.

"I was good at sports and was kind of popular, but I was also quiet and, believe it or not, a little shy."

Izabel grinned, picturing a younger version of the handsome man beside her—all lanky arms and legs just waiting for him to grow into the tall, strong rancher he'd become. She would bet the last of her meager savings that he'd been a lot more than 'kind of popular' but then again, maybe he hadn't noticed.

"When I meet Debbie, though, things changed."

The way he said the girl's name was almost reverent, like a prayer—or a plea for her return.

The tone of his voice blanketed Izabel's mood and her heart grew heavy at the sound. She waited for him to continue, but he paused for so long, Izabel feared he wouldn't start again.

"Debbie?" she coaxed.

He swallowed and nodded, but he didn't look up. "Debbie Jensen. Debs. She moved to town my sophomore year and completely changed my life."

"Sounds wonderful," Izabel said, for lack of anything else to say, and though she didn't begrudge his prior happiness, she couldn't help the pang of jealousy that stabbed through her chest.

"It was," he said sadly. "She was so damn pretty, smart as a whip, and so feisty. I was wrapped around her finger the first time I saw her." A soft grin pulled at his lips. "And she definitely kept me on my toes."

He paused again, but this time Izabel stayed quiet, anxious to hear what came next.

"In case you haven't already guessed, Debs was my high school sweetheart." He gently squeezed Izabel's hand and met her eyes. "But I don't want you to think I'm still holding a torch for her or anything, because I'm not."

Izabel nodded. "But something happened to her, didn't it?"

"Yes," he said, his eyes dropping to their hands. His thumbs swirled small circles on the backs of hers, as if that small movement calmed and anchored him to her, as well as to the present. He shook his head at something and then licked his firm lips before he spoke again. "We did everything together, were basically inseparable. Hell, at the time, I thought we'd grow old together..." He huffed a bitter laugh. "Obviously, that didn't happen."

He shrugged as if the pain in his voice didn't exist. This strong, sensitive man clearly didn't want to show how much he was hurting—how much he'd been hurting for years.

"What happened, Zack?" she asked quietly.

His breath seemed to halt, but then he released a heavy sigh and continued. "Like I said, we did everything together, and for the last two years of high school, we'd talked about attending Montana State University as a couple. We had planned to rent a house or apartment together, to study and work through everything together. We'd had it all planned and our futures were mapped out. Until..."

He stopped and swallowed, as if afraid of what came next. Izabel waited, letting him tell his story in his own time.

"I was so happy then," he said quietly. "I would've done anything for her, except...leave my family and the ranch."

"Is that what she asked you to do?"

"Sort of," he said with a slight shrug. "She said she'd changed her mind. That she wanted to get out of our small town, out of Montana, out of the 'backwoods hinterland' as she called it."

"Did she break up with you then?" Izabel asked gently, knowing how much first-time love affairs could hurt.

"Not exactly," he said. "She asked me to go with her. Maybe I had missed it somewhere—the hints about what she wanted—or maybe I just didn't listen. Maybe I didn't want to, but when she brought it up the summer after graduation, while we were cuddling in the barn—after rolling in the hay, so to speak—it had floored me. I'd been stunned and a little pissed..." He looked up, and Izabel was shocked by the sheen of tears in his eyes. "I love it here, I always have, and I never wanted to leave. I told her that—had never kept it a secret—but she said she felt differently. That the attitudes of the people here made her feel stifled and that she'd been accepted to one of the big schools in California." His voice cracked and he paused to swallow the bitterness the memories brought up.

"So she left Montana *and* you?"

He shook his head. "Not exactly."

Izabel frowned. "I don't understand."

Zack sighed and she realized his hands were shaking.

"That evening in the barn, we fought and said some awful things to each other." He paused, not looking at Izabel, seeming to gather his courage.

Izabel's heart felt like a stone in her chest. He blamed himself for his ex-girlfriend's choices; she could see it in the way he hung his head in shame, in the hard line of his jaw, and in the defeated droop of his broad shoulders. As if he had done something wrong to make him unworthy, or worse, that he hadn't been enough for her to stay. "It wasn't your fault," Izabel murmured. "She made her choice for herself, not because of you."

"But it was my fault," he nearly shouted, and when he met her gaze, Izabel's heavy heart clenched as tears fell from his warm, whiskey-colored eyes. "And that's not all."

"How?" she asked softly, wiping the dampness from his cheeks. "How was it your fault?"

He shook his head and dropped his gaze. "I said terrible, hurtful things. I wanted to lash out in any way I could to ease my pain. I didn't think about her or how she might be feeling. She tried to explain, but I wasn't listening. I…I told her to go, that I didn't need her. I made her cry. I made her…hate me…"

Izabel gripped his hands in both of hers, brought them to her mouth, and kissed his knuckles in an attempt to support and encourage him. To give him her strength while he crumbed before her eyes.

"She ran from me," he said quietly. "Tears streamed from her eyes as she dashed out to her little car. I should have gone after her, apologized, done something, *anything*, to keep her from leaving."

"You couldn't have stopped her from leaving if she wanted to go, Zack. Love isn't a prison. You know that."

He nodded. "Yeah, I do. I did back then too, but it wasn't love that stopped me. It was pride, anger, and a sense of betrayal that still lives inside me now. But none of that was why I should've stopped her."

Izabel shook her head, her brows drawn low. She didn't understand what he was trying to tell her.

He looked up and the devastation she read in his deep brown eyes broke her heart.

"I killed her, Izzy," he croaked, his voice so rough, she barely understood his words.

A soft gasp escaped Izabel's lips and her hand instinctively pressed against her chest.

"If I'd been more forgiving," Zack continued, "more open to her needs, we could've talked it out and come up with something we both could've lived with. But instead, I pushed her away and broke her heart…and she died because of me."

"You mean s-she's…actually dead? That's not just a metaphor?"

"Yes." His head hung lower than before. "She was sobbing because of my cruelty when she ran from the barn." He shook his head. "There was no way she could've seen the road clearly, especially not at night, but I let her go."

"A car accident?"

He nodded. "She took a corner too fast and lost control. Her car went off the road and rolled down the embankment. She wasn't wearing her seatbelt and was thrown from the car. The car...crushed her as it rolled over her on the way down the hill, but she didn't die right away." His voice sounded raw. "That would have been a mercy, but no... She suffered for God knows how long, all while I sat at home, stubbornly refusing to go after her. She bled out on the roadside, in the dark…alone."

His last word was an anguished whisper that burned through Izabel's chest. Without a word, she dropped his hands and wrapped her arms around his shoulders. A sob escaped him as she cradled him in her arms, holding him and aching for his loss.

His arms slid around her waist and he pulled her closer as he rested his cheek on her shoulder.

"I don't deserve this," he whispered, even as his hold on her tightened. "I don't deserve to be happy. I don't deserve you."

"That's not true, Zack," Izabel said as she sat back and cradled his face in her hands. "The two of you fought and she left. That doesn't make her death your fault."

"I could've gone after her," he cried. "I could've helped her, gotten help, something!"

"I hate to say this," Izabel said slowly, "and please, don't be angry or upset with me, but from your description, I doubt she would've survived...even if you did go after her and tried to help. The car crushed her when it rolled over her body; there wasn't any way you could've saved her."

He nodded and his stiff anger seemed to drain out of him as his shoulders rounded. "The cops said the same thing when they took my statement." He paused briefly, and when he continued, his voice was so low and hoarse, she barely understood him, "But if I'd gone after her, I could've apologized. I could've done that much, at least. I could've been with her when she'd needed me the most...and I could've told her I was sorry before it was too late."

Izabel cupped his jaw, her heart aching for him—and, if she was honest, a little angry that he'd spent so many years blaming himself. "If she loved you the way it sounds like she did, then she already forgave you, Zack. She never would've wanted you to torture yourself like this. Don't you think she'd have wanted you to be happy?"

"I suppose so..."

Izabel smiled sadly. "And don't you think she'd want you to forgive yourself as well?"

He sighed and looked up. "I don't know if I can."

Izabel dropped her hands to her thighs. "How long has it been?"

He blinked slowly and brushed at the dampness on his cheeks. "Almost twelve years."

"Have you told anyone else about this?"

"No," he said, shaking his head.

Her hands curled into fists in her lap and her chest ached for all he'd suffered alone. "Why not?"

It took him a moment to answer. "At first, I couldn't bring myself to admit my part in what had happened. My friends tried to talk to me, but I got angry with them. My parents knew I was upset and tried to help, assuming my change in temperament was because of the terrible loss, but I wouldn't let them. My sisters..." He shook his head at the mystery of Grace and Emmy. "They'd somehow guessed that I didn't tell them everything. Even when they cornered me in the barn to ask me point blank what I was hiding, I couldn't bring myself to talk about any of it.

"Eventually, things moved on, as they always do. People ceased to mention the accident or Debs around me, but I never forgot what I'd done."

Izabel cocked her head. "Don't you think you've punished yourself enough? Twelve years is a very long time."

Looking away, Zack rubbed his eyes. "I don't know."

"I do," she said, cupping his jaw with her hand, turning his face to hers and tracing his lips with her thumb. "It's time for you to move on, too. To let the past go."

"I can't forget—"

"I'm not asking you to forget," she interrupted, shaking her head. "I'm asking you to *forgive*. Forgive yourself so you can finally live the life you were meant to. So you don't have to pretend anymore. So you *can* find happiness again."

He pulled her hand from his face and gripped it in his lap as he stared back at her. "Will you...help me?"

His voice was so low and ragged and his eyes so desperate, it rattled everything inside her and wrung her heart with empathy. All she wanted was to help. She understood why he blamed himself, why he became the Casanova Cowboy—because he felt unworthy of love or happiness.

"If you'll let me, I'll do whatever I can."

His breath rushed through his lips in a relieved sigh. "You mean that?"

"Yes."

"And all the... I mean, me being a... Y-You don't mind my alter ego and what he made me?"

"You mean the Casanova Cowboy?" she asked with a tiny tip to her lips.

He nodded, his dark eyes intent on her face, and then he swallowed, as if bracing himself for the worst.

"You said that's not who you are; that you don't want to be that person anymore. Is that still true?"

"Yes," he croaked, then cleared his throat. "I want a normal life, Izabel. To have a wife, a family, and to have my kids grow up in this town, just like I did. There's no room for the Casanova in that life."

She smiled. "I don't care about your past, Zack. I only care about you."

He returned her smile and gently pulled her into his embrace. "I still don't deserve you."

"Yes, you do," she said next to his ear. "Just like I deserve a good man who will treat me right. A man like you, Zack."

His arms tightened. "You have me, goddess. For as long as you want me, I'm all yours. Only yours."

Tears stung her eyes at his profession of devotion. A warm feeling of completeness filled her chest and happiness swelled within her heart. But she wanted more. She wanted his hands and mouth on her skin, with no barriers between them while they sealed their commitment to each other. She pulled back to look into his soulful whiskey eyes. "Show me, Zack," she said breathily. "Show me how much you want me."

A devilish grin curled his lips and the skin at the corners of his shining eyes crinkled with delight. "Yes, ma'am," he drawled and brought his lips to hers.

Every inch of her body came alive the moment he kissed her. Heat flamed within her and her skin became sensitive, desperate for this man's touch. She squirmed onto his lap, closer than she had been, and he hummed with delight at her sudden nearness.

Slowly, Zach removed her clothes while he continued to kiss her lips, her neck, her collarbone, until she lay naked on the couch, gazing up at him. His eyes seemed to burn as he stared down at her—first at her face, then sliding down to linger on her breasts, and then to the dark thatch of curls at the apex of her legs. Her nipples tightened at the amber fire burning in his eyes, but he seemed hesitant. She held out her arms and beckoned, "Come here, Zack."

In the next instant, a surprised squeak burst from her kiss-bruised lips, when he scooped her up into his brawny arms and carried her to the bed.

"We're going to do this right," he murmured as he yanked back the blankets and gently placed her on the bed in the next room. "My goddess deserves better than...the couch."

Izabel caught his slight pause and knew what he didn't say—that she deserved better than *him.*

Aside from his half-open shirt, Zack was still fully clothed, but she could feel the heat of his body as he hovered over her. She wanted him closer with nothing in the way.

"I don't care where we are," she said, pushing his shirt from his shoulders and wrapping her arms around his neck, "as long as I'm with you."

A slow grin curved his sexy mouth and he quickly shook free of the shirt dangling from his wrists. Gently, he tugged her arms from his neck and removed the rest of his clothing before hurrying to the bed, her eyes drinking in every hard line, admiring the flex and bunch of muscle, and his impressive size in this amorous state. Something low in her belly twinged so hard it was almost painful, but anticipation drowned out the bad and left her mouth watering as she waited for him to join her on the bed.

Once he slipped beneath the covers, he gathered her close to his chest and Izabel closed her eyes with a grateful sigh. She loved how his big body and strong arms made her feel small, cherished, and safe all at once. How his skin almost seemed to burn hers, fusing them together. And she adored his significant arousal as it pushed against her belly. Knowing that he wanted her only made her heart beat even faster, but he lay very still, almost rigid, as if preparing to be hurt. She looked up into his eyes and saw a plethora of emotions shimmering in their whiskey-colored depths.

She could guess his thoughts, but she didn't want him to pull away, so she touched him instead. Her thumb traced over his lower lip as his short beard tickled her palm. "I want you, Zack," she whispered, then strained upward to press her lips to his.

In seconds, his arms tightened around her, his fingers delved into her hair, and his mouth slanted over hers to deepen the kiss.

They had kissed several times over their nearly three-month acquaintance and every one of them had been hot and needy, so full of desire that it could have singed their eyebrows had it been real flame. But something about this kiss was different. She couldn't put her finger on it exactly, but Zack seemed to let himself go, as if truly accepting what he had been and embracing what he wanted to become. It was sweet and sultry, dark and full of light, and everything in between. He had opened his heart to her, bared the pain and regret of his past, and now he seemed to be inviting her in for the very first time.

And it made her love him all the more.

Slipping her arms around his sides, she traced the line of his spine down to the hard, sculpted muscles of his rear end. She squeezed him, letting her nails dig in just a little, while pulling him closer. She pressed her hips to his, rubbing against his thick, hot shaft.

He sucked in a gasp and pulled back just enough to end that tantalizing kiss. She felt his long body shiver as he pressed his forehead to hers and tried to catch his breath.

"Oh, what you do to me, goddess," he said, his voice low and raspy. "I'm trying to do right by you, but I don't know how long I can hold back with you doing things like that."

"Then don't," she told him, placing a quick kiss on his lips. "I want you, now, Zack. I don't want to wait. Fast and hard and wild will be perfect right now. Can you do that?"

His lips quirked. "I can do whatever you want, baby, but let me please you first."

He brought his head down to kiss her again as he rolled her onto her back. A sudden urgency seemed to hover around them, a need to touch, kiss, lick, and thrust—to seal their commitment to each other, for both of them to claim the other as their own. His mouth was hot on her skin, his tongue smooth and enticing as he sucked and nibbled her nipples—one after the other until she writhed beneath him, panting with increasing desire.

Then he took her lips again as his big hand slid down between their bodies to the triangle of damp curls between her legs, where he touched her exactly where she needed him to. His long fingers thrummed her sensitive nub, sending shocks of pleasure throughout her whole body. Her breast grew heavier, the tips hard and aching, wanting more of his attention—and they got it.

She whimpered when his fingers stopped their strumming of her delicate, yet now swollen flesh, but moaned when they moved back to her breasts. He kissed and licked his way down her body until he reached the apex of her thighs. And when he simply lay there, she looked down.

His big, long-fingered hands cupping her breasts was one of the most erotic sights she'd ever witnessed, but the look of awe and outright hunger on his face as he stared at her most private area had her squirming on the bed.

"Zack," she whispered intently and then gasped when he lifted his burning eyes to hers. A barely controlled passion blazed in those amber depths, along with a yearning and possessiveness that she'd never seen before. She frowned, but the slow grin that curved his mouth rose goosebumps across her skin.

"You are the most beautiful thing I've ever seen, Izabel," he murmured, his warm breath sweeping over her heated flesh, making her shiver.

"I bet you say that to all the girls," she joked in an unsteady voice.

His face turned serious and he shook his head. "No, I may have given compliments, but I've never said that, and as long as you want me, I will never say it to another soul."

The somberness of his words washed away any doubt that may have still lingered in the dark corners of her mind. He was giving himself to her, all of him, without reservation. That freely given devotion and his open vulnerability touched her more deeply than she'd ever known she could be. Her heart swelled, filling her chest almost to the point of pain.

"I know, Zack," she said, hoping to reassure him.

He drop his chin in a brief nod that implied something like, "Good," and then grinned at her again, right before he leaned in and used his tongue to trace around her needy flesh.

She moaned with pleasure and dropped her head to the mattress. He had a very talented tongue, and the heat from his mouth drove her wild as he licked and suckled her.

Minutes passed, or maybe it was hours, she didn't know, because Zack teased and tantalized her until she couldn't think. All she could do was feel, and with each touch, he took her higher, edging closer to the brink of something truly wonderful.

When he slid one long finger inside her and then a second, stretching her while pleasuring her, she moaned even louder. It felt so good, what he was doing to her, but she wanted more. More of him inside her, his body crushing hers. She needed his heat burning through her until they both went up in flames.

She was about to beg him to take her fully when her muscles tensed and she hovered on the edge of something thrilling.

"Umm," he hummed against her slick folds, and the vibration, along with his seductive mouth and those slippery fingers, drove her over the edge into a glorious world of light and more than pleasant sensations. She screamed with ecstasy, and he kept the waves of sensual bliss crashing through her until she slowly came back to herself.

Breathing in deep gasps, Izabel gradually drifted back to earth as the man who had driven her to paradise with his surprisingly adept carnal skillset pulled away from her. She moaned her displeasure as he leaned over to grab his jeans from the floor, but then smiled slightly when she realized what he was doing. *Protection.* She'd told him they needed to use it this time. A part of her wanted to forget it and continue as they had been, but she knew he wouldn't do that. He was protecting her from any unwanted consequences of their union, but would they really be unwanted?

Having shielded his length in the condom he'd pulled from his pocket, Zack grinned at her as he crawled up her body to kiss her once more. She could taste herself on his lips as his talented tongue delved deeply into her mouth. Responding wholeheartedly to the play, she wrapped her arms around his neck and pulled him closer. Despite her attempts, however, he wouldn't lower himself any farther. She arched her back until the smattering of hair on his chest tickled her tight nipples, but he still resisted her urging. Instead, he propped himself up on his elbows, keeping his body above hers, while he kissed her silly, and no matter what she did, she couldn't get any closer to the seductive heat of his well-hewn body.

Just when she wanted to scream in frustration, she felt the head of his erection slip through her folds. Not yet demanding entrance, but sliding back and forth over her, slicking his cock with her juices and over-stimulating her wanton desires.

How could she still be this hot, this turned-on? Especially after the extraordinary climax he'd just given her? But the sensations were there, growing ever more intense as he slid along her moist flesh. With each pass, he taunted her swollen nub, making her whimper and cry out with the molten need to have him inside her.

"Please, Zack," she cried against his lips. "Please..."

But he held back, and she wanted to cry in desperation. He was more than ready to take her—she could feel his iron stiffness and the smooth satin of his skin, the enticing heat of it as he skimmed his length over her.

When he finally lifted his head to look down into her eyes, she sucked in a needed breath before she met his gaze. What she read on his face made her heart flip and flutter in her chest. So much emotion, so much love, spilled from his amber eyes that she felt the burn of tears in her own. How could she ever have doubted this man's heart? It was there now, in his eyes, begging her to stay, to love him. He didn't say the words, but in that moment, she could feel his affection all around her, and she believed in it.

"My goddess," he murmured and she cupped his face in her palm.

"My cowboy," she replied with a smile that seemed to stretch from ear to ear. Because he was hers and she was his. There was no doubt about how she felt for him now, and there was no going back.

Laying beneath him, she stared up into his expressive gaze and hoped he could read all the feelings rolling through her by the expression on her face. She hadn't noticed how still his body had become, but when the tip of his cock pressed against her entrance, her breathing stopped. A second later, she gasped. He was inside her, all the way to the hilt, and he held himself there while she drew in deep breaths and grew more accustomed to his girth.

He brushed back a stray lock of her curly hair and searched her face. "Did I hurt you?" he asked, a wrinkle of worry appearing between his brows.

Smiling, she shook her head. "No, just a pleasant surprise."

He chuckled, the deep sound rumbling through his chest. "Good."

Then he began to move and Izabelle lost all thought. The only thing that mattered was this man and how he made her feel.

How *much* she felt scared her, but it also felt...right. The way he stretched her, filling her completely. The heat and sensation his movements created inside her. The way he looked into her eyes, as if she was the most beautiful, most precious, most loved woman on the planet. All of it filled her heart and brought a lump of tender emotion to her throat.

This time, when her orgasm came, he was right there with her, staring into her eyes until his body gave one last plunge deep inside her. Then his head flung back, eyes tightly closed, and he groaned, "Oh, Izabel!"

Then he collapsed over her, his arms sliding around her and locking her to him, but she didn't mind. She clung to him just as tightly.

That had been the most wonderful experience she'd ever had. Her heart was so warm and light, as if it wanted to float out of her chest.

She gently stroked his back, tracing the muscles and then the line of his spine, all the way to the chiseled curve of his backside and back again. Despite wanting to tell him how she felt, she held back, a little afraid of the extent of her feelings for him now.

They lay quietly together, neither wishing to move, until Zack chuckled.

"What's so funny?" Izabel asked, slightly offended that he'd be laughing after something so precious.

"That...was...fantastic!" Zack said, his voice muffled by the mattress beneath her. He kissed her neck and without losing their physical connection, he held her close and rolled onto his side.

When he pushed back her unruly hair to look into her face with the brightest, happiest smile she'd ever seen, a little of her trepidation dissipated.

"Did you enjoy yourself?" he asked.

"You can't tell by the look on my face?" she teased. "Or my screams of utter ecstasy?"

His cheeks turned rosy and he suddenly seemed shy. She touched his face, brushing some stray tendrils from his forehead. "You're right," she whispered with a smile she hoped conveyed everything she didn't say, "it was fantastic."

His smile returned and his arms tightened around her. "I've never felt that way before," he said as if in awe.

She frowned and pushed back a little. "You've never felt what way?"

He closed his eyes and inhaled slowly before he opened them again. "Happy. So damn happy, and content, and...well..." he shrugged and grinned, "happy!"

"I'm glad," she said, pulling him close again. "I'm happy, too."

"Will you stay?" he asked, his tone unsure.

She looked at him. "Of course, I'm staying. Especially if you're making breakfast in the morning again."

His eyes softened as they traced over her face. "Anything for you, goddess."

Her heart lurched and then settled, a warm fuzziness filling her chest. How did she get so lucky?

"You're a wonderful man, Zack MacEntier. Don't ever doubt that."

He lowered his gaze. "You may have to remind me of that every now and again in the future."

"Will we have a future?"

His eyes snapped up and his brows furrowed. "Absolutely."

She pushed against his shoulder until he rolled onto his back and then she rose and straddled him. "Then I'll be happy to remind you as often as you need me to," she said, leaning in to brush her lips against his. "I can start now, if you like?" She kissed his cheek and jaw, then nuzzled his neck.

He sucked in a deep breath. "That might be a good idea," he said as she nipped at his collarbone and his big hands slid slowly up her thighs. "I think I might've forgotten what you just said."

She giggled and lifted her head. "Well, we can't have that, now can we?"

He shook his head, his face a mask of mock solemnity.

"I care about you, Zack," she said, truly serious, "but I don't want to get hurt again, either."

His face softened, and he cupped her cheek in his large palm. "The last thing I want is to hurt you, Izabel. I know I don't have a great reputation, but if you'll give me a chance..." He sighed, his eyes shifting as if looking for the right words before settling on hers once more. "If you give me a chance, I'll make certain you never regret it."

"Just you and me?" she asked. "No...side deals?"

Damn, how she hated to ask that, but he smiled and slid his fingers through her springy hair.

"No, baby. Just you and me. *Only* you and me."

She nodded and leaned forward. "Good," she murmured right before she pressed her lips to his, sealing their promise to each other in yet another scorching kiss. Then she proceeded to remind him just how wonderful she thought he was, in exactly the same manner in which he'd favored her earlier.

Neither were disappointed as, after another round of slow rousing intercourse, they blissfully fell asleep in each other's arms.

CHAPTER 26

The loud cacophony of the state fair thrummed in Zack's ears. The music from the rides and gaming booths mixed with the chatter of the crowd, as well as the happy sound of children shouting, screaming, and laughing, gave the now well-lit field on the outside of town the feeling of a large backyard party. Lights flashed and people occasionally jostled Zack and Izabel as they slowly walked hand in hand through the carnival booths. They passed Zack's favorite waitress from Betsy's Diner, who greeted them with a big smile, and a little later, Zack nodded a hello to a couple bartenders from Tony's Tavern. The man had smiled in acknowledgement, but the woman looked unhappy about something. Zack hadn't noticed more than that as he continued through the throng with Izabel at his side. He didn't mind the crowd or how Emmy and his other friends kept flashing knowing smiles his way. How could he when he had the most wonderful and amazing woman at his side.

He grinned, thinking back to their time at the cabin last week. They'd stayed two days and spent the time building their connection and loving each other...sometimes several times a day. If it hadn't been for his responsibilities at the winery and the ranch, he'd have asked her to stay all week—and he knew she would've agreed. Unfortunately, that hadn't been the case.

How they'd ended up at the fair with all his friends, his sister, and her friends, he didn't know, but he couldn't make himself care.

"Step right up, sir," one of the booth barkers called, "and win that lovely lady a prize."

Zack glanced over and saw the man looking directly at him. He looked at Izabel and grinned. "You want a teddy bear, goddess?"

She turned to examine the offerings and then met his eyes with a smile of her own. "Maybe just a small one."

He chuckled and led her to the booth. The game consisted of throwing darts at small balloons. Not too hard, but Zack knew that the targets would move easily and their under-inflated state would make them harder to break—even with the, no doubt dull, point of a dart. Still, he was confident he could win her a prize.

"Which one do you want?" he asked her as they stopped at the short counter.

Her gaze drifted over the offerings, inspecting each for one that struck her fancy. He knew right away when she spotted it.

Her green eyes sparkled when she turned to him. "That one," she said excitedly, pointing at a small white teddy bear with yellow sunflowers against a blue background on the soles of its feet and the inside of its ears.

"Very country," he teased. "Am I rubbing off on you?"

"I happen to like the country, thank you," she replied in a snotty tone that was so out of place for Izabel, it had to be fake.

He laughed and she tossed him a bright grin. "I suppose you may have had a little to do with it, too," she admitted, squeezing his hand. "And I think the bear is cute."

"You're sure?"

"Yes!" She giggled and he had to smile. Her excitement was addictive. It bubbled in his chest, thrilling him and making him feel a little anxious, too. "How many balloons to win that little guy?" he asked the man behind the counter, nodding toward the little white bear.

"Ten," the man said. "And it's four darts for five dollars."

"Who-wee," Zack said jokingly as he turned to Izabel. "That's a pricey toy."

She raised an eyebrow at him. "Worried you can't do it?"

He laughed at her challenge—something he seemed to be doing a lot more of since Izabel entered his life. "Of course, I'll do it," he said, then turned to the vendor. "Give me twelve darts."

The man grinned, selected the requested darts from a collection of red plastic cups on a shelf behind him, and exchanged them for the cash in Zack's hand.

Carefully, Zack raised the first dart and lined up his shot. Calling on all the dart-throwing skills he'd honed over the years with his friends at the bar, he tossed the dart at the board full of colorful balloons. The small projectile struck a blue balloon straight on and with a *pop*, it lodged into the corkboard behind it.

"Yay!" Izabel clapped and cheered him on.

"What's going on?" Emmy asked as she and the others came up behind them.

"Zack's going to win me a teddy bear," Izabel said, the smile on her face a mile wide and so gorgeous, it nearly blinded Zack.

Emmy met her brother's gaze. "He is, huh?"

Zack shrugged and picked up another dart. Let Emmy imagine what she liked, he didn't care. Izabel cared for him and his world now seemed to finally be righted. It wasn't perfect, but it was damn close.

Seven more darts flew at the board, all ending with a resounding *pop* and a loud cheer from Izabel and their group of friends who had formed a half-circle around them.

Izabel grabbed his shirt and pulled him down for a kiss.

Their friends clapped and cheered even louder for that, and he swore Aaron let loose with a rebel yell.

When she pulled back, Izabel's sparkling green eyes opened slowly and her lips curled up mischievously. "Just for luck," she told him.

"Mmm," he murmured just loud enough for her ears. "I'm going to need more of those when we get to the top of the Ferris wheel after I win this bear." He tapped her nose gently with his finger and grinned. "A whole lot more afterward, too."

She smiled. "I think I can be persuaded..."

His grin widened and he turned back to the balloon-filled board. Happiness swelled inside him, something he hadn't felt in a very long time. It seemed strange that the weight he'd carried for so long had lightened considerably. He glanced at Izabel and his wounded heart clenched with the strength of his emotions. She was beautiful and wonderful and...so much more than he'd ever imagined he'd find in a woman. And she cared for him.

How did I get so lucky?

"Come on, Zack," Cade shouted from his right. "You got this, man."

"Yeah, Zack, we know you can do this." That came from Addie, who stood beside Izabel with Cade's arm around her shoulders. The others took the opportunity to shout encouragement, too. Even little Bethany, Cord's baby daughter, clapped for Zack from the safety of her daddy's arms.

"All right, all right," he said, waving his hands for quiet. "Give me some room here."

They quieted as Zack shook out his arms and tried to relax.

Taking aim, he tossed the next dart, confident in his ability. But this time, the dart slipped to the side and the red balloon remained intact.

"Oh...!" his crowd of friends cried as one.

Zack's confidence waned slightly, but he pushed it aside. He knew how these games worked. He just had to concentrate a little more.

"Don't let it get to you, Zack," Cord said from his side.

He nodded. "Thanks," he said to his friend and leaned over to Bethany. "And thanks to you too, little one." He kissed her cheek.

Bethany giggled, then shyly tucked her face against her father's neck, making everyone chuckle.

He straightened and concentrated on the balloons once more. Only two more to go to win that little stuffed bear, and he intended to succeed.

Raising the dart in his hand, he focused, took aim, and let it fly.

Another balloon popped and his audience cheered loudly.

"Only one more," Aaron said, slapping his back.

Zack nodded and picked up another dart. He only had two left, so he'd better make this work.

When he missed, he started to wonder if he would actually succeed, but he couldn't give up now. Blocking out the noises around him, he persisted. He centered all his attention on successfully throwing the final dart in his hand. He inhaled deeply, then released it slowly as the dart flew from his hand.

When the last balloon popped, a loud cheer erupted from their little group of friends as they all patted him on the back, congratulating him on his win. Zack pulled Izabel in for a big hug, spinning in a small circle before placing her on her feet again.

The vendor handed Zack the little teddy bear, and with a huge grin, he handed it to Izabel. She cuddled it against her chest, then threw her arms around his neck to pull him close once more.

She hugged him tight. "Thank you, Zack," she whispered beside his ear. "I love it."

"Good," he said as he pulled back. "'Cause I don't think it would look right in my room."

She laughed and twined her finger with his.

"Where are we off to now?" Aaron asked as they started to move through the fair once more.

"The Ferris wheel," Zack said with a meaningful look at Izabel. "I have a debt to collect."

Izabel grinned, her eyes like clear, sparkling pale green jewels as she looked up at him.

"To the Ferris wheel, then," Cade said as they all turned toward the ride.

They made it three steps when a voice called out, "Hello, Izabel."

Zack felt her whole body tense before she slowly turned toward the voice. She stopped abruptly and a long silence followed as she stared at the strange man before them. Zack glanced between the stranger and Izabel, unsure what was going on. At first, she seemed worried, afraid even, but a moment later, she frowned.

"What are you doing here, Chris?"

Chris? Zack thought, stunned. *Is this her old boyfriend?*

"I need to talk to you," Chris replied, glancing at Zack, his hazel eyes sizing him up, clearly unimpressed. "*Alone*."

"About what?" Izabel snapped. "I think we've said everything we needed to say to each other."

"Izabel, please. It's important."

"Sure it is," she said with disdain. "How dare you follow me and show up here to ambush me. After everything you did? You should go."

Zack's chest filled with pride for the strong woman at his side. He would've gladly brushed the man off for her, but she was doing a fine job all on her own. Instead, he concentrated on looking as big and mean as he could to back her up.

"You'll want to hear me out, Izabel," Chris said, shuffling his feet nervously. "It's about the Simonson job."

Izabel bristled again, but something was different this time. "What about it? Didn't they pay you enough?" It was a snide comment on her part, but the bite in her voice had lessened.

"Please," Chris pleaded, "let me have a few minutes of your time. You won't regret it."

Zack glanced at Izabel and saw indecision cross her features. "Izabel?"

She turned to look up at him with wide eyes. When she sighed and held out her newly won bear for him to hold, he knew what her answer would be.

"Will you hold Sunny for me, Zack?" she asked, pushing the little bear into his hands. "This won't take long."

Before he could say a word, she turned and walked away, her ex-lover following close behind.

A part of him wanted to go after them, to tell them that whatever the other man had to say, he could say it to them both, but his feet wouldn't move. Was the bastard trying to get Izabel back? Did he have something that would persuade her to go back to Seattle with him? To leave Zack behind for the glitzy city life she'd always known? Could he even compete with that?

Zack shook his head. He didn't know how to even start, but he knew he wouldn't go down without a fight.

"Who is that?" Emmy asked from beside him, startling Zack from his dark thoughts.

"Her ex," Zack muttered.

"Maybe I should hold this," Emmy said as she gently removed Izabel's small teddy bear from Zack's tightened fist.

They stood there for a moment or two, the seconds ticking by while they watched Izabel converse with the man from her past. Her face, which originally held an angry expression for her ex, slowly softened to wonder. Chris handed her an envelope and she looked inside. When she lifted her eyes, they were filled with stunned surprise. Zack read gratitude and even some affection in her expression and his heart cracked a little.

"Are you just going to stand here?" Emmy asked quietly.

He frowned at his sister. "What?"

"Are you just going to stand here while he tries to win her back?"

Zack turned back to the one-time couple to see that Izabel had given the bastard a quick hug. Heat flared in his chest as his muscles tensed and a need to break something tightened his fists until his knuckles cracked.

"No," he growled as he started his march to break up the conversation and send the interloper on his way.

* * *

Izabel fumed as she stomped a few yards away to talk to the man who'd broken her heart so completely. She wanted nothing from him, didn't even want to talk to him, but something about his words and the tone of his voice told her to listen just the same.

When they were far enough away to chat privately, Izabel turned on him. "Okay, Chris, what is so damn important that you had to stalk me all the way to Montana?"

He managed to look sheepish at her demanding tone, which was a totally new look for him. "I don't suppose I could convince you to come back to me?"

She snorted in disbelief. "Ah, that would be a hard no," she replied. "I have someone new now, and he treats me far better than you ever did."

"Yeah," Chris said, shoving his hands into his pants pockets and kicking at the grass beneath his feet. "I kind of got the impression that the big guy wanted to break me in two."

"Maybe I should've let him," Izabel snapped. "What do you want? And what about the Simonson deal?"

"Well," Chris said, looking uncomfortable, "first, I want to...apologize for the way I treated you."

"Which part?" she asked, anger building inside her again. "For treating me like a child who didn't know anything all the time, or for stealing my work and passing it off as your own?"

"All of it," he said softly, finally meeting her irate gaze and looking far more contrite than she'd expected. "I was a tyrant, I know. I was a jerk, and I treated you badly. I regret that more than you know, but I truly hate that I stole from you and drove you to this." He waved a hand as if to encompass all of Montana.

"Well...that's good then," Izabel said, for the first time uncertain what she should feel. "And what's wrong with Montana?"

"Nothing, I guess," he said as he glanced around at the dingy carnival that surrounded them. The look on his face told her all she needed to know. Chris was nothing but a slick city boy, and she had learned there was more to life than glitz.

"I like it here, Chris. Don't go ruining your apology by being an ass again."

His eyes widened. "I didn't mean anything by that. It's...just not for me."

Scorn narrowed her eyes. "Clearly."

"Look, I came to admit my faults and apologize. I was insecure around you, Izzy," Chris confessed. "You are brilliant and beautiful, and I couldn't deal with the fact that I might lose to my younger girlfriend. I know it wasn't right, and I know you did the right thing by leaving me. I don't blame you one bit for that or for snapping at me now. I deserve it, and more."

"I can't say I disagree," she said, still wondering where this was going.

He lowered his chin and shuffled his feet. "I don't expect you to."

"So if you knew where I was," she said slowly, "you could've said all this in a letter or a phone call. You didn't need to come all the way to Montana to do this."

"Would you have read it if I sent a letter, or answered if I called?"

Izabel pursed her lips as if pondering his question. "You have a point..."

"That's what I thought," he said and shrugged. "I needed to talk to you, and I figured what better way than to meet you in person. Besides, the extra time and effort are part of my redemption."

Her eyebrows rose. "Your what?"

"My redemption. My lessons in learning to be a better man."

"Ah, I see," she said. "Like the twelve steps in AA, but for arrogant jerks instead?"

He laughed. "Yeah, something like that."

"So, what step is this? Seven, eight?"

"I don't know," he said. "I just want to be a better man, so that when I do meet someone again, I'll treat them better than I did you. So I won't lose them like I did you."

The sadness and regret that tinged his voice tugged at her heart. She knew Chris wasn't a bad man, just insecure. She could forgive him for that, but she had no interest in returning to him.

"Well, I suppose that's a good start."

"I also needed to come in person to give you this." He pulled a long white envelope from his inside pocket and held it out to her.

"What's this?" she asked as she took the envelope from his hand.

"Another of my lessons." When she only frowned at him, he explained, "What I did was wrong, and I don't deserve to profit from it. So that," he nodded toward the envelope in her hand, "is the first check of three from the Simonson project."

Izabel gasped as she pulled the check from the envelope and saw all those zeros. Her hand covered her open lips as her wide eyes lifted to look at Chris.

"I only kept a small portion for the work I've done, but the majority of it is yours," he said slowly. "And don't worry, now that I know you won't just throw them into the trash, I'll mail the next two to you when I get paid."

She couldn't help the little giggle that escaped or the quick hug she gave him. "Thank you, Chris. This means a lot to me and, though I appreciate your apology, I'm not sure I'm ready to totally forgive you yet."

He grinned as she stepped back. "It's a start," he said, and then his eyes widened as he stepped to the side as if he intended to hide behind her. But at the last minute, he straightened and turned toward the large man approaching them.

Zack's face looked like a thundercloud, and Izabel couldn't blame Chris for his reaction. If she didn't know him as well as she did, she'd be afraid of Zack, too.

"Are y'all done here?" he grumbled as he wrapped a possessive arm around Izabel's shoulders.

Izabel smiled. Didn't he know he had nothing to worry about*? I'll have to do something about that later tonight.*

"We're good," she said, wrapping her arm around his waist and snuggling into his side. "Zack, I'd like you to meet Chris Richards. Chris, this is Zack."

"Good to meet you," Chris said in his best boardroom voice and offered Zack his hand.

Zack frowned at the offering, but took his hand anyway. "You, too." His voice was still more of a growl, but at least he didn't look as if he wanted to beat the other man to a pulp.

"Chris just stopped by to discuss some business," she said.

"Yeah," Chris quickly agreed, "but I can't stay. I have a meeting tomorrow that I can't miss."

Izabel held in a chuckle. She knew that was a lie since she was certain that Chris had been here for weeks looking for her. Apparently, the town wasn't as small as she had thought.

"Well, don't let us keep you," Zack grumbled, and Izabel gave him a sideways look that had him clearing his throat.

"Thank you, Chris," she said into the gap. "And I hope the rest of your lessons go as well for you as this one has."

He smiled that shy, little boy smile she'd always found so endearing.

"Thanks. I do, too." He glanced at Zack. "Take care of her."

Zack's arm tightened around her. "You can count on it."

Then Chris said his goodbyes and left them alone.

"Are you okay?" Zack asked softly, his whole body taut, as if expecting the worst.

"I am great," she said with a smile as she leaned into his chest and went up on her toes to plant a quick kiss on his lips. "How could I not be when I'm with you?"

His smile wiped all the concern and doubt from his features. "Well, when you put it like that..." He chuckled.

Izabel glanced around, looking for their friends. "Where'd everyone else go?"

"To the Ferris wheel," he said as he turned her in the direction of the ride, "and that's where we're headed now."

"Are we? And why is that?" she teased.

"As if you don't know," he said, carrying on with the joke. "You owe me some kisses at the top of the Ferris wheel, remember?"

"Oh, yes, I do remember you mentioning that..." She glanced at his other hand. "Where is Sunny?"

"Who?"

"My teddy bear. The one you won for me. The reason for the owing of kisses?"

"Oh," he said, as if he'd forgotten all about it. "Emmy is teddy-sitting right now."

"Okay, as long as she knows he's mine," Izabel said.

"A little possessive, aren't you?"

"When it comes to you? Yes."

His smile widened. "Good."

"So, I was wondering..." Izabel said as they continued toward the line for the Ferris wheel. "How do you intend to collect said kisses at the top of the Ferris wheel? We don't know where or when it will pause."

"But I do," he said knowingly.

She glanced up at him with a question in her eyes. "How?"

"I slipped the guy running it a twenty to stop it with us at the top."

"Ah-ha." Izabel laughed. "So you had this planned all along."

"Yep."

"You are a clever man, Zack MacEntier."

"Yes, I am," he agreed. "I have to be to keep up with the likes of you, my darling goddess." He kissed the top of her head and hugged her close.

"I don't think that's going to be a problem, handsome," she said as she rested her head against his chest and wrapped her arms around him. He embraced her in return, and Izabel sighed with satisfaction. She could hear his heart beating beneath her ear, steady and strong, as solid as the man himself. He made her happier than she'd ever been and, right then, she vowed to do the same for him.

If it took the rest of her life, she would never let his heart break again.

CHAPTER 27

The next several days were a blur of steady work for everyone involved with the winery. From scheduling to inventory and everything in between, Zack, Izabel, and the Brodys had all pulled together to make the winery's opening day a resounding success. In fact, so many locals and out-of-towners from all around showed up that the owners and some of their close friends worked as servers and kitchen help to ensure their customers remained happy.

Zack had observed Izabel several times during the long hours of greeting and serving their patrons. He knew she was in her element—traveling from table to table and group to group, chatting and laughing with everyone she met—and she kept everyone pleased and in good cheer. And when they'd been overrun with more customers at dinner, it had been Izabel who saved the day with the rented tables, tablecloths, and chairs she'd had the Brodys' ranch hands set up the night before in the garden-like area surrounding the winery. The day had cooled enough that the customers were comfortable outside, and they loved that they were able to eat, drink their wine or microbrew, and enjoy the sunset over the wide valley before them. The long windows that filled the west-facing wall also allowed those dining inside to admire the beauty of a western Montana sunset.

With his family and friends' help—and Izabel's organizing and marketing genius—Zack couldn't have asked for a better opening day for the winery. They expected the work Izabel had done to keep customers coming in heavily for a few more days before it slowly tapered off to a regular income of new and repeat visitors. Zack's original plan to diversify appeared to be paying off and soon, his bills would be, too.

He wasn't going to fail himself or his family. He could finally breathe a little easier now, knowing they weren't going to lose their home or the ranch. He had partners and a plan for the future that could only get better from here. And he owed it all to one woman.

Once the crowds had dwindled after dinner, Zack, his family, and friends sat at a large table to celebrate their new success.

"Here's to Zack's bright idea," Cade said, lifting his mug of imported beer, "and to Izzy's brilliance! May their current success continue and rub off on the rest of our endeavors, too."

Everyone chuckled, lifted their glasses to a round of 'Here, here,' and drank to his toast.

"So how does it feel to be a business owner?" Aaron asked from one end of the table where Hawk and several other firemen sat.

"Good," he said with a grin. "I'm just glad it's finally done and that I had so much great help to make it a success." He lifted his glass to everyone. "Thanks to all of you for everything you've done to help with this venture that I had feared would never be finished...let alone be so popular."

"Well, we can thank Izabel for that," Addie added from beside her husband. "I told you boys she was a genius, and as usual, I was right."

"Yes, dear," Cade said, and the others laughed at their lighthearted play.

"Yes, that is true," Zack said, "but I couldn't have done it without Cade and Cord's financial help."

"Oh, no, we didn't do anything," Cord said, his expression surprised that Zack didn't already know this. "Izabel took care of all that."

Zack frowned and looked at the woman beside him.

She smiled at him shyly. "I didn't get a chance to tell you..."

"Tell me what?" Zack asked.

"Well, remember Chris stopping by at the fair?"

His frown deepened, disliking where this was headed. "Yeah..."

"He'd had a lot to say that day," Izabel said, "but mostly, he wanted to make up for the wrongs he'd done to me. One of the ways to do that was to pay for the plans he stole from me to get the job in the first place."

"Pay you...how?"

She shrugged. "With a check. And I expect two more of equal value to come in a few months. So I didn't see why I shouldn't jump on a fantastic investment when the opportunity opened."

"She means that she hounded Cade and me to let her take over part of the financial responsibility for getting this place and part of ours off the ground," Cord said. "She's very persuasive."

"Yes, she is," Zack said, shocked, thrilled, and a little uncertain about this new development.

"Well, I think it's a great idea," Addie said.

"So you do have more plans for the ranch?" Josh, the deputy sheriff and friend who'd assisted Zack so many times in the last few months, asked.

The conversation turned to Cord and Cade's ideas for diversifying both ranches even more.

"Are you upset?" Izabel whispered.

Zack looked down into her concern-filled gaze and shook his head. "No, why would I be upset?"

"I don't know..." She shrugged. "Maybe because I forced my way into your business when we haven't even clarified the *business* between us yet."

He smiled to settle her worries, reached for her hand, and lowered his voice so only she would hear. "Goddess, I want you in my life for as long as I can have you. You make me a better man, and I don't want that to ever change. We can talk about everything when we're alone, but for now, I'm happy."

Her eyes glistened with unshed tears and she smiled. "I'm glad."

"But are you happy?"

She nodded enthusiastically. "Yes, very."

"Good," he said and squeezed her hand. "Now, if you'll excuse me for a moment, I need to visit the little boy's room."

She chuckled. "Hurry back."

"You know I will." With a quick kiss on the cheek, he stood and headed for the hallway across the room.

* * *

A few minutes later, his business done and hands washed, Zack exited the restroom with a silly grin still planted on his face. He couldn't believe how his life had turned around so completely, and in such a short period of time. Nor could he fathom how he got just as lucky in love. Because, yes, he was in love—so deep and desperately in love that it terrified him, but he wouldn't back away. He'd spent too many years running and being afraid—of forgetting Debs, of getting hurt again—and he had no intention of running from it this time. Izabel was the one. Now if he could just dredge up the courage to tell her.

"Hello, Zack..." a low, sultry voice startled him as he turned toward the dining room. He spun on his heel to find the blonde bartender from Tony's

Tavern standing in the shadows at the end of the hall. Her face was made up more than he'd ever seen before and the spangled dress she wore was short and revealing. He remembered seeing her around dinnertime, but this was the first time he'd spoken to her.

She sauntered past him in a loose-hipped manner, her hand sliding down his arm as she passed, only to stop and turn to face him, conveniently blocking his exit.

"H-Hey there." He was taken aback by her presence in the dimly lit hall, the odd vibes that seemed to radiate from her, and the fact that he couldn't remember her name or if he'd ever heard it. Switching to polite business proprietor mode, he asked, "Are you having a good time?"

"Oh, yes," she said quickly, "and I'd love to have some more *fun* tonight." She placed her hands on his chest and slid them up around his neck. Before he knew what was happening, she had plastered herself against him and hauled his head down to kiss him on the lips.

Hell, she practically crawled up his body like a jungle gym!

He gasped in surprise and her tongue pushed into his mouth. Insistent and ardent, she wiggled against him, demanding—and clearly expecting—an equal response.

The moment she'd launched herself at him, Zack froze, stunned into immobility by her unexpected actions. Then an image of Izabel's face, if she learned of this unwelcomed indiscretion, flashed in his mind and a different sort of panic swelled within him.

The bartender's tongue had barely touched his when his hands shot up to grip her arms, pull them from around his neck, and push her away, while untangling her legs from his hips. Alarm had widened his eyes, but the woman looking up at him smiled warmly, her eyes soft and inviting. He didn't understand her sexual assault or why she'd kissed him since it was obvious he was with someone else.

"What are you doing?" he demanded, not caring if his irritation showed.

"Kissing you," she said in a low voice. "And I'd do a lot more if you take me home with you right now."

He frowned and shook his head. "I'm with someone," he said, pushing her back another step and letting go. Something wasn't right about this situation, or maybe it was just the woman before him. Warnings tingled the back of his neck, and all he wanted was to get back to Izabel, but the woman blocked his path.

"Never stopped you before." She smirked, reaching out to run her finger along his bare forearm.

The contact made his skin crawl as he yanked his arm out of reach and took a step back. "I'm not like that anymore," he said. "Now, please, get out of my way."

The woman's face instantly changed, turning from pleasant and inviting, to petulant and furious in a blink. "You don't want to do this, Zack. We have too much between us for you to leave me hanging."

His chin jerked back, completely stunned by her comment. "Between us? There's nothing between us. You served me beer and whiskey at Tony's; that is all that's between us."

Something feral flashed in her hazel eyes and Zack prepared to fight her off without getting arrested for assault, but she instantly shuttered the odd glimmer and smiled again. "I know you don't mean that," she said, shifting her hips and biting at her too-red lips seductively.

"I mean every word," Zack practically growled as he wiped his face to remove any residue her makeup may have left. *What is* wrong *with her?*

Deciding he'd had enough, Zack stepped toward her, once, twice, using his greater size to force her back and out of his way. She must've thought he had other ideas because her eyes lit up and her smile filled her face. He felt like an ass for being so rude, but he couldn't let her think he wanted anything more to do with her.

"Don't come near me again," he said with a dark glower as he slipped past her, ensuring no part of him made any contact with her. Her hands clawed at his arm, but he roughly shook her off and hurried into the dining area, praying she wouldn't make an even bigger scene by following him into the still-crowded room.

Wiping at his lips once more, he reached the end of the hall and turned toward his table, but as he stepped into the dining room, he could've sworn he heard the woman mutter, "You'll regret this, Zack MacEntier."

He had no interest in digging into her warped mind, so he ignored it and the shiver that tickled his spine, and kept walking. Whatever she thought was going on was her problem, and he wanted no part of it. What could she do, anyway? Lie and make up rumors about him? Tell Izabel that he'd been involved with her? He didn't think Izabel would believe the crazy woman, but he'd have to warn her just the same. He needed to make sure Izabel knew she was the only woman for him—that the Meriton Casanova was dead and he would never be resurrected as long as Izabel was in his life. But that could wait for another day. Tonight was about celebrating with his family, his friends, and the woman of his dreams.

* * *

They had finished eating, the dishes had been cleared, and few of the other diners remained as Zack and his friends sat sipping coffee and chatting the night away.

The woman who'd accosted Zack had left some time ago without another word, but the laser intensity of the glare she'd tossed his way had set off more warning bells in his head. He'd done his best to ignore it and prayed no one else saw her expression.

The first time he remembered ever seeing her was a few years ago when she started working at Tony's. He knew next to nothing else about her, but maybe it was time he did a little investigating. Or better yet, maybe he should have Josh do it—the last thing he wanted was to run into her alone. He wondered where she'd gotten the idea that something was between them. They'd flirted and she'd kissed him a few times, and even though she'd hinted about them getting together more than once, nothing about her had ever appealed to him. Maybe now, he knew why.

Their group had just begun to break up, grabbing their keys and preparing to head home, when several cell phones began to ring. Everyone looked toward the sound to find that all the firefighters at the end of the table had pulled out their phones.

"What's up?" Zack asked.

Aaron grinned and shoved his phone back into his pocket as several of the other firefighters headed for the door. "We're being called in to help with the fire up north. Sounds like the weather isn't cooperating and the wind is spreading it faster than they can handle."

"Are they calling the volunteers, too?" Cade asked as he wrapped an arm around his wife.

Aaron shook his head. "Nah, just the pros right now, but don't worry," he said as he reached the exit, "we'll keep y'all safe."

"Be careful," Emmy shouted as Aaron headed out the door. He grinned and lifted a hand in reply, then took off at a run to catch up with the other men he'd arrived with.

Zack glanced at his sister. He'd known she had a thing for Aaron, but he had hoped it would wear off. Apparently, that wasn't the case. Maybe he could ask Izabel for some advice in that department—how to make his sister give up on a playboy.

"I'm glad you all aren't going with them," Addie said as Cade helped her into her light jacket.

"Us too," he replied as he exchanged a telling look with his twin—as if a whole conversation took place in that quick glance.

Zack flexed his arm and bent it at the elbow, gently moving it back and forth, testing his flexibility. He'd been out of the sling for a couple of weeks, and the physical therapist was working to get his strength and mobility back, but if they got called to assist with the fire anytime soon, there was no way Izabel or his friends would allow him to go. His doctor would ground him as well, so he had no reason to even entertain the idea. But it still bothered him to see people he cared about running into danger, knowing he wouldn't be there to help.

"Hopefully, they won't need any volunteers for this one," Josh said as they headed for the door and they all nodded their agreement.

Zack stopped to quickly speak with the manager of the winery, thanking him and the rest of the crew for their hard work, before he hurried to rejoin the others in the parking lot.

"It was a great opening day, Zack," Cord said as Zack caught up to them.

"Yeah," Cade added. "I'm excited about the next project."

"Don't rush it," Zack replied. "We've still got work to do here."

"I know," Cade said, "but it's off to a good start."

Zack nodded and grinned as the others said their goodbyes, but a part of him still tingled with warning. The tiny hairs on the back of his neck rose and he got the distinct feeling someone was watching him.

He glanced around the parking lot, taking in the hills and the trees that surround the winery. Even with the lights and the illumination from the rising full moon, he could see very little. No suspicious vehicles were left in the lot, and no dark shapes were roaming the vineyard or hiding behind trees.

Stop it, he scolded himself. *You're jumping at nothing. She's gone. Tomorrow will be soon enough to find out what's up.*

He sighed as he waved goodbye to his friends, then dropped an arm over Izabel's shoulders as they headed for his truck.

"I suppose now that I can afford it, I should get my own vehicle," Izabel mused and looked up at him. "Any suggestions?"

"I don't mind driving you around," he said, "but I know you like your independence."

"Yes, I do."

"Okay, well, you should consider something that will get you around in all kinds of weather. Something sturdy, but easy to handle, and that will meet all of your needs. How about an SUV?"

"Hmm, that's a possibility," she mused as he opened the passenger door of his truck for her to climb inside. She turned to look up at him instead. "Are you taking me home tonight?"

He grinned at her. "That depends on where you call home?"

Her smile turned mischievous. "Anywhere you are."

The chuckle that bubbled up from his chest felt good. "To the cabin it is, then."

With an excited squeak and a quick kiss, Izabel crawled into the cab and turned her smile on him. "Well, get a move on. We're burning daylight."

He rolled his eyes as he closed the door on her giggles and rounded the truck to his door.

"You've been watching too many John Wayne films," he said as he slipped into his seat and shut the door.

"It was your idea," she told him.

He laughed as he started the truck. "I suppose you're right about that."

Placing his arm on the back of the seat, he tugged one of her silky curls before he backed out of the parking space and headed for home.

Izabel slid over to his side of the truck and rested her head against his arm with a contented sigh that made his chest swell.

"You make me happy, Zack," she said and lifted her chin to meet his quick glance. He wrapped an arm around her and hugged her close so he could kiss the top of her head.

"Glad to hear it, goddess. I hope to keep you happy for a very long time."

"Promise?"

Her heart had been in that one word. He'd heard it distinctly and his own thumped in eager reply. "Yes, goddess. I swear on my life, that's the absolute truth."

She snuggled against him and his heart swelled with all the love he wanted to give her. He still had to say the words though, and that was something he planned to do in the immediate future. Tonight would be the beginning, and he'd have the rest of his life to prove his worth by loving her the best he could and always keeping his promise.

CHAPTER 28

By the time they reached the cabin, the full moon had cleared the mountains and lit their little valley with an eerie, bluish-white glow. Not that Zack really noticed; he was too aware of the beautiful woman beside him to pay much attention to any other scenery.

He switched off the truck and turned to Izabel, his whole body humming with pent-up desire. Her green eyes seemed to glow in the low light and the smile on her face was radiant.

"Hello, goddess," he said in a low growl.

"Hello, handsome," she replied as she crawled into his lap. He held back a moan as she wiggled around to get comfortable between his body and the steering wheel—driving him just a little insane in the process—but she quickly settled. "So, what are your plans tonight?"

He pulled her close until there was no room between them and her sexy little bottom nestled directly over the exceptionally hard erection she had caused. "You know what my plans are," he murmured and kissed her.

Her soft lips opened for him instantly and he dived in, taking her mouth quickly, starved for the taste of her, and demanding her response. She didn't let him down. Meeting him stroke for stroke, her tongue darted around his in a playful game that had his heart thumping in his chest. When he ended the kiss, he pressed his forehead against hers and sighed.

"I know how you feel," she said between breaths, and her fingers fisted in his hair.

He grinned and pushed her big curls away from her lovely face. "How about we find a more comfortable location?"

She nodded and he pushed open his cab door. Gathering her in his arms, Zack slid from the seat and thrust the door closed with his hip.

Izabel laughed as he ran up the deck steps two at a time. "I can walk, you know."

"I know, but I don't want to let you go just yet."

She smiled as the cabin door swung wide and he carried her inside. Kicking the door closed behind him, he hurried across the moonlit room to the queen-sized bed they'd utilized so thoroughly before.

Kissing her, their lips never parting, he laid her out on the bed and then carefully covered her body with his own. Her arms wrapped around him as his hips settled into the cradle of her thighs, and he groaned with anticipatory delight.

"Oh, Izabel," he said, pulling back to look down into her passion-darkened gaze, "you are so beautiful, so much more than I deserve."

She shook her head, brushing her fingers against his face, skimming her nails through his short beard. "You deserve to be happy, Zack. You always have."

"You make me happy," he said and turned his head to kiss her palm.

It was time. He felt it in his heart, the expanding of his emotions until he thought he might burst. He must tell her. Now.

"Izabel, I want you to know that I—"

He paused when her body stiffened and her gaze narrowed with what looked like confusion.

"What? What's wrong?"

An instant later, her eyes widen with fear as she shouted, "Look out!"

He turned to look over his shoulder, but pain exploded in the back of his head and the whole world went black.

* * *

Izabel tried to scream, but Zack's limp body had crushed the breath from her lungs and buried her beneath his wide chest. Frantically, she tried to see over his shoulder, knowing danger prowled nearby, but she couldn't lift her head far enough. She tried to push Zack's heavy frame to the side so she could wiggle out from under him, but it was no use. One of her arms lay wedged between their bodies, while the other hand rested uselessly by his head. Even if she had both arms free, she doubted she could shift him far.

Heat swept over her and she cursed again, this time in frustration. She was trapped while a dark, and clearly sinister, shadow lurked somewhere in the room.

A chill of terror latched onto her heart as the scene played inside her mind once more. She'd seen it coming; she saw what looked like a cast-iron pan raise in the shadow's hand a second before it struck. She cursed herself for not perceiving the threat fast enough to warn Zack in time.

"Zack?" she whispered, trying to shake him awake. "Zack?" A new dread filled her heart when he didn't reply or move. "Oh, no. No, no, no." *He cannot be dead!* Her fingers fumbled along his neck, looking for a pulse. "Please..."

At first, her heart stalled when she couldn't find the normally strong pulse at his throat, but a moment later, she breathed a sigh of relief when her fingertips felt the steady beat of his heart.

"Oh, thank God," she murmured. Her hand slipped into his hair but stopped when it came across a large lump and something warm and wet covered her fingers. Pulling her hand back, she stared at the dark liquid coating them. It took her dazed brain a few seconds to realize it was Zack's blood. Whoever had struck him not only left a bump the size of her fist forming on the back of his head, but had broken the skin as well. Izabel knew a head wound would bleed profusely, but she couldn't stop the tight tickle of panic that welled in her chest.

"Zack?" she whispered urgently against his neck. "Zack, please, wake up!"

A loud crash startled her anew as something heavy hit the ground. Her breath sounded loud in her ears as Zack's arms moved upward one at a time. Izabel expected him to ease himself off her, but he stayed where he was.

What the...? Her mind flew through the possibilities, but only one made any sense. She felt his body jerk and shift, making the bed shake, and she knew the attacker hadn't left.

"What are you doing?" she asked in a quiet voice, not sure what was going on, or why, and terrified of what might happen next.

"Tying him up," came a soft, feminine voice. "Can't have him mucking up things more than he has already."

"What are you going to do with him?"

"Him?" The voice laughed and the maniacal sound sent a shot of dread racing down Izabel's spine. All the little hairs on her body stood on end at once.

"Nothing...at least, not right now," the voice replied. "I'll have lots of time to decide what to do with him after you and I have a little *chat*."

"A chat? About what?" Izabel struggled to keep her voice level, but it came out much higher than she'd intended.

"About how things are, and how they will be," the voice said, then grunted as Zack's body clumsily rolled off Izabel and onto the middle of the bed.

Izabel stared at his too-white face. Fear for his life and her own tightened her chest. She saw blood trailing down his neck and staining the collar of his half-unbuttoned western dress shirt. She remembered unfastening those buttons just a short time ago, remembered thc heat of his body, the muscles of his chest moving under her hands. He'd always seemed so solid, so strong, indestructible almost. Now, he was so still it alarmed her.

"Get up," the voice demanded, and Izabel had to drag her eyes from Zack's ghostly pale face. She looked over at the strange woman, and an odd feeling of recognition swept over her, but Izabel couldn't place where she'd seen her before. She was too concerned about Zack.

"Please," she pleaded. "He needs a doctor."

"He'll be fine," the woman who stood only a few feet from the bed informed her. "He's not your concern. Now, get up."

Something in the woman's hand glinted darkly in the pale moonlight and a new volley of terror bombarded Izabel. *She has a gun!*

Izabel untangled her legs from Zack's and slowly rolled to her feet.

"Up. Up," the woman said, waving the gun for emphasis. The thin jacket she wore made a swishing sound with each movement of her arm.

Izabel pushed onto her feet, her legs trembling beneath her, but she kept her eyes on the gun in the woman's hands.

"Good girl," the stranger said, her tone condescending.

Izabel straightened, unwilling to let this woman see just how terrified she was. She jerked her pink sweater to straighten it, quickly wiped her damp palms on her new blue jeans, and then lifted her chin once more.

"Now, move...toward the door. Go."

Izabel glanced at Zack and saw his eyelids flutter. "Zack?" she called, momentarily forgetting about the other woman in the room. "Are you all right?"

The woman turned to him as well, but Izabel didn't notice as Zack groaned and opened his eyes.

"Izabel? What the..." Confusion filled his expression and pain sparked in his eyes. He seemed to suddenly realize he was tied to the headboard of the sturdy iron and brass bed, and he tugged at it roughly. "Why am I tied to the bed? And why does my head feel like it's been hit with a cast-iron skillet?"

"Probably because you *were* hit with a skillet. One of your own, you ungrateful bastard."

Izabel's eyes flew to the other woman, unsettled by the venom in her voice and the truth of her admission.

"You?" Zack growled. "What the hell are you doing here? What do you want?"

Izabel's gaze fluttered between them, uncertain what was happening. How did he know her?

"You know what I want, Zack. You've always known, but you're too much of a playboy to do the right thing. So, I'm doing it for you this time."

"What are you talking about?"

"You are mine!" the woman screamed, and Izabel jumped in surprise and fear. "When will you learn that?"

"There's nothing between us," Zack said slowly, his gaze darting to Izabel and then back as he tugged at the bindings that fastened his hands to the solid bed frame. "I told you that before. There's never been anything between us!"

A stunned look crossed the woman's face and when she spoke, she sounded hurt. "How can you say that? After all the kisses...after all the love we've shared?"

"What?" Zack glanced at Izabel again, his eyes worried and confused. "I don't know what she's talking about, Izabel. I swear."

A shot rang out in the small confines of the cabin, and Izabel screamed, covering her ears with her shaking hands. Feathers flew into the air and gently floated around them. Sensing the danger Zack was in, Izabel dropped her arms and moved toward him. The woman saw her attempt to get closer to Zack and shoved her back so hard that Izabel landed on her butt in the living room.

"Stay away from him," the woman shrieked as Izabel fell.

"Leave her alone!" Zack bellowed as she dropped onto the hardwood, and the woman turned her venom on Zack once more.

"And you! That was just a warning shot," she said, feverishly gesturing toward the now-destroyed pillow with the gun. "You'd best take this seriously."

Too stunned to move, Izabel watched as Zack used his arm to brush the soft feathers that had escaped the bedding off his face. Time slowed and their world seemed to hold its breath. Downy white plumes descended slowly around the bed. They seemed ethereal, illuminated by the moonlight from the windows, as if an angel had just flapped his wings. It made the horrible scene appear, briefly, serene. But then everything slammed back into normal time once more.

"Why couldn't you just learn to behave?" the woman wailed with pain in her voice. "Why do you always make me hurt you?"

"Hurt me?" Zack asked, disbelief in his voice. "You've never done anything but force unwanted kisses on me. We have never been a couple, so how could you possibly have hurt me?"

The woman tilted her head, and Izabel saw the shine of tears on her cheeks.

"You built that damn winery to draw in more of your whores, didn't you?"

Zack opened his mouth to speak, but she ranted right over him.

"Oh, don't bother denying it, I know you did. It wasn't enough to cheat with locals, but you had to have other strangers, too." She waved the gun at Izabel. "Other *exotic* beauties."

"I don't know what you're talking about," Zack shouted, but the woman continued to speak as if Zack hadn't said a word.

"But you couldn't take a hint, could you? Even after I destroyed all your hard work, you couldn't just let it go and come back to me? No, you had to put everything you had into a building so you could have more playmates in your bed."

Izabel's mouth fell open and a boulder of cold dread settled in her belly. Could this woman possibly mean that she'd been the one who damaged the winery?

"That was you?" The question escaped before Izabel could stop it.

The woman chuckled and glanced at Izabel. "Of course. What else was I supposed to do when he couldn't keep it in his pants?"

She turned back to Zack, who appeared to have turned to stone at her revelation. "Now you have a new bitch warming your bed." She moved to stand over Izabel, then reached down, grabbed her arm beneath the edge of her short-sleeved sweater, and yanked her to her feet.

Izabel tried to pull away from her, lunging for the door and hoping she could make it down the mountainside to get help for them both. But the woman's fingernails dug into Izabel's arm, drawing blood, and she was jerked back to the woman's side.

She jammed the gun barrel into Izabel's ribs as a warning. "Behave," she whispered menacingly in Izabel's ear, "or I'll put a bullet in you now, right in front of your lover. And he'll be next."

Izabel clenched her jaws to keep her chin or lips from trembling as she stared at Zack's worried expression. Her vision blurred, wishing there was something she could do, but at the moment, she had little choice.

The woman tucked her gun away and pulled a cord that looked like it had been ripped from a lamp out of her jacket pocket. Quickly, she used it to bind Izabel's wrists together in front of her.

"Leave her alone," Zack said, jerking against his bound hands. "She doesn't have anything to do with this."

The woman kept coiling the cord around Izabel as she calmly glanced over at Zack. "You made her part of this."

The woman's erratic emotions frightened Izabel almost as much as her gun did, but Zack's distraction allowed her to slip a finger through the cord being wound around her wrists. She only hoped she could create enough space to wiggle free from it later.

Tying off the cord around Izabel's wrists, the woman gripped her arm, retrieved her gun, and once again shoved the barrel against Izabel's side as she hauled her toward the door.

"I would've taken care of this one months ago," the woman said to Zack, "if you'd just stayed out of the way."

Izabel froze and tried to swallow but her mouth was too dry. Her heart raced in her chest as a flush of terror tingled over her skin. This woman shot him...that day by the river. She'd been aiming for Izabel, but Zack had moved, just enough to shift Izabel. The bullet had passed through her hair and buzzed past her ear before slamming through his arm.

The danger she was in suddenly took shape and her legs began to tremble more than they already were.

"Why are you doing this?" Zack asked as he continued to struggle with the cord that trapped his hands. He rolled off the bed and stared at them as they reached the door. His eyes met Izabel's and she read his fear for her there, but she also saw strength and resolve...and something more she was afraid to name.

But how could he save her when he was tied to the bed?

The woman told Izabel to open the front door and, when the gun barrel dug painfully into her ribs, she did as instructed. The woman tugged Izabel to the threshold, intent on exiting the cabin altogether.

"Wait!" Zack shouted and a loud screech filled the air, the bed protesting as he dragged the heavy thing a few inches toward them.

"You can't seem to learn on your own," the woman said in answer to his previous question. She stopped and looked back at him. "And I won't let you make a fool of me again."

Zack's eyes widened briefly, but Izabel saw his flare of alarm. He recognized the danger as well as Izabel did.

"What are you going to do?" Zack asked, even as he hauled on the bed to get closer.

"I'm going to *remove* the temptation." The woman pulled Izabel through the doorway. "You stay right there now, ya hear? I'll be back shortly." She giggled.

"Zack?" Izabel's eyes widened as she searched his face.

"Wait!" he shouted, jerking at the bed with little success. "Wait...Sheila! Wait!"

The woman stopped in her tracks. The hand around Izabel's arm tightened, her nails digging into Izzy's flesh. She turned to face Zack. The silence around her, hard and brittle.

"Please," Zack cajoled, "come back to me. Sit down and we'll talk. Just like we used to. Please...Sheila?"

Izabel instantly understood what he was doing, but she didn't know if catering to this woman's mental fantasy was a good idea. It could backfire and make things so much worse.

A wicked smile curled the woman's tight lips. They seemed to pull back like a feral cat flashing its teeth before it pounced. A tingle of unease fluttered in Izabel's belly.

"My name..." the woman hissed, "is *Shelley*."

Zack's eyes widened and he stuttered over several words, trying to correct his mistake. "R-Right, of c-course, that's your name. How st-stupid of me. I'm sorry, Shelley. I still want to sit and talk with you though. Won't you come back?" The softness of his eyes, the slight smile on his face, the persuasive tone of his voice...he used all of his many charms in an attempt to sweet-talk the woman into staying and letting Izabel go. Izabel applauded his efforts, but was afraid for him as well.

The hand holding Izabel's arm trembled, but she didn't think it was fear or unease that caused it. Heat radiated off the woman's body, and the way she held herself, as well as the tone of her last statement, gave the impression of barely suppressed fury.

"There'll be plenty of time to talk when my work is done," the woman said in a low voice. Then she turned and hauled Izabel toward the trees behind the cabin.

"No! Wait," Zack bellowed from inside the cabin. Then, a loud roar escaped him and several grunts and creaks followed as Zack fought to be free of the bed. His cry had been heartbreaking to hear, but Zack was safe for the moment, and Izabel had one less thing to worry about.

They rounded the back of the cabin to find a small four-by-four truck parked there, and the woman forced Izabel to climb into the passenger seat.

"Now, stay put," she said, waving her gun threateningly. "You try to run, and I'll just shoot you and be done with it. Understand?"

Izabel nodded and the door slammed in her face.

Folding her arms against her chest and trying to hold on to her fear, Izabel's mind raced through possibilities, but it seemed she had no choice but to follow along until an opportunity presented itself or until she made one for herself. She turned her finger and wiggled her wrists. The cord loosened only slightly, but it gave her hope. Something had to happen, otherwise, Izabel feared she'd never see Zack again, never feel his touch, his kiss, or tell him how much she loved him.

That, she could not allow. None of this was his fault, and she would not be another reason for his guilt and shame to cut him off from the world again.

Taking a deep breath, she cleared her mind and sharpened her awareness, determined to survive whatever this woman had planned. She would live to see Zack again, and then she would show him everything that was in her heart.

CHAPTER 29

Zack dug his teeth into the electrical cord that bound his wrists, hoping to loosen a strand that might free him from the bed. Aggravation welled up in his chest when nothing moved, but he refused to give up. His head pounded, sweat dotted his forehead, and he fought the dizziness and constant urge to vomit. She'd hit him hard, and he was sure he had a concussion, but that didn't matter. He had to get free to save Izabel, but that wouldn't happen if he lost consciousness again.

An engine he didn't recognize started up outside and fear turned his insides to ice.

"Izabel!" he bellowed as terror clawed at his heart. He could not lose her now. He had so much to tell her, so much to give, but his alter ego had struck once again.

How he hated himself for what he'd become, for what his choices had done to his life—what they were *still* doing to his life. His stupid choices were going to get Izabel hurt! He roared with rage and fear, yanking at the bindings like a madman. His arms ached, and he'd moved the heavy bed halfway to the door, but the only other thing he'd managed to do was bloody his wrists.

The vehicle outside drove away and he screamed Izabel's name once more, but the engine drew farther away, growing quieter and quieter as the seconds ticked by.

He forced himself to listen carefully. The sound didn't seem to be headed back to the road, but rather up the side of the mountain behind the cabin.

Where was that crazy woman taking Izabel? There was nothing up there but denser trees and wild animals. Maybe that was the plan—to get Izabel lost in the forest, leaving her for a bear, a mountain lion, or a pack of wolves to find.

"No," he groaned as he fought to be free. He had to find her before that Shelley woman did something he'd regret forever.

Another wave of nausea struck as he chewed and tugged on his restraints. He paused and clenched his teeth, waiting for it and the wooziness to dissipate.

He had no idea how long they'd been gone—ten minutes, an hour?—when he heard another engine approach.

Was she back already? Was he too late?

"Oh, God, no," he moaned and his eyes burned with the threat of tears.

The sound grew louder, and Zack pulled himself out of self-pity and looked around for a weapon or something to subdue Shelley. He saw nothing. He wasn't close enough to the door to grab her or knock her over the head with anything like she'd done to him. All he had was himself.

He paused in his frantic search. Maybe that was all he needed. Maybe he could convince her he was ready to be her man. Maybe then, he could coax her into telling him what she'd done with Izabel.

Catering to her delusions made him almost as ill as the knock to his head, but he'd do it for Izabel. It was also a long shot, but at this point, he had very few choices. He sat on the bed and tried to look sexy and pleased that she'd returned.

He cursed under his breath. "Please, help me pull this off." He hadn't prayed for anything in a long time—not since Debbie's gruesome death, in fact—but right now, he'd take help from anywhere if it meant saving Izabel.

As the engine approached the cabin, Zack cocked his head, ignoring the intense surge of vertigo that stuck with the movement. This vehicle sounded different—the engine more powerful and...familiar. Was someone else coming up here?

No, he was the only one who ever came to this place—not even his feisty sisters came here. Even though he'd never brought anyone else to the cabin, they assumed it was his love-shack.

"So then who's driving up the road?" he muttered aloud.

Straining against his bonds, Zack tried to get a look out the large front window, but all he could see in the dark was a set of headlights as they stopped next to his truck. He heard a door open and close. It wasn't Shelley, he was certain of that.

"Help!" he shouted at the newcomer. "Help! I'm in here."

Boots hit the deck and a tall figure in jeans and a dark T-shirt crossed to the half-open door and threw it back.

"Zack?" Josh's voice almost buckled Zack's knees.

"Josh! Oh, thank God!"

"Are you okay," Josh asked as he walked into the cabin, quickly checking the surroundings, and then tucking his handgun back into its holster. When his eyes landed on Zack again, he halted and tilted his head, a curious frown marring his brow. "Are you...tied to the bed?" Awkwardness and a touch of humor tainted his question.

"It's not what you think," Zack said, frustration making his voice sharp. "Untie me and I'll explain."

Josh pulled out a pocketknife and sawed at the cord while Zack rapidly relayed what had happened.

"Shelley?" Josh asked incredulously. "The bartender from Tony's did all this?"

"Yes," Zack hissed as the cord finally came loose. He was free! "I'll bet she's the one who left that threatening note on my truck, too."

"But why?"

Zack blew out his frustration in a single breath. "She has this delusion that she and I are a couple. But I swear, Josh, I've never been in a relationship with her. Never been with her at all, except when she'd kiss me at the bar. I just thought it was fun flirting, but she blew it way out of proportion."

Josh cursed as he looked around. "Where is she now?"

"She took Izabel up the mountain about twenty minutes ago," he said, nodding in the direction he'd heard them go and pressing his fingers to his dizzy head. "I think Shelley's going to hurt her. I can't let that happen, Josh. I can't." He had tried to stay calm, to get his story across without losing control, but his last words came out like a sob as his trembling hands latched onto Josh's shoulders.

"Okay, Zack, take a breath," Josh said as he tugged Zack's hands away. "I'll get her back."

"I'm coming with you."

Josh eyed him askance. "You can barely stand. You're swaying, Zack, and you look like you're going to puke at any second."

Zack's stomach clenched as panic welled within him. "I'm fine. I cannot sit here and wait while she's out there in danger. I have to find her." He gripped Josh's shoulders again. "Don't you understand? Because you, of all people, should understand. I can't lose her now—"

"Fine." Josh raised his voice—though Zack wasn't sure whether he did so to stop Zack's babbling or to keep him from bringing up more of the past. Josh stepped back out of reach. "We'll go after them together, but I need you to be calm. Otherwise, you *are* staying here."

Zack's shoulders straightened and, despite the pain and lightheadedness, his spine turned to steel "No! I will not stay behind. I'll follow you if I have to."

"I know," Josh said sternly, "but I need you to keep a clear head. If you let your emotions rule, you'll only be a liability."

Zack nodded his understanding, grimacing internally at the new wave of queasiness that hit him, then followed Josh out to his truck.

"One more thing," Josh said as they climbed into the cab.

"What's that?"

"You will do as I tell you. If I say to stay in the truck or go back to the cabin, you will do it. Without arguing."

Zack clenched his jaw and pressed his lips together. He wouldn't leave without Izabel, but Josh would make him stay at the cabin if he didn't obey. He gave his friend a tight nod.

The deputy and ex-soldier studied him for a moment, then inclined his head. "Good."

Josh started his truck and as they headed up the mountain, he used his police radio to call for backup. Once he'd finished, the only sound in the cab was that of the truck's tires crawling up the hillside.

"What brought you up here, anyway?" Zack asked a few minutes later to keep his mind from conjuring all the terrible things that might've already happened to Izabel.

"I was headed to a friend's place," Josh said, his eyes glued to the bumpy path as they slowly continued up the mountainside. "I saw some light through the trees up here that got my hackles up."

"Light?"

"Yeah." Josh threw him a somber glance. "Firelight."

"Fire..." Cold swept through Zack's inside. "You think that forest fire up north has reached this far already?"

Josh shrugged. "Don't know. I haven't heard anything about it, but I suppose it might've. That's why I came up to check it out." He spared a look at Zack. "Don't worry, we'll find Izabel."

"I know." Zack nodded, then added in an apprehensive whisper, "We have to."

* * *

They had been driving uphill at a steady clip for several minutes before

Izabel dredged up the courage to speak to her kidnapper.

"Where are you taking me?" she asked quietly, eyeing the gun in the other woman's hand.

Shelley looked over at Izabel and sudden recognition struck.

"You're the bartender," Izabel blurted out, completely surprised she hadn't recognized her right off. But the make-up the woman wore had made her look different in the moon's ethereal glow—the harsher curves of her face softened in the darkness, her lips a touch more full. She looked quite pretty and less work-weary than she had the first time Izabel saw her. The dash lights in the truck, however, were not so kind. Izabel recognized the woman who'd been all over Zack that night at the bar before they'd first gotten together.

The woman's smile was frigid. "Finally figured it out, did you? Well, good for you. To answer your question," the woman said, slowing the truck over a particularly bumpy part of the trail, "we're taking a ride."

"To where?"

"Oh, just a little campsite," the woman said as she continued up the hill and through the thick trees. "Zack used to take me up here to camp. We'd build a little fire and make love under the stars. It's a beautiful place."

Izabel didn't reply. She knew the woman was delusional. She'd read the truth on Zack's face, and she knew he wasn't involved with this woman. In fact, Izabel would bet every penny of the money Chris Richards had given her that Zack had never been with Shelley in any way. But this woman had created a whole relationship with him—a detailed fantasy that Izabel had threatened just by being there.

How did one go about dissolving a delusion without getting shot in the process? She shook her head ever so slightly. She wasn't a shrink, nor had she ever been to one, but she had to do something.

The truck abruptly lurched to one side, and Izabel squeaked in alarm as her head slammed into the passenger side window, leaving a spidery crack in the glass.

A harsh laugh filled the cabin. "Don't worry, honey. You may have tried to steal my man, but I won't drag this out."

Izabel glanced at the woman's profile. *Somehow, that doesn't make me feel better,* she thought snidely. But maybe if she could get her talking...

"So, did you *sic* the protesters on Zack, too?" she asked.

Shelley laughed again. "As a matter of fact, yes, I did. A friend of mine is very involved with all that Earth Friends crap. He was very upset to hear about all the *horrible practices,*" her voice dripped with sarcasm, "Zack and the other ranchers were using around here. It didn't take much to convince them to cause trouble for a while. Unfortunately, the others discovered the error of their ways and left town too soon."

"A friend, huh?" Izabel mused. "Might this protester friend be a big guy with a beard?"

"Yeah." Shelley flashed her smile. "How did you know?"

"He attacked Zack in town a few weeks back," Izabel said. "Did you encourage that as well?"

Shelley frowned and shook her head. "No, Ed did that all on his own. He has a crush on me, you see, and he thinks Zack isn't good enough for me. He's probably right, but Zack is my *everything*."

"Why don't you date Ed? He seems to want you...more than Zack does." Izabel knew that mention of Zack's disinterest might anger the woman again, but she risked it anyway.

"Zack is my man," Shelley said in a dreamy yet possessive way that made the fine hairs on the back of Izabel's neck stand on end. "He loves me. It's just that he's had everything his way for so long... He'll learn this time."

Izabel didn't like the tone in which she spoke that last sentence. It gave her chills and had her fumbling for some other tactic to use.

Something off to the side and up the hill caught her eye, and she gazed past Shelley out the driver's side window.

Flickering blinked between the trees. It was too variable to be a flashlight or another vehicle; it reminded her of...a campfire. But that can't be right. It was huge. No, not a campfire...a bonfire.

Had the forest fire reached this far already? she wondered. *Or had this unstable woman started it to cover up—* Izabel's mind froze. Her widened eyes focused on the driver and found her smug smile.

"What are you going to do with me?" Izabel asked, her voice shaking with fear, no matter how she tried to keep it cool and steady.

The woman didn't reply, instead, she started to hum to herself. It took Izabel a minute to place the tune and when she did, her whole body went cold.

It was the chorus to "The Night the Lights Went Out in Georgia." Izabel only knew of the song because a friend of hers from school had loved country music and play that song, in particular, all the time—a cover version, recorded in the 1990s by a well-known female country singer whose name Izabel couldn't remember. What she did remember, however, was that the song was about the murder of a cheating wife, the wrong man was blamed, and he died for it.

It wasn't hard to make the connection to their current situation, but did that mean Shelley intended to murder Zack as well? Is that why she tied him to the bed, to make it easier for her to kill him later?

Izabel couldn't let that happen. Even if Shelley had some other plan for him, she would react badly when he rejected her and might shoot him again out of spite, or jealousy, or rage. Whatever may happen to Izabel, she would not let this woman harm Zack.

They drove for a few more minutes, and the farther they went, the bigger the flames became, until they rounded the intersecting foliage and at the end of a long, rough dirt path. The glow Izabel had seen earlier turned into an uneven, oblong circle of forest engulfed in flames.

Izabel glanced farther down the dark hillside, but saw no other flickering light. Off in the distance to the north, she could just make out another glow in the night sky above the foothills, but that had to be, at least, twenty miles away, if not farther. Too far for this isolated blaze to have sprung up from the larger one up north the firemen had left to battle earlier that night.

So where did it come from? Izabel wondered. *Did Shelley set it?* Her head snapped to the left to assess the other woman as she turned off the truck and pulled the keys from the ignition.

Shelley smiled as she opened her door and exited the small truck. Izabel suspected the woman's grin was because she thought her plan was nearly completed, but Izabel intended to alter those schemes—she just had to figure out how. She'd already scrutinized the inside of the cab for anything that might help her escape, but had found nothing. She would need to use the forest, the flames, and her wits if she was going to get out of this.

She wiggled her arms again and the cord loosened a bit more.

Shelley opened Izabel's door and waved the gun at her to exit. When Izabel didn't immediately move, Shelley growled, "Come on, get out."

A wall of intense heat slammed into Izabel and her heart lunged into her throat, beating so hard and fast she thought it might explode. She bit her lower lip to hold back a whimper of fear. She concentrated on forcing her trembling limbs to keep her upright as she slipped from the truck and on slowing the galloping beat of her terrified heart.

She would not die this way. She and Zack had just found each other. If something happened to her now, there was no doubt he would blame himself. She would not leave him like this or give him more undeserved guilt.

The heat of the blaze grew even more powerful once Izabel was on her feet beside the truck. The yellow-orange flames weren't more than ten yards away, licking hungrily up the sides of several tall trees and skating over the dried deadfall along the forest floor. The breeze that ruffled Izabel's curls felt hot enough to burn, even at this distance, and after speaking with the Brodys about forest fires, she knew how fast and unpredictable they could be.

Her legs suddenly felt too weak to move, and she clenched her bound hands to keep them from shaking.

"Move," Shelley shouted, then followed her command with a rough shove to Izabel's back.

She stumbled forward several steps, only to come to a stop once more, staring at the inferno before her. The branches of the evergreens shimmered in the heat and small drops of orangey-red dripped from the branches overhead, raining down glowing embers on the dried-out vegetation below. It seemed to grow, and change, and spread more rapidly than Izabel could fathom.

"I said, move!" Shelley shoved her again.

Izabel's shaky legs slowly stepped forward. She made it five steps before she stopped again and turned to her kidnapper. "Did you start this fire? Maybe to cover up what you're planning to do?"

"Smart girl," Shelley said, then her grin dropped away. "Move!"

"But why do this at all? Aren't you worried about the town? The hundreds...the thousands of people who might get hurt?"

Shelley laughed. "This town? I just moved here a few years ago. No one really welcomed me, no one wanted to be my friend. Zack was the only one who was ever interested in what I had to say. So why would I care if it burned to the ground? Now, move!"

"You don't have to do this," Izabel tried again. "We can help you. We can be your friends." She tried to make her tremulous smile look friendly and inviting, but Shelley wasn't buying it.

"You won't be around much longer," Shelley shouted, and when Izabel simply stood at the edge of the burning area, staring back at her, Shelley rushed toward her. "Why do you have to make this difficult? The outcome is inevitable."

Grabbing Izabel by the arm, she jerked her into the smoke and heat of the fire. Both women instantly began to cough. Thankfully, Izabel's hands were tied in front of her, and she used them to pull up the T-shirt she'd worn beneath her sweater to cover her mouth and nose, hoping it would help. It did a little, keeping the hot air from burning her throat, but the smoke was too thick and the heat tried to singe her bare arms. Her eyes began to water and she found it even harder to see. She had to do something now if she intended to survive.

"What about Zack?" she called to the woman hauling her through the flaming trees and brush.

Shelley glanced back at her but didn't stop moving into the flames. "Zack will be fine."

"But this blaze is growing fast, and we're not that far from the cabin. What if it catches fire and he can't get out?"

That stopped Shelley in her tracks. They both glanced back the way they'd come. Through the billowing smoke, Izabel could just make out the truck and how the fire had crawled a good distance toward it.

Shelley eyed the flames as her hand dropped from Izabel's arm. "Stay here." She held the gun pointed toward Izabel as she took several steps toward the truck. Her gaze darted in the direction of the cabin and she shook her head.

Izabel didn't wait to see what the woman would do next. Instead, she turned and ran. She'd spied an open area about ten yards downhill that appeared to have already burned through. The flames in that direction weren't more than three feet high, and if she could get to that area, she'd be safe—well, safer than she was now. Then she could work on getting back to the cabin to help Zack. She didn't have her phone—having left it on the bedside table in the cabin—but Zack had said there was no service out here anyway, so she had no way to call for help. Which meant, she was all Zack had.

She leaped over a fallen log that had yet to catch fire, then darted between trees and the flames, her eyes locked on the open space below, while she continued to cough from the hot, acrid smoke she couldn't avoid. She'd covered a few yards of burning debris when something struck the tree beside her with a loud *thwack*. Fiery tree bark splintered in every direction, sticking to Izabel's clothes and hair, scorching her skin where it touched. She shrieked in fear and pain, frantically brushing at the dying embers that had landed on her. She risked a quick look behind her and saw that Shelley was no longer distracted. Her face twisted with hate as she viciously pulled the trigger of her handgun. The shot went wide to Izabel's left, but it was closer than the last. Far too close.

Dashing to the left, Izabel put the large tree between her and any other bullets and kept moving. She went a few more yards, closing in on her goal, when Shelley suddenly blocked her path. She must've guessed Izabel's plan and had made her way around her. She'd stepped out from behind the trunk of a large fir tree only a couple of feet away, its branches crackling with fire over their heads.

Shelley laughed and the cold dread of panic swept over Izabel. Her heart beat so hard she could hardly breathe, and the smoke kept her coughing. She glanced behind her, but the way she'd come was now filled with fire, and the areas to her right and left weren't much better. Her smoke-burning eyes landed on Shelley once again, and she knew she had no choice as Shelley's arm swept forward, the gun still in her hand.

An image of Zack, choking on smoke, fire consuming him as he lay helpless on the bed flashed in Izabel's mind. Then it went blank and anger flooded every corner of her awareness. She screamed, shook her arms free of the cord that had bound her, and dived at her would-be murderer.

Her hands clamped onto Shelley's wrist and she used her momentum to slam it into the tree beside them. The weapon fell from Shelley's hand and clattered into the mess of deadfall that had yet to catch fire beneath the big tree. Apparently stunned that Izabel would fight back, Shelley didn't move as she stared at where the gun had disappeared. Not waiting for the woman to gather her senses, Izabel shoved her out of the way and darted past. She made it three broad strides when a terrified, pain-filled scream came from behind her. Unable not to, Izabel slowed to glance over her shoulder and then came to a stuttering stop.

There, in the path, stood Shelley. Flames danced along her arms and torso and flickered at the end of her blond ponytail. Izabel's stomach clenched and her heart constricted at the sight.

More screams emanated from Shelley's open mouth, but the flames would soon consume her whole upper body.

Izabel's legs trembled with the desire to run as far from the heat and horrible scene as she could, but her feet didn't move toward the clearing. Instead, she rushed over to Shelley and threw her to the ground. Izabel saw in an instant that the lightweight jacket Shelley wore had shrunk in the heat and with the flames, the synthetic material fusing to her skin. Not wanting to get more burned herself, Izabel used a stick and her freed hands to dig at the ground, and scooping up handfuls of dirt, she began to toss what she could onto the other woman's flaming clothes.

Izabel's lungs were burning from the smoke and heat by the time she was finally able to douse all the flames dancing over the other woman. She pulled her shirt over her face again and looked down at the immobile Shelley. The woman lay motionless, partially covered in dirt, and Izabel feared she may be dead, but then a soft moan of agony reached her ears.

Looking around, Izabel knew they had to move. If she moved quickly, she could still get to the burned-out area beyond the fire. Moving around the prone woman, Izabel leaned close to Shelley's ear. "I'm going to move you out of the fire," she said over the sounds of the blaze around them. "It might hurt."

When the injured woman made no reply, Izabel carefully turned her over. Shelley screamed, but Izabel didn't stop. She didn't have the time or the luxury to feel bad or to find another way. And for whatever reason, she couldn't just walk away and let the other woman burn to death. No matter what she had done, Shelley was still a human being and Izabel would do what she could to help.

Gently working her arms under Shelley's shoulders, she gripped her under the arms and dragged her toward the clearing.

Shelley screamed again, fighting against the hold Izabel had on her shoulders, crying and begging for Izabel to stop, but she kept moving. Soon, Shelley went still, and Izabel hoped she had only lost consciousness.

Coughing uncontrollably, her eyes too watery and gritty to see, Izabel inexorably kept going until she was finally able to take a clean breath. She blinked several times and took in her surroundings.

They made it. They were in the middle of the burned-out clearing. Izabel carefully turned the body so Shelley was laying on her belly once again, and then collapsed onto her butt as relief liquefied her muscles. A cool breeze swept up from the valley, rustling her hair and caressing her cheeks. It felt like heaven on her scorched skin, and she took several seconds to inhale all the clean air she could.

When her coughing finally diminished, she looked at the woman on the ground beside her. The inferno still blazed several yards away, which was just enough light to illuminate the blackened burns on Shelley's back, arms, and face. She couldn't tell the extent of the damage, but from what she could see, Izabel assumed they were extensive.

She reached over to gently press her finger to Shelley's neck—she would have used her wrist to search for a pulse, but the skin had merged with her clothing, mangling it so much, Izabel wasn't sure if she could find anything there. She waited a few moments, shifted her fingers, and then breathed a little easier. Shelley was still alive, though barely.

Izabel examined her surroundings once again. The fire seemed to be spreading uphill with the wind far faster than it was downhill toward Zack's cabin. She was thankful for that, but it didn't mean he wasn't still in danger. The fire was still moving toward him, just much more slowly. Plus, she needed to get to a phone to call the fire department out here, as well as to get medical help for Shelley.

She sighed with exhaustion and the aftermath of emotion—a result of nearly dying several times this evening. But she couldn't relax, not yet. She still had to walk back. Shelley's truck was on the other side of the flames and she had no desire to attempt to dash through them again to reach it. Besides, the blaze had likely reached the vehicle by now. No, she'd have to walk, and though she couldn't carry Shelley through the remaining brush and down the hillside herself, it shouldn't be too hard for her to let the firemen know where to find the injured woman.

Getting to her feet, Izabel wiped her face with her arm and started through the brush, toward the path that had led them here. She would get to Zack and call the authorities, and when everything finally settled into normalcy again, then...

"Then," she chuckled wryly, "I can have a nervous breakdown."

And what's good about that? she wondered at the lighthearted feeling that had come over her, but the answer came immediately. Zack. He would be there to take care of her. He was the bright spot in all of this, and as she trudged through the night-shrouded underbrush, her heart silently counted the minutes until she was in his arms again.

CHAPTER 30

Zack bit back the desperate need to urge his friend to drive faster up the old logging trail. Izabel had been gone for almost thirty minutes and there was still no sign of the truck that Shelley had taken her in. He knew the rig hadn't come back down, and there was no other way to get out of this forest without abandoning the vehicle and hiking. Shelley didn't seem like the backwoods-trail-hiker type to him, so he suspected the truck was her means of escape.

If escape had been her plan.

She'd left Zack tied to the bed and had implied she would return. What did she think he'd do when she returned without Izabel? He shook his head. It didn't matter. They were up in these trees somewhere, and he would find them.

Their cell phones were useless in this area, but the police radio Josh kept in his truck had no such issue. He'd already called his fellow officers for backup, and when they spotted the fire, he'd radioed for the fire department—at least, those still in town after the call out earlier—for assistance as well. Zack also suggested an ambulance, just in case someone had been seriously hurt.

"God, I hope that's not the case," Zack muttered to himself.

"We've almost reached it," Josh said, zapping Zack out of his dark thoughts.

Josh's eyes darted between the dirt path and the flames off to their left as they slowed to a crawl.

"I see that," Zack grumbled, forcing himself to breathe slowly and stay calm.

They'd already discussed their thoughts on where the fire had come from.

Both men had been around enough forest fires and firefighters to know this blaze hadn't been started by the other one up north, which was too far for the embers to have reached this mountainside, even with the winds they'd reported all night.

Several loud *pops* sounded from their left and slightly ahead of their position. The cracks kept coming, booming like bullets on rapid fire. Zack's stomach dropped to his toes and heat washed over his whole body, leaving little prickling sensations on his arms, legs, and scalp.

Josh cursed and slammed on the brakes, skidding them to a halt.

"What are you doing?" Zack shouted. "We've got to keep going."

"Those were bullets," Josh said as if Zack didn't know.

"All the more reason to go faster."

"I don't think that was someone getting shot," Josh replied, eyeing the brush around the truck. "It sounded more like a handful had been tossed into the fire."

"How would you know that?" Zack couldn't keep the incredulity out of his voice.

Josh glanced at him with a frown. "You didn't hear the doubles?"

Zack glared right back but didn't reply.

"Multiple bullets firing at the same time. Guns being fired by a person usually only fire one at a time; even an automatic weapon only fires one bullet at a time."

"You would know, soldier boy," Zack said. "I just want to find Izabel."

"That's just it," Josh said, throwing the truck into park and looking around again. "I think we have." He pulled his sidearm from his hip holster and opened his door.

"We have?" Zack muttered as he quickly followed Josh's exit through his own door. He could hear the crackling of the fire off to the side as he rounded the truck to where his friend stood.

Josh pointed his gun at the sky as he silently stared into the darkness.

"What are you doing now?" Zack muttered, his stomach and chest tightening with this new frustration.

"Shh," Josh said quietly and then glanced at him. "Listen." He nodded toward the blackness to the side, beyond the lights of the truck.

Zack turned his gaze and listened intently. After a few moments, his jaw clenched once again and he whispered, "All I hear is the crackling of the fire and—"

He stopped and cocked his ear toward the forest. Was that a voice he just heard? It was weak, as if very far away. He'd caught the sound but not the words.

Josh grinned at him. "It's coming from over there," he nodded toward the trees, "and I think it's coming this way."

Zack's heart thudded painfully. Was it Izabel? Was she hurt? Did she need help getting to them? Or was it Shelley? Did the fire separate them? Was Josh right in guessing that Shelley had caused this fire?

The thought turned his insides to ice. The only reason to do that would have been to cover something up.

Something like...murder.

Zack stepped toward the trees, intent on reaching Izabel, but Josh stopped him with a hand on his shoulder. "Neither of us are prepared to go dashing out there. We have no decent flashlight and we aren't dressed for the terrain."

"I can't just stand here," Zack growled. "Izabel may be hurt."

"Help..." the voice shouted clearly from the trees. It was a woman and she sounded much closer. "Can you hear me?"

At the sound of her voice, a little nearer now, Zack's throat suddenly swelled and tightened with emotion. His eyes watered and he couldn't say a word.

Josh tossed a smile his way and then raised his voice. "Yeah, we hear you, Izabel. Keep coming this way."

"Who is that?" she asked, her voice getting louder every time she spoke.

"It's Josh, Izzy. Zack is with me."

"I can see your headlights," Izabel shouted, though by to sound of it, she was only a few yards away.

Zack's urge to rush into the overgrown brush and pluck her from the darkness nearly overwhelmed him, but his feet stayed rooted to the ground. Josh was right. They could just as easily get lost or hurt going out there in the middle of the night with no decent light or gear. So, he stood, silently cursing as his boot toe tapped anxiously on the rough ground, impatiently waiting for Izabel to breech the wall of trees and brush.

Her footsteps rustled through the brush, twigs snapping with each step, as she slowly closed in on their location.

"Keep coming, Izabel," he croaked. "We're right here."

Several panicky heartbeats later, Zack watched as she stumbled through the wall of vegetation into the splash of Josh's headlights.

Black soot covered her face, arms, and hands, as well as the cute outfit she'd worn to the opening earlier that night. Her hair was a tangled mess of dead leaves and broken twigs. She looked frightened and exhausted, but she was still the most beautiful woman Zack had ever seen.

He dashed over and pulled her in close, relief flooding his senses as her arms wrapped around his neck.

"I was so scared," she whispered, her body trembling against him. "I thought I'd never see you again"

"Me too, goddess," he rasped, then pulled back and brushed her wild hair out of her face. "Are you okay? Did she hurt you?" His hands swept over her neck and arms as he spoke and then cradled her face.

"I'm fine." She nodded and then began to cough. When she finally ceased a minute later, she said, "Aside from the gritty eyes and the cough, I'm fine."

"Izabel," Zack said, pulling back to look into her dirty face, his heart heavy with desperation, imploring him to speak, and suddenly, he was certain that he could not wait one more second to tell her how he felt. "I was waiting for the right time, but I can't wait another minute. I love you. I love you so much, Izabel, I don't know what I'd do without you."

"It took you long enough." She smiled and tears filled her eyes. "I love you too, Zack."

He chuckled and pulled her in close, hugging her against his chest, thankful to have her back in his arms. And if he had his way, that was where she'd always be.

"Where's Shelley?" Josh asked from beside them.

Izabel trembled against Zack and her green eyes shimmered with tears when she looked up at him. She turned to Josh. "She's out there," Izabel said, pointing diagonally across the hillside. "I was able to drag her to the burned-out area below where the fire is now. She's safe, but she needs help."

"You dragged her out?" Zack asked, his hand gently rubbing what he hoped were comforting circles on her back.

Izabel nodded. "Yeah, she...got burned."

"How bad is it?" Josh asked, his serious policeman mask now fixed in place.

"It's bad," Izabel said. "She cried and screamed when I dragged her out. I couldn't carry her, but I know where she is."

In the distance, they could hear sirens coming up the hillside, and red and blue flashes lit the night sky. Help was nearly there.

"Zack," Josh said quietly, "why don't you take Izzy to my truck. You both look as if you're about ready to drop."

"We can walk back to the cabin," Zack said, wanting to get Izabel as far from the traumatic scene as he could. "Get out of your way entirely."

Josh had started shaking his head before Zack finished. "No, buddy, from what I've seen, you've got a concussion, and I want the paramedics to take a look at you. You'll probably need to go to the hospital for X-rays and observation, and Izzy should see a doctor, too."

Zack wanted to argue, but Izabel did need medical attention. He hesitated and looked at her in question.

"I think that's a good idea." She turned to Zack with those gorgeous green eyes and smiled just a little. "Let's go sit in the truck until the cavalry gets here."

Zack chuckled and shook his head as he wrapped an arm around her back and they slowly ambled to the passenger side of Josh's truck. "The cavalry?" he asked, astonished by how much she'd taken to the old films he loved. "Just how many John Wayne westerns have you watched?"

* * *

Josh had been correct about the paramedics wanting Zack to go to the hospital. But because Zack had refused to leave without her, the paramedics waited just long enough for Izabel to let the officers who had arrived right behind them know where to find Shelley.

He'd been annoyed by their insistence that he utilize the stretcher for the trip to the hospital. "She's the one who was traumatized," Zack had said, pointing at Izabel, but they wouldn't relent and Izabel wouldn't, either.

"I'm fine, Zack," she said, her tone holding just a touch of reproach. "You're the one who's injured. Please, just do as they ask."

He'd surrendered to the pleading in her eyes.

The trip had taken longer than he liked and sitting in the emergency room bed while they waited for the X-rays hadn't been any fun, either.

"Why does everything at the hospital take so damn long," he'd grumbled two hours after they arrived.

Izabel smiled at him and reached for his hand. "It won't be much longer. The nurse said the doctor was looking at the X-rays now. He should be here soon."

She'd had some time to clean up after the doctor examined her for injuries, and his sister Emmy had come by to loan her some clean scrubs and a brush to untangle her hair. She looked almost normal now as he looked over at her.

"Not soon enough," Zack complained.

Izabel squeezed his hand gently. "It doesn't matter," she said. "We're both safe and together. I could wait another twenty-four hours and not be upset as long as you're with me."

He returned her grin. "I love you," he said as he laid his head back against the mattress and fought the nausea that still threatened to up-end his stomach. It surprised him that each time he said those words, they got easier to say.

She gave him such an endearing look that his heart felt ready to explode with joy. "I know," she said with a mischievous smile. "Back at you, cowboy."

Another twenty minutes passed before the doctor finally showed. And though his news wasn't the best, it wasn't the worst, either.

"Because you lost consciousness, your concussion would be considered relatively severe; however, since you were only out for a few minutes, I think any traumatic brain injury would be mild. I'd like you to stay the rest of the night for observation and then come back in a week to see how your symptoms are faring or if any new ones arise. And, of course, if anything gets worse, you can always come back sooner."

"Great," Zack moaned.

The conversation hadn't lasted much longer before the doctor wrapped up his visit. "You both should get some rest now," he said, pointedly staring at each of his patients.

"May I stay here with Zack?" Izabel asked, and Zack's heart once again swelled in his chest.

"Yeah, doc, can she stay?" he asked, hopefully.

The doctor chuckled. "As long as you both rest, I don't have a problem with it. I'll let the nurses know." With that, he lowered the lights and exited the room.

Izabel got up and pushed the large reclining chair she'd been sitting in closer to Zack's bed.

"What are you doing?" Zack asked, smiling at her. "I should be doing that for you."

The glare she tossed him stopped him from doing just that. "Don't even think about it, sicky." She smiled a little, making her last word an endearment. "I'm going to line this chair up beside your bed, grab a blanket and pillow from the closet over there," she pointed across the room, "and then push back and cuddle up for a long nap. No help from you is needed right now. You rest."

Zack laughed. "As you wish, goddess."

CHAPTER 31

It was late the next morning when Zack finally got the all-clear to head home with instructions to take it easy for a while. It was just before lunch when they forced him into a wheelchair, and Izabel rolled him through the hospital and toward freedom for a second time in the last few months.

He couldn't wait to get out of this place and back home with Izabel. He'd dreamt about it all night long—well, except when they had awakened him to check on his status. He was still tired, but excited to get her alone again.

Izabel had been lucky not to receive any more serious burns than those from the bark embers that had fallen on her bare arms when Shelley shot at her and a general sensitivity from the wildfire's intense heat.

The fire Shelley had started last night had been defeated a little over an hour after they left the scene, so he and Izabel were able to return to the cabin, and, he hoped, to the activities that had been so rudely interrupted the night before.

Shelley had arrived at the hospital sometime after they'd been taken to the exam room—not that Zack cared all that much about what had happened to her. The woman had planned to murder Izabel and he suspected, he would've been next. To his way of thinking, she'd needed mental help as much as anything. Unfortunately, they'd heard from a nurse before they were released that Shelley hadn't survived her wounds. She'd been burned over eighty percent of her body, and those burns had been exacerbated by the synthetic clothing she'd been wearing, which had burned into her skin Had she survived, the scaring would've been horrific.

The generous side of Zack wouldn't have wanted her to suffer like that, but the vindictive part—the one that raged inside whenever he thought about what might've happened to Izabel—couldn't find any sympathy for Shelley's fate.

Zack had decided, however, not to press charges against the man who'd attacked him. Last night, Izabel had told him and the police about her conversation with Shelley on their way up the mountain and Shelley's connection to the protestor, Ed. Zack couldn't blame the man for standing up for the woman he cared about or for being fooled by her. Love did strange things to intelligent men. He had made one stipulation about the deal to Josh, which was that Ed must leave Montana immediately, and never come back. He hadn't heard anything yet, but now that the woman Ed had adored enough to risk prison time for was dead, Zack doubted the other man would argue the matter any further.

He turned his head to look over his shoulder at Izabel. "Hi, goddess," he said with his best charming grin.

She smiled. "Hi, handsome."

"You think you could hang with me for a few days? You know, so you can nurse me back to health and all that." He wiggled his eyebrows suggestively.

Izabel's face remained passive and she shrugged as they made their way down the hospital's pale yellow hallway on their way to his sister Emmy's department. "I thought you'd never ask." Izabel gave him a wink and he turned back around with a laugh, high on life once again.

They were just entering the trauma unit when someone called out to them from behind.

"Clear the way ahead," they shouted, and Izabel wheeled Zack to the side to make room.

Two paramedics and several hospital staff rushed down the hallway, shouting information about their patient and instructions on what they needed to do to help him.

"Hey, guys," Emmy said as she came up to stand beside her brother and Izabel.

They replied to her greeting, but all of them were fixated on the stretcher coming toward them.

"Do you know who it is?" Zack asked his sister, who shook her head as the group reached them.

"No, I've been upstairs," she said distractedly.

Emmy and Izabel both gasped at the seriousness of the man's condition, and Emmy pressed a hand over her mouth as the gurney rolled by.

Zack cursed when he got a look at the man on the stretcher. A firefighter by his clothes, and it appeared he'd been burned. Zack wasn't able to see the man's face or station insignia when he murmured, "I hope he's not one of ours."

Emmy stopped the paramedics who had passed off their charge into the care of the trauma center doctors and were making their way back to their ride.

"How bad is he, Noah?" she asked the closest paramedic, pointing toward the double doors the injured fireman had been pushed through.

"Not too bad, but bad enough," Noah replied vaguely.

"Who is it?" Zack asked, anxious and worried for the man.

"One of ours," Noah said sadly, shaking his head. "Aaron Monroe."

A soft cry of despair escaped Emmy's lips, and Zack's chest squeezed with regret. He turned to find his sister's face had paled drastically, her lips trembled, and he saw unshed tears in her glistening eyes. He took her hand in his, hoping to comfort her, but she didn't meet his gaze.

"Is he still in danger?" Emmy asked, and Zack was surprised by the steadiness of her voice.

Noah shrugged. "He's stable and should survive, but his recovery will be hard. Burns are the worst." He shook his head and then walked away with his partner.

Emmy stared at the doors where Aaron had disappeared behind.

"Emmy?" Zack called softly, but she didn't respond. Instead, she stepped toward the doors where Aaron would undoubtedly be getting the emergency care he needed. Zack's hold on her hand brought her up short, and she shook her hand, trying to free it. When that didn't work, she looked down at their clasped hands and finally met her brother's gaze.

"You don't have to go in there," he said quietly.

Emmy frowned, her gaze darting to Izabel and then back to Zack. "But I do, Zack. I'm a trauma nurse; this is what I do, and I'm damn good at it."

"I know that, but someone else can do it this time. It doesn't have to be you."

Emmy shook her head. "He's going to need help, even once he's out of here. He's your friend, Zack. Don't you want him to have the best?"

Zack stared back at her silently. He didn't want her getting involved with this case. He didn't want her to get too close to the man who would only hurt her in the end. But then again, Zack had changed his ways for Izabel. Who was he to say Aaron couldn't turn himself around as well?

"I don't want you to get hurt," he finally admitted.

Emmy smiled and touched his face. "You don't have to worry about me, baby brother."

"I will always worry about you...and Gracie, too."

Emmy dropped her hand from his cheek. "I know, but I can take care of myself, and so can Gracie. You know she won't tolerate being coddled, and neither will I. Especially not in this situation."

He nodded and released her hand. "Doesn't mean I like watching either of you get hurt. You're my sisters, and I love you both."

"And we love you, but we don't need you telling us what to do." She patted his hand. "Get used to it, Zack," Emmy said as she hurried away, her meaning clear—she would not change her mind. "I've got to go. See you at home." She waved and then vanished into the ER.

Zack stared after her, worry knotting its way through his vitals.

Izabel's arms wrapping around his neck from behind broke his trance.

"There's nothing we can do for him right now," she said, her lips caressing the shell of his ear and raising goosebumps on his arms. "How about we head back to the cabin and get started on that new life together you talked about? We can come back later to check on him."

Heat stirred in his belly and he smiled. He reached up to where her curls brushed over his shoulder and tugged one gently. "I like that idea."

"Good," Izabel said as she released him and reached for the wheelchair handles, but Zack grabbed her hand and tugged her to the side of the chair where he could look into her face. "Thank you, Izabel."

She smiled and leaned down to kiss him softly. "You are very welcome, handsome." Brushing her fingers down his cheek, she stood again and returned to her position behind him. She pushed and the chair began to roll down the hallway toward the exit. "Now," she said cheerily, "what did you say last night about going home?"

He smiled as images of her naked in his bed flashed in his mind. "I said, we needed to hurry and get back so we can pick up where we left off."

"Hmm," she said.

He could see her in his mind's eye—cute little frown, head tilted just a touch, her green eyes pensive. It was surprising how well he knew her already, and he couldn't wait to learn more.

"I'm not sure about that," she continued, dousing the furnace that had heated his blood. "At least, not for a while... But maybe we can snuggle and watch some movies."

He chuckled. "Okay, what do you have in mind?"

"Well..." she said eagerly as they reached the exit doors and Zack could finally get up from the chair, "I was thinking *El Dorado* or *Rio Bravo*."

He looked at her askance. "More John Wayne?"

Her lips pushed together and her brows drew down in an adorable pout as he slowly got to his feet. He took her hand and led her outside where the warm afternoon air felt good after the coolness of the hospital.

Once they'd exited the last set of doors, he pulled her into his arms. Emotions swirled inside him—fear that he'd almost lost her, joy that she'd survived, lust just because she was beautiful and his, and love. So much love, it threatened or overwhelm him. His eyes burned and he tightened his hold, resting his cheek on top of her head. Her hair still smelled of smoke, but he didn't care. Dizziness assaulted him, but still, he stayed where he was.

Her hands patted his back and her voice came to him, a little muffled by his shirt. "Hey? Are you okay?"

He nodded and she pulled back to look up into his face.

"What is it?"

Trying to grin, he ignored the tightness in his chest and throat. He shook his head. "Nothing's wrong. I'm just...happy. And it feels..." He inhaled deeply and released the air in a rush. "It feels fantastic! Thank you for staying with me. For loving me."

"You" she poked him in the chest to emphasize her words, "are a wonderful man, Zack MacEntier." She grinned and went up on her toes—her breasts sliding against his chest as she did, causing his blood to heat again—to plant a quick kiss on his lips. "And you make me happy, too."

"That just makes everything so much better."

"Good," she said, patting his chest. She pulled out of his arms and took his hand to lead him to the truck Josh had brought down from the cabin. "Now," she shot a glance at him over her shoulder, "about that movie..."

"We can watch them both," he said as he followed her, his eyes tracing the trim lines of her lovely body, looking forward to the day he'd be well enough to do more than just stare. "And all the others you wish to see."

"Really?"

"Really. Just remember, I liked the Duke first."

She laughed and it was the sweetest sound he'd ever heard.

"Hmm." She tilted her head. "Maybe tomorrow we can start on his war movies."

He laughed as she slipped away and hauled on his arm to get him moving once more. "Are you trying to make me jealous?"

She frowned over her shoulder. "Of course not; just eager to get close to you and watch some good movies."

His eyebrows climbed upward. *Well,* he thought, *can't get better than that.*

"I only watched them because of you, you know. It's not my fault that I like them so much. You started it."

"I remember." He tugged on her hand until she spun around and landed in his arms once again. Cupping her face, he lowered his head and kissed her right there in the middle of the hospital parking lot. Strangely, he didn't notice any dizziness or nausea; all he knew was the taste, smell, and feel of Izabel.

When he broke the kiss and rested his forehead against hers, they were both breathing hard. "I love you," he whispered, and not only did the words get easier, they meant more to him every time he said them, too.

"And I, you," she said before ducking under his arm and taking his hand to pull him forward again. "But if we're going to get through two movies tonight, we need to get a move on."

She turned at his truck and they stopped beside the passenger door. After a quick kiss, he carefully climbed inside. Once he was seated, Izabel went around to the driver's door and slid behind the wheel.

"I'm going to hold you to your word, you know," she said as she pushed the key into the ignition.

"My word?"

"Two movies tonight."

He laughed again. He knew she would insist he rest some too, but he loved her lighthearted teasing, which broadened the warm emotions inside him. This feeling of lightness and completeness, of finally finding what he'd been looking for, was better than anything he'd ever known. He'd never expected to be happy again, but he was, and he owed it all to the strong, brave, intelligent woman beside him. And he'd spend the rest of his life making her just as happy as she made him.

His lips curled into a wide grin as he stared at her easy smile. "Anything you want, goddess. Anything at all."

Epilogue

Izabel could feel Zack's eyes on her as they rode up the old horse trail behind his parents' house. The big sky overhead was a beautiful blue, with large fluffy white clouds shifting across its grand expanse, but the weather had turned a bit colder. She'd worn her new cowboy hat and boots, along with a pair of Wrangler jeans that Zack keep eyeing as if planning every way in which he could remove them. The red lightweight, though warm, jacket she wore had been a gift from Addie.

"You're going to need a lot more clothes if you plan to live in Montana year-round," Addie had said, picking up a gift-wrapped box. "We'll have to go shopping soon so I can show you the good stuff that Emmy revealed to me. Until then, though, you'll need this." She held out the box and grinned.

After opening the box, Izabel had been delighted with the gift and humbled, too. "Addie, this is a great jacket, but too expensive. I know it costs a small fortune. Let me pay you for it."

Addie had shaken her head, adamantly refusing the offer. "Nope. It's yours, and I look forward to seeing you in it the next time we go riding."

Izabel had run her hand over the jacket's smooth material. "That might be a while," she said sadly. "We're both still healing."

It had been almost a month since she and Zack had left the hospital and gone home to the cabin. The first night back, they'd nestled down together on the couch for a John Wayne movie marathon, but Zack hadn't made it to the end of the first one before he fell asleep. She hadn't minded, though. After all he'd been through, he needed the rest. She'd simply made him comfortable, pulled the blanket over the both of them, and cuddled up to his side.

She'd need to recover as much as he did. Breathing in the hot air and smoke had caused her a lot of respiratory irritation and some shortness of breath at first. Her throat and lungs had ached quite a lot in the beginning, but they both had grown better as time went on, though her voice was still a little raspy. Thankfully, the doctor had said she should fully recover from the physical damage that had been caused during the fire.

Luckily, there'd been few complications from Zack's concussion. He still got headaches and had a little trouble focusing sometimes, but the bouts were getting farther and farther apart.

"Turn right at the fork," Zack shouted from behind her, dragging her thoughts back to the present.

She glanced around at the assorted trees, bushes, and tall grasses, but saw nothing that resembled a fork. "What fork?"

"See the tall ponderosa?"

She frowned. "The what?"

"The big tree with the reddish-brown trunk, long needles, and few lower branches."

Looking to the right, she spied a tree that resembled his description and pointed. "That one?"

"Yes," he said with a little too much mirth in his voice for her taste, "keep to the right of it."

She did as he said and ended up having to hold her arm in front of her face to keep the sticks and some other low-lying limbs from poking or scratching her.

"Are you sure there's a trail here?" she asked doubtfully.

He actually chuckled this time. "Yes, I'm sure. Just keep going. The bush will thin out soon, and then you'll be able to see the far valley."

"Uh-huh," she said suspiciously.

"Really," he said, still attempting to convince her and hold back a laugh at her expense. "It's a stunning view. You'll love it, I promise."

"Why do we need to go up to this particular spot?" she asked as she shoved a larger branch out of her way, remembering the odd looks they received from his mom and sister just before they left for this trip.

"You'll see."

Izabel shook her head. He'd been very secretive about this little jaunt into the hills, and she was beginning to wonder if he wasn't just teaching her yet another lesson about how difficult living here would be. He'd told her so many stories about the wild animals and rough terrain that she'd about had it with his teaching.

Yes, she thought with more than a little irritation, *I was a city girl, but I've never been an idiot.*

Still, she couldn't get too upset about his overprotectiveness hidden in his overabundant teaching. Zack had been terrified by her kidnapping—had barely let her out of his sight since coming home—and he wanted her prepared for whatever she might run into in the woods. She'd learned a lot over the last couple of weeks, and the reasonable side of her was thankful for the education—while her other side silently grumbled about being annoyed, tired, and ready to call off this seemingly aimless trek into the bush.

Just when she was ready to shout that she was going back, the brush and limbs subsided and she could see the long, narrow valley on the other side of the mountain. The fir trees were a deep forest green, but the deciduous trees had all begun to change color. Assorted reds and oranges dotted the landscape amidst dozens of yellow and gold variations. She spotted some maples, with dinner-plate-sized leaves, and the white bark of birch trees on the far side of the valley. It was beautiful, just like all the other areas of Montana she'd already seen.

She tilted her head and checked her attitude. Maybe her irritation kept her from completely enjoying the view.

Zack exited the brush as Izabel dismounted. Holding her reins, she moved farther into the clearing, staying well away from the drop-off on the far side.

"What do you think?" Zack asked as he stepped up beside her, his horse munching on some grass behind them.

She smiled up at him before turning back to the view. "It's everything you said it would be."

"I'm glad you like it."

"But why was it so important to come here today?"

The small rocks beneath his boots crackled when he shifted his feet and he rubbed the back of his neck with one big hand. "Well," he said, "I'll show you, but first...close your eyes."

She gave him her best 'don't mess with me' glare. "What?"

His face paled slightly and his eyes darted around as if looking for something else to say.

She altered her tone and tried to soothe his discomfort. "Do I *really* need to close my eyes?"

"Yes." His emphatic, instant answer had the wheels in her head turning.

What's he up to?

"All right, but this had better be earthshattering." She sighed and closed her eyes. "Okay, now what?"

"Keep them closed," he said as he wrapped his arm around her back and guided her to her right. "Just a few steps...don't worry, I won't let you fall."

She chuckled. "I hope not."

He positioned her just where he wanted and then stood back. "Okay, open your eyes."

Izabel blinked a few times and looked around. For a second, nothing appeared to have changed, but then she noticed Zack had gone down on one knee in front of her.

Oh, my! Her heart did a little jig of joy in her chest.

"My dad proposed to my mom right here, on this spot," he said with his charmingly crooked smile. "Thirty-nine years ago, this year."

Her eyebrows rose. "Really?"

"Yep," he said, his grin growing more confident. "He said she'd led him on a merry chase before she finally accepted him."

With her earlier irritation forgotten, Izabel cupped his cheek in her hand. "Was he a rascal like you?"

He flashed her one of his sexy grins. "Probably not quite as bad..." he said, "but I'm sure he had his share of faults."

"Faults can make a person interesting," she said, brushing her thumb over his cheek and then dropping her hand.

He shrugged. "Maybe. I'm just glad you're still here."

She had a suspicion about where this was going, and she waited patiently for him to get to it. Pressing her lips together, she tried to keep the smile from her face.

"Izabel," he started. "I have something to say, and I need you to just let me say it. Okay?"

She nodded and murmured, "Okay."

Looking at the ground, he pulled off his black felt cowboy hat, set it amongst the weeds beside him, and then raked his fingers through his short hair. Then he straightened his shoulders and lifted those mesmerizing whiskey eyes to her face.

"I haven't been the best of men," he said, then waved his hand impatiently for her to wait when she opened her mouth to argue. "I haven't been and I know it, but you make me want to be a better man. I feel like I'm on the right path again, that I know who and what I am."

Izabel stood very still, hardly breathing.

"I've been lost for so long. The road back to myself, to the man I wanted to be, had been cracked and shadowed by a haze of fear and bad choices."

He reached for her hand and she let him take it.

"But you, Izabel Silva... You have been like the sun, shining your beauty and brilliance into my life, warming the cold corners of my heart, and bringing color back into my gray world."

"Oh, Zack..." Realizing she'd spoken, her teary eyes widened and she slapped her free hand over her mouth.

Zack smiled, his eyes bright and twinkling with humor at her comedic reaction.

"You are strong, and brave, and beautiful, my goddess. You deserve so much more than me, but I can't let you go."

His free hand had reached into his jeans pocket, and he lifted it between them. Held in his unsteady fingers, a sparkling, princess-cut solitaire engagement ring winked in the afternoon light.

When he'd first started to speak, her heart had begun to beat wildly and she'd been almost too breathless with excitement to speak, but as he lifted that gorgeous ring, she sucked in a surprised breath as he stared deeply into her wide, stunned, eager gaze.

"I love you, Izabel. I want to spend my life loving you. Will you marry—"

"Yes!" she shouted as tears spilled onto her cheeks and, dropping to her knees, she threw her arms around his neck.

"—me," he finished and laughed as she squeezed him tight.

"Yes, yes, yes! Zack MacEntier, I will marry you," she said, kissing his cheeks before smacking a quick peck on his lips. "I love you, too. So damn much. I was afraid you would make me wait forever."

"Oh, no. I'm not risking some other dude showing up to steal you away from me."

"That will never happen."

His arms tightened around her and he ducked his head to rest it against hers. "I was so afraid I wouldn't get the chance to tell you how I feel...how much I need you."

Her arms curled around his neck and dived into his hair. "I was afraid too, you know."

"Of what?" His words came out both protective and disbelieving.

"Of never seeing you again," she said quietly, and a little shiver wracked her body. "I couldn't let that happen. I was going to get back to you, no matter what. I wouldn't let her hurt you."

"My warrior goddess," he murmured, burying his face in her curly hair, and she heard the smile in his voice. "I would've come for you. You know that, right? I'll always come for you."

She nodded. "Yes. I know."

"Good," he said, giving her a playful smack on her behind before he let her go and got to his feet.

A small cry of surprise escaped her and then she narrowed her eyes. "Be careful, buster."

He chuckled and helped her up, but she couldn't help but smile—she loved his laugh.

Capturing her left hand, Zack slid the glittering diamond ring onto her ring finger, and she held it up to stare at the beautiful piece of jewelry as it sparkled in the sunlight. Then something terrible occurred to her; Zack was broke and the minor profits the winery had supplied so far wouldn't have covered the cost of his bills and this expensive ring.

"Zack?" she said, lifting her worried gaze to his face. "You can't afford a ring like this. Please tell me you didn't do anything drastic."

His face sobered and paled a little, but he smiled. "No, nothing drastic." He shrugged and reached for her hand. "I had another ring...one I'd bought a long time ago."

"For Debs?" she asked quietly.

He nodded. "I've kept it in my truck for a long time, but it wouldn't have been right for you, and I didn't think you'd want something that had been meant for another woman."

He glanced at her and she nodded, agreeing with his assessment, but amazed by his thoughtfulness.

"Well, I wanted to get you something meant for you. Something that reflects the woman you are. So..." he shifted his feet and stared at the ground, "I sold the other ring, and that money, along with some of the profits from the winery, bought this for you." He looked up expectantly, anxiety and hope filling his soulful eyes. "I hope that's okay with you...?"

Izabel swallowed the lump in her throat and blinked back tears. He'd finally let go of the guilt he'd carried for so long. He would always regret what had happened to Debs, but he'd finally moved beyond his grief. Izabel's heart felt so full that it seemed to swell beyond the cage of her ribs. She nodded, unsure if she could speak. "Yes," she rasped through her raw throat and even rawer emotions, "that is perfectly okay with me."

He grinned and some, but not all, of the concern left his face. "So," he said, bringing their entwined fingers to his mouth to kiss her knuckles, "when would you like to have the wedding?" His gaze smoldered down at her, but she still saw worry or tension in the fine creases around his eyes.

"Well, I'd marry you today, if you wanted." She felt him tense and understood his unease. "But I know this is all very new to you—and for me, too. I'd like to have a few months to send invitations—especially to my mom so she can have time to get here. Then we'll need to find a spot for the ceremony and pick out my dress..." She cocked her head as if deep in thought and tapped her chin with her forefinger. "Something silky that clings in all the right places, I think, with a short train and a little lace around the low neckline..."

Her description must have agreed with him because a growl rumbled up from his chest and he pulled her into his arms. "Are you trying to kill me with lust before we say, 'I do?' I can barely control myself just thinking about seeing you in something like that; I can't imagine what the real thing will do to me."

She tilted her head in the other direction and her lips curved up mischievously. "I guess we'll have to wait and see then, won't we?"

"Tease," he joked, poking the tip of her nose with his finger.

"Well, if you can't wait, I'm sure I can find something lacy to wear tonight in celebration of our...engagement." She held her hand on his shoulder and wiggled her fingers, admiring how the light danced in the square-cut stone.

"Do you really like it?" he asked in a more serious tone, and she heard anxiety about his choice of ring. "If you don't, we can go back together and pick out something else."

She cradled his face in her hands. "I love it," she said, and going up on her toes, she kissed his lips gently, then pulled back to look into his eyes, "and I love you."

A huge smile filled his handsome face. "I'm glad to hear it. It took forever to pick it out."

Her eyebrows lifted. "You pick this out? By yourself?"

He nodded.

"How did you know this was my favorite cut?"

"The square, you mean?"

"Yes."

"Well, I asked the sales lady if they had anything for a goddess. She said this one was a princess-cut, so I figured that would be the closest to a goddess I could get."

"Oh, Zack," she said, her heart melting. If she didn't already love him to distraction, that charming comment would've pushed her right over the edge. "You are such a good, sweet man, Zack. I can't wait to spend the rest of my life with you."

"I'm only trying to be worthy of you, Izabel," he said, placing soft kisses on the corner of her mouth, along her jaw, and down her throat. "I will spend the rest of my life making you happy."

Izabel moaned at the tender torture of his lips nibbling her ear. "Let's go home and make each other happy. We can share the news with our family and friends tomorrow."

He bit her earlobe gently and then sucked it into his mouth.

"Or maybe in a few days..."

He chuckled and bolts of desire shot through her body.

"As you wish, my goddess," he said, his voice low and tender. "As you wish."

The End

* * *

If you've enjoyed this story and would like to read the first book in the series, you can get your copy of *Broken Cowboy* at your favorite retailer today.

Your review means a lot to me and to others who may be deciding whether to purchase my books. So, if you enjoyed *Casanova Cowboy* please consider leaving an honest review at your favorite retailer. Thank you!

* * *

About the Author

Jamie Schulz is a contemporary western romance and dystopian cowboy romance author. She loves to write about heroes with vulnerabilities and strong, feisty heroines who are a match for the men they love. To her, every one of her stories, no matter how dark, must have a happy ending, and she strives to make them impossible to put down until you get there.

Jamie has been writing and making up stories for most of her life and hopes to one day reach the bestsellers lists. Her book *Broken Cowboy* won the Global Book Awards Gold Medal for romance and was a RONE Awards finalist. *Jake's Redemption*—a full-length prequel introduction to the Angel Eyes series' dark and terrible world—was also an award-winner in the Global Ebook Awards.

Cowboys, ice cream, and reading almost any kind of romance are among her (not so) secret loves. She balances her free time between reading her favorite romance authors—in genres ranging from erotica and dark romance to sweet historicals and contemporary romance—and spending time with those she is closest to. She lives in the beautiful Pacific Northwest with her family and their fur babies, and she enjoys hearing from her fans.

You can learn more about Jamie and her books on her website:
www.thejamieschulz.com
Sign up for her newsletter and never miss out on new releases and specials:
www.subscribepage.com/newsletter_sign-ups

And you can follow her on her social media pages:
Facebook (@TheJamieSchulz)
Twitter (@TheJamieSchulz)
Instagram (@thejamieschulz)
Goodreads
BookBub

ACKNOWLEDGMENTS

I'd like to say a special "Thank You" to my editor Silvia Curry, especially for her willingness to work with me and my odd schedule. And for acting as a "sensitivity reader" for the Brazilian social structures and practices as well as the racist content in this story. The racism was hard for me to read about when researching and I appreciate Silvia's personal input, which improved Izabel's backstory.

I'd also like to thank my graphic artist Lesia T (germancreative on Fiverr), as well as all my beta readers, proofreaders, and wonderful ARC reviewers, my social media followers, and all the others I may have missed.

I'd also like to send a heartfelt thank you to my family. I love you so much! Without you and your support, I couldn't keep doing this, so thank you for everything!

Thanks to all my friends for your praise and encouragement, you're all precious to me. And once again, a big thanks to Sam, the Facebook groups, Miss N. for everything (of course), Bryan Cohen, all my newsletter swap author friends, and everyone else I may have missed!

And mostly, to you, my dear readers. I truly appreciate the time you take to escape into my stories. I love your wonderful comments and the devotion of each of you. Thank you so much!

Made in the USA
Las Vegas, NV
10 June 2024